Praise for
Three Roads Home

"Travis Thrasher is an author to watch. Every book gets better."
—FRANCINE RIVERS, author of *Redeeming Love* and *A Voice in the Wind*

"Writing with a sweet and tender touch, Travis Thrasher plucks our heartstrings. *Three Roads Home* is a wonderful collection celebrating real, mature love."
—ANGELA HUNT, author of *The Shadow Women*

"With a unique style, Travis Thrasher has given his readers intriguing glimpses at love in all its complexities. I loved *Three Roads Home!*"
—ROBIN LEE HATCHER, author of *Firstborn* and *Ribbon of Years*

"*Three Roads Home* is an absorbing collection that beautifully portrays God's limitless love. Thrasher's characters are sympathetic and believable."
—LORI COPELAND, author of Brides of the West: *Faith, June, Hope, Glory,* and *Ruth*

"Travis Thrasher weaves together three colorful threads in a tapestry that will certainly give readers a glimpse of themselves. *Three Roads Home* takes us on an unforgettable journey, one that shows us the scenery and pitfalls, the detours and destinations of love."
—KAREN KINGSBURY, best-selling author of the Redemption Series

THREE ROADS HOME

THREE ROADS HOME

HOME

Stories of First Love &
Second Chances

TRAVIS THRASHER

WATERBROOK
PRESS

THREE ROADS HOME
PUBLISHED BY WATERBROOK PRESS
2375 Telstar Drive, Suite 160
Colorado Springs, Colorado 80920
A division of Random House, Inc.

Scripture quotations are taken from *The Holy Bible, New Living Translation,* copyright © 1996. Used
by permission of Tyndale House Publishers, Inc., Wheaton, Illinois 60189. All rights reserved.

The characters and events in this book are fictional, and any resemblance to actual persons or events
is coincidental.

ISBN 1-57856-643-6

Copyright © 2003 by Travis Thrasher

All rights reserved. No part of this book may be reproduced or transmitted in any form or by any
means, electronic or mechanical, including photocopying and recording, or by any information
storage and retrieval system, without permission in writing from the publisher.

WATERBROOK and its deer design logo are registered trademarks of WaterBrook Press, a division
of Random House, Inc.

Library of Congress Cataloging-in-Publication Data
Thrasher, Travis, 1971-
     Three roads home : stories of first love & second chances / Travis Thrasher. — 1st ed.
     p. cm.
     ISBN 1-57856-643-6
     1. Domestic fiction, American. 2. Christian fiction, American.
     I. Title.
     PS3570.H6925T73 2003
     813'.6—dc21

                                        2002155488

Printed in the United States of America
2003—First Edition

10 9 8 7 6 5 4 3 2 1

There is only one person I could ever dedicate this book to.

She is my best friend, the love of my life,

and the somebody God allowed to come across my path.

———

This is for you, Sharon.

ACKNOWLEDGMENTS

With special thanks to the following:

Erin Healy, for believing in this book before anyone else did

Sigmund Brouwer, for helping it find a home

Anne Christian Buchanan, who continues to guide me along and
challenge me as a writer

Dudley Delffs, for your insight and enthusiasm

Ron Beers, for giving me my first break

Bill and Mary Thrasher, my parents and biggest fans

Warren and Willamae Noorlag, my in-laws, for allowing me to marry
your daughter and be a part of your family

Anne Goldsmith, for continually sharing wisdom on fiction and for
making me laugh in the process

Cindy Martinusen, for your interest and encouragement in my writing

Don Pape and the other fine folks at WaterBrook, for taking a chance
on me

The Haskells, the Macks, the Odells, the Pearsons, and the Swobodas,
for being there

And the many authors I've been privileged to know who have shared
their talents and insights with me along this wandering road

Somebody

PROLOGUE

Charissa Thomas found her husband sitting on the couch, staring at her laptop. It lay open on the coffee table and plugged in just as she'd left it a couple of hours earlier.

"Hey, honey. Sorry I'm late. I wanted to—"

"What is this?" Trevor asked in a hushed voice.

"What?" she said, grinning at his unusually serious tone.

"This." He pointed. "This e-mail."

She looked at him and then at the computer. Nothing registered. Charissa felt a slight chill pass over her as she stooped to put down the gift bag in her hand.

"I know I'm late, but—"

"What have you been doing?"

Trevor's stony expression surprised her.

"What do you mean?" she asked as she approached the couch.

"Who is Greg?"

"Greg?" she mouthed, not understanding the question or its tone.

"Give me a break," he said, standing and walking away from her toward the stairs.

The typically unnoticed creak in the floor between the couch and the stairs let out a grinding rasp as Trevor walked over it.

"What are you talking about? Greg who?"

"Greg. E-mail Greg. Don't lie to me, Chris. I know. I read his e-mail."

The vicious tone in his voice startled Charissa. She felt frozen in the middle of her family room, unsure whether to move toward Trevor or the computer or just leave the room.

"What e-mail? The only Greg I know is from work."

"Yeah, that'd be him."

"What are you saying?"

"There something you want to tell me?"

She looked at her husband with fear, curiosity, and anger all tied together. The family room's shades remained down, hiding the after-noon sunlight that she usually let pour in.

"Trevor, I still don't know—"

"Where were you just now?"

"I was…I told you, I was…busy." She thought of the gift bag at her feet. "Why?"

"Who were you with?" Trevor asked, his face red and mouth tight.

"No one. What is this?"

"What is *that?* That e-mail. I read it, Chris. I know. I know every-thing."

"What are you saying? What are you accusing me of?"

"Just tell me," he said, tears in his eyes.

She moved toward him now, frightened at whatever was happening. She reached out to touch him, to assure him whatever he thought was wrong could be made right. But Trevor pushed her away, his demeanor unwavering.

"I'm leaving for Germany in minutes. I'm gonna be gone a week. And just as I'm ready to leave, I get…this."

"What were you doing on my e-mail?"

He let out a sharp laugh and shook his head again. "You wouldn't get it. It doesn't matter anyway. Just tell me the truth."

"You think I'm having an—" She couldn't even finish the sentence. "You can't be serious."

"I'm very serious."

She bit her lip. "Trevor—"

"Just tell me the truth. For once."

"For once?" she asked. "What's that mean? After all these years, you still don't—"

"I don't *what?*"

"I can't believe it." She desperately fought tears that still came.

The doorbell rang. He cursed and looked toward the doorway and back at her.

"I don't deserve this," he said.

"And I do?"

"Is this why these past few months have been like this? How long has it been going on?"

Charissa shook her head. "I can't believe you go into my e-mail and…and…*accuse* me…"

"Next time do a better job of concealing your personal love notes."

"What?" she asked, furious and bewildered.

The doorbell rang again.

"I'm leaving."

"You don't trust me."

"No," he replied. "Not anymore."

"Have you ever?"

He only shook his head, as if the question was out of line.

"Then what are we even doing together?" she uttered loudly enough for him to hear.

He didn't answer, didn't say a single word to her, didn't even look at her as he strode past her. He opened the front door, handed his garment bag to the waiting driver, then walked out the door and shut it.

The silence smothered her.

Charissa sank onto the couch, sat there feeling the tears running down her cheeks. Only when she knew he was gone, truly gone, did she look at the open e-mail on her computer screen.

"Oh dear God," she whispered before the tears intensified.

No wonder Trevor was upset. But he never even gave her a chance to explain. After all these years, he still didn't trust her.

She looked over at the gift bag resting forlornly on its side close to the front door, spilling its brightly colored tissue. Inside sat a going-away gift for her husband, one that would have surprised even him. Since this trip was scheduled to last a whole week, Charissa had wanted to give him something special.

Now this.

As she reread the e-mail again and again, she kept thinking that the door would open and that he would come back in and finally hear the truth. He had to come back home. He had to walk back through that door and resolve things. He couldn't leave thinking the worst. Especially not now.

But the door didn't open again. For five hours, thirty-two-year old Charissa Thomas tried to make sense of what had happened in the silence of her home. Just when her anger cooled and her sadness subsided, Charissa received a phone call that would change her life forever.

It was her mother, telling her a plane headed for Germany had just crashed into the Atlantic Ocean.

From: Imperiopoint@aol.com
Date: June 12
To: CST61795@aol.com
Subject: parting thoughts

I begin this e-mail by stating the obvious. I love you, Charissa. Nothing and no one in the world can change that fact....

TUESDAY, JUNE 12, 9:50 P.M.

Charissa ached.

She sat in the unlit closet next to the master bedroom and wiped tears off her face. The smell of Trevor's cologne still lingered. Breathing in, she tried to regain whatever composure she could. She refused to let the ominous voices linger in her mind, though they had been haunting her since her mother's call almost an hour ago.

he's gone

In the bathroom, she applied some fresh makeup and puckered her lips in a defiant no. She rejected going there and letting the waters of despair and sadness flood her already wrecked soul. Everything was too fresh, too sudden, too soon, too...

Too what? she asked herself. *Too much? Too final?*

No, she screamed in her mind. *Stop it, Chris.*

gone

No.

She wanted to rip away the voice inside her head. Yet it wouldn't leave her.

Charissa entered the busy family room minutes later and glanced at her father, who gave her the saddest smile she'd ever seen on his always-optimistic face. She noted absently that he seemed to have a slight sunburn on his bald head.

The television blared details from the cable stations reporting the news of the possible tragedy—CNBC, MSNBC, CNN, and a series of others. Her older brother, Doug, monitored the channels for any new details, as if managing the remote was the only thing he knew he could handle.

"You okay?" her swollen-eyed mother asked as Charissa sat down next to her on the couch.

She shook her head and stared at the television. A distant memory brushed over her as she recalled buying the thirty-six-inch set with Trevor. Why remember such a mundane, meaningless thing? She didn't know. The only thing she could remember about that shopping trip was that it had excited Trevor.

Around her sat most of her immediate family: her mother and father; Doug, who sat close to Penny, his wife of two years; and Aunt Sheila, her father's sister, who lived in Deerfield. Sheila's arrival ten minutes ago had done something to Charissa, as if greeting this relative she didn't see that often confirmed the worst. Sheila's sweet smile had done nothing to comfort Charissa, who hugged her aunt and then excused herself for a few minutes.

The only one missing now was her older sister, Lisa, who had to drive down from Milwaukee.

The faces in the room looked spent, shattered, beyond any hope, even though they continued to offer words of optimism.

"Still no luck in contacting Trevor's parents?" her mother asked her.

"Robert's been at a convention in New York, and I don't know how to reach him. He's due in tomorrow. And Trevor's mom—well, I tried a couple of relatives, but they have no idea where she is. She still travels a lot on business. And it's not like we have a lot of contact with her. I might not even be calling the right number."

"Did you check in Trevor's study?" her father asked.

I can't go in there. Not yet.

"No," she replied without an explanation.

"He probably has the right number somewhere on his desk."

"Henry, maybe you can just go and look?" Evelyn VanderVelde said to her husband.

"Sure." He stood up and asked if anybody needed something.

"You know, I'll make a pot of coffee," Sheila said, tapping her brother's back. "Go on."

"You'd think more stations would have information," Penny said to Doug. "Check back on CNN."

From the kitchen, Aunt Sheila politely asked where the coffee was. Charissa heard her mother answer. Nothing about this felt right. Yet even in the midst of it, between her mother's phone call and turning on the television and getting the first knock on the door, Charissa still found herself acting more or less the same as usual. She had spent ten minutes straightening everything in the house, knowing her family was coming over. She had called Trevor's business partners, tried to call his parents. After her mom and dad came in and greeted her with hugs and tears, she found herself horrified that the gift bag containing Trevor's going-away present still rested near the front door. She managed quietly to carry it upstairs to her bedroom. Now was not the time to try and explain anything else to her parents.

The television volume magnified her anxiety.

"Could you turn that down a little?" her mother said, watching Charissa as carefully as she did the screen. "Can I get you anything, sweetie?"

Charissa smiled and shook her head. She thanked God again that her family was close by. She didn't know what she would have done if they lived on the West Coast like their friends Sheridan and Genevie, far away from her parents and siblings. The family managed to get together several times each year, celebrating either a birthday or a holiday. Their presence now made Charissa feel a little safer, a little more calm. The breathlessness and nausea that overtook her when her mother called were mostly gone now.

"When's Lisa supposed to get here?" Penny asked.

"She left a little before nine. Traffic's not too bad, so she should be here soon."

Thinking about her sister on the highway gave Charissa a shiver of worry.

Lord, please protect her and bring her here safely.

She wished she had prayed the same prayer for Trevor when he left that afternoon.

Details Charissa and the rest of the country knew: Transcoastal Airlines Flight 421 containing 217 passengers and crew took off from Chicago O'Hare bound for Frankfurt around seven that evening. That was the same flight number Trevor had scribbled down on a sheet of paper a couple of days ago and posted on the refrigerator door. Sometime after eight o'clock, the plane fell off the radar scope, and the Coast Guard was dispatched. News of the disaster began to spread about thirty minutes later as the networks and cable channels began reporting on it, with cable channels covering the story intensively. At that point there were only speculations, nothing confirmed.

By a quarter of nine that night, the media confirmed the 747 had crashed into the ocean. Some reporters were already labeling the incident a disaster.

Is it truly a disaster? Charissa wondered now as she sat hypnotized by the television screen. A disaster meant deaths. And no deaths had been confirmed yet.

The channel she was watching showed a map of the eastern states with possible locations in the Atlantic where the plane could have gone down. Underneath the illustrations were haunting words:

Transcoastal Flight 421 Missing.
Plane Down over Atlantic. 217 Unaccounted For.

Phrases and words that stung. Missing. Unaccounted for. Presumed. Unofficial.

"There have been survivors of crashes in the ocean," Doug mentioned to the room.

"We don't know anything official yet," her mother added.

"Are you sure he was on that flight?" Penny asked Charissa.

"Yes. He wrote it down—I've got it on a sheet in the kitchen."

"He could've changed it."

"I don't think so," Charissa said.

"Who is your travel agent?"

"I'm not sure he even has one. Trevor's always handled his own business travel. He likes to look for Internet deals. Or Peggy at work might have done it."

Penny stood up and said she would go upstairs to try and find information on how the flight was booked.

"It will be a while before they announce anything," her brother stated. "They always try to make sure they have the right info before saying anything."

"How will they know where to look?" Evelyn asked.

"I guess it depends on where they lost contact with the plane," Doug replied.

"You never know," Charissa's mother said, mostly to her.

They family continued to talk as if their very conversation might help. As if the generalizations and suppositions could make this all go away, could make Trevor come back. Charissa knew they only meant the best. She also knew there was nothing anyone could say now that would make things better.

"Do you want some coffee?"

Charissa looked up and saw her aunt standing there with a cup. "No, thanks."

Things weren't going to get better. They might never get better.

Trevor, where are you?

The phone rang, and everyone looked at Charissa. She let it ring a couple of times before her aunt picked up the receiver.

Charissa watched her aunt and expected the worst.

This is it.

"It's Lisa," her aunt said. "She's about fifteen minutes away."

As Aunt Sheila spoke to her sister, Charissa blocked out the voice. She blocked out everything for the moment. She fixed her eyes on the television and let her mind loose to wander anywhere from here. Memories that had been submerged for years seemed to float to the surface, like an inflatable raft appearing to rescue her.

CHARISSA

To tell you about the Trevor I fell in love with, the Trevor I lost forever, the Trevor whose memory still haunts me, I have to go back to the very start. And I can still point to the fact that on the first day I saw Trevor Thomas walk past in the hallways of Grace Christian High School, I felt an attraction to him. Somehow, deep inside, I knew that a guy like him could change my life, could literally uproot my stable existence and pull me down an unexpected path with him.

Little did I know where that path would take me. Where it would take us.

I guess it's natural to wonder, if I had it all to do over again, what I would change. But I'm not really sure I'd change much. Or even anything.

Because the thing was always this: I wanted to go down that path. When I met Trevor in my junior year of high school, I very much wanted to uproot many things about my life.

I still sometimes flip through the pages of our 1988 high-school yearbook. The Grace Christian Crusaders. Located in Elmhurst, Illinois, with a student body of just under four hundred, Grace was the absolute worst place a person could transfer to in the middle of his junior year.

You can see it in the yearbook pictures—the happy faces, the comfortable-looking, close-knit groups. And the pictures don't lie. Many of us had been together since kindergarten, attending Grace elementary and junior high before arriving at the high school. And by the time we reached eleventh grade, most of us old enough to drive and many of us rich enough to have our own cars, we knew who our friends were—as well as who everybody was, who had more money, whose father did what for a living, who had dated whom, who was Mr. Popular and who was Ms. Outcast.

Nobody really put names or definitions on these things—they just evolved. Unfortunately for me, with the junior year a couple of months old, I already knew I was in trouble.

I guess you could have labeled me cute in high school. But you'd also have to say I was fairly quiet and shy. What Grace knew about me, besides the fact that I just got braces which I tried to hide by keeping my lips close together no matter what, was that I had dated Kyle Zielstra all of my freshman and some of my sophomore year. I broke up with him because I wanted something more—or more specifically, someone different—in my life. I think maybe I wanted to *be* someone else. But my breakup with Kyle, of course, meant that my group of friends suddenly changed.

On top of that, my best friend—my best growing-up friend, I should say—decided to change schools. Ashley was a daring, outgoing girl who had always helped balance my introverted nature. So when she told me she'd decided to go to a big public high school near her home, I felt a combination of panic and dread. I felt literally alone, starting over that year in many ways.

All to say that when I first saw Trevor, I kinda related to him. I knew how hard it would be for him to break in. Most of the kids going to Grace High were 100 percent Dutch and were Christian Reformed, and while that didn't mean that all of them were fine, upstanding students or came from the same tax bracket, it did mean that most of them shared many things in common. Many of the students had at least one or two relatives in their class. And as I said, many had known each other all their lives. People would have labeled most of Grace's students as clean-cut, preppy, well off, maybe a little arrogant or naive about the outside world.

Into that closed society—and right past my locker in the hall—walked Trevor Thomas in his cargo pants and his T-shirt that read "The Smiths." I didn't know the Smiths were a rock band from England, nor did I know that Trevor had just moved to Illinois with his father. All I knew at that point was that Trevor Thomas was tall and lean and wore his hair the way James Dean used to. And, yeah, I thought he was cute.

But mostly I remember thinking something else:

What's going to happen to him now?

I noticed several things about Trevor that first day. His locker was across the hall from mine, a universe apart in my eyes. Somehow he got stuck between Jason DeGroot and Alex Huizenga. There are a couple of good Dutch names for you.

Jason was a dark-haired overtalker and overachiever who tended to lord it over everybody. I used to think that the guy, who resembled a young Alec Baldwin, would eventually go into politics or some other leadership position. Amazing how the years can change you. I ran into him not long ago, and he was the manager of a family restaurant in a south suburb. Not exactly a failure, but not quite up to the standard of his swagger and big talk in high school.

Alex Huizenga was sort of the poster boy for Grace High. Hundred-percent Dutch, blond-haired and blue-eyed. Played soccer, basketball, and baseball. Had always been on the homecoming court and tried to be involved in everything he could be involved in. And while I liked Alex as much as I knew him, there was one thing that didn't add up about him. His friends.

In a way, of course, Alex was friends with everybody. I'd see him laughing and joking with Jason all the time, since their lockers were right together. And Alex *liked* everybody, but his friends were three of the wilder guys in our class: Nick, John G., and Tank (a name derived from Tankerton). I mean "wild" by Grace standards—not really hoods or burnouts, but people you knew would party on the weekends and might do things they shouldn't be doing. Alex's student-council, Mr. Clean image didn't fit with them, but he hung around with them anyway.

I saw Alex chatting with Trevor between class periods that first day. Trevor showed almost no expression on his face. His eyes looked almost melancholy, yet revealed very little of how he felt or what he thought. Alex patted him on the back, and I thought that perhaps it was good luck for Trevor. Not a bad thing for a new guy to be befriended by the big man on campus.

It was only then that I noticed the blue splint on Trevor's right hand. A brace of sorts, like a portion of a glove attached to the edge of his pinkie and fourth finger.

Kim Hoekstra, who went to my church and had ridden my bus since first grade, was one of the few friends I still felt close to. We talked about Trevor during lunch break in the girls' rest room.

"Did you see Amanda hug Trevor Thomas?" Kim asked me.

I shook my head and looked at my curled bangs to see if they needed hair spray.

"Amanda, Kelly, Rachel, too—all of them formed a circle around Trevor, and then Amanda hugged him."

"Give me a break," I said.

"Well, he's fresh meat, you know. A guy in this school that she hasn't dated."

"What'd he do?"

"Just smiled. I think he sorta blushed. Didn't say much."

"He blushed?" I asked. Trevor Thomas didn't look like the blushing type.

"Yeah. Amanda invited him to a party this week."

"It already looks like Alex likes him."

Kim grinned at me. "He's not the only one."

I told Kim to be quiet. Sure, I liked what I saw. But I was sure that Trevor Thomas would never notice me, never remember my face out of a flock of students. I doubted I'd even get to meet him anytime soon.

Soon came a couple of hours later.

Freddie Jones was introducing Trevor all around. Freddie was our whiz kid, the one who was too brilliant for his own good but also didn't have a clue. He often dressed like a disheveled thirty-year-old, with wrinkled button-down shirts and coffee-stained slacks and muddy dress shoes. His pudgy face and wide smile were easy to make fun of, but most of our class actually liked Freddie and his energetic spirit. Somehow that spirit had connected with Trevor's, and Freddie seemed to have declared himself Trevor's official tour guide to Grace High.

"Chris, hey, hold on."

I stopped as I walked down the tiled hallway toward art class. Freddie hurried up, guiding Trevor by his arm.

"This is Trevor Thomas," Freddie said.

I know.

What do you do when you meet the man you're going to marry? Of course you don't know this at the time. The thought is a million miles away. But I wish I had done *something*. Instead, I just smiled and stood there, at a loss for anything to say. Trevor grinned and looked at Freddie as if he was crazy. When I didn't say anything, he quickly spoke up.

"I'd shake but, you know—" He held out the hand with the splint.

"Trevor's from Michigan. Just outside of Grand Rapids. But no, he's not Dutch."

Freddie laughed and flashed gaping teeth that needed to be scrubbed hard. He looked ten years older than his age. I tried my best to appear at ease.

"She's Charissa," Freddie told Trevor.

"Sorry," I finally said, keeping my lips tightly clenched. "Hi."

"You've met Kyle Zielstra, right?" Freddie began. "No, you know him. Short black hair. The baseball guy—I told you. This morning after first period—yeah, that was him. Charissa dated him for a long time. Right? I mean, not anymore, but for a real long time."

I wanted to tell Freddie thanks so much for bringing that up. Not that it had *anything* to do with anything, except probably to keep Trevor away from me. Nice. Very nice.

Trevor watched me as he let Freddie talk. It almost looked like he held back a guffaw.

"How long have you gone to Grace?" Trevor asked me.

"My whole life."

"That long?"

"I've known her for eight years," Freddie blurted out. "Right? Eight years, I think."

"So what do *you* think?" Trevor asked me.

I swallowed and felt like a fool, not knowing what to think or say and wishing Freddie had prepared me for this.

"I enjoy it," I told him, wishing I could think of something witty to say. "It's a good school."

"Great thing starting over junior year, huh?"

Freddie gestured down the hall. "Hey, there's Amanda. She wants to talk to you." He started off down the hall, tugging at his falling, beltless pants to keep them up.

Trevor stood in front of me, looking around, probably wondering how he got stuck with this quiet, uninteresting girl.

"So, Charissa VanderVelde," he said.

I nodded.

"I'll try to remember that."

"That's okay."

"Trevor, come here," Freddie shouted from down the hall. He was standing next to Amanda Bennett and her group of friends.

You know Amanda Bennett. There's at least one Amanda Bennett in every grade of every high school in every state in this country. Perfect hair, perfect teeth, perfect skin, perfect body—plus a bubbly personality. I hated feeling this way, but I couldn't stand her.

"My new best friend calls," Trevor said.

He held up his right hand and waved. He realized I was looking at the splint. "It's not as bad as it looks," he said to me.

"Did you break something?"

He nodded. "They had to reset the bone and everything. Gave me some drugs and I didn't feel a thing. Remarkable stuff. I just won't be playing tennis anytime soon. Which isn't surprising, since I never played tennis before."

"Trevor—"

He grinned as he headed off. "I'll see you later. Nice to meet you."

A few minutes later Trevor strolled into the art room. I was already sitting behind a messy canvas that tried to pose as something vaguely resembling art. I stopped painting as I watched him talk to Mr. Maynard and show his injured hand. Mr. Maynard did his usual disorganized shuffling around and finally found his class roll, then Trevor was excused from class to go study in the library. Before Trevor left, he noticed me and smiled.

I can't tell you how amazing that smile made me feel, knowing that he'd spotted me and made it a point to let me know he did. That smile made me believe that maybe people could start over—not just new students from another state, but also girls everybody thought they knew and hardly anyone noticed and who desperately wanted to change their lives.

Looking back, I can't believe I even dared to think it—but I did. I was thinking that with Trevor Thomas, I just might have the chance to be someone different.

From: Imperiopoint@aol.com
Date: June 12
To: CST61795@aol.com
Subject: parting thoughts

...I sit here thinking of all the reasons why I love you. Is it strange to hear these words coming from me? Maybe it is. Maybe I should have written them before now. I know I can't let any more time pass without sharing how I feel. I need to tell you everything. Maybe this is my last chance....

TUESDAY, 10:25 P.M.

Lisa was holding Charissa's hand and talking about the news coverage on the car radio when the phone rang. Again.

Silence coated the room as Charissa picked up the cordless phone. Doug quickly turned the volume of the television down.

"Hello," she said as calmly as possible.

Ever since answering her mother's call earlier that night, Charissa jerked every time the phone rattled. And it had been ringing nonstop, with family members and church friends and Trevor's colleagues and fellow teachers from her elementary school calling to see if she was all right. She was amazed at how many people knew or were wondering if Trevor was on board the plane.

"It's not them," she mouthed to the group as she stood and walked away from them toward the kitchen. In their faces she saw the same mix of feelings that shot through her each time she answered the phone—disappointment that it wasn't Trevor, relief that it wasn't some stranger's voice from Transcoastal Airlines calling to deliver nightmarish news.

In this case, though, she also felt a surge of gratitude to hear the voice of Genevie Blake, one of her closest friends from college. Charissa had left a sobbing message on her answering machine thirty minutes earlier. She wanted—she needed—to talk to somebody about the day's events—including what had happened before Trevor left.

"How are you doing?" Genevie asked her in a motherly tone.

"Not good."

"I'm so sorry. We just got home. We'd heard about the crash on the radio, and then I got your message. I'm so sorry, Chris."

"Thanks." Charissa carried the phone slowly across the kitchen and into the unlit silence of the living room.

"Are you with anyone?"

"My family is here."

"That's good. I wish I could be there too."

Genevie lived an hour north of San Francisco.

"That's okay. I'm glad you called."

"They don't know any more details, right?" Genevie said.

"Not yet," she replied.

"Has anyone from the airline contacted you?"

"No. My father has been trying—the lines have all been busy."

"We're going to be praying for you guys. And for Trevor."

The soft worn cushions of their living room couch felt comforting to fall back into. Their living room couch. *Their* couch. Was anything *theirs* anymore?

"Gen?" Charissa said after a brief silence.

"What?"

"Trevor and I argued before he left on his trip."

"I'm sorry."

"No, I mean we really argued. He got—I mean he found an e-mail sent to me from this guy at my work and—it's so horrible…"

Charissa began weeping softly in the stillness of the room. The voice on the other end of the cordless phone said that things would be okay, told her to just slowly relate what had happened. Charissa finally managed to in the midst of deep sobs.

"He thinks I'm having an affair. He saw an e-mail sent to me. I never saw it. It's from Greg."

"Greg? Who's Greg?"

Charissa clenched the receiver.

"He's a teacher at my school. I barely even know him. I've talked with him a few times. This was his first year. He teaches sixth grade. I just—I don't even know how he got my personal e-mail. Not that it's a secret, it's just—it's horrible. And now Trevor thinks I was having an affair. After all we've gone through. I still can't— Oh dear God, this isn't happening."

"Trevor knows you wouldn't do anything like that," Gen's calm rational voice assured her.

"No, he doesn't. We haven't been doing that well lately, Gen. I mean, I knew things weren't perfect. But all marriages go through that, right? But this happens, this stupid e-mail. He refused to believe me. I didn't even know what to say. He left without saying good-bye, and I just thought…"

"He knows deep down. He knows you would never do anything to hurt him."

Charissa sat in the dark and looked back over her shoulder to the brightly lit kitchen and family room. The scent of freshly ground coffee beans filled even this room, and she could make out the flicker of the television reporting news that was never going to get any better.

"He's gone, Gen. He's gone—"

"Don't think that."

"It's true. I know it's true. I knew something horrible might happen the moment he stepped out that door. He died thinking—"

"Charissa."

"that I was having an affair."

"Stop it," Gen ordered. "Right this instant. Don't do this to yourself. You don't know what happened. Not yet."

"I can't just sit around like this." Charissa stood up again and began pacing the dark room.

"Listen, Chris, all couples go through hard times."

"Not like this, they don't."

"No, I guess not. But you know, Sheridan and I haven't always had an easy road. There've been times—especially after we had Elisabeth. But that's why you rely on the Lord, Chris."

Charissa thought of the last time she'd seen Genevie and Sheridan. It had been at their wedding a couple of years ago, a small and intimate beachside affair. She and Trevor had ended up vacationing a few extra days in San Francisco. Snapshots from that trip flickered through her mind. Very pleasant snapshots.

"I just don't know what to do."

"You have to wait. And have faith."

"I didn't even—"

Charissa stopped herself.

"What?"

"Nothing."

"What is it?" Genevie asked.

Charissa knew she couldn't say anything more.

"I should go."

"Call me if—if you find out anything. And keeping praying, Chris."

"I know. I'm just so angry. I'm not sure I can pray. I don't know what to pray for."

"Pray that Trevor is safe. Pray for a miracle."

A miracle.

Charissa wiped at her wet cheeks and cleared her throat.

"I picture him alone on the plane thinking all these horrible thoughts and then the plane going down and him never getting a chance to know the truth—"

The tears came faster now, and Genevie stayed on the line, murmuring words of comfort and mostly just listening. But she offered one final bit of wisdom before she hung up.

"No one knows for sure what exactly happened with the plane," Genevie said. "Don't you dare give up hope. Or give up on God."

TREVOR

He didn't want to be in this house, around these people, listening to Def Leppard and making stupid small talk. He didn't want to explain to anybody why he had moved or what his father did for a living or anything else about his life. He wanted to tell the next person who made a remark about his New Order T-shirt to get a life. Or tell the girls with the wine coolers and rising volume to shut up and grow up. But he stayed by Alex and listened to him talk and sipped on his bottle of Budweiser and took in the scene.

It wasn't one of those ridiculous scenes out of *Fast Times at Ridgemont High* or one of those John Hughes pictures that had 250 drunken high schoolers wrecking an upper-class home in the suburbs. This party consisted of around forty students, mostly juniors and seniors, all relatively well behaved and arrogant in their sophistication. There was no keg—simply bottled beers and wine coolers and some heavier stuff in the kitchen that you could mix. Everybody had to take their shoes off before entering Kelly's house, even though her parents weren't home. Kelly was one of Amanda's friends, a dark-haired junior with suggestive eyes and a habit of wearing tight clothes.

"That's Dan," Alex told Trevor in a snide voice just above a whisper. "Wait until the end of the night. We'll have to carry him home."

"His parents don't mind?"

"They're in denial or something. Sorta crazy."

"This kind of party common?" Trevor asked.

"Yeah, I guess. You get some bigger ones. Depends on who's having it. This is pretty low-key. Most of the parents would freak, you know. But hardly anybody gets out of hand."

Kelly walked up to them and joked with Alex about a sophomore girl named Debra. Alex disregarded her comments and asked if she knew Trevor.

"Hey, Trevor," she said with a curled smile and raised eyebrows. "How does this compare to Michigan parties?"

Somebody   25

"Tons better than the ones I've been to."

Trevor didn't add that he had been to maybe two or three "parties" back home. There was no point in any real conversation anyway. He had noticed Kelly's glazed eyes and the way the smile wouldn't leave her mouth.

"You'll have to tell me all about your old school," she said, touching Trevor on his arm.

Yeah, that was subtle.

She walked away a little unsteadily. Trevor noticed her short skirt and then laughed.

"Think she likes you," Alex said.

"I think she's had one too many wine coolers."

"So, what do you think after a few days? Any girls you're interested in?"

"Well, Kelly I want to marry."

Alex looked at him, puzzled at his deadpan expression.

"No," Trevor said.

Alex seemed surprised by Trevor's quick response. "Come on. There's gotta be someone."

"Amanda and them—they're hot."

"Amanda—I wouldn't get involved with her."

"I don't plan to."

"She's dated at least six guys in our class. She goes for older guys anyway."

"You ever gone out with her?"

Alex laughed. "That'd be a little weird."

"Why?"

"She's my cousin."

"Ah."

"Now, Kelly—she's actually pretty cool. A bit of an airhead sometimes, but you know."

Trevor nodded, not saying anything. He still couldn't believe he was here—in this living room, around these teenagers, in this new locale. A new town, a new state. It still didn't even feel real. Like the beer he drank and the slight buzz it gave him, it felt phony and temporary, as if it was going to wear off and he'd wake up and find himself back in Michigan

before everything happened. Before that afternoon when he discovered
the truth and decided to do something about it and ended up ruining
everything.

"You know—I could set you guys up," Alex was saying.

Trevor looked at his new friend. "Who?"

"Kelly."

"That's all right."

"Why not?"

"Did she say something?"

"Sort of. Amanda said something."

"I'm not looking for a relationship."

Alex laughed. His yellow polo shirt looked freshly dry cleaned and
was untucked over jeans and boots.

"Kelly's not really looking for a relationship either."

Trevor smiled an obligatory smile. Even after a few days, he had
begun to figure out the landscape of the school, and he had decided it
was a smart idea to placate Alex, to smile at his jokes and get his innu-
endos and follow after him like so many other students did. Alex wasn't
the sort of guy Trevor liked. In fact, he hated phony rich smug types.
But perhaps Alex would prove him wrong. Maybe Alex would prove to
be real. Trevor doubted it. But he could see that his time at Grace would
be easier if Alex Huizenga was on his side. And at this point, he was
ready for his life to go a little easier.

On the way home, with his head feeling light and drained from too
many beers, Trevor leaned back in the passenger seat and watched the
passing side streets. Alex drove the black year-old Pontiac Grand Am
while the sounds of U2's *Joshua Tree* CD rumbled out of the stereo.

"Like these guys?" Alex asked.

"Yeah."

Trevor was still thinking of Kelly's good-night kiss, a simple kiss on
his cheek before leaving. Trevor had not had time to move his head, had
not known what was coming, and hadn't had anything to say afterward.
Alex had laughed and patted Trevor on the back like an affectionate
older brother as they climbed into the car. He would have been sur-

prised by how angry the kiss made Trevor. It made him think about another dark-haired beauty who used to kiss him often.

Emily still lived in that two-story brick home back in Michigan. She probably had already forgotten about him. But he knew that everything that happened back home would stay with him for a long time. Kelly whatever her last name was—she was just another attractive, over-privileged girl who was trying to get to know the "new guy." Yet Kelly had no idea what the new guy was like, what sort of baggage he carried. Nobody knew, and he had no intention of letting them know.

Bono wailed, the Edge's guitar riffs echoed, and Trevor just sat there wondering what it would be like if he could go back a few years and do everything over. Emily. The stuff with his mom. Everything. It all had changed as quickly as a stolen kiss. And though he kept trying to tell himself he didn't care, the truth was he cared way too much.

From: Imperiopoint@aol.com
Date: June 12
To: CST61795@aol.com
Subject: parting thoughts

...Why are we even together? Sometimes I've wondered this myself. I know that if I'm honest enough with myself, I'll admit I've never deserved someone like you. And even though they say opposites attract, I'll never know quite why I attracted you. But you—I know why I'm with you. Why you attracted me. Why I fell in love with you....

TUESDAY, 10:50 P.M.

Light from the kitchen reached into the darkness of the living room where Charissa knelt on the floor next to the sofa. Her forehead rested against the soft cushion of the couch. She had just finished talking with Genevie and decided to take her advice.

"Dear God. Please. Please."

She lost control for a few minutes and just knelt there, her face against the cushion, waiting for strength to continue.

"I don't know why you allowed this to happen—where the plane is—if Trevor is okay or not. I don't know what happened. I just pray—dear God, I pray, let Trevor come back. I know this might not happen, but I know you can make anything happen if you want it to. Please, God, let me see him again. There's so much we need to talk about, so much I need to tell him. Forgive me for being distant and for arguing with him—forgive us for arguing this afternoon. Please, God…"

give me a miracle

"…bring him back to me."

After another long minute she stood, wiped the tears from her swollen eyes, and walked back into the family room.

"I haven't been able to find anything about a travel agent." Penny had just come downstairs and now stood next to the couch where Doug still sat.

"I'm pretty sure that was the flight," Charissa said. "But thanks."

The short, red-haired woman nodded, her eyes on the television.

"It's just, you never know."

"He would have called," Doug told his wife. "If he was on another flight, he would have called."

Maybe not, Charissa thought.

"Do you know the hotel where he's staying in Germany?"

Charissa nodded. "I called. But it was an overnight flight, so he wasn't supposed to check in until tomorrow."

"What about any people traveling with him? Do you have anybody else you can call?"

"Pen—come on."

"I'm just thinking of anything we can possibly do."

"God's the only one in control of this right now," Henry VanderVelde said.

"I don't think prayer's gonna do anything at this point."

Penny's remark hit like tear gas in a crowded room. Evelyn's eyes widened as she glanced at her husband. Doug shook his head and mouthed the words *shut up* to his wife.

"I think prayer is the only thing we *can* do at the moment," Lisa said.

Charissa looked at her older sister. Lisa's eyes had sharpened, and her face had become flushed.

"Prayer isn't going to help all those passengers in that plane."

"Come on." Doug glared at his wife.

"I'm just being real. There's a lot of things we can do besides pray."

"Penny, please," Charissa began.

Control. I need control. I can't keep breaking down.

"If God is really up there, why would something like this happen?"

"This is not the time," Henry said to Penny.

"What?"

"You know what," he said.

"Not every single person believes what you do," Penny's nasal, deliberate voice stated.

Charissa glanced at her father and saw the anger in his face. Her mother's eyes had filled, and she knew either Lisa or Doug was on the verge of saying more.

"Please—don't—all of you."

"I'm sorry, Chris," Penny said. "I just—"

"I know, it's fine. But—all of you—I can't do this if you guys are arguing. I just can't take another big debate about the existence of God. Okay? Please. I need everyone to—I need calm right now. Please."

Henry shot his daughter-in-law a warning look but said nothing more. The phone rang again, and Aunt Sheila stood up.

"How about I monitor the phones?" she asked.

"Thanks," Charissa said in a whisper.

Penny left the room, and the front door opened and shut. Doug sighed and glanced at his mother, then he handed the remote to Charissa and left the room as well.

"Why does she always have to—"

"Lisa, no."

Lisa shook her head and then looked at her sister.

"I'm sorry, Chris."

"You didn't do anything. It's nobody's fault."

"None of us can question God's will," Henry said to the room. "It's nobody's right to do so. Who can know what the Lord thinks?"

Charissa recognized the reference to Romans 11:34. She nodded at her father, then couldn't help noticing his muscular and mostly hairless legs exposed between the Nike shorts and bedroom slippers he wore. He must have forgotten to take off the slippers when they left their house fifteen minutes away.

She surprised herself by smiling, though she knew it was just the start of a very long night.

CHARISSA

How did we ever end up together? Good question. I would love to be able to tell a romantic story that begins with Trevor's spotting me in the hall and falling for me on the spot, then continues with his asking me out and my turning him down and his not giving up on me and my finally giving in to him. But it didn't happen that way. The way it did—I know I'll never forget the series of events that led to our friendship and eventually to something more.

Yet even as I write that, I know I'm afraid I might forget some of those events or overlook some of those simple words.

A month after Trevor arrived at Grace, I spoke to him again. One time. One solitary, insignificant time. We spoke about, of all things, Twix candy bars.

Several times I'd seen him purchasing a Twix during the morning break. Sometimes he'd bring it down the hall where Alex and his group lingered. Other times he'd open it and eat alone, not seeming concerned about what people might think. Sometimes I wondered if Trevor even noticed most of the other students around him.

On this day I was standing behind him after his morning break purchase. He turned around and almost bumped into me. I remember being aware of how tall he was. For a moment we stood facing each other, the crowd pushing us together as though we were slow dancing.

"Excuse me," he said, teal-colored eyes looking down at me in a polite glance.

"Another Twix?" I tossed out like a beggar producing a tin can, desperate for somebody to fill it.

"You bet. Every day."

He didn't smile at first, but the look on his face seemed lighter than his usual deep, contemplative look.

"I hear those are good for you." Even as I said it, I was kicking myself for how lame it sounded.

"Really?" He raised one eyebrow. "Funny, I don't get that feeling."

I moved past him and bought a package of Starburst. As I left the crowd of students buying doughnuts and candy, I saw Trevor leaning with one leg against the wall. He chuckled and glanced at the candy in my hands.

"And *those* are good for you?"

I looked at the package and shrugged.

"I hear Starbursts don't digest well," Trevor said without a smile.

"Are you serious?"

"Yeah. They're made of a special plastic substance found on a distant planet. Neptune, I think."

"Neptune, huh?" I nodded and felt myself blush. "Sounds pretty deadly."

"Oh yeah. It is. I think I should at least sample one to make sure this is the safe kind."

"Go ahead."

As he took one and nodded in approval, I wanted to say something clever. I wanted to prove to him that no, I wasn't the boring girl he probably assumed me to be. I wanted to show that I could be funny, that I could talk in front of him, that I could hold a conversation just like Amanda and Kelly and any of those other girls. But I simply smiled and wondered if my face was red.

"Thanks," Trevor said.

I nodded and said sure and then began to walk away.

My entire high-school experience summed up by a simple conversation about a piece of candy.

It was the field trip to downtown Chicago, to the art museum on Michigan Avenue, that finally made Trevor and me something more than just hallway acquaintances

A large group rode there on a bus—several classes of us, all taught by laid-back Mr. Maynard. I looked around for Trevor after sitting down but couldn't find him anywhere. I sat with Gina, one of the few girls I talked to in art class. Remember having those classes that *none* of your friends had? For me, it was art. Ashley would have taken it with me—I'm sure of that. And she would have talked all throughout class as we worked on our projects, and it probably would have been one of my most enjoyable classes. Instead, I sat in my usual place next to a sophomore named Gina, who didn't talk much but at least knew my name and could carry on conversations with me.

The two buses departed, and we were given passes for an afternoon in the museum. The multilevel building was enormous, from the steps in front to the high-ceilinged rooms and massive corridors containing expensive works of art. I began walking around with Gina, not very interested in the paintings but glad to be out of school.

After half an hour I grew bored with studying the famous paintings and reading descriptions of who painted them and what they were called. (The dull-sounding titles, like *Afternoon on the Pond* and *Girl in Blue,* didn't help.) Then I rounded a corner to yet another large open room and saw Trevor sitting on a bench, studying a picture.

To this day I wish I could remember that painting. It'd be nice to say, "We started it all sitting in front of a Monet," and to be able to remember that exact painting, but I don't have a clue what it was. Trevor wasn't interested in art either, it turned out. He was simply zoning out, waiting for time to pass, sitting down and looking at the wall and thinking God knows what.

That's sort of the point, actually. God *did* know that Trevor would be there and that I would somehow have the courage to walk up to him and ask if he liked the painting.

"Yeah, it's okay," Trevor said, looking up at me.

"You could spend a whole day here and never see the same thing twice."

"I know. Have you seen Maynard? He's describing all his favorites. I don't think he's even noticed that most of the kids are out on the steps or down in the gift shop."

"I'm sure he loves it here."

Trevor wore jeans and a sweater since it was November and had already started getting cold. I felt awkward and wished I'd made a better dress selection than my jeans and button-down white shirt underneath a jean jacket.

"Want to sit?" he asked, moving over.

"Um, okay."

I sat down next to him and looked at whatever painting was there but didn't *really* look at it. Instead, I just wanted to talk to Trevor and be with him. I wondered if he still remembered meeting me that first day or if he remembered our glorious conversation about candy.

"Charissa, right?" he asked.

"Yeah."

"I'm Trevor."

"Yeah, I know."

He nodded. "It's easier knowing the new guy's name."

"You like art?" I asked, my voice shaking but quiet enough that I hoped he wouldn't notice.

"Well, I'm not exactly anti-art. But I took this elective 'cause I figured it'd be easy. My father teaches art."

"Where?"

"Covenant College."

"Oh yeah. That's not too far away from here."

"He takes the train in every day."

"I'm thinking about going to Covenant."

Trevor made a *hmm* sound, a dismissive grunt of sorts. I didn't know what it meant, what he was thinking, so I said the only thing that came to mind.

"So your father teaches art?"

Of course I knew this, because he'd just told me.

"Yeah. Taught art back in Michigan."

"Why'd you guys move?" I asked.

Trevor glanced at me and then looked back at the ground. "New job. A change of scenery. My parents' divorce. You know, the typical stuff."

"Oh. Sorry."

"No, it's okay. It took them twenty years to officially sign off on the fact that they weren't ever meant to be together. I'm living proof of a miracle, to be honest. Not sure how they ever stopped arguing long enough to start a family."

I cleared my throat and looked to my left for a second.

"Sorry," Trevor said. "Nothing like a little divorce talk to suddenly make a conversation awkward."

"No, it's okay."

"So, I see you working away on your paintings every day in class. You big into art?"

"No, not really. It's just for class, I mean."

"What are you interested in?"

"At school?"

"Yeah. Or life in general. Anything. What do you see yourself doing years from now?"

"I wouldn't mind being a teacher."

"Hmm, a teacher. What, teach at a college or something like that?"

"No," I said. "Probably younger. Maybe elementary. I love children."

"I would never be able to teach." Trevor shook his head and looked deep in thought. "Plus, they don't make squat. My father's a great guy. I just—I want a different life than his."

We both looked at the painting in front of us. Mr. Maynard's voice drifted in from another room. He was the sort of teacher who was so immersed in his love of art and teaching it that he tended to forget that he was dealing with teenagers who sometimes didn't necessarily share that same level of passion.

"Uh-oh," Trevor said.

"What?"

"We're going to get roped into his lecture."

"Oh yeah."

"Hey," Trevor began, studying me for a second before going on. "You want to stay in here?"

"In this room?"

"No, in this museum. It's a gorgeous day out. Want to go walk down Michigan Avenue?"

I didn't even know exactly what he was talking about doing. Leaving the museum? Walking down Michigan Avenue? What for— shopping? talking? just walking?

"Sure," I said.

"Let's go before Maynard sees us."

As I followed him, Trevor asked me what time the bus was leaving to go back home.

"I think four."

Trevor checked his watch. "So we've got an hour to kill."

In a few minutes, we were walking with the crowds on Michigan Avenue, past department stores and expensive shops. We walked side by side, and Trevor acted more upbeat than I'd ever seen him. After we'd gone about six blocks, he spotted a café and asked if I wanted to go sit inside.

"Yeah, that'd be great," I said.

I didn't know what we were doing or what Trevor was thinking. He was simply excited to be downtown, next to tall skyscrapers and designer clothing stores. He kept asking questions like how often I came to downtown Chicago, what I thought of the city, how long I'd lived in the suburb of Hinsdale, what the city was like during Christmas, and how bad traffic was on the interstate.

We sat at a round table with two chairs in the corner of the small café. We both ordered sodas and sat for a few minutes looking through the window that peered onto Michigan Avenue.

"Sorry for talking your ears off," Trevor said.

"That's okay."

"It's cool to be in the city. I've only been here a couple of times in my life."

"Really?"

"Yeah. We didn't come to Illinois very much. I don't have much extended family, and the few relatives that I do have are in Michigan."

"I've got a few cousins that live in Michigan."

"Any relatives at Grace?" he asked me.

"No."

"No relatives?" Trevor joked. "Wow. That's a rarity."

"I know."

Trevor sipped his soda and looked around the café. The walls were adorned with Chicago pictures—the lake, Michigan Avenue, famous residents like Michael Jordan and Walter Payton and Mike Ditka.

"I'd rather come in here and look at this art," Trevor said.

I agreed with him. Other than that, I honestly didn't know what to say. I felt like an idiot. I was sure he'd eventually realize how boring I was and move on.

"What's your favorite class?" he asked.

I thought for a moment and then told Trevor it was probably chemistry.

"Chemistry? Seriously?"

"I like Dr. Schiller."

"Yeah, but chemistry," Trevor said, exaggerating the word like it was a curse.

"It's not that bad."

"I'm in algebra, and it's awful. But since I'm the new guy, they give me a lot of leeway."

"Do you like Grace?" I asked.

"It's interesting."

"Interesting how?"

"You got a lot of politicians and lawyers walking around the hall-ways."

I scrunched up my eyebrows and tried to figure out what that meant.

"You know," Trevor said. "People that'll say whatever they need to whenever the time comes. Phonies. Hypocrites. That sort of thing."

"Like who?"

"You know them better than I do," he said. "Why don't you name off some people?"

I simply smiled.

"There were a lot of cliques and all that nonsense back at my old school, but people weren't as rich. Or as snotty."

"Not everybody at Grace is rich."

"So, are you?" Trevor asked.

"Not really. I mean, I guess we do okay, but we're not in the same league as some of the others."

"Well, that's good. 'Cause you're not snotty either. I wouldn't put you in the Amanda Bennett category."

I was surprised to hear him say this since I always saw him hanging around with Amanda and Kelly. I sipped my soda and then decided to ask a question that had been niggling at me ever since I sat down next to him at the art institute.

"You're going out with Kelly, right?" I asked.

Trevor looked at me with a puzzled look. "What do you mean 'going out'?"

"Seeing each other. You know—dating, whatever."

"I did some stuff with her and some others. Is that what people are saying?"

I nodded. I was glad I'd had the nerve to ask him since I was dying to know. Kim had told me just a few days ago that Kelly and Trevor were an item, and I had overheard Kelly and Amanda talking about Trevor.

"I mean, it was this one thing last Friday, and she asked me—it was with a group. Alex was there. It wasn't a big deal."

"I just—that's what I heard."

"No, no, no," Trevor said, shaking his head. "Kelly, believe me, nothing's going on."

"Okay."

Trevor looked at me, frustration on his face. I blushed and looked down at my drink.

"That was pretty quick," he said.

Quick to blush? I wondered. How could he say that?

"I mean, it was just one date. And suddenly everybody's saying we're a couple?"

"No, I just—I'm sorry."

Trevor nodded and moved to grab his glass and accidentally hit it, sending it flying onto the concrete floor. It shattered into what sounded like a thousand pieces.

"Aw, man," he said, cursing under his breath and realizing it came out louder than he intended.

"Sorry about that."

"No—" and I wanted to apologize, saying this was my fault, that I shouldn't have brought up the whole Kelly thing.

Trevor looked at me and started to laugh.

"What?"

"Nothing," he said.

"No, what is it?"

"Nothing, it's just, the look on your face."

"Is funny?" I asked.

"No, it's—it's cute."

I didn't know if the old blush had stopped before a new color came.

Trevor stood and found a waitress to clean up the glass. He joked about ordering another drink but decided against it.

"Sorry," he said to me again.

"It's fine. I'm—"

"I shouldn't be so—so whatever about the whole labeling thing. It's just—Kelly." He laughed. "Tell whoever that I'm definitely *not* going out with her. You might want to tell her that too."

"Kelly and I are not exactly the best of friends," I said.

"Really? See, my respect for you continues to grow. Tell me more."

"About what?"

"About you. Like, do you have brothers or sisters?"

"One of each," I said. "Both older."

"Did they graduate from Grace?"

I told him yes and then suddenly found myself telling him about me. Telling him about Charissa VanderVelde. This was new ground for me. And I could have told him anything. I could have lied and made up stories, and he would have believed them because he didn't know me. But I didn't lie. And even though I told him my simple story of living in Hinsdale most of my life and growing up going to Grace with the same friends and the same church and the same everything, Trevor listened to my every word and appeared interested. I found it amazing that he would even remotely care.

The only time he stopped listening was after he glanced at his watch.

"Oh man."

"What is it?" I asked.

"This is not good," he said.

The buses had left half an hour ago. And though we ran back to the front of the museum and ran up the steps and looked around to see if anybody had stayed behind, we realized that the buses had gone back to school without us.

All Trevor and I could manage to do was laugh. I told him I couldn't believe they'd left us behind.

"Maynard doesn't strike me as the most observant teacher at Grace. Am I right?" Trevor asked as we stood on a curb waiting to hail a cab.

"Yeah. But still—I'm surprised someone didn't say anything."

"Half the people don't even know who I am."

"I've only gone to this school all my life," I told him with a smile.

"Well—if I'd been on that bus and didn't see you, you know what I'd do?"

"What?"

He thought for a moment. "I'd get out of the bus to find you." He paused, then added, "And tell them to go on without us."

The sixth cab driver told us he'd take us back to the suburbs for fifty dollars. More than the cost of a limo, about ten times the cost of a train ticket. Trevor simply nodded and told me not to worry about anything, that we should take the cab.

We sat in the back of the taxi, in stop-and-go traffic on the Eisenhower expressway headed west, without a care in the world. I don't remember exactly what we talked about, but conversation never stopped. Not once.

When we got back to school, we saw the two buses parked on the side of the school next to the parking lot with a few students waiting for their rides. The buses must have arrived fifteen or twenty minutes ahead of us.

"We'll have to go find Maynard and tell him what happened," Trevor said as the taxi circled around to let us off. "Just in case there's an APB on us or anything."

I was prepared to cover half the cost of the taxi ride, but he surprised me by paying for the whole thing. He grinned at me after shutting the cab door and surprised me yet again.

"You know, you're a pretty expensive date," he said with a laugh.

From: Imperiopoint@aol.com
Date: June 12
To: CST61795@aol.com
Subject: parting thoughts

...I love you first and foremost for your gentle and kind spirit. Your sympathetic heart. Your sensitive nature, fragile and breakable and yet so giving. Your smile.

I remember your smile the most from my first few weeks at Grace. So much had happened before I came. So much of me hated being there. And amid a bunch of unfamiliar, uncaring high schoolers, that smile stood out....

TUESDAY, 11:20 P.M.

Doug walked in and ran a hand through his blond, thinning hair. His eyes had a faraway expression, almost as if he were sleepwalking.

Even after so many years, Charissa found her brother difficult to read. Like her, Doug kept a lot inside—not just his thoughts and feelings, but an entire life. The few things he ever talked about with her included professional football, about which she knew practically nothing; cars, mostly for the sake of Trevor; and people from their old high school. Their relationship seemed to exist only because of their parents and the fact that they lived close to each other.

Doug stood at the island in the kitchen and waited for Charissa to finish filling her glass with ice.

"Sorry about all that," he said.

"It's okay."

"Penny had no right—I told her so. She just doesn't get it sometimes."

"It's fine," she said.

"I told her to just go on home."

"You didn't have to."

"No. It's just—it wasn't right."

She saw tears edging his eyes. He didn't say any more, but already this was more than she would ever have expected. Penny clashed with the family on a regular basis, but Doug had never once publicly questioned or even disagreed with her before tonight. His sending her home only compounded the intensity of everything that was happening.

"Do you want anything?" Charissa asked him before he sat down.

He let her pour him a glass of Coke from a can. She filled her glass with the same for herself. From the kitchen, she continued to watch the television. Her father was back on the phone with Transcoastal Airlines. Judging by his silence, she figured he was on hold again.

A stack of bills on the kitchen island caught her eye. She examined them and wondered what they consisted of. Trevor usually took care of these things. He took care of many things.

My car. Money matters. Insurance—what about life insurance? Where would I even begin to look? And does looking mean I'm considering him— I can't.

Her mind exploded in a meteor shower of thoughts, each more impossible than the one before. She started flipping through the bills and noticed a credit card statement with a balance of $2,467.08. Hadn't they already paid this off? How did they run up the Visa card again?

A blanket of worry wrapped around her. She could actually feel her body temperature rise. She took another sip from her glass.

There's so much I don't know.

What about their mortgage? And the rest of the bills? And of course, those car payments? The house was only two years old, Trevor's car practically new.

What am I going to do?

She remembered her father's statement earlier: *Who can know what the Lord thinks?* But what was the Lord thinking about how she was going to take care of all the endless bills? What about their house? What about the life they'd worked so hard to build?

what about

But she wasn't ready to ask that last question. Instead, she crossed the kitchen toward the door that opened onto the laundry room and the garage. Maybe Trevor had taken his car, she told herself. Maybe she just hadn't heard him leave.

She knew better, of course. And when she turned on the overhead light, the black two-seater still sat there in the garage, the security lights blinking every few seconds.

Still there, next to her white SUV.

Charissa went inside again and walked past the laundry to the kitchen. She found the extra set of keys in a drawer and took them back outside. She clicked off the alarm and opened the door of the almost-new vehicle.

Trevor's baby. A 2002 Audi TT two-seater convertible. Black with a tan leather interior. Unbelievably sporty. Incredibly expensive. The list could go on.

She slid inside the car and closed the door. The top was still on. She breathed in the new, leathery scent.

How long had Trevor talked about buying this car? How often had they argued about such a meaningless possession? He had finally given up pleading his case and driven home in it one day. He had told her they could afford it, that he worked hard and that he wanted to drive something he absolutely loved.

She had not driven the car yet. Not that he hadn't let her. She simply didn't want to.

I'm left with this car. And the payments.

She couldn't believe the thought. It was so utterly selfish, so utterly trivial. In light of everything, who cared?

I never drove the thing. Not once.

The interior felt confined, silent, almost majestic in its cleanliness. The dials and knobs in the car looked simple and European, in contrast to the complicated stereo and phone system above the shiny gearshift. Charissa studied everything for the first time.

The car. The TT. The stupid TT. One of the top items on the list of things argued about. Charissa questioned whether they could afford such an expensive car. He resented her questioning, told her to trust him. In Charissa's mind, a sporty German two-seater had just seemed foolish. Especially since they'd been thinking about the whole family thing. Not just talking. Arguing. She winced at the memory.

The car, the careers, the baby, the new house, the bills, the money, the budget, the business—month by month, they found new items to add to the list.

So this is what I'm left with. A list.

It was a foolish and melodramatic thought. She knew that. She knew it even though she fought back more tears. She knew it even as she glanced down at her lap and pressed her hands against her still-flat abdomen.

What are we going to do now, Lord? What are we going to do now that we're alone?

She breathed in, then stared hard at the controls of the car. Silence. Nothing but silence.

She heard the slight click as she inserted the key. The engine purred to life. She didn't turn on the lights, didn't open the garage door, didn't do anything. Her hands rested on the steering wheel, but she had no idea where she wanted to go.

TREVOR

The basement of the two-bedroom house on Martin Lane in suburban Lombard served as Trevor's room. His holding cell, as he liked to think. His mattress lay on the floor, a desk next to it. Against one wall was a bookcase his father had built. On it sat his stereo and hundreds of records and cassettes. On each side of the bookcase hung five-foot-tall posters of his favorite rock groups: Depeche Mode, the Cure, The Smiths. This Sunday evening, as he listened to Depeche Mode's *Music for the Masses* and waited for Alex to stop by and pick him up, Trevor replayed the conversation he'd had with his father earlier that afternoon.

"I really wish you had come to church with me," his father had said.

Robert Thomas was a medium-size man with thick curly hair that should have been cut two months ago and a goatee that made him look too artsy for his own good. For him to suggest that Trevor attend church with him was ludicrous.

"Don't start," Trevor said, not even looking up from the football game.

"I'm just asking."

"I get five days of church," Trevor said. "One more day isn't going to help."

"School isn't church."

"Really? Then what do you call Grace *Christian* High? Sounds sort of churchy to me."

"I know—but it's still just a school. You need—"

"You know how I feel about church," Trevor said.

His father was standing in the living room, looking at Trevor with desperate eyes. Trevor hated those eyes, hated how often he'd seen them look that way, hated the way they made him feel. It wasn't enough that his parents had gotten a divorce, and an ugly one at that. What killed him was the fact that his mother had so thoroughly and utterly defeated his father—and Robert Thomas wore that defeat on his soul every day.

"I'm not going to make you go, you know that."

Trevor chuckled. "Yeah, I'd like to see you try."

"Trevor—"

"Church really did a lot for us, didn't it?"

"You can't judge them all—"

"No? I can judge the only church I know. Good ol' Pastor Wood—there's some grace for you. Christian love. What a godly man."

"He had his reasons."

"Yeah, right. I don't want to see any more Pastor Woods and their reasons. There's enough hypocrisy at Grace."

His father stared at him. "I'm sorry you feel that way."

A singe of guilt burned him, and Trevor smothered it. He didn't want to think about it here and now.

"I'm not saying that about you—"

"I know I haven't been the best example," Robert told his son.

"Look, you couldn't help what Mom did. I just—I can't deal with any of that stuff now."

His father nodded and walked away.

Now, a few hours later, listening to music in the solitude of his bedroom, Trevor thought of the conversation and his father's words and the embarrassing change in his father's once-positive personality. A failed marriage, the loss of a job, being ousted by a church. Trevor would feel defeated too. Instead, he felt shame. He wanted the memories simply to go away.

Music allowed him to slip away. So easy. So simple. Chords and verses and minor keys and words like the Depeche Mode song that played now. Amazing that a group from overseas who had absolutely nothing in common with Trevor could speak to him so clearly. Like now, as Dave Gahan's deep voice sang that "God is saying nothing."

Trevor had to agree with him. He believed there was nothing ordained, nothing predestined, nothing God-given in his life. It was the only thing that made sense. If God existed—and that was a mighty big *if*—he didn't give a flip about Trevor or the Thomases and especially not about Robert Thomas.

Trevor knew his father worried that he'd lost his faith. Maybe he had. Or maybe he'd never had much faith to begin with.

Steps sounded behind him, and Alex showed up smiling.

"Ready?"

Trevor nodded and turned off the stereo. He picked up a few cassettes and grabbed his jacket before heading out.

He would have thought that being befriended by Mr. Grace Christian High meant swallowing big doses of religion and being bored out of his skull. Instead, Trevor was amazed to find what Alex Huizenga and his friends did for recreation.

Trevor sat in the backseat of John G.'s SUV between Tank and Nick while Alex rode shotgun. They listened to the industrial rock group Ministry and didn't talk much.

John G. found the parking lot next to an empty office building.

"Cops never come here," he said.

They stepped out of the car and walked to the edge of the woods nearby. Trevor knew the drill by now. Normally he would only smoke a little; he hated the way marijuana burned his throat going down. The first time he'd smoked with these guys—the first time he'd ever smoked—he had inhaled from a pipe and had managed two seconds before gasping and coughing. The guys laughed, and Alex assumed his mentoring, big-brother stance as he put an arm around Trevor and told him it was all right. The Obi-Wan Kenobi of pot smoking—that was Alex. He didn't smoke as much as the other guys, especially not as much as Tank, but he still had his share.

Tonight would be no different. After half an hour of smoking, they'd drive around sipping bottles of schnapps and listening to music. They laughed a lot, talked about people at the school and things they wanted to do in college, but nobody ever got too out of hand. Trevor always got the feeling that Alex still needed to be in control of things, even things like getting high.

He didn't mind going along with it. These guys would never be close friends—he wasn't interested in making friends at Grace anyway. But he liked being part of something, even though he didn't really know these guys any better now than on the first day of school. The pot made his problems ease a little, made the memories of his parents' divorce seem distant and the mistakes made with Emily like a moot point. But even in the midst of these four guys, laughing and joking and drinking, listening to music that pounded against his eardrums and his head, Trevor still felt alone, apart.

And on this Sunday night, as he sat in the backseat feeling light-headed and empty, a picture of someone came to mind. Someone he barely knew, even though he probably knew her better than anybody else at the school. Someone who actually seemed real, someone he simply enjoyed being around. Not that he had been around her much, but still. Charissa's smile came to mind.

He found himself wishing he was with her.

She probably wouldn't feel the same if she knew what he was doing now.

From: Imperiopoint@aol.com
Date: June 12
To: CST61795@aol.com
Subject: parting thoughts

...I never wanted anything serious in high school. To me, Grace was a way station for something bigger and better. I knew I'd soon be going to college, and the rest of my life—a career, a marriage, a family, all of that stuff—could be taken care of then.

It never occurred to me I'd meet someone like you....

TUESDAY, 11:40 P.M.

"What are you doing?" Lisa asked as she opened the car door.

"Nothing."

"Nothing's going to get you killed. Turn that off."

Charissa shut off the engine for a moment.

"Is this new?" her sister asked.

"Yeah. Trevor bought it a few months ago."

"Looks expensive." Lisa got in and started examining the interior.

"He never told me how much he paid for it. He just said we could afford it."

Lisa nodded and studied her sister.

"Let's go for a ride."

"I've never driven it," Charissa said.

"So? You know how to drive a stick, right? Well, let's go."

"No, really, I need to stay—"

"For what? For more news on nothing? Let's take a breather. I'll tell Mom and Dad—and grab my cell in case they need to call."

"Really, Lisa—" But her sister was already out of the car and through the door to the laundry room.

In a few minutes, after moving their parents' car in the driveway, Charissa and Lisa drove down a street headed toward nowhere in particular. They rode with the top down—another of Lisa's orders.

"This thing is fast," she said.

"Yeah."

"Floor it."

"No."

"Come on," Lisa shouted over the wind.

Charissa pushed it up to seventy-miles an hour, twenty over the speed limit. As her hair streaked back and her eyes watered from the wind, she felt a weight lift off of her. She knew it was partly because she had left the house and partly because for a few seconds her mind was on something else. She also realized this grace period was merely a

tease. She'd be back home soon enough, waiting for news, trying to pre-
pare herself for…for whatever.

"Let's go to Krispy Kreme."

"No, Lis."

"Come on. It'll be good for us."

"I'm trying to watch out for sweets."

"One won't hurt you."

"I already feel sick to my stomach."

"Okay then. Anywhere around here you *do* want to go?"

"No."

They stopped at a light, and a truck full of young guys pulled up
next to them. Someone shouted "hey," and Lisa turned, waving at
them.

"What's going on?" Lisa called out to the strangers.

"Lisa—don't!"

The light turned green, and Charissa jammed the gas pedal down.

"So, that's the secret to picking up men," Lisa said. "All I need to
get is one of these little things." She patted the leather upholstery.

Charissa didn't say anything. Lisa put a hand on her bare leg.

"Chris—I'm just trying to get your mind off things."

"I know. I appreciate it."

Charissa turned on the radio and tried to find an AM station with
any new updates. Lisa turned it off.

"They'll call if they hear anything."

"Where should I go?" Charissa asked.

"There, down the road." Lisa pointed to the Dairy Queen. "Let's go
get something. We can drive through."

"Lisa, I told you—"

"I know, I know. I'll get something. You can share."

The two sat in the half-full parking lot outside a Target store, just down
the road from the Dairy Queen. Lisa worked on her large Oreo Blizzard
that Charissa had taken a few bites from. It helped a little to realize that
Lisa knew her well enough to know her favorite dessert, ice cream, and
her favorite flavor, cookies and cream.

"It looks like it might rain," Lisa said as they looked up to the sky.

"Wonder what Trevor would do if we got the inside of his little TT soaked?"

Charissa didn't answer. Lisa took another bite and stared at her sister.

"You're already acting like he's gone."

"He is."

And he's been gone for quite a while too, Charissa thought.

"Don't say that."

"Why?"

"'Cause you just can't, Chris. You can't start thinking that way."

"Lis—"

"What?"

Charissa wondered how much she should tell her sister. She decided she could tell her anything. Now was not the time for censoring her thoughts, as she so often did with those around her.

"Things haven't been great between Trevor and me."

"Meaning?" Lisa asked, finishing the bottom of the Blizzard.

"Meaning we've been arguing a lot lately."

"About the car?"

"No." Charissa held back her emotions as she stared up at the cloudy sky. "Well, that, too. We argue about basically everything."

"Married people do that, I guess. Not that I'd know. But isn't it normal to argue?"

"Not the way we do."

"What do you mean?"

Charissa tried to capture it in a sentence. Or a paragraph. Or something that could communicate to her sister exactly what had gone wrong between her and Trevor. But no words did it justice. "It's—I don't know—it's like we just don't connect. We don't rely on each other anymore."

"Trevor adores you, Chris. He always has."

Charissa shook her head. Tears worked their way to her eyes again.

"You two were always meant to be together."

"I thought so," Charissa said. "Now I'm not so sure. Maybe it was all a big mistake."

"Don't say that." Lisa's tone caught her attention. "What I did to Michael—now that was a mistake."

"What?"

"Well, maybe in the long run, it wasn't a mistake. But calling off the wedding, breaking up with him like that—I wonder every day if that was what I should have done."

Her words surprised Charissa. She had always wondered if there was a darker secret her sister had never shared, something she had learned about her fiancé. Michael was a good-looking, dark-haired jock who had gone on to move up the corporate ladder.

"I always thought there was something—some reason."

"Just that I believed in my heart he wasn't the one," Lisa said. "I didn't think he was the one God picked out for me. Now—now I wonder if it works that way at all. Maybe we're supposed to just make a choice, hopefully a smart choice, and then God gets involved after we say 'I do.'"

"What do you mean?"

"I mean that he's the only one who can make marriages work. Look at Mom and Dad, for instance."

Charissa thought of her parents and their rock-solid marriage. "Well, yeah, but that's them."

"I think it's God. God's always been part of their life together, and it shows. I think you have to just put your faith and hope in him and trust that things will work out."

"It's hard. With Trevor, I mean. His business has boomed, and it seems that the more successful it's gotten, the more distant he's become. He's always traveling, always doing something for work. I was so proud of him at first, doing so well, after he'd floundered around for so long. He's really a hard worker. It's just—I wished he worked harder at other things."

Lisa reached out and took her sister's hand. "I've said more than I probably should—as if I knew anything about marriage anyway. But I do know that Trevor loves—"

Lisa's phone rang, jolting both of them. She opened the receiver and said hello, then waited as someone gave her news.

"Okay. We'll come on home."

Charissa's stomach tightened, and she felt nauseous again. She breathed in and knew the news Lisa was going to tell her. She knew there was nothing to do but continue through this nightmarish sequence of events.

Tell me. Just get it over with and tell me.

"They found someone," Lisa said. "They didn't say who, but they found somebody."

CHARISSA

I came to know the Lord at an early age, and my faith was an ever-present backdrop to my teenage years. My parents always read from the Bible and prayed after every meal. Our Sundays consisted of church morning and night, and we often had activities during the week as well. But church was something I enjoyed, not something I dreaded.

Since I went to a Christian school, I never had to wear my faith like a badge of honor. It was assumed that all of us students were Christians. But we still had to cope with things like labels and cliques and reputations. My label was conservative and bashful. I wasn't really part of a clique—I was kinda on the outside my junior year, though I did hang around with some of my church friends. My reputation—to be honest, I didn't think I even had a reputation.

This doesn't mean I wasn't interested in a social life. I was curious about the popular group and the parties I heard about, and part of me wanted to be part of it all.

I got my chance at John G.'s New Year's Eve bash.

I heard about plans for a party even before Christmas break. John G., so called because his middle name was Gregory and his parents insisted he keep it as a title, was one of the richest kids in our junior class—the sort of guy who didn't care about wealth simply because he had grown numb to living in a world full of it. His house was not so much a house as a mansion—located in Burr Ridge, an upscale suburb with sprawling lawns and giant castlelike homes. His parents had said it was okay for him to have a party. A big party.

Two things excited me when Kim told me about the party. First of all, the fact that I was even being considered to go. Before this, I might have been at one party during all of high school. But John G. liked me well enough—we knew each other from the time I dated Kyle, and I think for a while he might have even been interested in me. That was during our freshman year, before the cliques were set in stone and the idea of John G. dating me made no sense to anyone. In fact, sometimes

I still got the slightest hint that he might like me, and I know that after Kyle and I broke up, he talked with me more often.

Of course, everybody knew and liked Kim, the friendly outspoken jock who liked to tease guys. It probably wasn't much of a decision to invite Kim and me. John G. wanted a big party, and we made the cut.

The other, more important reason I was excited about the party was that I knew Trevor would be there. Since our memorable Chicago experience and the cab ride back home, we hadn't spoken much. It wasn't that he avoided me; he just didn't make it a point to find me. Occasionally he would see me in the halls and make a joke about something related to the art institute or the cab ride home. But besides that and the art class we shared, there weren't many reasons for us to spend time together.

I thought the party might change that—give us a chance to make another connection. I didn't know what sort of connection, but any connection would have been fine by me.

Kim and I ended up at John G.'s house around nine o'clock on December 31. We had been told to dress up. And this instruction, of course, had provided hours' worth of conversation. Should I wear a dress or skirt or pants or what?

Most of the outfits in my closet consisted of khakis and jeans, plus some long skirts, and some boring, traditional church clothes. I had asked for a dressy outfit for Christmas and received several floral sweaters and dress pants, none of which would work. So Kim and I went to the Oak Brook Mall and found something that might work: a narrow black skirt that ended a few inches above the knee.

This was big for me. I always hated wearing anything, absolutely anything, that drew attention to me. I still do. Anything that shows too much of my legs or my shoulders or anything else makes me uncomfortable. But Kim insisted that I buy that skirt.

"You've got such a cute figure," she said as I stood in front of the dressing room in the black skirt and its matching long-sleeved lacy top. "You *have* to get that."

"I don't want to look like a floozy."

"You're not going to look like a floozy," she said with a laugh. "You'll look stunning. You'll finally get Trevor's attention."

"Kim," I said in shock. I looked around in horror, as if Trevor might be in the dressing room next door with his ear against the door

"Well, that's what you want, isn't it?"

I ended up getting the skirt and the top and a pair of black high heels with strapped tops. All for this party.

But now, as I walked up the long, car-lined driveway toward John G.'s brightly lit house, I doubted my decision. Was my outfit too revealing? Would people think I was trying too hard? What would people be doing in there? Where would I put my purse?

Questions filled my mind as I followed Kim into a house full of mostly juniors and seniors and people I didn't know. John G.'s parents were on the premises, but they made a point of staying out of the way. I think they were spending the evening with some friends in the guesthouse in back. I never even saw them until the end of the evening.

The big table in the dining room was loaded with elegant hors d'oeuvre and a crystal bowl filled with pale-colored punch. Kim whispered to me that there was booze in the basement. It was kinda an open secret. But I didn't feel comfortable drinking alcohol. I never had, and didn't feel any big need to suddenly start. Did I think it was a sin having a glass of wine? Deep inside, I honestly didn't know. But punch suited me fine, and John G. seemed happy to pour me a glass of it.

"Lookin' very nice tonight, Chris," he said to me in a perfectly gentlemanly tone. "Glad you could come."

These words surprised me. The host of the party saying this to me. I don't know how many people were in his house—a hundred or more? Music bellowed through the cavernous living room with its sleek white furniture and high ceiling. Kim and I mingled—what a sophisticated thing to do as a junior in high school. The dress, the punch—you might have thought we were adults by the way we all acted.

Kim and I eventually gravitated to the luxurious den, where we stood next to a gargantuan entertainment center that hosted a large television and various boxes controlling the compact discs and everything else. For a while we talked to John G. and Jason DeGroot and some others about the house. John G. was in rare form that night, more talkative than usual and paying much more attention to me than ever before. As he spoke, I glanced around the room and finally spotted Trevor.

He walked across the hardwood floor by himself, holding a glass of punch in his hand. His gaze found mine for a second and moved on. And then his eyes shot back toward me in an obvious double take.

It was a glorious moment.

He paused and looked as if he was going to say something, to call out at me across the room. Several people walked between us, and then I saw him again, stopped, looking right at me. I turned my head back toward Kim and John G. and tried to appear as though I was listening to them.

Again, I glanced at Trevor, and this time he smiled. When he saw me looking his way, he waved at me—as if he hadn't recognized me at first. That seemed strange to me. I mean, sure, my hair was worn in a different way, in a low ponytail that fell over one shoulder. And sure, I was dressed up. But I was the same girl he'd seen so many other times.

What is it about a short skirt and heels that sometimes makes guys act so strange?

For just a minute I thought Trevor would walk over and talk to me. Then he apparently decided against it and walked into the kitchen.

But I wasn't worried. The night was still young.

All that night we kept seeing each other and not talking to each other. It felt like a game we played. I remember around ten o'clock I noticed Trevor talking with Kelly. She wore a skirt that made mine look conservative, and she draped herself over Trevor in a way that embarrassed even me. He didn't encourage it, but he didn't seem to mind either, and for some reason, this infuriated me.

Something had happened between us with that earlier glance. I don't know what it was, but it was *something*. And so far, he had yet to even talk to me that night. So when I saw Kelly throwing herself at him like that, I decided I would not make the first move. I had done my part by showing up. Now it was up to him.

At one point in the evening, Kim asked me about him. I shrugged and said I wasn't sure what he was thinking. I didn't tell her about our shared fleeting looks earlier—or that he hadn't said a word to me all night.

John G., on the other hand, made it a point to stay around me. I had always thought he was good-looking—big and dark and muscular—and he made me feel comfortable. I found myself in a conversation with Alex and the others, with John G. by my side making me laugh. Trevor saw me with this group, with *his* group, and didn't come up to us even then.

I didn't know if I could have the same effect on him that seeing him and Kelly had had on me. But I tried. I laughed a little harder and tried to look as if I was having fun. And so this stupid charade of sorts continued for a while.

Midnight eventually came. And in my mind, the inevitable happened. Trevor found me and told me how beautiful I looked and how he'd barely recognized me at first but now wanted to be near me during the countdown to the new year so he could kiss me gently on the lips and tell me he had always thought I was adorable and he simply couldn't control his feelings anymore.

Of course, this didn't happen. I didn't talk to Trevor at all. I kept seeing him around others, acting a little more boisterous than usual—it didn't occur to me then that he had been making regular trips to the basement—and he kept seeing me around John G. Then the countdown came, and John G. hugged me, and Trevor Thomas was nowhere to be seen.

The party started going downhill when Tank came up to John G. with his white shirt untucked and soaked and spotted.

"Dude, we got a problem."

So far the party had been mostly uneventful in terms of problems. John G. and his group had ordered several people to leave after being rowdy and spilling drinks and causing a commotion. It was almost like an unspoken code. Everyone knew that alcohol was available, but no one was supposed to act drunk or let on to John's parents that there was booze anywhere on the premises. Now the short but stocky Tank looked angry and concerned.

"What is it?"

"It's Trevor. Man, he's sick. And he's upstairs."

My heart sank, and I followed them up the off-limits stairs to John G.'s parents' bathroom. Between a two-sink marble counter and a

Jacuzzi, a figure wrapped himself over the toilet bowl in a way that almost appeared to be a joke.

John G. looked at the mess around Trevor and cursed.

"I tried to help him, and he threw up all over me," Tank said. "This is uncool."

I stayed in the room for a few more minutes as I watched John G. try to move Trevor. I saw half of Trevor's face, his eyes mostly closed and his crusted lips moving as though he was saying something. Both of Trevor's arms clasped the white bowl, and I noticed his brown hair damp from probably dipping it in that same bowl.

I couldn't believe what I was seeing. I felt sad, sick, and completely bewildered.

What had happened to Trevor tonight? What did he do to himself? I knew *what* he'd done to himself, but why? Why tonight?

Then he dry heaved, and I knew I had to leave. I couldn't see this. I couldn't see Trevor like this. I didn't want to get sick myself.

John G. cursed, and he and Tank talked about what they needed to do. On my way downstairs I saw a concerned Alex walking past, looking like a parent about to ground his child for something awful the kid has done.

Kim and I left a few minutes later, just after John G.'s parents came upstairs to discover the spectacle.

From: Imperiopoint@aol.com
Date: June 12
To: CST61795@aol.com
Subject: parting thoughts

...And why? Why did somebody like you cause this train of thinking to derail? Why did all my plans suddenly go on hold? Because I knew I loved you—and I knew that you might be the person God chose for me. And I think I realized this early on. It might surprise you when....

WEDNESDAY, 12:26 A.M.

please God please God please

Charissa's hair whipped in front of her face and across her mouth and behind her again as she sped down the road leading to their subdivision. No longer refreshing, the air felt like bitter breath blowing on her face. Lights flashed by in a surreal rhythm. Sitting in Trevor's car with her sister beside her, racing through the neighborhood where she and Trevor drove every day, speeding past the elegant stone gates and the various houses that slightly resembled their own—everything felt dreamlike.

She turned onto Portsmouth Court and drove down the road. Their house, a twenty-five-hundred-square-foot structure where they had lived for a couple of years, stood at the end of the drive, all lit up and adorned by cars. And empty. Twenty-five hundred square feet of emptiness and smashed dreams.

They pulled in the driveway, but a car Charissa didn't recognize blocked them from pulling into the garage. Lisa exhaled, closed her eyes for a second, then gave her a glance that said *here we go*.

Charissa knew her sister had been praying, and she wondered what God thought about all these sudden prayers. All these voices calling out for the life of Trevor Thomas. Did he deserve to live? Did Charissa deserve to beg and demand that Trevor's life be spared? Would any of this make any difference?

"It's going to be okay," Lisa said behind her as Charissa opened the door to the house.

They all sat together in the family room—a still-life portrait of loyalty and nervousness. Her brother in a chair in the far corner, the remote still clutched in his hands as if everything depended on his TV vigil. Charissa's parents sitting on the plaid sofa along with Aunt Sheila. Lisa and Charissa on dining-room chairs, their hair still windblown from their drive. And Bart and Megan Markson, a couple from Charissa's small group at church, sitting awkwardly on the love seat.

The Marksons had greeted Charissa with hugs and tears as she entered the room. At first she thought they had good news. But she'd quickly learned that nobody knew any more than the initial report about a survivor. Bart and Megan had simply been offering their love and support and trying to appear as positive as possible.

Charissa was vaguely aware that she was falling down on her hostess duties. Ordinarily she would have talked with Bart and Megan and asked how they were doing and whether they wanted something to drink. Now she could barely say anything to them or to anyone else. Part of her wished she were alone so she could focus on the television as if it were her own personal viewfinder. Everything else seemed pointless and peripheral.

The group watched the television as the cable news channel listed details about recent air disasters. Her mother had suggested they change channels, but Charissa had told them no, she wanted to watch. She wanted to learn about the possibility of survivors.

"I don't think I can watch this," Evelyn said, going into the kitchen.

"Just don't change it," Charissa said.

A flight that went down in China last year. No survivors. A plane that seemed to explode in midair. No survivors. A 747 that plummeted into the Pacific a couple of years ago. No survivors.

The news confirmed how she felt, what she believed. Trevor had to be gone. The news that somebody had survived this airline disaster, that a person had actually lived, was almost unfathomable. It might be true, but it still seemed surreal.

Was this what true, genuine shock felt like? Her senses felt overloaded and numbed at the same time. Yet she continued to watch the television even as her mind wandered on to what had happened to her and Trevor, to their marriage.

Charissa thought of the last year. Of the lonely evenings and the five-minute calls before she slipped into an empty bed. Of her busy days teaching third grade at an elementary school in St. Charles. Of living in a house built for four and wondering if the other two would ever come—and if she even wanted a family under the circumstances. How could they raise a child if they couldn't even communicate with each other?

It was the little things that had told her everything. The standard "How was your day?" as he passed by her searching for a remote to turn on the evening news. The standard peck on the forehead as a goodnight. The morning send-off as personal as an attendant giving you back fifty cents in change on the tollway.

Little things mattered.

Oh, to have the little things back now, Charissa thought. *There's so much about them I'd change.*

More news about past plane crashes, this time a little more positive. Portugal. Ten survived. California. Twenty-five percent lived. The recent National Airlines flight she remembered hearing about that had somersaulted on a runway in Nebraska. Almost half the passengers had survived that crash. The newscaster was saying that somebody had survived a plane crash that had nosedived into the ocean.

Somebody survived.

The reporter's words brought her more fear than consolation. A thousand what-ifs rattled in her mind. Oppressive and growing, the dread she felt consumed her. She wished she could say that the prayers were working, that her family's presence helped, that hearing anything about faith and love soothed her ache. But each minute of waiting cemented another brick around her flickering candle of hope.

somebody

A distant time, distant place, distant memory filled Charissa's thoughts.

You've always been that somebody.

She could hear the words as if he were sitting next to her on the couch.

TREVOR

The thing was, he had no one to blame but himself.

He wanted to say and believe that he didn't care what they thought or what they said or did. He told himself this again and again as the weeks and months passed.

They're just passing by. They're just scenery. They don't matter. None of them matters because they'll soon be out of my life—just like all the others. They'll be gone, so I can deal with their glances and their whispers and whatever else they do.

Trevor knew he was feeding himself lies. When he was alone in his room at night, he knew he had made a stupid mistake, and it had cost him a lot. His reputation at school—not that he really cared about that. But also his friends. The friends he'd told himself didn't matter. They mattered.

Being grounded by his father for what seemed like the remainder of his teenage life wasn't the worst part of it. What was he going to be grounded from? Not hanging around with friends he didn't have? Big deal. If his father was smart, he'd have forbidden him to listen to his music or watch television. The grounding and the lecture about mistakes didn't make much difference to Trevor.

No, the worst thing had been the call a few days after the drunken incident. A call Trevor couldn't do anything about except listen.

He could still hear the highlighted comments from Alex:

"You really disappoint me, Trev... You let us down... There are things you just can't do... A lot of people heard about what happened... You gotta apologize to John G.... That was uncool... You just don't understand..."

Trevor had listened and said little except "sorry." There wasn't much else he could say. It was as if he had sinned and needed to come before Father Alex for absolution—only there was no absolution. As if Alex were a sinless soul who had allowed Trevor to walk with him for a while but no more.

Now, months later, Trevor realized this conversation was the last one he would ever have with Alex.

Their lockers remained next to each other. And Alex would say hi. But Trevor knew. He'd known the moment he got off the phone with Alex that things were forever different. He had violated an unwritten rule, crossed a line he hadn't even known was there.

In this crowd, apparently you could do some things—like smoking dope and drinking and partying a little—but other things were completely unacceptable. Having parents and other kids find out about the partying was unacceptable. Not handling your liquor was unacceptable. But letting down your cool friends and embarrassing them—that, apparently, was unforgivable. There was no being sorry, no going back. Break the rules, and you were out. Even if no one told you the rules.

Trevor still didn't understand exactly how it all worked. He just knew that Alex ignored him along with the others—John G., Tank, Nick, even Amanda and Kelly and their friends. This small webful of friends sure had a way of biting you.

In response to being ostracized, Trevor had done what he did best—retreated. Took the bus back and forth to school. Spent breaks in the study hall. Ate lunch alone, even when Alex and Nick were in the same room, often across from him, often just a few seats over, acting as if they didn't even know him. He walked the hallways by himself and smiled a tight-lipped courtesy smile at those who knew him and probably felt sorry for him, even girls like Kelly who probably felt obligated to go with the flow. He didn't like being ignored, but he kept reminding himself that he was just passing through anyway. In the long run, none of this mattered.

What he regretted most about the whole incident was that certain people—like Charissa VanderVelde—seemed to be legitimately disappointed in him. She didn't shun him like the others. But Trevor felt shame whenever he was around her. He knew she'd seen him that night—a lot of people had. And while few of the others' opinions mattered to him, her opinion did.

Trevor knew Charissa wasn't like Alex or Kelly or John G. She was different. And maybe if certain things hadn't happened, he could have been different too. Different in a good way. Maybe he could have had more in common with her. Maybe he could have been worthy of being around someone like her.

Instead, he stayed far away. From Charissa, and from everyone.

Then April came, and with it came the biggest surprise of the year.

It was at lunch, right after the usual twenty-minute session in line and the five minutes he took to wolf down a burger. He had his books and was walking toward the library when he heard someone behind him calling.

"Trevor?"

He turned and saw Charissa and stopped. She walked up to him, her bright blue eyes and slender face so comfortable to look into. She appeared nervous and slightly out of breath.

"Um, do you have a few minutes?"

He wanted to laugh and say something darkly comical, but instead he edited his thoughts and simply replied "Yes."

She cleared her throat and bit her lip and began to speak.

"You know, there's this awards banquet at the end of the year. I know it's in a month, but I was wondering if…if you'd want to go with me."

Trevor stared at her and wondered if he'd heard her correctly. He started to say something snide, then stopped. He could see the fear on Charissa's beautiful face.

"Well, yeah, sure," he said, not very convincingly. It came out wrong, as though he was questioning whether he wanted to go with her or not.

"You can think about it if you—"

"No. I'd—it'd be great to go. I just—are you sure?"

"Sure?" she asked.

"Sure you want to go?"

"Yeah. I told you—"

"With me?"

Charissa seemed to understand what his hesitancy was all about, but she didn't comment on it. She just nodded. "It's not senior prom or anything like that. It's just a dinner."

"Yeah, okay," he said, then said without thinking, "I promise I won't hurl on anybody."

Charissa gave him a sad, heartfelt smile.

"Sorry," Trevor said. "I shouldn't have said that."

"Things happen," Charissa said, and Trevor etched those words deeply in his heart.

They were simple words, but the way they were said, the expression on her face and the timing of the words, all meant so much more. They meant *I'm sorry about everything that happened* and *It's okay that you made that mistake* and *I know what's happened to you and I'm sorry* and *I still think you're an okay person.*

And as much as Trevor didn't want to admit it, he knew he hadn't felt like an okay person for a long time. It went way back before the New Year's Eve party. It went back to the year before, to everything that happened in Grand Rapids.

He wished he could go back and simply change what had happened, what he'd done. But he knew he'd never, ever be able to.

From: Imperiopoint@aol.com
Date: June 12
To: CST61795@aol.com
Subject: parting thoughts

...And now—now where do we go? What can I say to you?
Perhaps there are too many things to say and it is too late
to say them. But I will try to put them in writing, hoping you
will see them someday. Hoping they will mean something to
you....

WEDNESDAY, 12:52 A.M.

"I just want some answers."

Charissa could hear her father's voice on the telephone in the living room. She focused on his words and tried to ignore the television.

"That's not an answer," her father claimed in a voice she rarely heard.

A pause. Someone from the airline was trying to say something, anything. Probably some young kid who didn't know anything and was being overloaded with phone calls like this one.

"The nature of the accident?" Henry said in disgust. "What do you mean the nature of the accident? I think it's obvious what the nature of the accident is."

A quick silence.

"I don't want a *sorry*. I want an answer."

A different answer.

"Look, this is the third time I've tried calling you guys and the first time I've actually talked to a human being, and I need to—"

Charissa turned her head.

"I know—," her father began. "Yes, but—"

Charissa stood up and walked into the kitchen so she could hear her father better.

"Okay?" he yelled. "Okay? The plane went down into the Atlantic. How are they going to be okay?"

The crowd in the room looked at Charissa. Everybody who knew her father knew he was always levelheaded and never shouted. Hearing him like this made things worse. If he was angry and desperate, then how was she supposed to feel?

Her father walked into the kitchen, the phone clutched in his right hand. He shook his head and didn't seem to notice that everybody was watching him.

"Nothing. They're saying nothing."

Charissa's mother stood and took the phone. "Next time I'll call."

"That girl didn't know a thing. It's almost like she was reading a statement instead of just talking to me."

"She might have been," Evelyn said.

"Maybe they don't know anything," Charissa's aunt said.

"I don't buy that," he said.

"They have to be careful what they say," Evelyn said. "They don't want to get people's hopes up or discourage them either."

In the family room, Doug stood up and turned up the volume as he called out, "Hey—they've got something on the survivor."

Charissa and her family and the Marksons leaned toward the television to listen to the reporter, who stood in the terminal at O'Hare.

"Transcoastal Airlines has confirmed that one person has been found alive, although the survivor's name has not yet been released. The passenger list will not be released until there is more information about who survived and until next of kin for the others have been notified.

"What we do know about the search efforts is that rescuers located the approximate area where the plane went down, but so far the wind and high seas have hampered rescue efforts.

"One of the rescue divers did mention a lack of the typical sort of debris around the crash site. This gives reason to hope that the plane might have entered the water at an angle or even floated for a short time instead of slamming into the ocean. This of course would increase the possibility for survivors. The airline says it will provide us with more information as it becomes available."

Charissa's mother looked over at her.

"I wonder what they did with the survivor."

"He would call," Charissa said.

"You don't know that. He might be injured or—"

"If it was Trevor, he'd call. He'd make sure we knew."

"There might be more," Doug said.

"How can there be?"

"They just said so, didn't they? They might find a lot of them on a life raft or something. Remember the airline that went down in Africa—"

"That was a chance in a million. A miracle. You can't count on a miracle."

"But miracles do happen, sweetie. And you can definitely pray for one."

"Excuse me," Charissa said. "I need to go get some air."

As she went to slip on her shoes, her mother followed her.

"Can I come?" Evelyn asked.

"I guess so," she said, "if you want."

The two of them stepped outside into the warm midnight. If it weren't for her mother by her side, Charissa might have started running down the street until she couldn't run anymore. Instead, she picked at the clingy shirt that stuck against her sweaty shoulders and walked in silence for a few moments. Evelyn didn't speak, just kept up with her.

Waiting.

Charissa

Why did I ask Trevor to go to the awards banquet? The same reason he appealed to me during those first few weeks of school when nobody knew him and he seemed to be looking for a place he had yet to find. He'd found that place for a while, but now he found himself exiled from most of the students in our class. Though it was partly his own fault, I still felt bad for him. I also found him strangely intriguing, this silent guy who walked our hallways with so much about him still unknown. I wanted to get to know him, to see who Trevor Thomas really was.

Because of the New Year's Eve incident, Trevor was grounded from driving until the end of the school year, so he asked if I could drive us there. I told him I didn't mind, that I could drive one of my parents' cars. I took my mother's gold Camry and followed the directions to Trevor's home in Lombard. It was a modest ranch house with an unkempt lawn and deteriorating driveway.

I knocked on the door and Trevor answered.

"Hi," he said, looking slightly bothered.

He looked handsome in a black sports coat and a tie. I wore a new dress that I hoped he would comment on, but instead he mumbled something about his father.

"He wants to meet you," Trevor said as if the thought was hideous.

"That's okay."

Trevor's father was a melancholy, amiable man who greeted me with a handshake and then complimented me with words that should have come from Trevor.

"What a marvelous dress," Robert Thomas said to me.

"Yeah, you look really nice," Trevor added, falling into the too-little-too-late category.

We made small talk and ended up on the subject of Covenant College, where Trevor's dad was an instructor.

"I'm thinking about going to Covenant," I told him.

"Any chance you can get this guy to come along?"

"Not a chance," Trevor said. "I don't care if my tuition would be free."

"Well, it'd never be free, but my teaching there sure helps."

"Let Mom pay for school; she can afford it. In fact, I'm going to find the most expensive college out there."

"Something tells me you wouldn't be able to get in," Robert said.

"See what sort of abuse I get from him?" Trevor joked to me, but he wasn't really joking. "Not only does he ground me for life, but he also taunts me."

His dad didn't respond. "You two have a wonderful night," he said. "It was a pleasure to meet you, Charissa."

We got in the car and I started toward the banquet hall where the event would be held. We talked about Trevor's father, and I asked him how often he spoke with his mother.

"Less often than I speak with you," he said.

I glanced at him, wondering if that was a jab at me or not. I realized he didn't mean anything by it but was just telling the truth.

"Is that hard?"

He shook his head. "I don't want to talk to my mom. Ever again. Period."

After a couple of silent minutes, Trevor changed the subject. "So what exactly happens at these awards banquets anyway?"

"They hand out awards to people in sports and academics, that sort of thing."

"Hmm, Something tells me I'm not going to get one."

"I'm a finalist. That's why I'm going."

"For what?"

"The science award," I said, slightly embarrassed even though there was no reason to be.

"'The science award?'" Trevor laughed. "Wow, you must *really* like chemistry."

I didn't say anything. It wasn't that I loved science that much; I was just a diligent student.

"Does everybody go to this thing?" Trevor asked, changing the subject.

"A lot of people do. It'll be fun."

"I'll just have to trust you on that," he said.

Trevor did trust me, even after we arrived and entered the large banquet hall with a congregation of people he either didn't know or didn't care to know. The mingling at the beginning was almost painful, with Trevor at my side holding a punch glass and saying next to nothing. Kim and her date, Westin Cole, stood and talked with us.

Several people did double takes as they noticed Trevor (a) being there at all and (b) being there with me. I didn't mind. I sort of liked those looks. John G. probably gave us the biggest double take of them all.

I wanted to tell Trevor, "Don't mind them—don't mind any of them," but I don't think he did mind them. I guess he had gotten used to being snubbed and ignored.

Throughout dinner Trevor remained silent, smiling whenever someone at our table made a joke and commenting only whenever someone asked him a question, but it was obvious he wasn't having a good time. I could tell by his body language and by his reticence that he was only there because I had asked him to come.

The awards started with academic prizes such as math and English and science. I lost to Freddie Jones, who ended up winning several of them. Then there were the choir awards and the drama award and the athletic trophies—Kim was soccer player of the year—and so on. It wasn't exactly an exciting evening. By the end of it, I knew I probably shouldn't have asked Trevor to come.

As we walked out of the banquet hall, John G. came up to us and blocked us from leaving. He was about the same height as Trevor but weighed maybe thirty pounds more because of his big frame.

"You know, they forgot to give out the drunken wreck award tonight," John G. said to Trevor without blinking.

Trevor politely smiled, nodded, and began to walk around John.

"Hey, what's your problem?" John G. said to Trevor, grabbing him by the shoulder.

The look on Trevor's face could not be disguised. His eyes smoldered, and his face hardened and flushed. He gritted his teeth as he looked at me.

I know he would have probably punched John G. at that second had I not been with him. But I was the only reason Trevor was there in the first place.

"Get your hand off me," Trevor said, yanking his shoulder out of John G.'s grip.

"You think you're really special, don't you?" John G. asked, smiling maliciously.

Trevor still looked angry, giving John a frigid stare. He turned to me and then opened his hand for me to take it. I didn't hesitate to put my hand in his. He grabbed it and continued walking with me.

I've thought for a long time what this meant and why he did it. I sometimes think that if I had not held Trevor's hand, he would have gone on to use that hand in some other way. Like balling it into a fist and ramming it against John G.'s nose. Like making that smug smile on John G.'s face disappear. Instead, he held on to my hand, and we walked out of the hall in silence.

Trevor finally let go when we got to my car.

"Sorry about that," he said.

"You didn't do anything," I told him.

"Yeah, I did." He paused for a second and looked up at the sky and breathed in. "That's why it's so frustrating."

From: Imperiopoint@aol.com
Date: June 12
To: CST61795@aol.com
Subject: parting thoughts

...I love your beauty. I know I don't compliment you enough.
Years ago, when a poufy-haired blonde with braces talked
to me in the hallways of school, I could tell you didn't know
how attractive you were. I knew. Yet even I have been
surprised at how a cute young girl could grow into the
breathtaking woman you are now....

"I can't remember the last time I was up so late," Charissa told her mother.

The two of them passed a lone house with its outside lights on. Most of the other two-story homes slept in darkness, the gleam of the widely spaced streetlamps lighting their slow walk. Charissa still couldn't see stars and wondered how long the clouds would hover overhead.

"It's quiet," Evelyn said.

"I remember always sleeping with my windows open at home, hearing late-night cars during the summertime. Remember the Johnson brothers? How they'd always come home late at night? Sometimes I'd hear them and watch them from my bedroom."

"I didn't know that."

The memory was random, as were many of her thoughts this night. Charissa didn't say anything for a few minutes. Her mother simply kept pace with her, both in stride and in conversation.

"Do you remember what you told me about Trevor during my junior year? When I was thinking about asking him to the awards banquet?"

Her mother thought for a moment and couldn't remember.

"You said to take a chance. That's what I remember. That nothing could happen if I never even tried. And that's what did it, you know."

"I remember now."

"That night—that was the first time I realized that we might actually have a shot at being together. At *really* being together. When I thought that Trevor might actually like someone like me."

"Someone like you? Why do you put it like that?"

"We were so different. So completely different. And for the longest time, I always thought we'd have no chance. But that night changed things."

Her mother glanced over and nodded to show she was listening, letting her talk, letting her share her thoughts as they came.

Charissa looked ahead toward the winding curve of the street. "I always thought I'd marry somebody safe, you know. Someone like Kyle. Remember him? The responsible, steady, *safe* guy. Then Trevor came to school with an unknown past and this aloof sort of air."

"I never knew Trevor to be aloof," Evelyn said.

"He changed. College changed him a lot. He's a lot different from that kid who moved here his junior year."

"How so?"

"He's different in so many ways. And I used to think that was a good thing. He's so responsible and focused, and I know that's why he's successful. But his job—it's like he's poured all of himself into Imperio."

"That what happens when you start up a company." Her mother's voice was gentle.

"I know. I've just— Things haven't been that good between us lately. And now this."

Evelyn turned toward Charissa and took her hand. Charissa couldn't remember the last time her mother had made such a gesture. Instead of making some sort of trite and antidotal reply, her mother remained quiet.

"I just wonder if God is somehow judging us for all the—"

"Oh, Charissa, you know better than that."

"It's how I feel," Charissa said.

"God doesn't work that way. Bad things happen, Chris. We don't know why. Sometimes we're not meant to know why. But that doesn't mean God is out to get us."

"It's just, I feel—I really feel this is somehow my fault."

"But how could it be?" Evelyn asked, clutching Charissa's hand.

Charissa breathed in. Her free hand wiped her eyes.

"Trevor's been talking about having a family for a while now. And part of me—I just didn't know. I wondered if we should—how could we raise a child when we didn't even have time for each other? And that's been another thing. I just can't help thinking I'm being cursed for being so selfish."

Evelyn stopped and faced Charissa, her blue eyes piercing deep inside her daughter's soul.

"Charissa, you need to stop this."

"I can't help it."

"Starting a family is a big decision. And despite all the hints your father and I might have made to you—probably have made to you—it's not something you should do to please us or anybody. I just—it's your own business. Yours and Trevor's. And it's something you both have to feel is right."

"I know."

"You're not being judged for anything."

"Then why now?" Charissa said. "Why is this happening now?"

"I don't know."

"Why did God allow Trevor to die when—"

Her mother interrupted her with a hug. "Honey, you don't know that he's dead. You have to keep on hoping. Keep praying. Remember that God *wants* you to keep coming to him. He can do anything, Chris."

"Mom, please."

"And he'll will hold you, sweetheart. The Lord will take care—"

"Mom, I'm pregnant."

Her mother started to say something else, then gasped. The transformation from a mother trying to set the example of depending on God and not giving up hope and trying to comfort her daughter all crumbled at these words.

It should have been a time for joyous tears. Instead, her mother pulled her closer and began to weep against her face.

"Oh, sweetie, I didn't know. Oh no. No."

Her mother couldn't hide it. She couldn't say "It's all in God's plan" or "Let go and let God" or any other trite saying that compensated for what she really felt. This time it was too much, and all she could manage for the next few minutes was tears.

Charissa knew her mother wanted a grandchild. She'd said so for years, She had dreamed of this moment as hopefully as she had dreamed of Charissa's wedding day. But she had never expected it to be like this. Charissa struggled with the irrational sense that she had robbed her mother of something.

"I'm so sorry, Mom."

The apology seemed to startle her mother. "What do you mean, Charissa? This is wonderful news. Except—I just— Are you okay?"

"I'm fine."

"How long have you known?"

"Not very long," Charissa said. "I just found out a couple of days ago. I wanted to tell Trevor before—"

"Oh no."

"She nodded. She knew what her mother was asking.

"Trevor didn't—"

"No, Mom."

Charissa looked around and saw they were crying on someone's shadowy driveway. It would just top the night off if someone called the cops on them for disturbing the peace.

"Let's walk back," she said.

They spoke for a few moments about the baby, but Charissa asked her mother if they could change the subject.

"I can't—I can't talk about it right now. Not with all this. I just needed somebody to know."

She knew there was very little her mother could say. They still held hands as they walked back toward Charissa's house.

"Things can't end like this," Charissa said. "Whatever happens, I just know—they can't end like this."

TREVOR

In another life, Trevor would have driven Charissa home. He would have coasted down her street and pulled into her driveway and turned off the engine and the lights in his sporty car and looked over at Charissa and kissed her good night. He would have told her how beautiful she looked and told her he'd call her tomorrow and watched her get indoors safely and then driven home.

Instead, Trevor sat next to Charissa as she drove down Roosevelt Road toward his neighborhood. He didn't know how to end this night. He knew that Charissa liked him. He didn't know *why* she liked him, but he could read her body language and her glances well enough. And while he was flattered and thought she was a pretty and pleasant young woman, he knew he didn't belong with her. He didn't deserve her. There were so many reasons why they shouldn't be together, and those reasons sounded off in his mind as she turned down a side street a few minutes away from his house.

"Hopefully it wasn't a completely awful night," she said to him.

Let it go and be polite and wish her a good night.

That's what his head told him, but his heart said something different.

"Charissa," he began.

"Yes?"

She kept her eyes on the road, this slim, tall blonde with the sweetest of smiles, with a tender soft voice and an incredibly humble, gracious heart.

"Thanks for asking me to come tonight," he said. "For picking me up and bringing me home."

"Oh, it's all right."

"And for being such a beautiful person."

Charissa turned and looked at Trevor and then quickly turned and glued her eyes to the road again.

"You know—you're one of the only good things I've come across this past year. Not only at Grace, but in my whole life. I can't begin to tell you how thankful I am to have met you."

A part of Trevor told him to stop this, to stop this nonsense, to just shut up. But he ignored that voice.

"I didn't say this—I mean, my father did, and I agreed—but you really do look gorgeous tonight. And I never told you this either, but you looked breathtaking on New Year's Eve. I'm not just— Hey, you just missed my house." He turned and laughed out loud.

"Oh, I'm sorry."

They both laughed nervously as Charissa slowed the car down and turned it around. She pulled into Trevor's driveway and put the car in park. She stared down at the steering wheel.

"Charissa," Trevor said, getting her to look at him. "You know—I couldn't wait to talk with you at that godforsaken party. And every time I tried, there was John G. Or Kelly. And I thought, you know, I'm not going to be able to talk with you. I was never able to tell you how stunning you looked."

Charissa looked away. Trevor saw the shadowed outline of her face.

"I just wanted you to know that. I…I'm not even sure why you asked me to come with you tonight. There's this part of me that wants to kiss you good night. But I don't know what you'd think—where things would be between us. And right now, more than any sort of heavy relationship, I need to know I have a friend there at school."

Charissa glanced at him with her lips curling into a soft smile. "You do."

"Thanks. For tonight. For driving. For everything."

"Sure," Charissa said. "I'm glad you came."

"Could you do me a favor?" he asked.

"What?"

"Call me when you get home."

"It'll probably be after eleven."

"That's okay," he said. "I want to know you made it home safe."

She nodded, and Trevor said he'd see her later.

Twenty minutes later, Trevor picked up the phone on the first ring.

"Hi." The delicate voice sounded as though she were right next to Trevor.

"Thanks for calling," he said. "No flat tires or anything?"

"Trevor?" Charissa said.

"Yeah."

"What you said—"

"Uh-huh."

She paused for a moment.

"Thanks," she said, then told him good night.

From: Imperiopoint@aol.com
Date: June 12
To: CST61795@aol.com
Subject: parting thoughts

...I can picture your hand balled up beside your chin, your mouth slightly open, your eyelids closed. Your curled-up body, protected and safe under a shelter of blankets. This is when you look the most beautiful. Without makeup, without your hair brushed just right, without any pretense. When I wake before you do and just lie there and watch you—this may be when I love you the most....

Wednesday, 1:53 a.m.

When they walked into the house, Charissa's father and brother were standing in the hallway. Charissa knew what they were going to say.

Get it over with and tell me now.

"What?" she asked.

"The person they found. It was a woman."

Charissa nodded. She had already assumed it wouldn't be Trevor. She glanced over at her mother, who had kept an arm around her shoulders. Evelyn looked flushed and out of breath.

"Any more news?" she asked her father.

"No. I think I'll try the airline again."

Charissa walked into the family room and sank down on the couch. The Marksons were still there, staring at the television and just waiting for her to say something. Like her family, they looked tired and shell-shocked. She could only imagine what she looked like.

"There's nothing more on the news," Bart told her, "except on a couple of the cable channels."

She nodded as her father walked into the room.

"The airline didn't have any new information to give me. They said they can't give out any official information on the survivors. They said there could be more by the end of the night."

Charissa nodded again.

"The person I talked to said they've contacted most of the families."

"Then what about us?" Charissa asked.

"She was going to check. Said they'd be calling back soon."

"They should have called us already. It isn't right to make us wait so long."

"You should get some rest," her mother said.

"Not yet," Charissa said.

"We can let you know if—"

"No, I'm fine, Mom. You guys can go on home."

"No. We're staying here."

"You didn't hear from Trevor's dad by any chance?"

Her father shook his head.

"Nobody's called. When's he supposed to get in tomorrow?"

"I'm not sure. Sometime in the morning. He was supposed to call."

"I was thinking, if we knew his flight, maybe we could have him paged—maybe pick him up. He ought to hear about this from one of us."

Charissa wondered where her father-in-law's itinerary might be. Trevor's study, maybe. She shook her head.

"I don't think he ever gave it to us."

Maybe that made her feel better about the truth—the reality that she didn't want to go inside the study. Not yet. She couldn't do it just yet. Walking in there felt like raising a white flag, officially recognizing the reality she already believed. God would see that and know she had given up and was paying last respects.

The entertainment center that held the television also displayed several framed photos of the two of them. Some recent, artsy black-and-whites. Their wedding portrait. One framed snapshot that had been taken during their senior year of high school.

She wished she could have the night of the awards banquet to do over again. And their first kiss. And prom. And everything that happened in college. And his simple yet surprising proposal in the hallway of her parents' house. She wished she could start over again and relive those moments, those and a thousand others. Just so she wouldn't end up taking him, and them, for granted.

God, if I could just go back.

CHARISSA

It was *H.M.S. Pinafore* that helped me really get to know Trevor Thomas.

It started four months after the awards banquet, during the first month of our senior year. I'd seen Trevor only a couple of times during that summer, running into him at his job in the produce department at a Jewel grocery store in Lombard. These encounters were brief. We smiled and said hi. I blushed a little. But Trevor never called, and I certainly couldn't bring myself to call him.

School started, and not much had changed. Our lockers were in a different location, we had different classes, and a whole slew of freshmen were learning the ropes of high school. But everything else was more or less the same. Including my feelings toward Trevor.

What exactly were those feelings? If Kim or one of my friends had forced me to write them down on an index card, I doubt I would have been able to fill in much of it. But I certainly felt something. An attraction, a curiosity, a longing. All that and more.

I was beginning my fourth year of choir. It was one of those things I'd simply started and didn't see a need to quit. I could sing decently, though I'd never want to sing a solo, nor did I expect to be asked. As with many other activities, I was content to be part of the crowd, quietly blending in without anyone noticing me.

This year our choir director, a hyper string bean of a man named Mr. Dodson, told us that choir and the drama classes would be teaming up to produce a play called *H.M.S. Pinafore*. Actually, it was more of a musical—or, as Mr. Dodson called it, an operetta—set on a Victorian sailing ship. There were various solo parts, but most of our choir would serve in the chorus as pairs of "sailors" and "maidens." And instead of assigning the parts to us, Mr. Dodson decided to let us choose our partners.

Though Trevor wasn't in choir, and even though I had spoken little to him during the month of September, I decided to ask him to be my "sailor."

I looked for him at break and found him purchasing a Twix bar.

"Still like those?" I asked him.

He smiled and nodded. "Some things never change."

"Hey, can I ask you something?"

We moved away from the crowd and stood against the wall. Trevor looked at me with his stern blue-green eyes. He ate his candy bar methodically and ignored the students who passed by us.

"Have you heard about the musical that choir and drama are going to be doing?" I wasn't about to call it an operetta.

He shook his head. I told him about *H.M.S. Pinafore* and about the fact that the chorus members needed partners. Right away, he began to chuckle.

"What?"

"I think I know where this is going," he said.

I paused for a second, smiling and waiting for him to say more.

"Charissa, I can't sing worth anything."

"You don't have to sing."

"Isn't that what a musical is? Isn't that what you'll be doing?"

"I don't sing. I mean, I do, but not like anybody can hear me."

"Will I have to try out?" Trevor asked.

"I don't know. Maybe. It doesn't matter. I asked Mr. Dodson, and he said that I could have a partner who isn't in choir."

"What am I supposed to do?"

This looked like a losing battle. I told him I wasn't sure what he needed to do, except that there would be afternoon practices several times a week.

"Wow, that's sounds like loads of fun," he said with only a tinge of sarcasm.

"I know—it's a huge thing to ask. I just—there's nobody to be my partner. I mean, there are a few. Freddie. Jake. Others."

"Freddie's in choir?" Trevor asked about the guy who initially introduced us. "Can he sing?"

"No."

"He'd make a great partner," Trevor said with a smile.

"That's what I'm afraid of."

Trevor thought for a moment and looked at me with curiosity. "*H.M.S. Pinafore.*"

"It won't be bad."

He looked like he was weighing the decision, thinking very hard.

"If you want to let me know—"

"It's okay," he said.

"What?"

"I'll do it."

I admit that I was surprised Trevor would agree. He later told me that if anybody else had asked him to do it, he would have said no without thinking. But he didn't mind agreeing to do it with me.

We stood facing each other, holding each other's hands, singing one of several songs we had been practicing for weeks now. Trevor and I, along with the rest of the couples singing to one another, were supposed to look "lovingly" into each other's eyes. As we sang, Trevor would widen his eyes and move his eyebrows and force a silly expression to make himself look like some B-movie actor pretending to be Dracula right before biting into his victim's neck. I always started to laugh and then had to contain my laughter as Mr. Dodson shouted instructions and watched all of us practice.

"Stop it," I whispered as we took a break and listened to more instructions.

I wiped my hands against my jeans, afraid of their being too sweaty for Trevor to hold.

Trevor didn't take this play seriously, even though I learned that he actually could sing quite well. Sometimes we would sit and watch the lead singers perform their parts, and I would look over to see Trevor's "this is nonsense" expression on his face. Other times he'd shoot me a grin or raise his eyebrows or give me some other expression that made me laugh.

Trevor had asked if I wanted him to drive me home after the rehearsals, so several times a week we would spend fifteen minutes in the car riding toward my house. It was out of the way for him, but he told me he didn't mind.

One overcast October afternoon, with the performance several weeks away, we landed on the subject of prom.

"That's one of the things I hate about prom," he said.

"What's that?"

"That people start talking about it months before it even comes. People make such a big deal about it."

"That's because you only have one senior prom."

"Just because you're a senior doesn't mean you have to go," Trevor said, shaking his head.

"So you're not going to go?"

"I don't really want to."

"What's so wrong with it?" I asked him.

"Nothing," he said. "I'm just not into proms."

"You don't have to be so detached from everything."

"I'm not detached."

"Yes, you are."

"I came here after the start of my junior year. How can I not be a little detached?"

"Prom's not so bad."

Trevor glanced at me. "You guys go out on a boat, right? You dance and have a fancy meal, and everybody compares their night to your night. Who has the nicest dress and the longest stretch limo and who's doing what afterward? I don't know. Doesn't sound wonderful to me."

"Okay, okay."

There was silence except for the sound of a slow rock song in the background. I had grown used to hearing different musical groups in Trevor's car that I had not heard before, bands with odd names like the Cocteau Twins, the The, and Front 242.

"Who's this?" I asked him to change the subject.

"You've never heard this?"

"No," I said.

Trevor pulled out one of the half-dozen cassettes from the seat divider between us.

"Depeche Mode. I play them all the time."

"They sound kinda different."

I tried to make out the cover of the cassette in the darkness. He turned on the light and glanced at me as I examined the tape.

"Most of their stuff has a pretty strong beat, but this song is mellow. It's one of my favorites. Called 'Somebody.'"

I remained quiet for a few moments, listening. I thought it was a pretty song.

"Trevor?"

"Yeah."

"Do you regret agreeing to be in the play with me?" I asked.

We reached my driveway, and Trevor pulled into it. He let the engine idle.

"No, it's been fun."

"Seriously?" I asked.

"I mean, I can't wait to get it over with, but yeah, it's been fun. I enjoy making you laugh."

"Mr. Dodson doesn't like it when you make me laugh."

"What's he going to do? Kick me out of choir? Oh, wait, I'm not even in choir."

I looked at him and paused for a second, a smile on my lips, and our gazes locked. In the darkness I could still make out the outline of his face, the curve of his lips. In my mind and in my dreams, I had kissed him good night a thousand times.

"See you tomorrow," I said, then opened the door and went inside.

From: Imperiopoint@aol.com
Date: June 12
To: CST61795@aol.com
Subject: parting thoughts

...I've always loved how shy you are. How hesitant you can
be in a crowd. How unsure you sometimes are around
others. You never want to say an unkind thing, and you
never want to be the center of a group's attention. I've
always admired this, since it's so different from how I am.
I'm quick to judge, quick to react, quick to speak my mind.
You've always regarded your reserved nature as a weakness.
I see it as a blessing....

WEDNESDAY, 2:14 A.M.

"Transcoastal Airlines Flight 421, which departed Chicago O'Hare Airport at approximately 6:00 P.M., went down in the Atlantic Ocean roughly two hours later. The flight carried 212 passengers and 5 crew. Everyone at Transcoastal Airlines is deeply saddened at this tragic accident and would like to extend its deepest sympathies to the families of the passengers and crew of Flight 421."

Charissa sat in front of the television once again, watching the bulletin scroll past on the bottom of the screen. Nothing new. The Coast Guard had been called out. One passenger had been rescued—no name, but they confirmed it was a woman. A spokesperson for the airline commented that a passenger manifest would be released once all the families of the passengers were contacted.

What about me? What about my family?

The airline still had not called. Charissa's father had tried calling several more times. Once he'd gotten disconnected, another time he'd been put on hold until he hung up, and yet another time he'd been told that Trevor Thomas was not listed as being a passenger on the flight.

"Can I get you anything?" Charissa's mother asked, her hand caressing her daughter's head.

"No." Charissa smiled at her mother with an expression that said *I'm okay.*

"Maybe you should lie down for a while."

"I just don't think I could—"

"We'll be down here. Why don't you go on up? We'll let you know if we hear anything else. You need to rest."

"I won't be able to."

She glanced at the Marksons, and Megan nodded.

"We're going to go soon."

Charissa wanted to apologize for practically ignoring them. She didn't know what to say.

"It will be good for you," Lisa said. "You should try to sleep."

"I've got to put Trevor's car up. Before it rains."

"I'll do it," Lisa said.

The TV continued to blurt out facts and information and interviews. Two hundred seventeen on the plane. One survivor.

There had to be more, right?

It had been so many hours. So many hours in the cold waters of the Atlantic. The deep, seemingly eternal abyss of ocean.

She thought of Trevor drowning. Of dying on impact.

She felt as if she might be sick.

"Maybe I will go upstairs for a short while."

"I can go with you," Megan said with her round-faced eagerness.

As Megan began to follow her, Charissa stopped for a moment and looked pleadingly at her friend.

"Megan, I'm sorry. I just—I need to be alone."

Charissa had already gotten enough pep talks and had heard enough God-is-good and don't-you-dare-give-up speeches to last her awhile. She simply wanted and needed to be on her own now.

She felt beyond exhausted, though she knew sleep was probably impossible.

"Are you sure?"

"Yes. I appreciate your being here. I just need some time by myself."

"Okay," her friend said, letting her continue upstairs alone.

Charissa walked into her bedroom and sank on the edge of the bed, her thoughts still lost in a stormy Atlantic.

If I pray, will God hear me?

She thought again of what happened before Trevor left. He died believing a lie. He believed she had been unfaithful, that she didn't love him, that she loved someone else.

Trevor, how could you be so wrong? How could you not trust me?

Why would God allow something so horrible? How could things end like this?

How would she go on?

TREVOR

Don't get too close.

A familiar voice kept telling Trevor this. And yet, throughout the rehearsals and finally through both the Friday and the Saturday night performances of *H.M.S. Pinafore,* as he and Charissa sang phrases like "For he is an Englishman" and held each other's hands and looked into each other's eyes, Trevor knew that he was already far too close. There was something about Charissa that made him feel right, that filled a huge void inside. The emptiness would disappear whenever Charissa was around, when her soft voice and comforting grin and generous spirit were evident. Sometimes he would drop her off and actually feel the emptiness creep back inside as he drove home.

On the night of the second performance, after the final bows had been taken and the punch-and-cookies reception was finished, Charissa asked Trevor to come over to her house on Sunday night. Trevor wasn't sure if it was a date or a get-together or what exactly it was. Charissa just said that she was having Kim and Pete Starkenberg over and wondered if he wanted to join them.

And Trevor said yes. Even as the voice continued to warn him over and over.

Watch what you're doing.

But he knew exactly what he was doing.

"So this was all a ploy to get Pete over here with Kim?" Trevor asked.

They sat on the couch barely watching a John Candy movie while Kim and Pete splashed outside in the swimming pool.

"Yeah. All Kim's idea."

Trevor squinted at Charissa and feigned suspicion. "You don't say."

"Sure you don't want to go swimming?" she asked.

"In October? I don't think so."

"The pool's heated. And there's a hot tub. It's really kinda nice."

"I'll give them some privacy."

"But this movie—"

"Isn't Candy's best," Trevor finished.

"Sorry. Pete brought it."

"Tell me something," he said, serious and gazing into her eyes.

"Tell you what?"

"What kind of socks are those?" he asked.

"What are you talking about?"

"Those things."

He pointed at the tiny tennis socks she wore. They barely fit over her feet, with the edges just slightly over her heels.

"They're tennis socks."

"They barely cover your feet."

"They're supposed to do that."

"They look like they were made for a three-year-old."

She laughed. "I like them."

"How do they stay on?"

"They stay on."

He made a funny face. Throughout the movie, he continued to tease her about the tennis socks. They sat close together on the couch, moving closer. Trevor teasingly touched her feet as he made fun of the socks.

After the movie, Trevor and Charissa sat on the couch watching television. Kim and Pete came in after drying off and changing. Pete said they were taking off, that he would drop Kim off at home.

"You don't have to go yet," Charissa said when Trevor stood to leave. "Not if you don't want to."

Trevor looked surprised. "Sure that's okay?"

"My parents have already gone upstairs. They don't mind."

It seemed comfortable and natural to lounge on the couch watching television and talking. They laughed about Kim and Pete wanting to use her pool.

"It seems like it worked. Pete sorta likes her, right?"

"I think. I'm not sure. She hopes he's going to invite her to the prom."

"Ah, the glorious prom."

She nodded, then changed the subject.

They talked for the next two hours. Eventually they found themselves on the subject of college.

"So, are you ready?"

"No," he said.

"I can't wait."

"You're going to Covenant, right?"

"Yeah."

"My dad still wants me to go there because I'd get a tuition break and he can keep an eye on me. But I don't know where I'm going. Hopefully somewhere far away. And somewhere easy to get into. Who knows?"

"You probably should know pretty soon," Charissa said. "Most people have already decided these things."

"I don't like to look into the future too much."

"How come?"

"I find it can be disappointing when things don't work out. When life takes different turns."

"How so?" she asked.

Trevor looked across her family room and remained silent for a moment. For a while now he had wanted to tell Charissa about Emily but didn't know how to. He wanted to tell her many things but wondered if he could ever really do it.

"Let's just say you never know what's going to happen. I used to think—well, actually believe—that God had a plan for everybody and that he helped work these plans out."

"And now?" Charissa asked.

"Now I think that half the time it's just pure luck. There isn't some grand plan for everybody. What happens, happens. I mean, I'm not saying we don't have any control over our destinies. I think what we do does matter. But still…"

She waited for more, but nothing came.

"So what do you think will happen to you?"

He grinned. "I'm thinking of maybe going on Broadway. I mean, after my successful *Pinafore* premiere."

"Seriously," she said, nudging him on the shoulder.

"I don't know. Maybe I'll end up at a college somewhere in California or Florida. That's my criteria—close to a beach and far away from here."

"Nice criteria."

"Better than Covenant. Seems half the senior class is going there."

"It's a good school."

"Well, I don't know what the future holds. And I don't want to think about it."

"I like looking ahead to the future," she said.

"Oh yeah?" He adopted the serious tone of a job interviewer. "And where do you see yourself in six years?"

"Teaching at a Christian school. First or second grade."

"Married?" Trevor asked her.

"Hopefully."

"Children?"

"Not right away," I said. "Though I'd like children one day."

"Me, too," Trevor said. "In about fifty years, that is."

"And you?"

"What?" he asked.

"What about you? Where do you see yourself?"

"I want to run my own business. Doing something. I don't know what. I just—I don't want to have a boss telling me what to do. I don't want to be part of some big cooperation. I want the freedom to run my own life. And of course, I want to make a lot of money, be successful. Not like my dad."

"You're kinda ambitious for a guy who doesn't like to look at the future."

"What can I say? I'm a teenager. I'm supposed to be contradictory."

"Do you see yourself being married?"

"Sure," Trevor said. "Maybe. I'm in no rush."

They continued talking about their future for a while, then flipped the television back on. They were shocked to realize it was after midnight.

"Are you tired?" he asked.

"Not really," Charissa said, though her drained eyes gave her away. "But I know I'm going to be tomorrow."

"I better go," Trevor said. "I hope your parents don't mind me staying here so late."

"Nah, it's okay, as long as they know where I am. But your dad might mind."

"He knows I'm with you. He calls you an answer to prayer."

Charissa gave him a bewildered look, and Trevor knew he probably shouldn't have told her that.

"It's just—you know, he gets concerned about all the biker chicks I bring home."

Charissa laughed, then grew serious. "Thanks for helping set up Kim and Pete."

"Sure. I'm just wondering. Was this a date for them?"

"A date?"

"Yeah."

"I guess they'd say it was."

He nodded. "So then, what is this for us?"

"I don't know."

"Is it a date? We're not out, so perhaps technically it isn't."

"What 'technically' would you like to call it?"

"Technically speaking?" he asked with mock graveness. "I'd say a date."

Still talking, they meandered through the rooms toward Charissa's front door. Then they stood by the doorway for a moment, suddenly silent. The hallway was dim except for the glimmer of light from the night switch on the wall.

Trevor smiled briefly. The voices inside him were quiet. For once, he had no reservations about where this was heading.

"So, you'd be okay calling this a date?" he asked.

"Yes."

They were speaking in whispers next to the front stairs. Charissa looked gorgeous, and Trevor finally asked something he had longed to ask for quite some time.

"Can I kiss you good night?" he asked her.

Speechless, her mouth already slightly open, Charissa nodded.

He moved closer and gently kissed her on the lips. She let the kiss linger, as he moved his hand softly behind her neck. She looked up into his eyes, shadowed in the low light of the front hallway, and saw the smile in them.

"Thank you for tonight," he said.

What she said in response surprised him.

It would be a memory, and a statement, he would never forget.

From: Imperiopoint@aol.com
Date: June 12
To: CST61795@aol.com
Subject: parting thoughts

...All of these words and thoughts and feelings I've written—
it's taken me so long to share them with you. You've
deserved a little taste of them each day over the years
we've been married. Instead, I've taken you for granted.

There is a comfort in knowing you're always there, that your
love for me remains strong and secure. But has this comfort
tricked me into forgetting how to love you back, how to meet
your needs? And is that comfort even there anymore?...

Wednesday, 2:47 a.m.

"Dear Father, you've been there for me all my life, ever since I came to you when I was five. You've blessed me. You've given me such a wonderful family. Such a wonderful life. I really can't ask for anything else from you. You allowed me to meet and fall in love with Trevor. You made him fall in love with somebody like me. You gave us some of the most incredible years of our lives. Even though we've had problems, I can see that our life together is a gift.

"Now I'm lying here in this empty bed in an empty room, knowing that Trevor might be gone. And I know I can't keep coming to you asking to bring him back—even though you know how much I want that. I don't know your will, Lord. No one does. But I can only pray that if Trevor does come back, Lord, we will honor you with our marriage. Please forgive me for the mess I've made of everything in the past few years. Forgive me for being so selfish and so petty. Forgive us for the arguments, for the horrible things we've said to one another. And forgive us for believing we could make this marriage something out of our strengths. It has nothing to do with us, Lord. I know that. I've known that. I've just been too stubborn to try to let you handle things.

"Dear Father, I pray—I beg you to bring my husband back to me. Dear God, please. I know I don't deserve to ask. But I feel things have been left half-done. I have so much left to learn about Trevor. There's so much I want him to know about me. Our marriage *can* honor you, Lord. I want it to. I want to have another chance.

"I don't know why—I just wish I could know, Lord, why he doesn't trust me. Why after all this time he was so quick to accuse me, when I hadn't done anything wrong…"

Charissa paused and felt an anger rattling inside of her. Perhaps it was a righteous, justifiable anger, but then again perhaps it was a evil spirit convincing her pride to swell and her wrath to rule. *Remember his last words to you, Charissa,* said a voice inside. *Remember what he said to you.*

She tried to overrule the voice, but Trevor's accusations kept playing in her head again. She hated that her last memory of the two of them consisted of lies and an argument.

It doesn't mean anything.

But the voice said that it meant everything. That it summed up their relationship and that after all this time and so many years and everything that had happened, Trevor still assumed the worst about her. If he couldn't trust her, what kind of relationship did they have?

"Lord, please let these doubts leave me. Please let me know—let me hear your spirit. Lord, please help me. Help me tonight. Help me and

he died believing a lie

"help my child. Help me to remember the good things, Lord. Help me to keep my eyes on you

seven years down the road with nothing to show not one thing

"and help me not to give up. God, help me. Please, God."

She kept on begging and pleading, and eventually she could feel the voices fade. She was left in silence in this room, drained. She felt so minuscule praying to the God who created her life and every life around her. She felt undeserving asking God for help. Yet she recalled her mother's reminder that God allows us and even commands us to put our petitions before his feet.

God can do anything.

She knew that, too. God had brought her and Trevor together.

"But why, God? Why bring us together, just to have it end like this? Why, if there is so much left to be said, to be done?"

She wished God could actually speak to her out loud, the way he often did in Old Testament times. She wished an angel of the Lord would come down and explain his will. She wished for something divine, something amazing, something—

Something miraculous.

Once again a voice whispered in her head. Except this felt like another spirit. A gentler, more loving one, speaking from her memory in Trevor's voice.

Everything about the way this happened—everything is a miracle.

Please, God, let there be room for one more miracle.

CHARISSA

I wondered if I had tried too hard. If I'd moved too quickly. If I had said the wrong things. If I'd uttered the wrong words. I tried to figure out what I'd done wrong, what I didn't do right, but nothing I could guess or suppose with my friends would have come close to being the truth.

So I got through most of the Monday after my date and first kiss with Trevor. I didn't see him until that afternoon. At first I thought he might have missed school that day, but then I saw him walking past during lunch.

I wanted to follow after him, to find him and talk to him and tell him I couldn't sleep and all I could think about was him and us. But why wasn't he coming to me? Why didn't he want to find me and talk to me today? And so I felt a cloud of doubt cover me until the minutes after the last bell of the day rang and I walked toward the bus I assumed I would be taking home.

"Charissa?"

I turned and saw him and tried to act nonchalant, but knew I failed miserably.

"Can I take you home?" Trevor asked.

I looked at him and desperately tried to control my emotions. I nodded and told myself not to ask him what was going on, not to say anything yet. I wanted him to talk. I wanted him, for once, to make the first move.

"Sorry I haven't been around today," he said.

I nodded again. I knew it would be pointless for me to simply shrug off the doubts and frustrations of the day. We walked to the car in the parking lot as a cold drizzle began to fall.

He opened the door for me and then started the car and pulled out of the parking lot without saying anything. It was only when we were on the street headed toward Interstate 83 that he began to talk.

"Charissa, I made a mistake last night."

I looked at him and braced to hear words I feared. He didn't want to be with me and never had. How could he have ever wanted to be with somebody like me? Last night was a fluke, a fantasy he allowed to happen because he probably felt sorry for me. That was it. He felt sorry for me. Or maybe he was just leading me on.

You know that's not true, a voice told me.

"I really had a great time last night," he said.

Rain fell down harder against the windshield. For once, we didn't have the backdrop of gloomy, angst-filled music piping through the stereo.

"I did too," I said.

"Charissa, I got home and I…I realized what a mistake I made."

I thought of what I'd said that night, and I knew I shouldn't have said it. Why had I opened up my heart to him so easily?

"I shouldn't have— I didn't mean for things to happen."

"What things?" I asked, my voice trembling and my hands shaking at my sides.

"Just— I let stuff happen that shouldn't have. I don't— Look, Charissa. I think the world of you."

So then why are you telling me this?

"That sounded lame," he continued. "I adore you. I think I always have, ever since I first got to know you. There's something about you—something inside of you that's different from the rest of the girls around here. Different from most girls I've met. That's why I've kinda kept my distance most of the time. It's almost like I told myself to stay clear."

"Stay clear of what?" I asked.

"To stay clear of you."

"Do you want that?"

"No. I mean, yes, sorta. With college coming and everything else going on—I just don't think it's a good idea."

"You said yourself you have no idea what the future will bring."

"But that's exactly my point. Look, I once believed I knew exactly what my future would be—and who I'd be with. I used to be in love with a girl named Emily. We dated my freshman and sophomore years—I honestly thought I'd be with her the rest of my life. She was…

she was everything to me. And one day I realized she'd fallen in love with one of my closest friends."

I watched him as he spoke straight ahead, watching the window and the falling rain and the gliding blades of the wipers.

"It was right about the time when everything caved in on top of me. Right before I learned we were moving and—well, right about then. Emily decided to tell me she didn't want a long-distance relationship. In fact, she didn't want any kind of relationship, at least not with me. She wanted one with someone else. My best friend."

He laughed harshly and continued.

"Remember when I first came to school? Remember how I had busted my hand? I did that on my friend's face. I— Everything just went black." He cursed under his breath. "I remember blaming pretty much everybody, but most of all I think I blamed God. I think I still do."

"I'm sorry," was all I could say.

As the rain came down harder, Trevor pulled his Volvo into a gas station and parked the car for a moment. He cut the ignition and faced me, taking my hand.

"Charissa, you shouldn't be with someone like me. Not with everything—not with all the stuff I've done. I don't deserve you. I don't know why I'm even here, sitting in this car, having this conversation. It's like the last thing in the world I would have ever expected."

"But why?" I asked him.

"I didn't want anything to happen while I was at Grace. After everything back home—I just wanted to come here and not make any ripples and serve my time and get out of here. Of course, I failed miserably in trying to do that. Now I'm your basic social outcast."

"No, you're not," I said.

"It doesn't matter. What matters is—last night was wonderful. It meant a lot to me."

"Then why—"

"None of this is supposed to mean anything to me," Trevor barked. "Grace is supposed to be a way station. I'm supposed to forget about all of this in seven or eight months and leave it all behind. And I don't think I can do that with you—not if we continue on the road we're going down."

"Why does that have to be so bad?" I asked him.

"I told you—"

"I don't care about your past," I said without hesitation. "Or about the mistakes you've made, or about the things you believe. Trevor, I want to be with you."

"I can't," he said. "I just can't."

"Please," I said, allowing tears to come into my eyes. I know I must have looked desperate.

"This has gotta stop. I'm sorry."

"No—"

"Charissa, I'm sorry."

I shook my head. This was wrong. Everything about this was wrong. The feelings I had couldn't simply be dismissed. They weren't trivial feelings. And this was not a trivial matter. I didn't know a lot about relationships, but I knew Trevor's reasoning made no sense. If you cared for somebody, if you loved someone, why couldn't you try?

But who says he's at that point? said a nagging, doubting voice.

Then I remembered the look in his eyes the night before. The look when we'd kissed by my front doorway. The way he'd smiled and looked at me, like he was seeing me for the first time. All of that meant something. I knew that Trevor knew it too.

"Why are you so scared?" I asked him.

He shook his head as if to say he wasn't.

"Why?" I asked again.

"I'm not scared," Trevor said unconvincingly.

I looked at him with a stare that longed for, that demanded, more. But nothing else came.

"I need to go home," I told him.

When we arrived at my house, Trevor turned toward me and tried to take my hand again. I shook my head and opened the door and climbed out of the car. I heard his voice call my name, but I shut the door behind me and walked into my house.

I told myself in those moments afterward that I was finally finished chasing after Trevor Thomas.

I had already wasted too much time on something that would never happen.

From: Imperiopoint@aol.com
Date: June 12
To: CST61795@aol.com
Subject: parting thoughts

...I see all the things I could have said. Everything more I could have done. I think of a thousand things I've never told you, and I wonder if you would believe them if I did. I wonder if there's room and time for you to believe in them—and to believe in me—once again. I know I've had a hard time believing—and trusting—in you. You need to finally know why....

WEDNESDAY, 3:15 A.M.

The storm unleashed itself over the early morning like a newborn's strangled tears. The house slept, but Charissa only lay still with her eyes forced shut. The sound of an engine outside allowed them to open, prompted her to climb out from underneath her covers and walk over to the bedroom window.

The dark house scared her—its silence and its size. Had everyone left while she was asleep?

I can't be left alone here, she thought. *Not here, by myself.*

The car engine shut off, leaving only the sound of rain pouring down outside.

For a moment she saw only the steady downpour backlit by the streetlight. Then she peered down at the driveway and saw him sitting in the TT with the top down. He waved at her, and she grabbed her chest. Then she glided across the room toward the open doorway and down the steps to the front door.

She unlocked the front door and opened it. Rain pounded down sideways, sprinkling her robe and bare feet. Undaunted, Charissa followed the curving sidewalk toward the car and the figure on the driveway.

Lightning struck in the background. The rain felt soothing on her bare feet, refreshing against her forehead. She walked to the drenched figure sitting in the car.

"Chris, I don't know what to say," her husband told her.

"I can't believe it's you."

He appeared to be crying. She wondered if the rain merely gave that illusion.

"I have something I need to tell you," she said to him.

"I already knew."

"But how?" she asked him.

"Your glow, Chris. You couldn't hide that from me. I already knew. I was just waiting for you to tell me."

"I wanted to—"

"It's too late," he said, starting up the car.

"Why? What are you saying?"

"Good-bye, Chris."

She went to touch him but found herself alone again in the shadows of early morning, standing on her sidewalk, wet and cold.

"Trevor!"

Her screams went unheard until the third one woke her up. She heard the bedroom door open and her mother's voice call her name.

Charissa looked out the cracked-open window. The outside summer night revealed no storm, no rain, and no tears.

Perhaps she had shed enough for everyone.

TREVOR

He knew by Christmas break that he had made a mistake, but of course it was too late. And as the new year arrived and Trevor found himself alone, counting down the seconds left in 1988, he realized that once again he had brought his pain upon himself. He had thrown away the one and only good thing about Grace—possibly the best thing about his high-school years—because of his fear.

Why are you so scared?

Charissa had nailed him on that. He knew deep inside that he was scared of everything. The unknown. The future. Relationships out of his control. Being broken and humiliated again or let down and lied to. Being a failure like his dad. His fears covered the walls of his life like the black-and-white posters covering his bedroom walls, and he had no clue how he could stop being afraid.

His father would have told him to pray about it. Get on your knees and pray. But how could he pray? Praying meant you had to believe. It meant that you had to ask forgiveness before asking for what you wanted, and you had to forgive others, too, had to stop being angry at all the people who had ruined your life. And Trevor wasn't sure he could function without his anger.

Praying was for people like his father, who lived in a washed-up world of broken dreams and shattered promises. Or people like Charissa, who were naturally good and kind. Or like the others at Grace, the others he didn't want to be around anymore.

He knew he was throwing himself a pity party, but it was a party he didn't want to leave. And so the days and the weeks and the months passed, just as the faces and the people and the hours passed him by at Grace. Period after period. Day after day. Until the morning he realized how stupid he had been. On this day, just weeks away from graduation, Trevor saw Charissa VanderVelde pass him in the hallway. He stopped and turned and looked at her.

And as suddenly as that, he realized he needed to win her back.

* * *

The prom he had called a crock, the prom he'd said was pointless and worthless, ended up being his last chance. He decided to go by himself, not so he could continue to wallow around in misery but so he could declare his feelings to Charissa.

If he simply tried to connect with her during school in the hallway, it would seem lame and pitiful. At this point he needed something dramatic, a grand gesture. She knew how he felt about the prom. For him to show up there just to see her would show her exactly how serious he was, how important she was to him.

He knew that she was attending the dance with John G. and that she didn't hold any deep feelings toward John, so he didn't particularly care if he ruined their magical night. In fact, he hoped he would. He would ask Charissa to dance and tell her what an idiot he'd been and talk her into breaking off her date with John G.

Maybe he could make up for lost time.

So Trevor rented a tux and arrived on the boat downtown alone. He didn't sit with anyone he knew during the meal but waited, biding his time, counting off the minutes until the music and the dancing started. Then he climbed the steps to the upper deck, which looked out over the lake and the glittering Chicago skyline. He waited some more until Charissa found her way up there too. He had counted on her needing a break from the noise and activity below.

She held a plastic cup of punch and just watched him walk toward her. She didn't smile, didn't say anything, just stood there looking glorious in the long black dress that showed off her graceful neck and shoulders.

"Hi," he said, trying to gauge her body language and the expression on her flawless face.

"You're here," she said, though he knew she had seen him earlier. "That's a surprise."

"I couldn't stay away. There's somebody I need to see."

Charissa studied him and waited for more. She took a sip from her glass and looked out toward the city.

"Charissa, I'm sorry. About everything."

"It's okay," she said. "It's done."

"No."

"No?" she asked, looking at him. "What do you mean 'no'?"

"It's not done."

"Yes, it is."

"Charissa, I'm sorry. I know I should be here with you."

"It's no big deal," she said with a shrug.

He glanced at her red lips and could still remember kissing them. He could still recall the words she had said that night.

"It is a big deal, Charissa. All I wanted— I just came for one thing."

She moved her body slightly as she looked away from him again, back out to the skyline.

"Please," he said, "just look at me for a minute."

He could tell she didn't want to, so he stepped closer to her. He could smell her light perfume, see several strands of her hair blowing in the soft breeze, and sense her apprehension. He called her name again, and she looked up at him.

"I just want to dance one dance with you. That's all."

"I can't," she said.

"Yes you can."

"They're almost to the last song of the night."

"So that'll be perfect," Trevor said.

"I can't."

"Why?"

"Because," she said.

"Because of John G.?"

Mentioning this name was all he needed to do. He knew that this was a cordial date at best. Would she regret not dancing the last dance of her senior prom with John G.? Trevor believed in his heart it wouldn't matter to either of them.

"That's all I want," Trevor said. "One dance."

"And that's why you came tonight?"

Trevor nodded.

"That's a pretty expensive dance."

"I told you before—you're an expensive date."

Charissa didn't smile at his remark, and he instantly regretted it. She gave him a sad look.

"You never did actually ask me out."

He nodded. "I can't make up for past mistakes. But I can ask you for this dance."

All she did was nod.

He took her hand and led her down the stairs. As they reached the dance floor, the Billy Idol version of "Mony Mony" finished playing, and the deejay announced the last song of the night. Charissa looked a little guilty as Trevor led her onto the dance floor. He held her slender frame against his own, his hands resting on her sides and his cheek pressed against her hair.

In just a few seconds, both of them recognized the song.

"Isn't this 'Somebody?'" she asked. "The one you played for me in the car?"

Trevor told her it was.

"Did you ask them to play it tonight?" Charissa said, moving to look at him for a moment.

"No."

"Yes, you did."

"I didn't. I swear."

He was telling the truth. And for the first time in his entire period at Grace Christian High, Trevor believed that something was not just a coincidence. The significance of this one song being played as they danced their one and only dance almost overshadowed the mistakes he had made.

Almost.

It was while he was holding Charissa in his arms and gliding gently with her to the slow beat of the song that he realized he had lost her. Something about the way she held herself, the way she remained silent and didn't look at him, told him that all she had agreed to was a dance.

He closed his eyes and listened to the words of the song and dreamed that this was another time, a better time when Charissa and he were together and they didn't have to worry about anything except one another.

Trevor moved so he could whisper in Charissa's ear.

"I'm sorry for being scared," he said to her as they continued to sway together. "I'm sorry for standing back and not doing anything."

He felt her head nod, knowing that she heard his apology but that it was still too late.

"I'm sorry for not realizing how wonderful you are. For not telling you sooner."

Again she simply nodded.

"I'm not going to forget about you after we graduate. No matter what happens or where I go, I'm never going to forget about you, Charissa. Never."

The singer continued to croon about the somebody he wanted to share the rest of his life with, the somebody who would care for him passionately, the somebody who'd help him see things in a different light.

"You've always been that somebody, Charissa," Trevor spoke softly into her ear.

The song ended. When they finally separated, Trevor noticed the tears in Charissa's eyes. He wanted to say something else to her, but he knew he had already said enough.

"Good night," she told him, then walked across the dance floor to where John G. stood waiting.

From: Imperiopoint@aol.com
Date: June 12
To: CST61795@aol.com
Subject: parting thoughts

_____

...I'm so afraid that I've already lost you. That regardless of
what I say, it's too late.

I know that the last few years have been difficult, with the
business and the traveling and your job and the whole topic
of starting a family. I know that in many ways I've pulled
away from you and hurt you. I just hope and pray that we
can start over again....

WEDNESDAY, EARLY MORNING

Waves of sleep crashed against the beaches of Charissa's consciousness. She woke in small, fuzzy increments, when she would open her eyes and not remember whether she had been sleeping, when she would remember the alarm clock showing the same exact time, when she would become chilled and cocoon herself with blankets, then awaken damp with sweat.

Waking now, she shivered. But this time she didn't feel cold.

"Dear Father. Please."

Silence interrupted her words. Had she spoken them out loud? She didn't know.

"Please, God, let him be alive. That's all I ask."

Tears came, or was she dreaming again? Echoes of things she wished she could say to Trevor surrounded her. Things she needed to let him know.

Her imagination began gliding over the ocean, through clouds and over raging seas. What could he have been thinking as the plane went down? Was he brave? Did he pray, and did he think of home? Was there even time to think? Was he scared?

He died believing a lie. A lie I let him believe. I didn't even tell him it wasn't true.

More tears. She'd thought the well was dried up, but no. Not yet.

"He can't be gone, God."

Images attacked her. Memories of times she had turned away from him, times when she should have asked him how he was doing, times when her frustration had got the best of her.

You did nothing wrong.

"I've done so much wrong," she told the voice.

The pitch blackness gave her a strange sense of security. She feared the morning, when she knew she would have to face the truth. Now, in the pit of night, things could remain unknown. Not just what had happened to Trevor, but what had happened between the two of them. How they had left things.

The emotions and voices inside her waged war. Her forehead was covered with sweat even though she still shook. Was she crying? Angry and betrayed, she tried not to pray. But she couldn't help doing it. She prayed almost without meaning to, in between the waves of hurt and betrayal and anger.

It'll be daylight in just a few hours.

Perhaps things had been bad between her and Trevor. Perhaps she had made mistakes. But she would never betray his trust, his love.

How could he

A breath. And another. The world, even in darkness, spiraled

die

and twisted and turned

not trusting me?

until she finally closed her eyes and fell into a sleep so deep it hid her from dreams and nightmares.

CHARISSA

You would have thought that Trevor was this great love of my youth that I simply couldn't let go. That is how the memory of our brief moments together grew inside me, mushrooming almost into fantasy. Yes, there had been those moments, and there had been those feelings, but I had assumed I would simply move on and grow out of them.

So why, during the spring semester of sophomore year of college, did my thoughts still wander onto a missing Trevor? Why did I keep thinking about him even though I had a boyfriend?

I vividly remember a night when Dan Rice dropped me off from a dinner and a movie. He gave me a nice, polite peck on the cheek and told me he'd see me tomorrow. Dan was always polite and always friendly, the perfect guy for me in a lot of ways. What was it about that kind of guy, the steady and stable and staid sort, that made me want to yawn whenever nobody else was around?

On this night, I vowed to finally do something I'd been putting off.

Dan Rice was a good guy, and for a while I'd done the thing I thought I should have been doing—moving on with my life. But I was beginning to realize I had never ended the chapter with Trevor.

After our brief encounter at the prom, where we danced one slow song and he apologized and then I resumed my date with John G., we talked only a couple more times. We said a quick and awkward good-bye at graduation, and that was it. My link to Trevor was forever gone.

Except, of course, for his father. Robert Thomas still taught at the college I attended. So on the morning after this night out with Dan, I decided to go see Professor Thomas to ask about Trevor.

I found him in the ceramics building, looking for some cutting materials. He recognized me right away.

"How are you?" he asked.

"Good, thanks."

"I've been meaning to look you up one of these days. I always figured I'd run into you on campus."

"Sorry I haven't said hello sooner."

"How are your classes?" he asked.

His hair still looked bushy, his face dotted with several days worth of beard, his jeans smeared with clay and grime. I could see Trevor's smile on the man's face, and I found myself longing to see him again.

For a few minutes I spoke about my elementary-education classes, but then I worked up courage to ask what I'd come to ask.

"How's Trevor doing?" I asked.

Robert Thomas rubbed his lips and thought for a moment.

"I don't see much of him. He still lives at home. You know he's going to the College of DuPage, right? The junior college not far from where we live."

"I didn't know that," I said.

"Yeah. He stays out late, sleeps in. I'm not sure he ever goes to class. I worry about him."

"He's not in any trouble or anything, is he?"

"I don't know, Charissa. I really don't. You know, you should call him sometime."

"I don't think I can."

"He asked about you not long ago. During one of our rare evening conversations when he was actually home."

"Yeah?"

"I know he'd enjoy talking with you."

"I don't think— I just—I was just wondering how he is."

"Lost—that's how he is," Robert Thomas said. "Did he ever tell you I prayed that he'd end up with a girl like you?"

I nodded. The memory stung.

"I still pray. Even if it's not you, I pray that at least he finds somebody like you."

"That's a nice thing to say," I said.

"Can I tell him I saw you?"

"Sure. If you want to."

Part of me wanted to ask him to give Trevor a message, but I didn't know what the message would have been.

Still not over you, but not sure why.

I didn't understand what I still felt for Trevor. All I knew was that it felt different from my feelings for Dan. Night and day different.

Something about that had to change.

From: Imperiopoint@aol.com
Date: June 12
To: CST61795@aol.com
Subject: parting thoughts

...I don't know if there's a chance for us or if your heart belongs to another. The worst thing is wondering whether you'll ever love me again. You have to understand, Charissa. Your love for me, your faithful pursuit to win me over, your patience with me over the years—without these, I am nothing. Nothing....

Wednesday, 5:12 a.m.

She knew the constant nudging meant something, but she wasn't sure what. It kept distracting her from the sleep she craved, the oblivion she had almost reached. She was surprised by how heavy her eyelids felt.

This is what being high must feel like, she thought. Numb. Completely numb. She had cried all of her tears, prayed all of her prayers. And sleep—sleep had rolled over her like a fog, blotting out every thought, every feeling. One, two, three—how many minutes or hours had passed?

"Cee?" a voice was saying.

But no one called her that anymore. She'd always hated the baby nickname, hated being the youngest in the family. Having everyone else talk for her and tell her what to do and leaving her out because she was too young. Always the "caboose," the afterthought. Maybe that was why she was always so quiet and shy.

The nudging continued. "Cee, wake up."

But Trevor never seemed bothered by her reticence. Trevor never called her Cee. Maybe that was why she'd always felt so comfortable with him. Like it didn't matter how shy she was, like being bashful was quite a beautiful thing. Trevor had always made her feel this way. Not by his words. By his attitude, the way he made her feel wanted. Trevor—

"Cee, I'm leaving."

"Yeah?" she finally mumbled to her father.

"I just wanted to tell you—Doug and I are leaving for O'Hare."

"What?" she murmured. She sat up and realized she still wore the same shirt and pants she'd had on yesterday.

"We're going to the airport, see if we can get an answer from some-body there. People have been camping out there."

"Anything more—"

"No. I'm sorry."

"They didn't find any more survivors?"

"Not that we know of."

"Is Mom going with you?"

"She's asleep. I gave her a pill to sleep—she had a hard time last night. She'll probably be out for a while."

"Are you okay? Can I get you anything?"

"No. I'm fine. I just—I just wanted you to know we're going. Lisa is still here. Sheila, too."

"I want to go—" Her eyes were almost back to normal. The room was dark except for a hall light that pierced in.

"I think you'd better stay here. I don't think we'll find out much. And you'll want to be here when Trevor's dad calls."

She had forgotten that Robert was due in from New York this morning. She wondered if it had dawned on him that the plane crash on the news had any connection to his son. Probably not. He would have called if it did.

"Okay," she told her father. "I'll stay here."

He brushed the blond hair out of her face. She couldn't remember the last time her father had deliberately touched her. He wasn't that sort of man.

"Cee?"

"Yeah?"

"I want you to know your mom and I are here for you. We're not going anywhere. We'll stay here with you—anything you need. We'll be here. You understand that?"

She nodded and saw something odd in his shadowed expression.

"God's really throwin' a curveball here," he muttered.

"Dad?"

"It's times like this—I don't know. I really don't. But I'm tellin' you, we're not going anywhere. We're going to stay by your side no matter what. No matter what."

Charissa wondered what her mom had told him.

"You just, you get some rest." His voice shook. "We'll be back. Okay?"

"Yeah."

She sank back against a pillow and understood the look on her father's face.

Fear.

TREVOR

He followed the girl to a red sports car he didn't recognize. A Mazda perhaps? Toyota? Who cared? It was a two-door. She climbed in and leaned to open the passenger door for him. He got in and looked over to see long legs in a short skirt. His eyes took an extended time to blink before he opened them again.

The girl with short black hair and a white face with red lips lit a cigarette and asked if he wanted one. He took one and began to smoke as the car started down the street. Nightlife blurred past him. He watched the lights and the intersections and the strangers outside and then glanced back at the stranger across from him.

"I live in Wicker Park," she said. This meant absolutely nothing to him.

He vaguely wondered how he had gotten here. To this point. Not only tonight, but in his life. He looked at the young woman driving the car and wondered where this evening was headed. He knew. He didn't want to admit it to himself, but he knew.

Where am I, God? His own prayer startled him. He hadn't even meant to think that. It occurred to him he might finally be losing it.

Then he thought of his mother, and the thought angered him. It had no place in his mind, not anymore. It was the past, and the past should simply be. He thought of the last year and a half and knew that nothing had changed. Absolutely nothing, except that he was now skipping classes at a junior college and going nowhere with his life. He still felt alienated and alone and guilty, and doing what he was about to do wouldn't change a thing.

I need someone tonight, he told himself. The girl was talking about something, but he didn't hear her. He hadn't heard her all night. He had smiled at her attractive face and had nodded and acted as though he were listening to her, but he hadn't really heard her and still didn't know her name.

Is this how easily it happens?

But he wanted it to happen—wanted it because that's what happens in the real world. Not the tiny, sanctified world of the holier-than-thou Christians who lived only in their little universe. No, this was the way things were, and he was just doing his part. Right? Wasn't that all this was?

Nothing really matters.

He felt dizzy, and he looked at the world passing by his window. The music blared through the car, the college radio station playing classic alternative music. The girl gushed about the music and how she loved it, and Trevor laughed because all of this was ludicrous and meant nothing.

I'm so tired, he thought.

He had gone out with friends tonight. Friends. The sort of friends that reminded him of Alex from Grace. The kind who stood next to you and laughed and talked but never cared who you were. They were just some guys, and he had gone out with them and had ended up meeting her. Whatever her name was. And she had asked if he wanted to go back to her apartment, and he had said yes, absolutely.

Would anyone care? Would God care?

God is saying nothing, Trevor thought. *Isn't he?*

They stopped at an intersection, and Trevor looked out at the masses partying the Thursday night away and wondered if anybody in the city actually worked. As he reflected on this, the song came on and made him stop and look at the stereo.

"Oh, I love this one," the girl said as the light turned green and she clutched and shifted. "Do you like Depeche Mode"?

The familiar song played over the radio, and instantly Trevor found himself thinking of Charissa.

I'm living a lie.

"I want somebody who cares," the singer sang, transporting Trevor back to high school and back to that final dance and back to the moment when he knew it was over with Charissa.

"We're almost there," the girl said, and this Trevor did hear.

"Let me out," he asked.

"Excuse me?"

"Could you let me out?" His voice was louder than he wanted it to be.

She gave him a puzzled look. "What are you talking about? Are you sick?"

"Very," he said.

She pulled over quickly, and Trevor opened the door and climbed out. He didn't shut the door behind him.

"Hey! Trevor! Where are you going?"

Trevor began walking down the concrete sidewalk, the song still in his mind, the picture of Charissa very much in his heart.

I need to find her.

Yet he knew he needed something else even more. Somebody else. He realized he had been running for a long time.

Lord, I'm lost.

He walked through the cool spring night and looked up into the sky and wished he could see the thousands of stars above him. The glow of the city blocked the beauty of the heavens he knew were up there.

Where are you?

He heard the voice in his heart. But he couldn't tell if he was asking the question or if someone else was calling him.

Trevor walked until he recognized where he was. He sat down on a bench outside a closed restaurant and looked around him. He rubbed his forehead and finally began to feel a little more sober.

Where do I go from here?

And all he could think of was one place. One person. He couldn't go on like this. He was a mess. And he didn't know what she would do or what she would say, but he knew he needed to find Charissa.

Maybe she couldn't be with him.

But maybe she could still help him.

From: Imperiopoint@aol.com
Date: June 12
To: CST61795@aol.com
Subject: parting thoughts

...You say that I've never fully trusted you. That even after we shared our wedding vows, something has always been between us.

You're right.

I know I should have told you all this years ago. That way, even if you couldn't take away any of my hurt, you could have at least understood my perspective. But I couldn't do it, Charissa. I couldn't make myself drag that memory back into the open. I had to keep it buried....

WEDNESDAY, 5:29 A.M.

Downstairs, in the dark kitchen, the sun only starting to come up, her father and brother already gone, Charissa found herself alone. Alone, standing on the cool ceramic tile and leaning against the kitchen counter. Alone, looking at the coffee maker and debating whether to make a pot. Unable to sleep and unable to talk with anyone.

this is what it will be like for the rest of your life

Wake up, Chris. Smell the coffee. And the bacon. And everything else that makes you snap up and out of it and on to something else. This is your life now, and it ain't gonna get any better.

"Jesus," she pleaded. "Jesus, help me."

She couldn't breathe through her stuffy nose. She looked over the kitchen island toward the dark living room, then down the hall to the stairs. She realized that Trevor would never be coming down those stairs to get a cup of coffee.

I don't think I can do this.

She thought of all the talk she'd heard last night about God. Thought about all the sermons and debates she'd heard about God's will and human freedom and the power of prayer and why bad things happen to good people. And at the moment none of it seemed to make any sense. The preachers could say whatever they wanted. The pastors and the know-it-all doctors and authors and counselors could spout out a million opinions and truths. But in this silent moment all she could see was that her life was over and she had no control over anything that was happening. Not a thing. Probably God didn't either.

Mom knows this. So does Lisa. So does Dad. His look betrayed him. It's all too wrong. Too awful. Can't be God's will. A will for what? Heartache and bloodshed and pain and brokenness?

come to me all you who are heavy-hearted

I can't come now, Charissa thought. *I don't want to come.*

he leads me through the valley of darkness

For what? What for? I don't want to be led through this.

She wanted to be angry. Charissa, in the still of her empty house, wanted to curse God. She wasn't a Job and never would be. She didn't have the faith to praise God in the midst of this agony. She was a doubting Thomas, worse than a doubting Thomas. She doubted God had anything to do with this. She doubted that God and his Son saw her now as she wept. She doubted that God heard her prayers.

Yet she continued to pray them.

And as she did, something made her finally stand and ascend the stairs.

For a few seconds she hesitated in the doorway of Trevor's study. Then she took a step further and entered the room. She found it remarkable that nothing happened. No bright lights or crackling noise. She simply turned on the light and looked around at the same room she had seen hundreds of times before.

She opened a closet door with photo albums tucked away in the corner. On the top of half a dozen books lay the most recent they had made. It was a simple beige-colored volume with a date marked in its center title. Two years ago. She picked up the album and opened it.

A monogrammed business address for Brad Corbin Photography was printed at the bottom of the interior cover. Charissa thought of the blond-haired photographer, an old friend Trevor had looked up a few years ago. He was a local guy who specialized in black-and-white shots. Trevor had thought it would be interesting to have Brad take a series of photographs of the two of them over the course of a year.

She brought the binder over to Trevor's desk and sat in his leather armchair. She tilted his computer keyboard against the monitor to make space on the desk and began to go through the album. She remembered posing for the camera down at the lakefront, at the park, in their backyard, on the streets of quaint Geneva, where Brad's studio was. Portrait after portrait depicted a couple some would call good-looking, apparently happy, living the American dream.

Half a lifetime lived on through smiles and poses in this and other albums. Charissa shivered, wondering if all she had left of that life was a series of images on chemical-coated paper.

We let it all get away from us, Trevor.

The wasted opportunities in her life with Trevor haunted her. There were so many words left to be said. So many things left to do—taking trips, raising a family, growing old together. A future that would never happen.

She turned the page to a shot of Trevor and her walking hand in hand on a downtown street. She couldn't even remember when it was taken. Had things begun to go wrong between them when that was taken? How long had the passion and love they shared been fading? How long since the smiles actually meant something?

She saw a picture of Trevor outside their home in a sports coat and tie. Coming home from a business meeting, making time to allow someone to take pictures of them outside their beautiful house.

The American dream.

How could it ever be a dream if you never trusted me?

The chair squeaked as she leaned back in it. Her eyes wandered over the various items on the desk and back to the computer monitor.

She suddenly found herself turning on his computer and logging on to their e-mail service. She waited as the computer dialed and the phone line screeched.

She didn't know what she was looking for. Maybe there was nothing to find. But she waited.

And waited.

CHARISSA / TREVOR

The crowd around us waited for the green. The light changed, and the mass of businessmen and women and tourists and students moved across the wet street. I held Dan's hand as we stepped into the intersection and tried to keep under the umbrella he held. I didn't see the figure next to me until he called out above the pounding rain.

"Charissa?"

I turned and saw Trevor standing in the street, looking at me with astonished eyes. He looked different—a little stockier, his hair short and spiked.

Dan didn't see him. He kept leading me toward his car.

"Wait. Dan, hold on."

We stopped, and I waited for Trevor to catch up. Drops streamed down his face from the rare July evening downpour.

"What are you doing here?"

He only looked at me as I still held Dan's hand and leaned under the umbrella.

"The concert—I was at the Chicago Theatre to see Pearl Jam."

"Really?" I called out.

"We gotta get out of the street," Dan yelled.

We moved to the sidewalk and slipped under a small overhang that partly shielded us from the rain. Dan reached over and tucked my arm under his elbow.

"Dan, this is Trevor."

"Who?" he asked.

"Trevor Thomas," I said louder.

"Oh," Dan said, nodding and shaking Trevor's hand.

"This is Dan Rice. He goes to Covenant."

Trevor kept his eyes on me. I found myself wishing I had called him or written him or sent him an e-mail or done *anything* to have simply made this meeting less awkward.

"It's been a while," he said.

"It has," I said weakly.

I noticed Trevor staring at me, then at the tall figure next to me, then back at me.

"How's school?" he asked.

"Good. I've got one summer-school class. One more month before we get back into the real grind."

Dan groaned. "Don't say that."

"How was the concert?" I asked.

"Oh, great. I went with a buddy who lives down here. I was just about to head back to the suburbs—I took the train downtown."

"Where do you go to school?" Dan asked.

"Oh, I just—I was going to College of DuPage."

"Where?"

"It's a junior college. Wasn't sure where I wanted to go. It's pretty easy. And it's close."

"I've talked to your father a few times at school," I said, trying to change the subject.

"Yeah, he told me he saw you."

We both nodded. The downpour seemed to taper off. Dan fidgeted as if bored and ready to leave.

"I guess we should go," I said.

Trevor nodded. "Yeah, well, good to see you. And nice to—"

"Yeah, you, too," Dan said.

I smiled and thought of what I should do. Hug Trevor? That'd be too strange, and how would I explain it to Dan? Trevor might not even let me hug him. What should I say to him? "Good-bye, nice running into you"? "See you later"? Would I ever see him later?

So what I did was remain silent. No big surprise. *Good ol' Charissa.*

"You know I…," Trevor began but didn't finish.

I waited, but he simply told me to have a good night.

I gave a little wave, and then Dan and I started toward the parking lot.

"That was Trevor, high-school Trevor?"

"Yes," I replied.

"What are the chances?"

I shrugged and shook my head.

"When was the last time you saw him?"

"Our graduation day."

"Been a while. I can't believe he got Pearl Jam tickets. I tried getting them, but they sold out in a few minutes. I heard that Wiley was going to the show. We'll have to get the rundown from him."

"Chris?"

Dan looked to one side, and then we turned and saw Trevor.

"Um, Dan? I— Can I talk to Charissa for a few minutes?"

Dan looked at me and saw me nod in approval, so he started to move away.

"I'll just be a couple of minutes," I told him.

"How about if I walk ahead and get the truck? I can pick you up."

I nodded. Dan walked away without another word to either of us.

"I couldn't just leave, Chris," Trevor said. "Not like that. Actually, I've been thinking of calling you."

"Are you all right?"

"I'm fine," he said.

"Really?"

"Want me to lie?" he asked with a grin.

"No."

"You know—it's like I've been stuck back in high school. Remember what I used to talk about—that Grace was just temporary, that going on to college was when I'd start getting serious? Well, somehow the plan didn't work. But—I think things are going to be different."

"What do you mean?"

"I don't know. I can't explain now. I just—I'm really sorry for what happened between us."

I found myself thankful for this moment to have arrived. "Me, too."

"No. I'm *really* sorry. I think awhile back I suddenly realized—and now, seeing you again—looking so beautiful."

"Trevor—"

"I know. But you know something? Sometimes. I'd like— It'd be great to just go back."

"What do you mean? Back where?"

"To the start. To have a chance to do things over. Do them right this time."

The truck rolled up beside us. I glanced up at Dan and then back at Trevor.

"I didn't think I'd ever see you again," Trevor said.

"I know."

"I'm glad I did."

We said another round of good-byes, but the words were forced and under the glare of two lights beaming from a Chevy truck standing next to us.

The truck drives away. He turns and walks the other direction.

Yet they still remain together.

He walks down the sidewalk, off the curb and under the dripping canopy, across a side street, by a cab and past a newspaper stand, over a bridge and toward the train station.

She sits in the passenger seat, listening to ESPN radio. Dan talks and she replies and he talks some more.

The sky is clearer now, the storm over.

He looks up to the sky, pieces of the jigsaw night appearing.

Not far behind, heading toward the expressway, heading west toward her home, she looks out at the passing traffic.

Steps.

Lanes merging.

A train car waiting.

A two-seater convertible cutting them off.

Railroad tracks.

Four car lanes.

Miles.

Years apart.

Start.

A word lingering in his mind. And in hers.

Start.

Back to the start.

Back to the start of it all.

Years removed and destinies apart and roads traveled and yet this night arrived with a timely, predestined intersection. One more step, one hesitation, one minute earlier or later—

But no.

Their paths crossed.

"How" is all he can ask.

"Why" is all she can think.

"Stupid" he knows.

"Past" she faces.

Start. Back to the start.

And the train waits. Passengers bump arms. He stalls. Wants to stop and turn around and do something.

"Chance" she believes.

"What if?" he answers.

Voices around them aren't answered. For the moment, they are still together. Even two years after the fact, they're back together. They can close their eyes and see each other and know each other's words.

He makes his way down a crowded aisle.

She sees a passing sign.

He turns around, calls on help from above.

She thinks a silent prayer.

I know now.

Maybe.

I've failed so badly.

I'd give anything—

Lord, help me.

Lord, be with him.

Give me another chance.

Give us another chance.

I want to believe.

To start over again.

Forgive me.

From: Imperiopoint@aol.com
Date: June 12
To: CST61795@aol.com
Subject: parting thoughts

...When I met you years ago, I wasn't simply at a crossroads because of changing schools. There was a reason my dad and I moved to Chicago. It wasn't because he was changing jobs or because of some way he failed with my mother.

It ultimately ended up being because of me. Because of something I discovered. Because of something I did....

WEDNESDAY, 5:47 A.M.

The e-mail from Trevor was waiting in her in-box.

Tears sprang to her eyes, and her breath gave out for a few seconds. She felt utterly confused and elated and destroyed when she opened up the message with yesterday's date on it.

> I begin this e-mail by stating the obvious. I love you, Charissa. Nothing and no one in the world can change that fact.

Last words, typed in an e-mail.

an e-mail

from a dead man

She read on, wondering how he could be saying all these things, wondering why now. Why had he taken so long? And why had he sent it—

She stopped for a second and wiped her eyes and breathed in.

He sent this before he left on his trip.

She closed the e-mail for a second and looked at the list to find out when Trevor had sent it.

The time the e-mail had been received was 6:33 yesterday evening. Trevor's flight had taken off around seven.

She shook her head and thought deeply for a moment. Where would he have sent it from? He always carried his laptop with him on trips. He could have sent it from the executive lounge at O'Hare—that private area where business travelers and frequent travelers could make phone calls and relax and work on their computers.

And send long farewell e-mails.

She saw her hand on the mouse shaking uncontrollably. She had a few more tears in her. She clicked back on the e-mail and continued to read. Pausing, rereading the words, Wiping her face. Reading on.

And Trevor's words cut through her. *Your gentle and kind spirit... It never occurred to me I'd meet someone like you... This is when you look the most beautiful... I see it as a blessing... You need to finally know why...*

And as she reached the end, the very end of the e-mail, when she finally could look down through the tiny, piercing hole Trevor had opened in his soul and understand him a little better, she wept. Wept for the man he was, for the pain he had suffered, for what the two of them had lost and for the beauty of what he had left her. She held her face in her hands and sobbed, knowing that it was all over.

These were his last words to her—a precious and awful gift. Somehow, God had allowed him to say these things so she wouldn't have to be left with the nagging doubt that he no longer loved her or the question of why he no longer trusted her.

Did it make his suspicions acceptable or her loss any lighter? Of course not.

But these words—these words she kept rereading to herself. The things he was telling her. It was not like Trevor to actually write these beautiful words, but she knew that only he could have written them. He knew her better than she would have dared to guess.

This is what he left me with. She smiled ruefully, then reached down to touch her stomach. *And...you.*

The computer hummed in the background, and she sniffed and wiped her nose and felt woozy and knew she needed to lie down. She felt faint and began seeing small dots of stars.

Am I going to pass out?

She stood and barely made it back into their bedroom. Or her bedroom now. Her bedroom in her house that she owned by herself.

I hope and pray we can start over again.

This was one of the many things Trevor had written to her. She wished she could hit the Reply button and know without a question that he would read her response. There was so much she needed to tell him.

And now we'll never get the chance.

CHARISSA

For the second time in my life, I found myself ending a relationship with a guy I knew would be good for me—but this time was a little different.

This time I kept wondering what *good for me* actually meant. How did I really know who was good for me and who wasn't? Did it boil down to passion or practicality?

And this time I prayed about it a lot. Prayed about what was right, about what God had in mind for me. And ended up convinced that Dan Rice wasn't supposed to be part of my future.

I remembered having reservations about ending my high-school romance with Kyle, but I was young and hadn't known what love was or could be. And now, as I walked down the sidewalk to the coffee shop to meet Dan, I knew that what we had could not be considered love either. I had known love once, and only once, even if it was brief and never fully realized. Part of me still longed for that kind of connection, still dreamed that it could happen again. Whether it did or not, I knew it wouldn't be happening with Dan.

The August afternoon made me wipe sweat off my forehead. I knew I'd be ordering an iced coffee, though I doubted I'd have a chance to finish it.

Dan greeted me with open arms. I tried to sidestep his hug and ended up receiving half of it. I saw confusion on his square face, a question in his dark brown eyes. He had an iced coffee waiting for me.

"Mocha, right?" he said with uncertainty.

I nodded and thanked him.

"Everything okay?" Dan asked me.

We sat, and I took a sip of my drink. For a minute, a terribly long minute, I didn't nod, nor did I say anything. I had asked him to meet me here, at this time, simply to talk. This was unusual, and the tone in my voice must have told him something. Dan knew everything wasn't okay.

I took a deep breath, praying for strength.

"I can't see you anymore."

The deliberate words, the steady way they were spoken, and their concise bluntness surprised both of us. He looked as if he thought I was joking, and he sat crinkling his eyebrows at me.

"What're you talking about?"

"I need to break up with you." I didn't know how to put it better.

"What? Why?"

"Because I just—I don't think I'm as ready for this as you are."

"Ready for what?" Dan asked.

"Ready for us. To be serious."

He laughed. "I don't have to be serious. It doesn't have to be serious."

"I just—I don't want to hurt you."

"I don't understand. Where did all this come from?"

"You're a really great guy, Dan. I know you'll make some girl really happy."

He shook his head and continued to stare at me in utter disbelief. He sipped his orange drink and wiped his mouth and forced a grin.

"So what did I do wrong?"

"Nothing. I just—I just don't see any point in going down a road I'll eventually get off of."

"But why would you do that?"

"I just will," I told him. "I don't feel right about us."

"How do you want to feel? Chris, I swear, I don't have to—we don't have to be serious or anything. I can take it easy."

"I know you can. But I don't think you should have to."

"Just tell me what you want," Dan said.

I looked at him with eyes that didn't blink and felt someone other than myself speaking and acting. I was being strong, but I knew this was a strength that was not my own.

"I've told you what I want."

And it's not you.

The good-bye took another ten minutes. Dan tried to ask more, to get me to explain how he could change, to offer solutions, and I tried to avoid telling him outright that I didn't love him and didn't believe I ever would. It wasn't his fault. It wasn't anything he did or didn't do, or any shortcoming on his part. I knew it was all me—and, of course, my feelings for Trevor Thomas.

When I finally said good-bye to Dan, knowing I'd see him soon around campus, knowing I would still talk to him and make some further explanations, I wondered if I'd have an opportunity to explain this to someone else.

On the sidewalk, I prayed another prayer.

"Dear Lord, I don't know how or when, but I ask that you allow me to see Trevor again and that you give us the chance to start over. Somehow. I know you can do anything you want. And I believe you don't want me to be with Dan."

I continued walking.

"Let me know if you want me to be with Trevor."

This was answered only two weeks later.

From: Imperiopoint@aol.com
Date: June 12
To: CST61795@aol.com
Subject: parting thoughts

...One afternoon during my sophomore year of high school, even before I discovered the truth about Emily and my best friend cheating on me, I uncovered another cheat. Another fraud. My mother.

I know you've wondered why I have such a bad attitude about her. It wasn't just that she divorced my dad and gave up custody. It's how it happened.

I was driving by with several friends, and I saw my mother and her boss in the parking lot of a dry cleaners. They were walking together, holding hands.

I might as well have walked in on them having sex. It meant just as much to me. And I knew, even at that young age, that this wasn't a friendly, brother-sister, Christian love sort of holding hands.

That was when I began to spy on my mother. When I learned about her midday meetings with her boss. I found out she had been cheating on my father for a long time.

It took me just about a week to tell Dad everything. And soon after I did, my whole life changed....

WEDNESDAY, 6:23 A.M.

The gift bag lay in the corner of the bedroom, under a chair that served no other purpose than holding clothes that needed to be cleaned. For the first time in a long time, Charissa sat on the armchair and dug through the tissue paper to find the contents inside.

She pulled out a box the size of a large Christmas ornament. In it were nestled the two items she was going to surprise Trevor with. She could close her eyes and imagine him opening the box, bringing out a pair of white baby tennis sneakers. Tiny little doll-size shoes with miniature laces and a sports logo and everything.

Shoes that would have told Trevor the truth.

This was to be his going-away present. Their starting-over present. A present to say that things were getting better, that another life awaited them.

Another life did await us. But that us *didn't include Trevor.*

She put the box back in the bag, wadded the tissue back in the top, and slid the bag back under the chair. Standing, she walked aimlessly across the room and finally ended up resting on the bed. With her eyes already closed, she summoned up the energy to pray.

"Please hear me. Oh, God, please hear me. Hear me, Father. I need you so much now. I'm so scared. So hurt, so lost. I can't do this alone. I don't understand what happened. And why? And why now?

"God, please. I need you to bring Trevor back to me. Perform a miracle and do something unthinkable. You're the Creator of life and everything, and I know you can do this, Lord. Please, God, I want another chance.

"Please forgive me for taking our marriage for granted. For not giving Trevor the reason to feel he could open up to me. Forgive me for hurting Trevor. Forgive us for not being more faithful to you, for not praying together, for not being closer. God, I know I wasn't as loving as I could be. I know I pulled back. Forgive me, Lord.

"Father, please let Trevor be safe. I don't know how—just—that's all

I can ask. Maybe I shouldn't— I should just be praying that your will would be done. But I have to ask. I can't help it.

"Bring him back to me, Lord. I'm so scared that my last words will be— You know them, Lord. You heard them. If they were— Oh, please, Lord, bring him back. In your Son's precious name, please, God. Please."

Charissa curled up in a ball on the king-size bed. A thousand memories flowed through her mind as the tears rolled onto her pillow. She breathed heavily and cleared her throat and sniffled and wondered if sleep could possibly come and then didn't think about anything anymore except the finest day of her life.

The day when she finally knew that she and Trevor would be together.

TREVOR

On a mid-October night, close to ten, Charissa picked up the phone and called Trevor's room. One of his suitemates answered.

"Trevor, it's for you," Cliff said.

Trevor picked up the phone and said hello.

"Studying?"

The voice startled him. So far, he had only had one conversation with Charissa, and that was when he first came on campus and told her he was moving into a dorm. She'd been stunned to know he had decided to attend Covenant after all.

"It's a new concept. I'm trying it out."

"Good for you," Charissa said.

"How are you?" he asked her, trying to sound as natural as possible.

"Can we talk?"

"Yeah, sure. What do you want to talk about?"

"I mean, can we meet somewhere and talk?"

"All right. Want me to come up?"

"No. Not here. Maybe downstairs in the dorm lounge."

"That would work. Sometime tomorrow?"

"Actually, I was thinking of now."

He looked down at his grubby torn shorts and mustard-stained T-shirt. Then he shrugged.

"Yeah, that'd be fine. See you down there."

Several minutes later Trevor walked into the crowded dorm lounge. It was a large room that held several couches and love seats as well as a big-screen television. A group of students were gathered around it watching a science fiction series. He saw Charissa standing there, wearing jeans and a sweatshirt, her blond hair pulled into a ponytail.

"Not very private," he said.

"No."

"Do you want to go downstairs?"

"To the laundry room?"

"We could talk better there," Trevor said.

"Okay."

The downstairs steps led to a nondescript room that housed several washers and dryers. The machines were in use, but no one was there. Trevor walked over to a table and sat on it.

"So. You want to talk."

"Uh-huh," she mumbled.

"About?"

"Why'd you change schools?"

"Now?" Trevor said as he chuckled.

"What?"

"You want the story *now*? After I've been here a month and a half?"

"I told you when you got here—"

"I know, I know," he said. "And I haven't, have I?"

"No. I haven't felt pressure."

Trevor looked at her and nodded. He glanced around the white, stark room, which was decorated only by signs about how to use the washers.

"So you want the story now? Tonight?"

"That's what I had in mind," she said in her soft voice.

He marveled at how beautiful she looked. Simple and understated and beautiful. "But why now?"

"I—to be honest, I don't know. I just thought—I had a nightmare the other night."

"About my coming back?" Trevor asked.

"No. About your leaving and *not* coming back."

"Leaving what?"

"College," Charissa replied.

He nodded. "I don't want to complicate things."

"You coming to school here complicated things," Charissa said.

"Yeah, I guess so," Trevor said. "Okay. Fine. Let's see. Well, when I graduated, I wanted to get as far away as possible."

"I remember that."

"But it was too late to get into most schools, so I ended up still living with my dad and going to COD. Great plan, huh? And for those two years I did nothing worthwhile. Nothing. I just sort of drifted.

With everything. Grades. Friends. Habits. Everything. I guess my dad told you about that."

She nodded. "So when did you decide to come to Covenant?"

"The night I saw you downtown after the Pearl Jam concert."

"Are you serious?"

He nodded. "I already knew something but couldn't admit it."

"What was that?"

"I was disobeying God."

"You were what?" she asked. "Since when did—"

"I knew what God wanted for me. It was crystal clear; I knew it years ago. But there was this other voice that said, No, do it yourself. Don't buy into God and his so-called love. Don't do what he wants you to do. But you know—these last few years, since my parents divorced—I realized I've basically been miserable."

"I'm sorry."

He gave a snort of laughter. His eyes narrowed and his cheeks tightened.

"You're sorry? There's no way you should be sorry. You were the one thing that helped out during all that time. You tried and tried again to connect with me, and I kept pushing you away. I think deep down it was because I was afraid of how God might be using you in my life."

"What do you mean?" Charissa asked.

"I don't think anybody could have had an impact on my life back then—except you. I mean, I couldn't stand my mother, and I had no respect for my father, and most of the kids at school were too caught up in their own world to even notice me. And I didn't want to have faith and have a God I had to answer to. But I know I've been wrong. And that night after the concert, after seeing you—I went home and asked God to forgive me of everything I'd been doing and show me what he wanted me to do."

She smiled. "Trevor, that's amazing."

He nodded, knowing he could barely explain how he felt and what he believed in his heart and how special that night had ended up being.

"For a long time, I've been angry," Trevor said. "I was angry with God about the whole Emily situation. And about my parents getting divorced. Even after meeting you, I was angry. And I couldn't see why

God put someone like you in my life just so I could leave them and hurt them. I couldn't believe God would do that. I finally realized *God* hadn't done it. It was my own stupid fault. But then I thought it was worth one more try."

She looked down at the floor. "A lot has happened the last couple of years."

"I know, Chris. Maybe too much for you. But that's why I came here to Covenant. To give it a chance, if you want to give it a chance. If it's over between us, for always, that's fine. I have to accept it. But I still have this sense that God put us together for a reason."

The hum of the washing machines covered their silence for a couple of minutes.

"I'm not rushing you," Trevor said. "I didn't even want to tell you all this so soon. I don't want you being scared, thinking I'm a nut case. It's just—everything about the way this happened—everything is a miracle."

Charissa looked at him with sympathetic eyes. "I don't think you're a nut case."

"It's like, I was so afraid of something happening when we first started hanging around with each other. And after things did happen, I was even more afraid. You nailed me on that one, remember? You knew I was scared, and you were right."

Trevor slid off the table and walked to the washer she leaned against. He looked down at her, inches away from her face. Her smile made him feel safe, free, and lost.

"In some ways, I'm still scared," he said.

"Me too."

"While we're standing here being scared, would you mind if I kissed you?" he asked.

She shook her head no but said nothing. He saw her looking at his lips as he bent to kiss hers. It was a soft, sweet kiss.

"Thank you," he said.

"Trevor—"

"Yes?"

"I need to tell you something."

"Okay."

"I don't know if you heard—about Dan and me? We broke up."

Trevor nodded. "I probably wouldn't have kissed you if I hadn't heard."

"Who told—"

"People talk," he said.

"It's just—all of this, so soon after— I mean, I should probably—"

"Yes, you probably should."

Charissa began to walk away, then turned for a moment.

"I'm really glad to hear all of that," she said.

"Thanks."

"That doesn't mean—it doesn't mean I'm not still afraid. I mean, I kinda got burned the last time."

He nodded and knew she had every right to feel that way.

"I promise you, Chris. I'm not going to push you away again. Not if you give me another chance."

From: Imperiopoint@aol.com
Date: June 12
To: CST61795@aol.com
Subject: parting thoughts

...And now, so many years later, that awful experience with my mom still eclipses so many things in my life. To see how she humiliated my dad and how easily she left us both— that just did something to me. I've tried to forgive her and give it to God and leave it all behind me, but sometimes those feelings of being rejected still reach up to bite me. Like they did this morning.

All of which is to say: I know I should trust you. I know I should believe in you. And I know that I should have told you these things—all of these things—years ago.

All I can do now is ask your forgiveness—and ask whether we can try again.

You've already given me so many second chances, Charissa. But I'm asking for one more. Give me another chance to be the kind of husband you deserve....

Charissa lay underneath the covers, her heart sad and her mind barely asleep. Her hand rested close to her cheek, her eyes closed. With one part of her mind she heard the door open and the light footsteps walk across the carpet. But she didn't even respond when the mattress sank under the pressure of the man sitting down next to her.

"Chris," a familiar voice said.

She opened her eyes and looked up and realized she was in a dream again but decided not to wake up.

"I'm sorry, sweetie," her husband said, looking down at her and stroking her cheek.

She squinted her eyes and wanted to begin with all the things she still wanted to say. Instead, she broke down instead and started crying tears that felt too real to be allowed in a dream.

Trevor leaned over and pulled her close. She wept into his chest.

"I'm so sorry, sweetheart," he said. "I'm sorry for everything. For the last year. For the last few years. There's so much I need to tell you."

"No," she mumbled, "you don't understand."

"Wait, listen. I don't know—I don't know if anything is happening between you and that guy."

"What?"

"But I don't care. I love you, Chris. It's been so long since I acted like it. But you need to know I love you too much to let go of our marriage. I'm not going to let anyone take my place."

"Trevor?"

"I won't let you go. I went away and thought of all the reasons I love you. There are so many. I wrote them up in an e-mail—some of them, anyway. I wanted to tell you the rest in person. I want to spend my life showing you every single reason why."

"What's going on?" Charissa asked.

"I'm sorry."

She sat up and placed a hand on his lips, on his cheek, then on his forehead.

"No," she said, crying again.

"What?"

"No. No, please, God, no."

"Chris. Please tell me it's not over."

"You can't be real."

Trevor looked at her, squinted his eyes and appeared confused.

"What do you mean. Of course I'm real."

"But you—you're gone."

"I'm what?"

"No," she said. "Let me be." She was breathing hard, feeling feverish. "Let me wake up."

"You are awake, Charissa."

"Let me know— I can't go on— I need to know—" She touched him again, afraid that doing so might ruin everything.

Trevor took her hand in his own. "What are you talking about? I'm right here, sweetie."

"The plane, the crash—"

A slight pause. "The what?"

"You're dead."

"What are you talking about?"

"I'm dreaming. No. Go away. Please."

She scrambled to her feet and looked back at Trevor, still sitting on the bed.

"Charissa. I'm here. Look."

She walked over and looked down at him as if it was the first time she had ever laid eyes on him.

"Where've you been?"

"I, well, actually I drove up to Michigan. I ended up at a motel—"

"But—but what about the e-mail—the plane?"

"I never got on the plane."

Charissa's knees buckled, and she fell to the floor, continuing to cry. *Dear God, please let this be real. Please, Lord.*

Trevor came to her side and gathered her in his arms.

"Chris, what's wrong?"

please God please dear heavenly Father answer my prayers and let this be a miracle

She choked out her words. "The plane you were in—the accident—it went—the ocean."

"What are you talking about?"

"You don't know?"

"I've been by myself thinking and driving and writing. I didn't—I mean I haven't— It was just yesterday. I couldn't just leave you, not after everything that just happened between us. But I didn't know where to—"

"So you really are there?" Charissa asked him again through tears.

"Yes. Oh, sweetie, yes. Are you— Oh, I'm so sorry. I didn't know. I swear I didn't know anything, but listen, I'm here."

"No, no. I'm sorry too."

They embraced, and Charissa cried into her husband's strong, unmoving arms.

"Trevor, I love you so much."

"Do you?"

"There was never anybody else."

"The e-mail?"

"Nothing—I'd never even read it. I don't really even know the guy. I promise you that. I don't know— I was trying to be nice because he was new, and maybe he took it the wrong way. I just couldn't believe you'd believe something like that."

"So nothing—"

"Nothing is going on. Nothing ever happened."

He let out a deep sigh. "I wasn't trying to be nosy, going into your e-mail. I just wanted to leave you a funny good-bye message that you'd get once I was gone. But then I saw—"

"Shh. It's okay. I'm just glad you're here."

"I was killing myself all night wondering how and why this happened. All while you— Oh, Chris, I'm so sorry. It must have been—you must have—"

Fresh tears started down her face, and she nodded. "But then I found your e-mail. Just a little while ago. Trevor—"

"I sent it from the airport. After I finished it, I knew there was so much more I needed to say. I just—I didn't know what to say and how to say it. So I decided to rent a car and just drove off. Didn't even listen to the radio."

"You're here," Charissa repeated. "You really are here. That's all that matters now."

"I am."

"Don't ever leave me again."

"I won't," he said. He kissed her gently, then held her face with both hands and looked into her eyes. "I've been gone too long anyway."

They kissed again, a deeper, longer kiss. Finally Charissa broke away.

"Trevor," her voice choked out. "I need to tell you something."

He raised his head at the gravity of her tone.

"What is it, Chris? Is everything all right?"

"It was something I was going to… Well, I…I wanted to surprise you before you left."

"So what is it?"

She knew she was babbling, but she couldn't seem to stop. "I wanted it to be the right time—the perfect time, you know. But I just—you need to know. And well, here it is."

The tears came first. Then the gift bag and the little box. Then more tears. And then, as the sun peeked in through the bathroom skylight next to their bedroom, the weight of the world suddenly off Charissa's shoulders, she embraced the somebody she knew God had chosen just for her.

CHARISSA

So I've finally reached the end—the end of my story about how we ultimately got together. I know this hasn't even begun to sum up every emotion I ever felt about you or every situation we ever encountered. But I know that, regardless of how our wedding goes and the rest of our lives unfold, a new chapter in our love story began on that glorious night I came back to you.

I know you remember what happened, Trevor, how we met and finally got together. But I'm writing this to let you know all the things I felt and wanted to say but didn't.

These pages are my wedding gift to you—the unspoken words I never managed to utter.

I heard the distinguishable sounds of Trevor Thomas as I opened the door to the two-bedroom dorm suite. I had asked one of his suitemates, Marcus, if anybody else was in the room. Marcus told me no, that the other guys were out and that Trevor was, as usual, by himself. As I walked through a hallway littered with bags full of disregarded textbooks and various shoes, I recognized the Morrissey song that was playing right away. It was "Last Night on Maudlin Street." I'd been around Trevor long enough to know this.

I followed the music, stopping behind the barely open door. I tapped on it hard enough for Trevor to hear, hard enough to get his attention. Then I pushed the door and walked into the room to find him on his bottom bunk. He lay sideways, his head propped up by his arm and elbow, his face pointed toward the textbook he was studying. I could see his confusion as I stepped toward him.

"Hi," I said as I reached to turn off the music.

It was only a couple of weeks after our conversation in the laundry room. I walked to the edge of the bed and sat down on it. He didn't move, just remained on his side glancing up at me.

I took his free hand and held it in both of mine. Then I brought it up to my lips and kissed it.

"Chris—," he said, but I only shook my head.

I rubbed the side of my face against his hand, allowing it to stay there, allowing him to stroke my hair.

Then I moved to kiss him on his cheek, then on his lips.

"What's going on?" he asked me as he finally moved to sit up next to me.

I smiled at him, looking into his gray eyes, his sad eyes, longing to know every thought and feeling this man held deep inside.

There was so much I wanted to say, but the words escaped me, as they often had. And yet, I think this was good. I think it was perfect because words would have done such a poor job of summing up everything inside.

I nodded. That's all I did.

He only shook his head, not understanding, not comprehending.

"What are you—"

I smiled and interrupted him with another kiss. This kiss was longer, and he put his hand on the back of my head. Gently he held me close.

As we kissed, I realized I didn't know whether God had ordained this moment from the beginning of time. Or whether he would allow Trevor and me to stay together and grow in our love and discover all there was to know about each other. I didn't know how long we would both be given together. But I knew that for this moment, God was smiling down on us.

I believed in my heart God wanted us to be together. I still believe it.

When we moved apart, Trevor's eyes looked full, his face relieved.

"I love you," he said to me.

My eyes leaked tears, and I wiped them away and kissed him again.

"I know," I said.

And we were finally together, just like that.

Simple.

A simple miracle.

From: Imperiopoint@aol.com
Date: June 12
To: CST61795@aol.com
Subject: parting thoughts

...And if I only had one chance left, one chance left to be with you, what would I wish for? If I could receive a single solitary gift from God and begin again with you, where would I start? What moment would I go back to?

I know.

It'd be the night of our first date, by your parents' front doorway. When an adorable young blonde of eighteen looked up at me after our farewell kiss with tears of joy, surprise, and so much more. When she said words that ultimately would change my life forever.

"I love you, Trevor."

I couldn't believe you thought so much of me, of us, of the night. I couldn't believe that you, who were usually so quiet, would work up the courage to tell me this.

I remember leaving wondering how in the world I could have affected someone that much. I wondered how I had ended up at the home of such a special and sensitive young woman. What in the world was she doing with me?

That's the moment I'd go back to. I'd go back to see that look again. I'd go back to remember when I realized just who you were, Charissa. And when I first had thoughts that you were the one, for some reason I'll never know, that God had picked out for me.

In Care Of

ONE

Are we allowed to say good-bye?

I wonder as my gloved hand reaches for the sculptured brass handle of the door, the force of the wind pushing me into it as if by divine intervention. Yet, as much as I believe that God controls the fates we often so casually overlook, I know this is an action I am taking on my behalf and my behalf alone.

Behind the door, away from the gusting snow and chapping cold, someone waits.

After all these years, I still can picture her smile.

All I need to do is walk into the hotel lobby as easily as I might grace the entry hall of my church, where the waiting greeter always grins and shakes my hand.

Just push that handle and go in.

The door opens with surprising ease.

Two

It's the previous September. I glimpse a sweep of hair across shoulders and feel a compulsion to jump up and turn the woman around. After all this time, I still envision the outline of her face, can still see the smile on her lips, can still feel her gaze go right through me. And I stop breathing, thinking that it's she, almost forgetting why I'm here.

Until the brown-haired woman turns. With her coat off and the maître d' leading her into the restaurant, she's a stranger looking past me. She strolls through the crowded tables toward an attentive man who waits at a table for two—just like the one where I sit. I wonder if they're married and casually study the talkative couple for several minutes before concluding they aren't.

The stranger, pretty in an unassuming and natural way, doesn't really look anything like the woman I knew. Same height, similar walk, the hair color—that's all. But still. It makes me wonder why she came to mind.

Already on my second glass of iced tea, I take another sip and keep watching the entrance to the cozy eatery. We've eaten at Giuseppe's in nearby Bristol, Tennessee, once before, almost half a decade ago, and have spent the remaining years vowing to come back. Yet after sitting here for twenty-five minutes, I realize we're going to have to wait longer. I glance down at my tie and wonder how long it's been since I've worn one. I find myself missing the office days for a moment, then realize the absurdity of those thoughts and quickly abandon them.

The phone on my belt vibrates, and I open it, seeing the name *Isabel* scroll across the top.

"Giuseppe's takeout," I say.

"Sorry," my wife's exasperated voice starts out. I can already predict everything she'll say.

"You okay?"

"Yes. It's just—this day—what a nightmare. I was a little late getting away from the office, then came home and got a message from Mona. She's sick and can't make it."

"That's okay." I glance at the waiter who's asked me half a dozen times if I need anything. I want to ask him if his duties include child-care.

"I've tried for the last half-hour to get a baby-sitter."

"No one around?"

"It's six on a Friday night. What do you think?"

"I'm thinking no."

"I wish your parents lived closer," Isabel says.

"I know."

"I'm sorry, honey. I know you had this night all planned out. Mona's usually reliable."

"It's okay. No biggie. How're the kids?"

"They're fine. Think Giuseppe's would mind a six- and a nine-year-old?"

I laugh and look around at the elegant, childless crowd. "Frankly, I think they'd make us check them at the door. Look, we'll do it some other weekend."

"Tonight was going to be perfect."

The small black box sitting on the bare stretch of white linen captures my attention. I pick it up and examine it once again. "We'll just do it again some other Friday," I tell her.

"I'm sorry," she says again.

"It's fine. Our anniversary isn't for another few weeks. We can shoot for then. Look, I'll be home in about an hour."

"Okay. Love you."

"Love you, too."

The waiter comes, and I give him a five for the iced tea and tell him to keep the change. I can tell he is unimpressed. He gives me a mildly sympathetic look, as if I've been stood up, and I resist the urge to explain. I grab the box on the table, and as I stand to leave, I open it up again.

The diamond pendant resting inside is big enough to be featured on one of those romantic commercials where the good-looking couple sneaks away from a party and the male model gives his cover-girl bride some gargantuan diamond ring or necklace. Nowhere in those commercials is the possibility that the baby-sitter gets sick or that there are even waiting children at home or that life isn't nauseatingly perfect.

I walk past the hostess station and almost make it out the door when I hear someone call my name.

"Mr. Conroy?"

I look back and see a woman who might be in her twenties, though the more time that passes, the worse I get at judging another's age. She's a pretty girl with short, stylish brown hair and a perky grin. Her black pants look painted on, and her revealing top is held up with tiny straps. I find myself wondering what her father would think of such an outfit, then realize how the passing thought ages me.

"Uh-huh," I answer.

"I just want to say that I'm a huge fan. I've read all of your books. I was at your book signing in Johnson City when you signed *A Harbor in the Tempest.*"

"Thanks," I say, glancing around the entryway to make sure we're not blocking the door.

"I wish I had a book you could sign," she says.

"I wouldn't charge you," I say with a cordial smile.

I can tell the girl is nervous and excited to meet me. This not only amuses me, but it also gives me a slight jolt of energy, the way a star running back might feel whenever he touches the football. I assume her date for the evening waits somewhere in the restaurant.

"All my friends are reading your books."

"Great," I reply.

"I'm actually writing my first novel, or at least trying to. I teach fourth graders."

I think about telling her I'm the father of a fourth grader, but I quickly squelch that impulse.

"I'd be happy to take a look at something of yours," I say. "You can send it in care of the address in the back of the book."

"Really? Are you serious?"

"Sure." I am.

Her excitement is contagious, and I can't hold back the beaming smile that covers my face. She nods, then awkwardly shakes my hand.

"Well, I just wanted to say hi. *Out of a Million* made me cry. It's my favorite book I've ever read. You really are a remarkable writer."

There are perhaps a hundred things I'd like to say, but instead I simply say, "Thank you." I step past the young woman and outside into the tranquil autumn evening. The sun still hovers in the distance, and I walk to find the vehicle I parked more than half an hour ago.

Once inside my SUV, I hear the woman's voice again in my head and feel a sensation I haven't felt in a long time.

It's not the actual compliment that makes me feel this way, but the woman who said it. There's just something about a flattering remark made by a beautiful woman.

My thoughts slither toward the earlier, split-second mistaken identity. Toward another beautiful woman who often paid me flattering compliments. A lifetime ago.

Where are you?

Just a thought. Simple, meaningless, safe. A thought I ask only myself.

As I drive back home, slipping in a CD for background music, I suddenly realize how long it's been since I've had that kind of praise from a woman—my wife included. I don't mean a simple "good job" affirmation or the "I love your book" compliments I get at book signings, but the gushing accolade that makes me smile and flush. And even though I know Isabel loves me and have always liked that she is not the gushing type, sometimes I find myself feeling just a little deprived.

A distant thought nags at me, a tug from years earlier, yet I ignore it and drive on. There's no reason to compare memories of the past with the present. I know that in my heart, in the unspoken recesses only I can access, the past will always outshine anything that happens now.

THREE

The letter arrives in a yellow bubble-wrap package along with twenty others. It's the sixth letter I hold in my hand, the only one without a sender's name and address. Years ago I would have found it remarkable to receive one of these, let alone twenty, all forwarded from my publisher after a mere week's worth of accumulation. Now I open them routinely, scan them, toss most in a box in my closet, slide a few into files. Time can take a toll on everything, especially the things that mean the most.

This is a Tuesday 10:45 P.M. project, with the kids in bed almost an hour ago and Isabel quietly reading upstairs. I have read three letters and one card so far. A woman in Texas wrote me a one-page note telling me she's read all but two of my novels and *Out of a Million* is still her favorite. Another is the kind I get often, from a woman who picked up a copy of my book in the library and is looking forward to reading the others. There's a thank-you note for *Turnabout,* my second novel, and finally a letter from a reader who is excited about my upcoming novel, *Immersion.* My standard, joking reply to such comments flits through my mind: *Hope you feel that excited after you finish it.*

The envelope I hold now feels heavier than usual. The address on the front is spelled out neatly:

Stephen Conroy
In Care of Random House Publishers

The familiar New York address is printed underneath. I wonder how many of these letters Random House receives on a daily basis and how anyone keeps track of the mail for all the hundreds of authors they work with. Add to that hundreds and thousands of e-mails they probably get daily, messages that rarely find their way to the authors. At least they don't find their way to me.

I slit open the letter with a fancy opener given to me by the first publisher I ever worked with, Triten House. It was a Christmas present, part of a pen set. The letter is heavy cream stock folded into thirds, the writing painstakingly scribed in neat blue. I find it odd that it begins with the words *Dear Steve*. Very few people except family and friends call me that.

Dear Steve,

I often wondered when the day would come. When I would come across your name and hold one of your books in my hands. *Moonlight* was the first. I wish I could say I've read all the others, but I didn't know you had written any until I found this in a Wal-Mart of all places and picked it up and then saw the name. You always held so many dreams for your writing. Congratulations on achieving them.

It's been a long time. Too long, in fact. And even as I write, I fear what you would say in response. I wonder if you'll even answer this letter.

I don't know exactly how to begin or what to say. How we left things—how *I* left you—I know now it shouldn't have happened that way.

I finished *Moonlight* and felt compelled to write. I just had to, even against my better judgment. It was a remarkable novel, Steve. I saw so much of you—so much of the Steve I once knew—throughout its pages.

Now, half a lifetime past, it feels as though there is too much to say, and simple words do the time little justice. Part of me wishes you could know all about my life, though part of me fears you might not even care to know. I will spare you the details except to say I ended up back in California. I guess that won't surprise you.

As for you—your bio reveals very little about you except where you live and the fact that you have a family. I even went on your Web site to try to discover more, but all I saw were photos and information on your other books. You still look the same, just a little more mature, and it looks good on you. I see you live in Johnson City now, not too far from Knoxville.

I just wanted you to know that I loved *Moonlight* in more ways than I can ever possibly share. I've often thought of you, of us, and wondered what might have been. Anytime a snowstorm comes, I think of that night. I'm sorry for everything that happened, for the mistakes made.

Congratulations on your successful writing career. I look forward to reading your other books—the future ones, too. And maybe, possibly, hearing from you again.

Nicole Marsh

Mailing and e-mail addresses hang at the bottom of the letter like dangling grenades.

I glance around my office, suddenly guilty. I haven't done anything wrong, yet just seeing Nicole's name after all these years brings a wave of shame over me.

I read the letter a second time. The last sentence pricks my neck.

And maybe, possibly, hearing from you again.

For so many years, I convinced myself I would never hear from her again. And the cushion of time set in and allowed me to be more and more comfortable as those years passed. And even though I've thought of her from time to time—as when I thought I saw her in Giuseppe's only weeks ago—the years have been mostly empty of feelings about Nicole.

Until now.

Holding the letter in my hand, I realize what part of me has known for years:

I still love Nicole Marsh.

FOUR

What did you say?

> *You heard me.*

> *Maybe I didn't.*

> *Maybe I didn't say it.*

> *Stop it.*

> *I have to get going.*

> *Say it again.*

> *Why? You already know—it's not any big surprise.*

> *No one's ever said it.*

> *Come on.*

> *And meant it.*

> *Hmm.*

> *Is that a good hmm, or a contemplative, what-am-I-doing-with-this-girl hmm?*

> *I love you.*

> *I know.*

FIVE

Winter is still a couple of months away, and as I open my eyes to the sound of my wife drying her hair, I remember the letter from last night. I know I should tell Isabel about it, know she'll want to read it, know this might prompt a discussion about Nicole Marsh. It's been years since we've talked about her. There never seems to be an appropriate time. Not that the subject of past loves could ever feel appropriate in a normal conversation.

I find a familiar mug for the already brewed coffee and begin working on the first of several cups. Natalie enters the kitchen dressed for school. She starts to get herself a bowl of cereal, and I compliment her on the colorful bow in her hair.

"Anything exciting happening today?" I ask my nine-year-old.

"We've got tryouts for the play," Natalie says in a familiar, matter-of-fact tone. After all these years, it still stuns me that a girl can be like her mother in so many different ways.

"Want to sing a song for me?"

"It's not even eight, Dad," she says as she rolls her chocolate-colored eyes and works on her Golden Grahams.

Natalie's long, raven hair mirrors her mother's, along with her dark, expressive eyes and tiny mouth. I would think she was beautiful even if she weren't my daughter. A part of me dreads her upcoming junior high and high school years. I still feel that one day there will be a knock on the door and the authorities will tell me I'm not a fit father, that I have no clue what I'm doing, and that I certainly won't be able to hack Natalie's teenage years.

But I know Natalie takes after her father in at least one thing—not being a morning person. Bonding with my children over a huge breakfast is not for me. Simply being awake and seeing them off to school is about all I can manage. But at least I keep on doing it.

A light-brown-haired tornado tears through the kitchen, and I tell my six-year-old to make sure he eats breakfast.

"What do you want?" I ask Jake.

"Chips."

"No," I tell him. "You're not eating chips for breakfast."

"I want chips."

"Come on. How about some wonderful fruit?"

"Yuuuuck," he says as he runs off.

"Jake, come here." This is a morning tradition as routine as hearing the alarm go off. Jake wants to do anything except sit still.

Eventually I get him to eat half a blueberry muffin as the other half crumbles over the wooden floor.

I wander to the family room to watch the *Today* show on NBC. I sip coffee and listen to the morning news and check the weather in all parts of the country and discover that it's going to be an unseasonably warm day.

Isabel walks into the room wearing black pants and a red, button-down top.

"You look nice," I tell her.

"Thanks," she says as she strolls by and tells Jake to clean up the mess he's made.

I venture a couple more sips before tackling my morning duty: making lunches. I'm glad I don't have to go to school and eat sandwiches that have been incubating in a little plastic Baggie all day. I hated bagged lunches growing up. I still have more tolerance for making them than for eating them.

Isabel manages half a cup of coffee and eats a blueberry muffin. She cleans up the mess left by Jake.

"Going anywhere today?" she asks me.

"Yeah, I was thinking about working on the shed in the backyard. Get some lumber, perhaps finally buy a hammer."

"Ha-ha," Isabel replies, rolling her brown eyes the same way she's taught Natalie to. "Can you go to the grocery store for me?"

"Ewww," I say.

Jake runs by me holding a toy and mimics the sound I just made.

"I have a list. It's short."

"There better not be any makeup or hair products on that list. I always end up getting you the wrong stuff."

"Don't worry. It's just the basics."

"All right," I say.

Isabel rounds up the kids and makes sure she has everything. I give her the bagged lunches.

"Have a good day," she says.

I nod and watch her, feeling I should tell her about the letter from the night before but knowing now is the wrong time. I give her a quick kiss and wonder when the right time will come.

Moments after they're gone, with the house to myself, I grab my coffee cup and head to my office. Normally these are my most productive writing periods, when Isabel is at her part-time job as a paralegal. This is her first year back at work after nine years of being a full-time mom. We don't really need the money, but I realize this is something she wants, maybe even needs. Sitting around the house in sweatpants is not her idea of fun or productive.

Maybe seeing *me* sitting around the house in sweatpants was what drove her back to work.

I turn on my computer but find myself restless, avoiding the story I'm just getting into. Writing a novel is like taking a long cross-country journey. The hardest part is getting going, making sure you have all the items you need to take with you, double- and triple-checking that the route you're taking is the best way. So often you leave your driveway and start north when you realize you actually needed to head southwest. I've never written a novel without a certain number of false starts. And it never seems to get easier. Part of me thinks it only gets harder.

After avoiding my work for an hour, I pick up the letter from Nicole and read it again. Sunlight spreads into my office. Somewhere in California, far away from this spacious house on a rolling mountainside in Tennessee, is a woman one year younger than me who decided to write this letter and finally reconnect after all these years.

I wonder if I can do the same.

Six

No true story is linear, regardless of the structure set into its pages. I've discovered that stories often resemble dirt paths that meander and break up and resume and intersect at different points. It is only where the roads meet that the tale really matters.

The story of Nicole Marsh and me began with my junior year of high school and ended a year and a half later. Since that time, I have lived another twenty years without hearing from her. Fourteen of those years have been spent married to Isabel, nine as the father of Natalie and six as the father of Jake. And with my thirty-eighth birthday three months past, I thought I knew the cards life had dealt me, as the cliché goes. My hand was quite good, great in fact, and there was no need to gamble anything away. Yet somehow, a wild card has ended up in my possession, and I find myself unsure what to do with it.

The morning after receiving Nicole's letter and reading it another half-dozen times, I rummage through plastic storage boxes in the basement storeroom searching for pieces of my past. By now I should be writing, plugging away on my iMac toward my daily word count, sometimes not managing the two thousand words I generally shoot for, occasionally becoming inspired and cranking out more.

Part of me knows I should have done this years earlier, that I should have been better prepared. I knew I would hear from Nicole eventually. I just never thought it would take her twenty years.

I poke around in a box full of old yearbooks. A few photo albums from our childhood are down here as well. What I'm looking for is a three-ring binder full of letters. Eventually, in a box full of old cards and folded letters, I spot the gray, nondescript binder. I doubt I've read a single word of its contents since my college days.

I carry the binder to my office and open the musty covers to reveal what looks to be a first draft of a hundred-page novella. It's written in a tight, close hand that makes the pages look like completed jigsaw puzzles, each neatly compressed and stacked. It's amazing how Nicole's handwriting hasn't changed in twenty years.

Why I ever opened up all of her folded notes to me and put them in this binder is a question I'll never be able to answer. I remember reading through them a few times in college. But every time I did, Nicole's flattering words only made me feel worse.

I never could erase the images of our last time together.

The first letter in the binder is the first letter she ever sent me, a letter that surprised me with its passion and its directness.

> Stephen,
>
> I can't believe what a sweet gesture the flower was! Thank you. And thank you for the wonderful note. I don't think I've ever received a more wonderful letter from any guy. Most of the guys I've met around here have been jerks, interested in only one thing. I doubt most of them even know how to write a letter.
>
> I have to tell you how adorable you looked during lunch yesterday. I really loved your outfit. I'm sorry to cause you to blush by saying that. It's not that big a deal! It shows your sensitive side. Really!
>
> I hope to get to know you better too. Being new at the school, I know it's going to be hard fitting in, especially after everyone's known everyone for the last couple of years. Everyone already calls me the California girl. The cliques seem just as bad here as my last school. Thanks for being so kind to me, and for being a gentleman.
>
> We'll have to do something, go out sometime. I hope I'm not being too forward in asking you out. I think we could have a fun time. I like being around you, more than most guys. My last few experiences with guys weren't too good. I'll have to tell you about them sometime.
>
> I've gotta go. Write back if you want. This geometry class is numbing—why in the world will I ever need this? Anyway, I'm thinking about you—is that bad to tell you?

I guess not. I guess you already know since I'm writing
you.

>See ya later.

Love, Nicole

She was sixteen when she wrote this, and I was a year older. Sixteen
and seventeen years old. And it wasn't that long before we were talking
about being in love and getting married. We used words like *fate* and
destiny and *happily ever after.* Could we really have been so utterly naive?

Looking down at the letter though, I can still feel a tinge of what I
felt when I read it. The little swell of pride and gratification and aston-
ishment to read such words from a beautiful girl who seemed to really
like me.

This notebook holds perhaps fifty or more letters from Nicole,
some two or three pages long. This was before e-mail occupied everyone's fingertips, when using a paper and pen was the best way to go. As
I remember, I answered most of them, and my letters were as long and
heartfelt as hers. I've often held my emotions and feelings close to my
heart, rarely expressing them except in fictional form. But Nicole was an
exception. Many things were different with Nicole. She brought many
things out of me.

I turn to the back of the notebook and check the date of the last letter. February 6, 1981.

>My dearest Stephen,
>
>>How could you say this is wrong? How could you
>leave just like that?
>
>>I realize what you believe. I don't disagree. In fact, I
>share the same beliefs. But how can you argue with love?
>You know how much I love you, and I believe you love
>me the same way. It doesn't matter what someone who
>doesn't know us says, someone either standing behind a
>pulpit or trying to act like a parent. My mom and dad
>talk like they know what people should and shouldn't do.
>Yet they got divorced and showed me how little they
>know about love. They made a *promise* to love each other,

and then they broke it. I don't ever want to do that. I don't want to regret loving someone. And I know I'll never regret holding these feelings for you.

The other night, when you left after everything—I'm sorry. I apologize for everything, even though I still don't think what we did was wrong. How could it be wrong, Steve? Tell me that. I heard the words you said, but they didn't make sense. Even you said you didn't fully understand them. I could see the frustration in your eyes. And there's no reason for it to be there. How much time do we have left together? Why can't we make the most of it?

The world doesn't understand what we have, how we feel. I love you like I've never loved another soul in my life. I wake up and instantly see your face, hear your voice. I can't wait to hold you close and feel your kiss. You can make me smile just by looking at me. I can't help these feelings I have. I know you feel the same way.

We need to talk about this upcoming weekend. Please let me know if you can see me this afternoon and if we can talk about all of this.

I love you.

Your teddy bear, Nicole

My heart blushes at her unabashedly sentimental words and also at the pain and confusion they betray. I remember this letter, one of the last ones she sent, the last one I kept. I remember feeling the same way about Nicole and thinking that no one understood us, that our love was exceptional and, because of that, could withstand anything.

I close the binder, wedge it into one of my crowded bookshelves, then just sit there thinking. It's been half a lifetime since a woman opened up like this to me, since someone I loved bared her soul with an intensity and fervor I couldn't begin to match.

I know it's dangerous to be reading these letters again and thinking about Nicole. Reminiscing is one thing, but Nicole is not a nostalgic childhood memory. There is still a part of me that belongs to her, that will always belong to her.

SEVEN

"Yeah, is Inspector Clouseau there?"

My brother laughs. "No, but there's a stud of a cop here who can take your sorry sack and lock you up."

"Sorry, I'm out of your jurisdiction."

"I've got friends over there," Randy says, his East Tennessee drawl much more pronounced than mine.

"What're you up to?" I ask.

"Just sittin' around watching television."

It's Wednesday night, and after a very unproductive day and an evening full of self-doubt, I've decided to tell someone about the letter. Randy is the only sibling I have, and although being older doesn't necessarily mean he's wiser, he often helps out whenever I need input or advice. I know I can tell him something and he'll never repeat it to anyone else.

"You got a minute?" I ask.

"Sure. What's up?"

I'm in my office again—a violation of my long-ago vow never to work in the evenings while Isabel and the kids are up. Back when I worked at the ad agency, keeping this promise was harder, especially since I'd come home and have to wait until Isabel went to bed before resuming work on my latest novel. I'm fortunate now to be able to spend plenty of daylight hours typing away, so I usually have no problem avoiding the office during the prime-time hours with the family.

Tonight is different, and this conversation needs to be held in private.

"Do you remember in high school—you were already in college— I dated this girl named Nicole?"

"That gorgeous chick from California?"

I chuckle at Randy's description of her. "Yes. Nicole Marsh. She was around for a few holidays."

"Yeah, I remember her."

"I just got a letter from her yesterday."

"What do you mean? Sent to your house?"

"No. It was forwarded from my publisher. You know, like all those letters I get."

"From your geriatric fan club," Randy says laughing.

"*Geriatric*. That's a pretty big word for you."

"Learned it from my little brother, Stephen, the famous author."

"Be quiet," I say. "Listen, Nicole and I were pretty serious back then."

"Didn't Mom and Dad have a cow about her? Didn't they ground you or something?"

"Yeah. They had some issues."

"They've always had issues," Randy says with a chuckle. "Whatever happened to her?"

"She moved away during my senior year."

"You ever heard from her since?" Randy asks.

"No."

"So what'd the letter say?"

"She read one of my books. She was talking about that. And saying that she wanted to write me before now. The thing is, I didn't tell Is about the letter."

"Why not?"

"I don't know. I just got it."

"You're telling me about it," Randy says.

"Yeah, but that's different. The thing is, I told Is about Nicole years ago, back before we got married. It's not something I can just casually bring up now."

"Why? 'Cause you guys were so serious?"

"Yeah, among other things. I just wonder—do I have to tell Is? Is it wrong for me not to?"

Silence over the line. Then, "You going to contact this Nicole? Write her back?"

"She did put in her address and e-mail."

"That might be a little weird—writing back to her."

"But would it be wrong?" I ask him.

"Probably. I mean, I don't know. Why don't you ask Dad?"

"You know what he'd say."

"Yeah, I know."

"I once thought I was going to marry this girl. We were pretty involved."

"Then it's probably a bad idea to write her back."

"Yeah, I figured as much," I say. "But what about telling Is?"

"I don't know. There's this guy in my Bible study that's always saying we should be up front with our wives about everything. So I asked him—what if I was surfing the Web and got on one of those porn sites? Do I tell my wife about that the next day?"

"You're not on the Internet, are you?" I ask him.

"No, I'm just talking hypothetically here. The thing is, he says we should always tell our wives what we're thinking and feeling. Well, I'm not so sure. Seems like it could cause problems. Besides, you know me—I'm not so good about the whole communication thing with Donna."

"Yeah, you are."

"Nah, not really. I joke around with her a lot, but I think it gets pretty old after a while. But you and Isabel talk a lot, don't you?"

"It's just—with this girl—it was a pretty big thing for Isabel and me. We talked a lot about it when we just started to get serious. You know—baggage from the past and all that."

"Everybody has that."

"Not everybody," I say. "Isabel doesn't."

"She's not exactly typical. You've always known that."

I agree with my brother.

"Look, why don't you sit on it for a while. Think about it. Like Dad always says, pray about it."

"Yeah, that's probably a good idea."

"Where does she live now?"

"Nicole?" I ask. "The address says somewhere in California."

"So you have nothing to worry about. It's not like you might run into her in downtown Johnson City."

"You never know. It was amazing that I ever met her in the first place."

"Look. You're this big-time author. It's not surprising someone from the past wrote to you. It'll probably happen again with someone else."

"Yeah," I say, knowing there was only one Nicole Marsh in my life.

EIGHT

It's amazing how ordinary the life you've always wanted can become. How you can spend years of a life working and hoping for your dreams to come true and then find yourself nonchalant about achieving them. I try to remind myself on a daily basis just how much the Lord has blessed me and my family, but sometimes in the middle of a busy life and a massive book project and all the other things going on, it's easy to take things for granted. In the middle of work on page seventy-eight of a still untitled novel that is due in the spring, I receive a call that's about to make my not-so-ordinary day job a bit more surreal.

"Stephen, my man!" The voice has a definite New York flavor.

"Alan!" I yell out, trying to match my agent's enthusiastic tone.

"Working on the next great American novel?"

"You bet," I say, curious about why he's calling me.

"Got a title yet?"

"I was thinking of *Bestseller*," I joke.

"Already been used. Olivia Goldsmith. How about *New York Times Bestseller*?"

"I like that even better."

Alan Dierge, rhyming with *dirty* except with a *g*, has been my agent for more than seven years. My first two books, both released by a medium-size publisher called Triten House, sold only moderately but managed to get Alan's attention. He added me to his short list of authors, most of them newcomers with potential. So far, according to Alan, I am one of the few that have paid off in terms of his investment, especially after I signed my most recent multibook contract with Random House.

"You better sit down for this, buddy," Alan says.

"I'm already sitting."

"Good. Listen, this is big. Think big. Huge."

"Well, I'd say Oprah had picked me for her book club if it were still going."

"No, it's not Oprah. Think again. Remember, we're talking big."

"Let me see. I'm going to be doing another book signing at Wal-Mart?"

Alan laughs. My book signing at the local Wal-Mart is an ongoing joke between us. I did it years ago, when I didn't realize how book signings really worked and before I started to gain any sort of name recognition. In three hours I sold a total of five books, most bought from people simply showing pity on me.

"How's does the *Today* show sound?"

"The *Today* show? NBC?"

"You got it," Alan says, unable to restrain his fervor. "I got the confirmation this morning. *Today* wants you to come on and talk about *Immersion*."

This *is* big. Huge, as Alan put it. I feel a prickle of goose bumps.

"Listen," Alan is saying, "this is incredible. Seems that Katie Couric is this big fan of yours. She's read almost all of your books and can't wait until *Immersion* comes out in February. So they want you to come on the day it hits the stores. You know, like Grisham and others do."

"No," is all I can say.

"Katie will probably interview you herself. Can you believe it?"

"Actually, I can't."

"So how does a trip to New York sound, buddy? It's been a while since you've been out here. I can take you to some outrageously expensive restaurant, and we can do the town and all that stuff. Bring Isabel and the kids. We can arrange a signing in one of the major stores, one of the flagships—it'll be huge."

I can't think of anything to say. After the gratifying sales and the incredible exposure of my last novel, *A Harbor in the Tempest,* I've continued to think that this dream I've been living in will soon end. The curtain will fall, and someone will whisper to me to get off the stage and get back to a regular nine-to-five job because people are bored with me and my writing. With *Immersion* only months away, I can already feel the familiar doubts. Prepublication jitters, as Alan calls them.

"Congrats, man," he tells me. "I'd send you a bottle of really expensive champagne, but I know you don't drink."

I laugh. "I should buy one for you."

"You know me—I never turn down free booze. But look, I gotta go. I'll be sending you more details. But it looks positive. February 9, right? The big Tuesday. Tell Isabel I said congratulations."

"Thanks, Alan."

"Feeling good about book number eight?"

"It's coming along. Slowly."

"I'm sure it's another winner. Take care."

I hang up the phone and just sit at my desk, glancing out my windows to the large backyard behind the house. I still can't believe the news.

Alan, for all his "hey buddy" attitude and animated chitchat, is one of the most serious and driven people I know. He's the kind of agent I need, a guy who loves my writing and believes in it and also makes me stretch as an artist while being ferocious about landing the big deal for me. He made me rewrite *The Long and Winding Road* three times before he gave it to Random House. It happened to be my breakout novel, selling more than seventy-five thousand copies the first year.

Sitting in my brown leather armchair centered behind my massive oak desk, I can simply turn around and spot my six published titles lined up side by side on the bookshelf behind me. To some this display might reek of self-importance, but that's not really why the books are there. To me they represent the accomplishments of a lifetime spent writing. Each book, slim or thick, hardcover or soft, reveals a little about me and a lot about my state of mind when I wrote it. They differ in terms of sales numbers and overall satisfaction, both from the publisher's side of things and from my own, but I can say I love them just as much as any parent loves his children.

I find *Moonlight* and take it off the shelf. Sometimes I do this with a book simply to remember what it was about. But *Moonlight*—I always remember *Moonlight*.

When asked, I usually tell people that I don't have a favorite novel. It's like asking which child is your favorite. But the truth is that *Moonlight* has always been special to me, a little orphan I adopted with its bundle of problems and ailments and odd little quirks. When people ask, I tell them it's a love story about two people who can't be together. It sold around fifteen thousand copies in the first year it was released, less than half the sales of the previous novel. But for an author, some-times sales don't matter. Sometimes awards and accolades and bestseller lists just don't make that big a difference. Sometimes you create some-thing you're passionate about and find yourself personally pleased with the results.

This is exactly what happened with *Moonlight*.

It is also the first novel Nicole read, a voice tells me.

That seems fitting, since it was written primarily with her in mind.

I find the remote control to the stereo resting on its shelf in the cor-ner of my office. A click, and the soundtrack to *How to Make an American Quilt* begins to play. This is one of five hundred soundtracks I own, this one I purchased without seeing the movie. The composer is Thomas Newman, a favorite of mine, and his haunting melodies help get me into the mood as I write.

The news from Alan seems to help too. Soon I'm cracking away at my keyboard, the words flowing, the story back on track, the end still far away but coming ever closer.

NINE

Can you just stop?

No.

Please. Just pull over.

I can't do this.

I just want to talk.

We can talk.

What is wrong?

I told you.

Please, Steve.

Fine. Look, I'm stopping. Okay. Good enough?

Don't get angry.

I'm not—I'm just—don't you get it? I'm not trying to be a jerk.

I know you aren't.

Then stop making me feel like one. Like I've done something wrong.

You won't be doing anything wrong.

Can we go now?

Just talk to me. Look at me.

What?

It's different. I mean, with you, everything is different.

It's not like this is easy or anything.

I know. I don't want you upset. I don't want you to worry at all. I just want—

What?

I just want to be with you. That's all.

TEN

"I want you to take a look at something."

Isabel glances over at me, and her narrow face focuses on the letter in my hand.

"What's that?"

"A letter I got awhile ago."

She sits at the breakfast table, a round wooden table big enough for six, doing bills. Isabel took over this chore shortly after we married and continues to diligently pay our bills ahead of their due dates.

Isabel begins to read the letter and then looks up at me.

"Who's this from?"

"Nicole Marsh," I say.

Saying her name comes more as a relief than as a confession. Isabel doesn't react.

"Remember—the girl I dated for a while in high school. The one who—"

"I know." She continues to read the letter and then ponders for a moment after finishing it.

I search for the right thing to say and end up just sitting there and waiting.

"How'd she get your address?"

I haven't included the envelope.

"It was forwarded to me by Random House."

"Oh."

This will bring up the past. We will have a long talk about everything that happened and what my feelings still are and whether or not I'll write her back.

"She lives in California now," my wife notes, handing me the letter. "You haven't heard from her since high school?"

Her casual tone surprises me. I know Isabel well enough to know that if something bothered her, she'd let me know.

"No."

"Did you write her back?" Isabel asks.

"No."

She nods and glances at me. Jake's padded steps brush on the wood floor and up next to me.

"Can we play on the computer?" he asks.

"Sure, no problem. Go turn it on."

He runs upstairs to my office and I stand there, facing Isabel. She looks young and pretty, especially with her hair beginning to wave around her face. It does that when it gets a little longer, a style I've always liked on her. She says it's just a guy thing, and she's probably right, but I'm glad she's letting it grow. It reminds me of the days when we dated and married, when those waves of hair fell down around her shoulders.

"Kinda strange, isn't it?" I say.

"Why would she say that about *Moonlight*?" Isabel asks me.

"I guess it's the only one she's read so far."

"Think she's married?"

"I guess. I don't know."

She shrugs, gives me a half smile, and turns back to the bills. I still find it remarkable how unconcerned she seems.

I go upstairs to find Jake and play one of the latest computer games installed on my computer. I tell myself to avoid getting into my e-mail. And at least on this night, I don't think about it again.

Did you write her back?

My answer to Isabel's question ended the discussion. She probably won't ask me about it again. If she didn't bring up any issues right away, none will be carted around for use on a later date. That's one of the things I appreciate about my wife.

I look at the empty box on my screen that is waiting for my words. And I know that Isabel asked the wrong question.

She should have asked: *Are you* going *to write her back?*

And what would she have said if I'd answered yes? *Good for you. Let me see it before you send it. Be careful.*

She wouldn't have said any of those things. She might have asked a few more questions. But as I think about it, I realize something is surprisingly different from those early days of dating. The grand question doesn't haunt Isabel anymore. She no longer has to wonder if she and I were destined to be together, if we fit in with God's plan, if we are a happily-ever-after. She knows the answers to all those questions.

Plus, she trusts me. I deliberately set that thought aside and begin typing the e-mail, not sure exactly why I'm composing the note I'm about to send. Part of me just wants to say something, like finally saying a word to the proclaiming man on the subway whom everyone's trying to ignore. I can't simply ignore Nicole's letter. All I want to do is acknowledge it, to not leave her hanging

the same way she left me

with the question of whether I ever received her letter.

I type a *Dear,* then delete it and start with just *Nicole:*

> Thank you for your kind letter. To say it surprised me is an understatement. I'm glad you found a copy of *Moonlight.* I always hoped that somewhere down the road you'd pick up one of my books and read it.

I stop the letter and back up, deleting the last sentence.

> That's always been one of my favorites, though it hasn't sold as well as most of the others.

I stop again and delete half of the last sentence. Why should she care about my sales figures?

> Those dreams of writing—God certainly did answer them. Can you believe that I'm going to be on the *Today* show in February? I'm very fortunate to have this day job. I hope I can keep it for a while.
>
> I could probably write you half a book to let you know how my life has gone. I honestly never thought I'd hear from you again. But I'm glad I did. Thank you for your letter.
>
> I apologize for

No need for apologies, I tell myself as I backspace and try again.

> I wish you all the best in life.
> Stephen

I read the e-mail over, and it sounds impersonal and phony. *I wish you all the best in life.* Even though it's been twenty years, she'll see right through that. Yet I have no idea what else to write. The things I really want to say, the questions and the comments I want to type out, this surprising mass of emotion her letter has dredged up—I can't write about those. There are things that should and will remain unspoken.

What about our last conversation? The last few moments we ever shared together?

I can't go there. All I can do is simply acknowledge her letter. No ulterior motives. And nothing to be ashamed of if Isabel asks me.

Then tell her you sent it.

I agree with myself there is no need. And agree to press the Send button.

I wonder where she'll be when she reads my response. I wonder if she'll write back, perhaps a simple short acknowledgment just like my own.

Part of me hopes she does.

Another part knows she will.

Eleven

Several of the "good" marriages depicted in my novels could have been based on my own with Isabel. Yet I'm the last guy on the earth to claim to have the definitive word on stable relationships, not to mention God-centered marriages.

It's one thing to sit in a Sunday school class or a small group and listen to a speaker or a friend talk about the value of putting God first in the marriage. Letting God oversee my relationships with my wife and my children is something else entirely. And I'll have to admit it's not that big an issue for me. At times I've wondered how in the world we're going to survive as parents, whether we'll have enough money for college, whether we'll ever have alone time again, but I rarely lose sleep over how we can have a more God-centered home. I wouldn't admit this in front of a crowd, but it's true.

Another truth is this: I'm not the same Bible-toting, on-fire Christian who grew up wanting to change the world. It's funny for me to write that, and I wonder what Nicole, who knew me back when I *was* the Bible-toting type, would say about it. I know, without a doubt, that coming to faith at an early age kept me out of trouble. And I know my faith is still real, still important to me. It just isn't the sort that prompts me to do family devotions at 7:30 in the morning or evenings with my family.

The older I've become, the more I've stopped thinking of faith as a set of dos and don'ts. I used to think more simplistically: You believed something, and you followed the rules, and everything would work out. Things don't seem so black and white to me anymore. I'm not sure if that's progress or backsliding.

I do know I was very naive growing up. And though I tried to do the right thing, I know I didn't have a clue about the power of passion and love.

"We finally made it."

Isabel studies the menu even though we both know she'll get either the lasagna or the pasta with meat sauce. There are many wonderful things about marriage, and knowing and predicting what your spouse says or does is one of these.

"I might get the lasagna," Isabel says, as if it's a big revelation.

If she said "I might get the shrimp fettuccini," then I'd be surprised. I'd also wonder where they took my wife.

We sit in a corner of Giuseppe's, a candle between us. In contrast to Isabel, I find about a dozen menu items that interest me. My taste buds are always up for something new and different.

"So, fourteen years," my wife is saying. "Can you believe it?"

"Absolutely not," I tell her.

Her black V-neck top dips below her collarbone, setting off the cobalt wool cuff pants she showed off for the first time tonight. A catalog purchase, she told me. And well worth the money, from where I sit. There's something breathtaking about a woman dressed up, with pulled-back hair and noticeable earrings and glossy lipstick. And tonight, with its official debut, the diamond pendant I gave her on the morning of our anniversary a few weeks ago.

"That looks great on you," I say.

She looks down and holds the pendant in one hand. Her beaming smile thanks me again.

"It's been a while since we've gone out," I say. "Without the kids, I mean."

"We tried a month or so ago."

"I was afraid it was going to happen again."

"Now we can celebrate our anniversary *and* the *Today* show."

"Or we could celebrate the anniversary tonight and the *Today* show next weekend by ourselves."

Isabel smiles and rolls her eyes. I know how she feels about leaving the kids for a night. Neither of us has ever been especially good at leaving them with someone else and having a great night out by ourselves. And if I was completely honest, I'd have to admit to having more issues about being away from Jake and Natalie than Isabel has.

"Actually," I say, "Alan invited you and the kids to come to New York with me."

"Oh, honey, you know I can't, especially with being so new at work," Isabel says.

"I know."

"I'm just getting back into the swing of things there. I don't want them to think I'm not serious about what I'm doing. Plus, I don't think we could get the kids excused from school."

I nod and take her hand and leave it at that.

The waitress arrives, and we order. I choose the special—ravioli stuffed with crabmeat. Isabel decides on lasagna.

Isabel and I talk the way we do on any other evening. She tells me about her day at the office, about the lawyers she works with, about the difficulties of picking up a career after years away. I tell her about Alan's call, about an opportunity to teach at a writer's conference, about what is going on with my brother. We don't talk much about my progress on the current book though. We rarely do. Isabel has read all my books and enjoyed them, but she always waits until they're out before starting them.

I learned long ago not to ask for input, for ideas on titles or suggestions on characters or anything related to the story. She seems to regard the writing as something remote and impossible, like a far-off land I constantly travel to but she can't.

I used to sometimes try and use her as a sounding board, the way I might use an editor or my agent. But these attempts always led to frustration. Isabel just didn't understand what sort of information I needed, and I didn't know how to ask for it. Over the years, we've more or less accepted that our minds just work differently. Most of the time, we can even enjoy the differences, just as we enjoy our anniversary dinner.

Our dinner date features no romantic words of love and hope, none of the exploration of our journey together that a Hollywood screenwriter might script for an anniversary outing. At the same time, there's no tension, no cold distance between the two of us.

This is marriage, I think. This is fourteen years of marriage. Being comfortable with the person across the table from you. Still appreciating her beauty and wit. Still being able to remember why you fell in love with her in the first place. And knowing, so many years later, that no sugarcoated reminiscing can ever take the place of affection and respect and a shared history.

We leave the restaurant. On the way outside to the car, Isabel takes my hand in a sweet gesture that tells me our night is not yet over.

TWELVE

I blow the snow off the driveway as flakes engulf me. The sun has already set, and I remind myself that I should buy a new snow blower, that this one is slowly dying. I can be the world's worst procrastinator until something like a snowstorm reminds me of something I forgot. It's been snowing since this afternoon. I know that tomorrow morning I'll be covering the same ground I'm walking on now.

They're predicting a foot, but where we live, sometimes a foot can be two. We live twenty minutes southwest of Johnson City, an easy fifteen-minute drive on U.S. Highway 23 just five minutes down the road from our house. We bought this house after the publication of *The Long and Winding Road,* when Is and I were both thirty-three years old. I had just signed a three-book deal with Random that not only guaranteed I could continue writing full-time but also allowed us to purchase the sort of home we might spend the rest of our lives in.

We knew the thirty-five-hundred-square-foot cabin was that home the first time we set foot in it. Isabel loved the enormous open kitchen and family room, with its vaulted ceilings, and I loved the downstairs with its fully finished basement that would be designated for storage, an entertainment room, and my office. There was a large bedroom in the back of the basement, complete with bathroom. The size would accommodate my many bookshelves and my large desk. It would also give me the privacy I needed so I could work while family life was going on upstairs.

The house resembles a mountain lodge, and people might think it is one as they steer up the long, winding driveway and stop in front of the tall but homey wooden beams. We live on a hillside, with one side of our property dropping down dramatically to give us a view of the rolling mountains and trees around us. Even from the basement you can look out through windows and see the stretch of lawn and forest outside. It's the perfect place to get away from the rest of the world and its busyness. That's one of the reasons I love this house.

The December night whips wind and snow at my uncovered face. As the low, steady engine of the snow blower whines away, I can't help thinking of another wintry night many years ago. Most of the time I refuse to unearth this buried memory, knowing there is no reason to bring it into the light. But tonight, as my ears grow numb and my nose runs and I'm wishing I'd worn a hat, I find the recollection warming—like hot cider that burns my tongue and the roof of my mouth.

Enough, I tell myself, the snow blocking my reason for a moment. Yet I continue to replay pictures in my mind, the events unstructured and loose and jumbled. I see the tiny stone house tucked back from the street, the snowdrifts cascading against one entire side of the house on the hill, the white cotton-coated windows, the flickering of a lit candle making the walls move.

I shake the thoughts. But they refuse to go away. I wonder whether they will still be there after another twenty years pass. Sometimes I find myself forgetting what happened last week, let alone last year. I ask Isabel where we were last Christmas, what we did for my birthday when I turned thirty-five. Yet some memories remain as vivid as an oil painting on a white wall—even those I wish I could forget.

I see long, light-brown hair brushed away from innocent green-blue eyes. Long lashes. A giving smile.

I can still play everything with a simple thought. Every moment, every action. And through it all I see those radiant, glowing eyes that seem so out of place with the rest of her. Uncomplicated, affectionate, insecure eyes. Eyes that tell me everything she doesn't say.

How did it ever happen?

I want to ask those eyes, that smile, that long-ago love. But I know Nicole is gone, has been gone for years. And so many things are best left in the past. Especially the night in question.

A blast of wind rushes at me, making me squint and stop moving. Perhaps this is God's way of telling me not to go there. I continue on, making a final circle back to the house. I can hear Nicole's words, not from years ago but from only a couple of months ago. Written words. I have them memorized.

I've often thought of you, of us, and wondered what might have been.

Anytime a snowstorm comes, I think of that night. I'm sorry for everything that happened, for the mistakes made.

Remorse. Regret. The same feelings I've often associated with that snowstorm. The reason I keep the memories stored in a deep recess most of the time.

I'm sorry for everything that happened, for the mistakes made.

Could this really be true? Could she after all this time have come to the same conclusion I reached years ago?

I head toward the open door of the garage located to the right of our house. I haven't heard from Nicole since the e-mail I sent to her. I don't figure I will. And in most ways, I'm glad.

I still wonder what would have happened if God had not sent twenty-four hours worth of snow down on us years ago. Could things really have been different? Did that one night truly change everything between Nicole and me?

I've often thought that the older I became, the less devoted I'd be to this theory. Yet now, so close to the landmark age of forty, I actually believe it more.

That all mistakes can be forgiven.

But consequences can last a lifetime.

THIRTEEN

So why'd you move here?

Issues. With my mom.

How so?

She tries to protect me from the world. From every guy she sees. Even though she goes around dating drunks. Makes a lot of sense, huh?

Why Knoxville?

My mom lived here for a while. Got pregnant with me and wanted to move off to make a new life for us. Figured Los Angeles was as good a place as any.

So what does she say about me?

To be careful.

What? Why?

It's not you. It's me.

What do you mean?

She knows me. I tell her everything. And she knows—well, she knows what kind of guy you are.

What kind is that?

A gentle one.

Harmless, right?

In some ways.

So your mom should like me.

She just—she's just afraid of my making the same mistake she made years ago.

What mistake?

Having me.

FOURTEEN

A glorious sun-streaked morning surrounds me as I wind up a morning's worth of writing. I glance up at a small, rectangular wall plaque my parents gave me a few Christmases ago and find encouragement in the simple quote:

"I am still learning."
—Michelangelo

One thing I've learned about this business of writing and publishing is that there is *never* a sure thing. No one can predict what will happen to a book. The beauty in creating art, even if critics don't necessarily feel that what you do is actually art, is that each new canvas or sheet of paper is the chance to try something new and either succeed or fail.

That idea in itself is certainly not original. There's a Hemingway quote on my desk that says it much better than I can:

For a true writer each book should be a new beginning where he tries again for something that is beyond attainment. He should always try for something that has never been done or that others have tried and failed. Then sometimes, with great luck, he will succeed.

At this point in my career, having produced a body of work that I'm proud of, I can't say whether I'm a success or a failure. My last book sold over a hundred thousand copies, but does that necessarily mean it was an artistic success? I don't know. And have I done anything that has never been done before? Of course not. At heart, my novels are tried-and-true stories that have been told a hundred, maybe a thousand times in far better books. But I do know that every writing journey I take is a different one, and that in writing, just as in life, there are many paths you go down as you near the destination. Sometimes these paths wander and lead nowhere. Other times they carry you to a place you've never been and change you forever.

Before switching off my computer, I decide to check my e-mail. There are two new messages in my box. The first one is from Alan, my agent, but I click on the second message. I remember its address from the brief e-mail I sent months ago.

The screen pops up, and I can almost hear her voice. To say it's soft is almost cliché—how many past loves ever have grating, irritating voices? But Nicole's voice was pleasant, always light in a way that made me want to grin, always subdued and never too loud. I can still hear her delicate laugh as I read her message.

> Dear Stephen,
>
> I was certainly surprised when I got the e-mail from you. Part of me wanted to e-mail you back without thought, but I hesitated and have done so ever since. I don't want to be inappropriate, and I hope that my letter, and now this e-mail, won't be deemed so. Your e-mail was short and somewhat impersonal, and I guess I can understand that, especially after all this time. You revealed very little. Yet since then I've had the chance to read some of your other books, and it seems as though I've been given this wonderful window into your soul. I write feeling I know you better than I knew you twenty years ago.
>
> I decided to read your books in chronological order from the dates they were published. *Evening Falls, Turnabout.* I just finished *Out of a Million.* So I have three more to go, but I'm still getting a pretty clear picture. You still have that sensitive side I fell in love with so many years ago, that romantic dreamer inside you that seemed so out of place in a high school full of crude and silly boys.
>
> Please don't object to these words I type, Stephen. Anyone else reading them wouldn't understand, but I know you do. I want you to know that the tender part of Stephen Conroy I was allowed to love—I know it's still there. Living a different life, one I don't belong in, but nevertheless still there.
>
> I wonder what it would be like to see you again. Just

to meet you and talk with you. I've read countless thousands of your words since first reading *Moonlight*. Yet still I wonder what you sound like, how the years have treated you. Most of all, I wonder what you'd think of me after all this time.

I didn't want you to know this, Stephen. I didn't plan on telling you this. But I guess I'm going to tell you anyway. My life since those days in Knoxville—what a life it's been. I thought I found love. Happily-ever-after, the sort of romantic and dreamy kind that they find in *Out of a Million*—I thought it was going to happen. But it didn't work out. My marriage ended a little while back. It actually ended several years ago, but the reality didn't hit until I signed the papers half a year ago.

That along with suddenly discovering a book by you—I don't think these things were accidental. You used to say that nothing happens by chance or luck, that God controls all things. I used to call you crazy for thinking that way. But I'm thinking differently now. I can't say who controls what in this world, but I do think that someone or something ended up bringing your book my way.

I don't know if I'll ever see or hear from you again. I probably don't deserve to, and it might not be a good thing. But, just as so many years ago when an unusual young man rescued me from a world of hurt—well, you seem to have done it again. Through your writing. And through your heart.

Thank you for not changing, Stephen. Thank you for being you.

I hope to hear from you again sometime.

Nicole

The words move me as few have in years. She thanks me for not changing, and I note that in many ways, from what I can tell, she hasn't changed either. She still wears her heart on her fingertips, writing away her soul's intent and hurt.

After so many years, you contact me. Can the world really be so small?

For the moment I can't help but feel a wave of sadness. And I suddenly wish I could see her again. Not for some reckless, forbidden romantic tryst. But to try to heal a hurting heart.

Even as I think it, I know I'll never be the one to bandage any of her wounds or even know how deeply she's been hurt. Nicole is not a part of my life now, and will never be.

I thought I could change her, I think. *I thought that love and devotion could change her.*

That was part of my boundless naiveté. I thought I could change this passionate, wonderful, damaged girl with real love and a genuine relationship. But the opposite happened.

Nicole changed me.

I close the e-mail, not deleting it, not replying to it, doing nothing to it. So close to the end of the year, only a week away from Christmas, I feel saddened to know that this woman might be all alone for the holidays—and that it's not really my concern.

I'm still learning. Not just with my writing, but with life.

I just hope I do a better job than I did years ago with Nicole.

FIFTEEN

We're a visual cliché: two guys in sweaters drinking eggnog by the fire. But when families gather around Christmastime, people do sit by the fireplace and drink eggnog. Not spiked eggnog, just good old thick, creamy Weigel's brand. Randy is telling me the latest "Incarcerated Idiot of the Week" story, which involves a guy breaking into his ex-girlfriend's apartment to try to steal their Christmas tree and getting attacked by the German shepherd he had given her for a watchdog.

"He even claims he's going to sue her," Randy says and lets out a bellowing laugh I can't help but echo.

"Too bad that wasn't on *Cops*."

"They could have a whole series devoted strictly to Knox County. There are so many morons running around. Hillbillies with their whiskey and guns. Gives us rednecks a bad name."

Randy's not exactly a redneck. He made pretty good grades at East Tennessee State before deciding to enter the police academy, and he advanced in the force pretty fast. But he does have that Southern-fried look, with his drawl and his extra chins and his laid-back demeanor. The two of us could pass as family—or kin, as they say around here. But somewhere along the way, he relaxed his attitude and his pants size. Everything about him is simply—unhurried. Agreeable. He usually shows up at family functions half an hour late and then stays far later than his wife, Donna, wants them to. His hair is thinning faster than mine—either a sign of things to come or a continuation of the destinies between brothers.

I know that my life and my relationship with Randy could have been a lot different if he had been someone else. We never competed growing up. He usually took the lead in whatever we did and has always been the guy to go to in a jam or when you need something fixed. Even though Randy is laid-back, that doesn't mean he's unreliable. You could trust your family and fortune to him and never blink once. As for what he thinks about his younger brother finding success in writing, he simply calls me Faulkner and tells me he'll get around to reading something I've written one of these days.

We're in the family room at his house, away from the family still talking and checking out toys and gifts in the living room. Out of nowhere Randy surprises me with a question.

"So, did you ever talk to that woman who wrote you? What's her name—Nicole?"

I don't think I've ever lied to Randy. There's never been a reason to, and most of the time, I bet he would see right through me.

"I e-mailed her back. A cordial e-mail. Just responding."

"And Isabel?" Randy asks.

"I told her about the letter."

"Did she read it."

"Yeah."

"And?"

"Nothing," I say. "Nothing really."

Randy nods.

"Nicole e-mailed me back just a week ago."

He looks at me and waits for more.

"A pretty deep e-mail. I mean, you know. We were pretty serious."

"Did you show that e-mail to Is?"

"No."

"Are you going to?"

I look around, not out of nervousness but rather to think about this. I've avoided deciding what to do about Nicole's last e-mail. There is nothing at all I need to keep from Isabel. She knows my past. She might question why I ever replied to Nicole's e-mail in the first place. And she might be uneasy about Nicole's response, some of her shared feelings.

Isabel wouldn't understand, I think. *How could she? How could anyone except Nicole?*

"I don't know."

Randy nods, not chiming in, not needing to suddenly give his opinion. "Well, if you need more brotherly advice down the road, let me know."

I nod and grin. He taps his belly and comments on how he ate too much ham at dinner.

Before we go, Randy looks me in the eye.

"And listen. Don't be a dork. Don't get into any silly trouble, okay?"

"You think I would?"

"You're a guy. I see a lot of guys gettin' in a lot of trouble. And they never mean to. Never."

Sixteen

I gaze out an oval window onto a platform of vanilla clouds as my mind skips over possible book titles. I've always found plane trips to be one of the best venues for brainstorming—better than sitting in my office at home, better than taking walks through the woods. I think this is because there is almost nothing to do except sit and think. I already have seven chapters of what is supposed to be my next novel, yet a title remains as remote as the specks of houses thirty thousand feet below.

A kid in front of me puts his nose on the window and peers outside with his Tigger glasses. I remember seeing him run around the gate area in Atlanta when I was waiting to change planes. I suddenly miss Nat and Jake and pray they're doing well. I wish that school hadn't kept them from going with me. Isabel, too—I wish she weren't so new in her job and could take off to go with me. I don't really travel that much, and being a full-time writer allows me to see my family more than many fathers can. But I still drag guilt along like a carry-on suitcase whenever I leave Isabel with the children. Guilt and worry—because my creative mind tends to work against me on these trips. What if my plane suddenly takes a nosedive into the Virginia countryside below? What if there's a fire or someone breaks into the house? A thousand awful scenarios play in my home theater of a mind, and all I can do is shut them off and pray to the Lord that he will continue to watch over all of us.

It's interesting, I think, how having children ups the ante for worry. Once you're a parent, you have so much more to lose. Before Isabel and I had children, we often remarked how we enjoyed the freedom of being on our own. But Natalie changed everything and changed it for the better. I never believed the fathers who told me how wonderful it was to be a father, how incredible it felt to hold their babies for the first time. I used to wonder if this indeed was true. Now I know. And I know I would do almost anything to keep them with me.

The flight from Atlanta to La Guardia is running ahead of schedule. I go back to my title brainstorming, trying to think of interesting metaphors and song titles and capture something fitting. The only ideas that sound vaguely promising have to do with the clouds: *Into the Clouds, Cloud Cover, Dancing on Clouds, Skipping over Clouds.* Unfortunately, they have absolutely nothing to do with the novel I'm working on.

The pilot announces the beginning of our descent toward the New York area. And I think again of the e-mail I received from Nicole—almost a month and a half ago now. As my eyes scan far down the horizon of textured white, glimmering from the noon sun, I wonder if I'll ever see her again.

The cab driver must have a death wish. The car races at seventy down a narrow street lined with cars and earmarked with pedestrians crossing. He slams on the brakes at a light, then steps on the gas again as if my arrival at the hotel in the next five minutes will guarantee him a million dollars.

I hold the door handle and wonder if my earlier prayers for safety on the plane will also cover this jolting taxi ride. The driver is quiet and unexpressive and faces ahead, barely looking alive. Yet he swerves back and forth, almost getting rammed by an SUV coming out of a parking garage, cutting off another taxi driver who looks to be doing the same thing, then barging out in front of a bunch of pedestrians who throw him furious looks.

Traffic is bad, and he keeps taking side streets to find an open lane so he can floor it again. I see avenues and streets I don't know or recognize. They all look the same to me. Sixth Avenue. Forty-sixth Street. I know that my hotel is located close to the theater district and Times Square. I've only been to New York twice before and don't remember the taxi drivers being this aggressive.

He finds an open block and soars down it. As he approaches the green light that turns yellow, he speeds up. A bicyclist turns right onto our street and almost gets plowed by my driver. We don't slow down as the bicyclist yells profanities at us and skids to a stop at the side of the street.

I really don't want to see someone die today.

At another point, blocked by two lines of vehicles, the driver turns the wheel and puts two tires up on the sidewalk, veering around the line of waiting cars only to stop at the red light. When green comes, the cab blasts out in front of the other line of moving cars and swerves in front of another taxi, which honks at us, then slows down for a pedestrian who almost gets her legs sliced off by our bumper.

When my driver finally stops outside the large Marriott surrounded by a myriad of other cabs, he tells me the fare and waits. I want to ask him what that mad dash was all about, why the rush, but instead I give him two twenties and tell him to keep the change. He thanks me and watches me leave the vehicle as if he's suddenly got plenty of time to kill.

As I emerge onto the curb holding my small suitcase, my laptop in its carrying case over my shoulder, I feel a few snowflakes melt against my chin. I'm thankful I've arrived before the storm that's supposed to move in tonight.

I check into the Marriott Marquis Hotel, Alan's choice for my Big Apple accommodations. He told me the hotel is convenient for Broadway shows and that we can take in one if I want. The Barnes & Noble where I'll be signing tomorrow afternoon is also close by.

As I open the door to my room, located at the end of a corridor on the forty-eighth story, I see a gift basket waiting for me on the table. This isn't a room; it's more of a hospitality suite, complete with a wet bar and kitchen and a living room with a big-screen television. The separate bedroom contains a king-size bed and an enormous adjoining bath.

The basket overflows with fruit, candy, chocolates, nuts, and cheeses—a handwritten note tucked among them. I pick it up and read.

> Welcome to New York. We hope your stay will be fun and rewarding. Best wishes on everything tomorrow.
> Your friends from *Today*

I laugh out loud, looking around the room and suddenly feeling like an impostor. I never cease to be amazed and overwhelmed the direction my life has taken. Here I am in New York City, in a suite at the Marriott just off Times Square, receiving a gift basket from a major network. Tomorrow morning I'll be interviewed by Katie Couric, and in the afternoon I will sign books at one of the biggest bookstores in Manhattan.

Surreal. Totally surreal.

I find a phone and call Isabel. The first thing I tell her is how much I wish she and the kids could be with me.

SEVENTEEN

"How is Paula these days?"

The tall man across from me—probably six foot three, with long, thinning hair and a chiseled face—nods and raises his eyebrows as if to say *Oh yeah—Paula*. He finishes working on his filet before speaking.

"We actually separated."

"What?" I ask him, completely surprised.

"Yeah, it's just—things have been a little difficult."

I try to remember how many years they've been married. Maybe fifteen, maybe more. Just a little longer than Isabel and me.

"I'm sorry to hear that."

"Things happen. So how're Isabel and the kids?"

It's the obligatory agent or publisher question. I don't doubt Alan's intentions and motives. He's been a trusted and encouraging agent, partner, and friend over the years. But I'm well aware we would not be sharing this expensive dinner in the city if not for a bit of luck—or, as I call it, divine intervention.

Someone gave Alan a copy of my second novel, *Turnabout*, two weeks before I sent him a letter asking if he'd be interested in representing me. I had worked with an agent named Samantha Yaeger on my first two books, and know that without her, I would never have gotten published at such a young age. She represented me, knowing I was ambitious and a good learner, and she made me work hard before sending out the first manuscript, *Evening Falls*. But after *Turnabout* came out to lackluster sales, I rarely heard from Samantha, and I began wondering if it was time to find a better agent.

Alan Dierge was one of several New York agents I wrote. As it turned out, he had just finished reading *Turnabout* and had idly wondered what else that twenty-nine-year-old author had written. Little did either of us know there were more books—better books, in fact—yet to come.

The fact that Alan is an atheist has never made me reconsider working with him. He values my writing and never seemed to have problems with my Christianity—either in my life or in my books. What I write is not explicitly Christian fiction, a popular genre these days. But it does steer clear of curse words and sex scenes, partly because I'd be ashamed to show that sort of writing to my mother. And besides that, the themes of my books can't help but reflect my world-view, so they really are Christian at heart. Alan actually seems to appreciate that. But he also helps me by pushing me out of my comfort zone, offering glimpses of a world I'm not part of but need to understand. After all, many of my readers are not Christians. The fact that they find my writing and my stories compelling enough to respond and tell me so is partially a tribute to Alan's help and support.

I decided long ago that the best way I could be a witness to Alan is through my actions and not through any rhetoric. I'm not the type to hand out tracts or debate the existence of God. Besides, Alan is extremely intelligent and well read and could probably argue circles around me. So I've always tried to show Alan that I still have a good sense of humor, can still be professional, and can still be a good friend and business partner to him even though we have different beliefs. When the time seems right, I try to share a little more directly. But I don't push it. I don't think that would work with Alan anyway.

After talking about Isabel for several minutes, Alan asks me a question I'm not ready to answer.

"Could you ever see yourself being with another woman?"

I think of Nicole and wonder for a second how Alan knows, then realize it's just a hypothetical question.

"Being with another woman? How?"

"You know what I mean."

"Like having an affair?" I ask.

"Yeah. Or a one-night stand. I know that it's probably not the *right* thing to do. But like tonight, if some beautiful woman hit on you, and you knew that there was absolutely no chance Isabel would ever find out, would you do it?"

"I'd hope not."

"I know. It's a moral issue, right?"

I only assume that Alan's marital woes have prompted these unusual questions from him.

"I mean, I'm human. I'm a guy. I see a gorgeous woman pass me, and I can't help but think about her. It's just—I made a promise to Isabel years ago."

"Yeah. Paula made one to me too. I guess she had a hard time keeping it."

I'm not sure what to say. I take a sip of my Diet Coke. I want to say something meaningful to him, something that will stick with him and perhaps allow him to question his own beliefs or his lack of beliefs.

"You know," Alan begins before I can think of anything, "what you have with your wife, with your family, it's really enviable. I'd give anything to have something like that."

"It's not perfect," I tell him.

He finishes his drink, and I wonder how many he had before I met up with him at the bar of the steakhouse.

"You've got an amazing life, Steve. You're going on the *Today* show tomorrow. Can you believe it?"

"I really can't."

We talk about what tomorrow will bring. Before we leave, I get back on personal matters.

"Hey, look," I say to Alan. "If there is anything you need—I mean, with Paula and you. I don't know if I can do anything. Just…let me know."

"Can you pay for my divorce lawyer?" Alan asks with a laugh.

"I'm going to say one of these cheesy lines you'll probably roll your eyes at, but that's okay. I pray for you, Alan."

"For my wayward soul?" he replies with a sarcastic grin.

"Just *for* you. I'll keep you guys in my prayers."

"At this point, I can use all the help I can get." He excuses himself to go to the men's room.

From my table next to an open glass wall that overlooks a busy avenue, I watch hundreds of nameless people stroll busily past one another amid the falling snow. Many of them are dressed up, probably going to see a show and perhaps having just finished a hundred-dollar meal like the one Alan and I just enjoyed. I sit and wonder how many of them are like Alan, lost and not caring a bit about being alone in a world full of hopelessness.

Thank you for Isabel, I tell God.

I could have been just like Alan, thinking that God is just another fictional fantasy like Bilbo Baggins or Harry Potter. Faith could have been one of those things other people had and did. Like a hobby, it could simply not be my thing. But years ago I prayed a simple prayer, knowing I was a sinner, believing in a real Jesus who also happened to be the Son of God. Countless times since then I've seen his hand in my life, and I can even see it tonight as I wait for Alan to rejoin me.

Could you ever see yourself being with another woman?

I hear Alan's question again in my mind and wonder how he could have hit so close to home. In my whole life, in all my thirty-eight years, the one thing I've never understood was why Nicole was allowed to come across my path. And why everything happened the way it did.

I mean, I'm human. I'm a guy. I see a gorgeous woman pass me, and I can't help but think about her.

And years ago, I met and befriended and fell in love with a gorgeous girl who forever changed my life. I was simply human, simply a guy. And even though I knew I shouldn't have done it, I made a mistake one storm-filled night.

Nicole believed in our love and said there was nothing wrong with two people sharing that love the way we did. The world didn't understand us, she said, and all the rules and the rights and wrongs just didn't apply to the kind of love we had. In the end, she said, it all boiled down to just her and me. A seventeen-year-old and a sixteen-year-old. Together, alone, with one another.

I couldn't tell Alan anything about Nicole, about the fact that I let the beauty and persuasiveness of the girl I loved convince me to abandon some of my deepest principles. And about how that one night changed everything between us.

I still wonder what would have happened to Nicole and me if I had simply said no.

EIGHTEEN

No one will ever know.
They might.
You called and told them. They're not worried.
I lied.
No you didn't. You just didn't tell them everything.
What about your mom—
What about her? She's not coming home.
I hope not.
Here—
What—
Hold my hand.
Think it'll die down out there?
I hope not.
At least we have enough wood.
Enough to be snowed in for a week. Could you imagine that?
Yeah, I can imagine what everyone—
Don't think about anybody else.
I just—
Tell me something.
What?
Do you really love me?
I'll always love you. You know that.
Then there's nothing wrong with this.

I wake up and wipe the sweat from my forehead. Then I remember I'm in New York City. I look at the clock. The digital numbers read 4:32.

In about three hours, I'm supposed to appear live on national television and talk about *Immersion.* I wonder if I'll look like a train wreck.

Standing up, I find the bathroom and then remember the minibar in the kitchen. I make my way into the next room and find the size of the suite daunting, too big. I locate a plastic bottle of water, probably priced around six or seven bucks, and drink half of it down with one gulp. I sit on the rigid couch in the darkness and wish the images of that night with Nicole would leave me alone.

They are not romantic or enticing or sweetly reminiscent of a long-lost love. I feel nothing but shame when I remember them. The same way I felt the morning after, a morning when I woke up and realized everything had changed and nothing could be taken back.

I would be lying if I said that the night before was awful and that I didn't enjoy myself. That's the whole point, really. I enjoyed myself the way a husband should enjoy himself on his honeymoon, experiencing something for the first time. Something wonderful, awe-inspiring, and truly God-given. Except there was nothing godly about our night together.

I knew—I truly believed, just as I believe now—that sex outside a marriage is wrong. But for a brief moment, a brief night, I let myself go. And ended up robbing both of us of what could have been.

I slip back underneath my sheets, but sleep has long since passed me by.

NINETEEN

By the time I'm sitting across from Katie Couric in a comfortable sofa chair, I've already met maybe a dozen people. A director, a makeup person, a *Today* show staff member who compliments me on my books. I fidgeted in the green room for more than an hour, waiting to get the call. Alan waited with me, and I know he's now standing behind the hot lights of the set. I've exchanged a couple of greetings with Katie during the commercial break, but now I keep quiet as I wait for her official welcome. I can feel my teeth chattering, and I breathe slowly, nervous and hoping I won't make a fool of myself on national television.

My interviewer exudes friendly, professional calm. She crosses her legs and shifts the papers in her lap. Then she flashes her famous smile as she begins to speak into the camera.

"Stephen Conroy has kept many readers up late at night finishing his novels. We're pleased to have him here today to talk about his latest release, *Immersion.* Welcome, Stephen."

I nod and smile and give her a weak, "Good morning, Katie." I feel like a goof, as if she's going to suddenly say *Wait a minute. Who's this dimwit?*

"So you live in Johnson City, Tennessee, right?"

"That's correct. Right at the foot of the Smokies. Beautiful country."

"Well, we're glad you made it here before all the snow. I have to tell you, I'm a big fan of your books. I picked up a copy of your last one and, as they often say, couldn't put it down. You've been writing all your life?"

"Pretty much so. I always hoped I could do it for a living, but for a while I was working a day job and writing late at night and on the weekends."

"Your first book was published when you were only twenty-seven."

I nod and wipe a bead of sweat off my forehead. "Yes. At the time I didn't understand much about publishing. I'm just fortunate that a publisher saw some potential in my work and took a chance with me."

Katie glances at her notes. "Your last book, *A Harbor in the Tempest,* came out a couple of years ago. That was about a family dealing with the aftermath of an almost unthinkable tragedy, the loss of a child. I just have to know—it felt so real. How did you end up writing something so personal?"

I smile, appreciating her words, trying to come up with a response.

"Thankfully, nothing like that's ever happened to my wife and me. We have two children and can barely fathom what life would be like if we lost them. But sometimes a writer works out his nightmares on paper. That novel grew out of wondering what life would be like if such a thing were to happen to me."

"And is that how your new book, *Immersion,* came about?"

I raise my eyebrows for a brief moment. "Well, I would hardly tell you that, would I?"

That gets a bit of a laugh from Katie. I add, "*Immersion* is a book about a man who discovers that his wife is having an affair and his life is basically not what it seemed. I got that particular idea from some people I know whose life always seems perfectly put together. But peel off some layers and you discover something different."

Katie gives me an earnest smile, another question ready. "It seems to me that the last few books you have written have been complex and even, might I say, dark. Why do you think that is?"

I laugh. "After I finished my first book, the agent I was working with at the time told me it needed more sex and violence. Well, actually she said I needed to 'spice it up,' but that's what she meant. I didn't go in that direction, but I did realize that true fiction, fiction that mirrors the world we live in today, sometimes needs to be dark and sad. There's a lot about life that's dark. But I always try to show some hope as well. I've never liked finishing another author's book and thinking, *I feel awful.*"

"You can see what I'm getting at though. I always wonder where novelists get their ideas, where their stories come from. Do you ever have a hard time finding something to write about?"

"I really don't." This question is common and a comfortable one for me. "At least I haven't yet. My problem so far has been making sure the story is compelling and that it makes sense. Thank goodness I have a great editor who guides me along."

"I have to say that I received an advance copy of *Immersion* and spent many hours reading it. It is—remarkable. The twist at the end— I can't say any more than it changes everything about what you've read. It's in stores today. And, Stephen Conroy, thank you so much for being here today."

"It's been a pleasure," I say.

Katie talks to the camera about what is next on the program and leads them into a commercial break. Before the crew closes in and Katie stands up for her next interview, she thanks me again and politely asks me to autograph the book she is holding. I scribble on the flyleaf, hand it back to her, and thank her again. I almost ask for her autograph as well.

I call Isabel on my cell a little after nine New York time, and she screams into the phone. She rearranged her work hours in order to see the show and tape it for the kids.

"It was great!" she says. "I can't believe you were on TV."

I've just spent the last few minutes being congratulated by Alan. He told me I looked professional and relaxed and that I "sold" the audience well. I wasn't aware of selling to anyone; I was just being myself. Now, as we sit in a limo on our way to a morning meeting at Random House, I hold the phone to my ear and listen to Isabel's take on the interview.

"Your new coat looked good," she remarks.

Alan suggested I model my appearance after another *Today* show regular, John Grisham. I copied his attire, going for a dressy-casual effect. Apparently my blue sports jacket was a good choice.

"Were you nervous?" Isabel asks me.

"When I first met Katie, I felt shaky. But she's very nice, put me at ease. She asked *me* to autograph my novel for her."

"I can't believe she's already read *Immersion*."

I grin. "Read it before you did."

"Oh, hush," Isabel says. She knows I'm kidding. "I've already gotten several calls this morning. One from your mom—"

"What'd she say?"

"She couldn't believe you were really on TV."

We talk for another ten minutes before the limo pulls up in front

of a towering building I've visited only one other time. I tell Isabel I have
to go and thank her for the encouragement.

"When's your book signing?" she asks.

"This afternoon. I'll call before then."

"Have fun."

"It'll be easy since I won't know anyone. As opposed to the signings
at Graham's."

Graham's is a local independent bookstore that always holds a book
signing for me once a new book is out. Some of the chain stores in the
areas have me sign too. And the difficult thing for me about local signings is remembering the names of people who clearly know me. After
you've written your name a couple of hundred names, your mind sometimes goes blank.

"Love you," Isabel says.

"Love you, too."

We climb out of the limo and head toward the mammoth corporate building. For just a moment I feel important, as if I belong here, as
if this is the obvious place for someone who's worked hard and done
well. I feel confident about myself and my work and the upcoming
meeting.

It's just a moment. A fleeting moment.

Get over yourself, I think.

TWENTY

At my very first book signing, I sold five copies. I remember sitting at a small table close to the front of the store feeling like I was selling Girl Scout cookies. The only difference was people *know* what Girl Scout cookies are. I was an unknown author, twenty-seven years old, signing a short novel no one had ever heard of. People would take one step in the store, glance at me and my little stack of hardcovers, and then head the opposite direction.

By the time I finish the book signing at the huge Barnes & Noble located close to Times Square, I've actually worn out my hand. I've gotten some sympathy, too; I can't believe how many people have asked me how the hand is feeling. I must have signed at least four hundred books.

The line has withered, and I stand, taking a sip of my bottled water as I scrutinize one of the remaining copies of *Immersion*. The cover is fabulous, done in reds and blacks that fit the mood of heartache and betrayal perfectly. My name is gratifyingly large on this one, a big change from the tiny font size on *Evening Falls*. I've signed extra copies for the bookstore and now give the store manager one for himself.

"Thanks so much for everything," I tell him.

A publicist named Jackie from Random House asks me if I need anything. When I smile and tell her no, she hurries off to check on something else. She's a skinny girl, probably just out of college, with a severely short haircut and sunken cheeks. I've felt sorry for her all afternoon, having to lug the heavy, hardcover novels from their shipping boxes to the table in front of me.

The bookstore manager is a round, balding man with a goatee. I can tell he views the signing as a success. Many of the people in line, the majority of them woman, still linger in the store—exactly what a manager hopes when he gets a famous author to make an appearance. Am I a famous author? I wonder. I guess I can say I'm semifamous, especially after my morning stint on the *Today* show.

I glance around and see Jackie walk up to me with some urgency.

"Mr. Conroy? A woman just handed this to me. She wanted me to give it to you."

I look at the cream-colored envelope and see the name *Steve* written on the front. Unmistakable handwriting in blue makes me sweep the store with my eyes.

"Who gave you this?" I ask Jackie.

She looks alarmed after seeing my surprise.

"The attractive woman in the long leather coat. She didn't want to give it to you directly, so she—"

"Where is she?" I ask, walking toward the front of the bookstore.

"I think she left. I don't know."

"What'd she say?" I ask as I approach the doors.

"She just asked if I could give this note to you. I told her she could give it to you herself, but she said she was in a rush and needed to go."

I open the doors to the bookstore and hurry outside. Streams of people pass by, all wearing winter coats and caps and gloves. I feel the sudden chill in the air and the falling snow. The wind whips at my open collar and my light sports coat as I glance in each direction. I see many leather coats, many on women, but nothing stands out. No one looks familiar.

The note in my hand weighs down my heart. Perhaps I'm just imagining the handwriting. Surely it can't be hers. How could it be? In New York City?

I walk back into the store and start to unfold the note.

"Stephen, we have a few more books we'd like you to sign." The store manager leads me back to the table.

I nod and glance at Jackie, who appears to wait for an order from someone.

"What'd she look like?"

"The woman with the note? Light brown hair down to her shoulders. Very striking—and tall."

All these years. Can she still be as beautiful as she was years ago? *What in the world is she doing here?*

I slip the envelope into my coat pocket and paste a smile on my face as I sign the last batch of books remaining in the store.

Snow continues to fall. The store manager, whose name is Art, tells me that the newscasters are now predicting the biggest snowfall in a decade. I wait for the limo they've ordered to take me back to the hotel. I've called the airport already and know that all flights in and out of the three major New York airports have been canceled, including my 7:15 out of La Guardia. Jackie uses her cell phone to make sure I have another night's stay at the Marriott. Before the limo comes, I call Isabel again.

"How'd everything go?" she asks.

"Great. The biggest one yet."

"Bigger than the last one in town?"

I remember when I signed *A Harbor in the Tempest* at Graham's and had everyone I knew, friends and family and church members, all coming to the store at the same time to purchase a copy.

"Maybe not that many. Look, have you heard about the storm here?"

"Is it that bad?" Isabel asks.

"Yeah. All flights have been canceled. I've gotta stay here for another night."

"The kids would've been asleep by the time you got here anyway."

"Yeah, I know."

"Call Alan and have another expensive dinner on him."

"Yeah, maybe," I say. "He told me he had plans tonight. He could blow them off—I know he would. But I don't want to make him do that."

"Is the Marriott nice?"

"Very. I wish you were here."

"Next time," she says. "Or I'll go with you when you get on Dave Letterman."

I laugh. "Yeah, right. Look, I have to get my luggage. My limo's here."

"Well, la-di-da."

"Hey, it's safer than riding with these crazy cab drivers. I swear I almost died in a taxi the other day."

"Call me later, okay?"

I hang up the phone and thank Art and Jackie again for all they've done. A driver opens the door, and I feel like royalty or someone important as I give him my suitcase and slip into the leather of the town car and hear the door shut.

I remember the note, take it out of my pocket, look at my name on the envelope. Tell myself it can't possibly be from Nicole.

I open the envelope as the car starts slowly down the packed avenue. Inside is a folded note card with a blaring initial *N* on its front. I open the card and see only a handful of sentences.

> Yes, it's me. If you're reading this, it means I'm too nerv-
> ous to say hello in person. Is there any chance you'd like
> to get together later this evening? I really need to see you,
> even just briefly. I'm staying at the Soriale Hotel. I will be
> in the lobby between seven and eight.
> Nicole

My head spins. I glance outside and see pedestrians moving through the snow and I wonder what Nicole is doing in New York and why she really needs to see me.

There's no way.

"How far away is the Soriale Hotel from the Marriott Marquis?" I ask the driver.

"A few blocks. An easy walk."

I look at my watch. It is almost 6:30.

I have no plans tonight.

I am alone.

No one will know, will they? And surely there's nothing wrong with just saying hello to an old friend.

I take a deep breath. Nicole never was an old friend. She still means more to me than that, even after all these years.

What would I say to her if I saw her? Hello? I'm sorry? Good-bye?

I think of her notes and e-mail and suddenly wish I'd never

answered her to begin with. I only did it once. I certainly didn't ask her to come looking for me—if that's what she did. This whole thing could be perfectly innocent—a business trip, a vacation. But something about it feels wrong.

Something about the fact that Isabel is home with the kids.

And I'm in New York.

All by myself.

Except for Nicole Marsh.

Twenty-One

What happens tomorrow?
It is tomorrow.
So then what?
Nothing.
How do you know?
I just know.
It's cold.
Tell me again.
What?
Say it again.
I love you.
We'll be okay.
When I leave—
Not another word.
Not even—
Not even a good-bye.
In the silence of my hotel room, I hear each unburied word.

Sometimes the years don't add up in my heart. Two decades can simply feel like two days—I can hear the echoes of teenagers' expressions and realize how foolish they sound now. At the time, I believed anything was possible. A part of that optimism died years ago, and I was sad to see it go.

I sit on the edge of my bed, drinking Coke and eating ice cubes. I hate being alone, feeling the absence of another around me and the boredom of sitting in this opulent but empty room. After an exhaustingly full day, I still feel the need to do something. Perhaps this is the same sort of longing that drove me to start writing years ago.

I know my empty feelings are due partly to the note that sits on the bedside table. All I can think back to are memories of Nicole. Memories fitting into one another like a jigsaw puzzle. The puzzle can never be finished. It was left undone years ago.

She said not a word, not even a good-bye.

And as if it were yesterday, I still remember that last glance. No words were necessary. Yet even now, I want to ask what burned behind it. Sadness? Regret? Anger? Or something worse? I carry that glance around whenever I think back on her beauty.

So much unspoken in so many years.

I still see the hallway—bright white cold. Her tall figure filling it, walking toward and then past me as I said nothing.

Those eyes. The wells of tears deep and impenetrable. The passion still filling them. How long did she remain strong? I wonder. Or did she ever shed a tear? Sometimes I've wondered if she simply left and never thought about me again.

That's why her letter stunned me.

I wish I could have said a simple "Good-bye, Nicole."

But the word *simple* no longer applied.

Not a soul around, her stride quick in jeans and a sweater as she passed out the door and past a life.

A life she's found again.

I look at the clock. The red numerals now read 7:35. I know I can still make it.

It's so easy to know what to do when offered situations like this on paper. When propositioned by a beautiful woman, do you— And of course you know the appropriate answer without needing to hear the rest of the question.

But nothing about this situation is predictable or expected. This isn't a proposition. I'm not even sure what it is. On the surface, it's a simple meeting in a lobby with an old friend. Yet I'm not fooling myself either. I know that even seeing Nicole is dangerous, that talking with her might be wrong.

I slip on my overcoat and leave the hotel room. I don't know if I'll make it to the Soriale or not. Perhaps I'll simply hit the sidewalks and let the wind and snow frostbite my heart.

All this time, and I have a chance to see Nicole again.

Am I strong enough to simply leave it at that?

Are we allowed to say good-bye?

TWENTY-TWO

The door opens with surprising ease. I slip into the warmth of the lobby. The décor is modern, ultracool, with sleek red and black couches and sculpted silver chairs shuffled around the carpet. Trance music plays in the background, as though I'm entering some underground club. In the back, stairs curve up to a mezzanine lined with tables and barstools that overlook the lobby.

A woman sells newspapers and sundries to my left. A glittering bar occupies the far wall opposite the stairway. My eyes scope the room in an attempt to be casual and observant at the same time. I don't see Nicole, but that doesn't mean anything. I take off my coat and make my way into the room.

Again, I scan the lobby. A couple, an older woman in her fifties smoking, a man sipping on a drink close to the bar. No one else. I notice a couple checking in, carrying luggage.

I sit down on a backless sofa. A woman comes up to me and asks if she can get me anything. I tell her I'm fine. I glance around to see if Nicole is anywhere to be found.

What are you doing here?

I don't honestly know. To say hello to an old friend. To say good-bye to an old love. Perhaps to—

You can't justify it.

There's no way. I'm curious, of course. I know this won't be some illicit, scandalous love affair. I mean, nothing can happen

You said that years ago.

because I'm different now. I know more. I'm stronger.

So many things are different.

Yet that doesn't change the fact that I'm here. Waiting.

My watch reveals the time as 8:03. I've been here more than ten minutes.

Nothing.

I feel like a fool. I continue to wait, glancing apprehensively at strangers, turning toward the sound of shuffling feet.

Finally, already thirty minutes past the end of Nicole's suggested meeting time, I stand up to go. I consider leaving a note, then realize that perhaps this is all meant to be.

It was stupid to come in the first place. Stupid and dangerous.

I survey the lobby once more. Nicole is not around. All the words I had in mind to say—the greeting, the questions I wanted to ask her about her life—will not be said. The images of her in my mind won't be compared to the real thing.

I guess that answers my question. Perhaps we aren't allowed to say our good-byes. Perhaps we should let the past remain untouched.

The wind chides me for going out in the first place. I walk the few blocks back toward the Marriott, my stomach full of nothing but knots. I contemplate eating but have no idea where I'd go.

I think back to another evening when I walked in a snowstorm, my car making it almost all the way up the hill to the wooded, secluded subdivision where Nicole lived.

In my heart I knew I should have never gone there. Everything that happened that night belonged to me. My sins that night were deliberate, not surprising. Over the years, I've realized just how much I wanted to be with Nicole that night and just how certain I was that I'd end up arriving at her home to find her mother, her only guardian, gone for the night.

We never knew she would show up the next day.

TWENTY-THREE

What's wrong?

Everything.

Don't give me that look.

What look?

That look.

I'm sorry.

For what?

Nicole, you know.

How could that be wrong?

What more do you want me to say?

Did it feel wrong to you?

I don't know how it felt. But I know it was wrong.

How could something like that be wrong? If you love someone, if you know in your heart that it's right, how could that be wrong?

Morally.

But we're not talking about that.

There are consequences to things.

Like what? What consequences can there be? Please—don't ruin something so special.

I'm not supposed to see you anymore.

That's just my mom overreacting.

She was really angry when she got home.

How could I know—I didn't think she'd get her boyfriend to plow his way home.

She knew something was up.

She's fine now.

She told my parents.

What's the worst that can happen?

I just want to know.

What?

Why did you cry afterward?

I was emotional.
Something was different the next morning.
I didn't mean for anything to be.
But it was. It is.
Steve...
What?
Let's don't talk about it anymore. We have the rest of our lives ahead of us. Nothing has to break us up.

Naive. Little did either of us know.

I walk through Times Square with the blaring colors and the panoramic visions blooming all around me. Crowds still meander by even though snow is beginning to accumulate. Wind deadens my face, and I glance up and see a monstrous billboard of a mostly naked woman. So simple, so meaningless. Another ad with a nameless model portraying something supposedly attainable, something obviously unforbidden. Something the world assumes you're going to glance at and then keep walking as though it's just another form of weather.

I feel loneliness and pray a simple prayer.

"Lord, watch over me."

I feel surrounded in this city of strangers, this haven of potential sin. I wonder if women know the temptations men encounter on a daily basis, on an hourly basis, where the media and the mind blend into two spiritually volatile things. Even years ago, when I thought I knew exactly what faith was and how to live it, I ended up walking into something I couldn't handle.

I feel thankful that I didn't see Nicole at the hotel. Regardless of what would be said or what attraction might be there, I know it's better to leave our history in the past. I only wonder now about the road her life has taken and whether she is any closer to finding the peace I claimed to have.

The last she remembers of my faith is conflict and an abandoned testimony.

My legacy to Nicole will always be that I failed her, even if she believes I did it out of love.

TWENTY-FOUR

I talk to Isabel for half an hour. Hearing her voice gives me stability, makes me feel whole again. I find myself longing to be next to her. After all our years together, I cherish the grounded feeling of knowing my wife is there. Waking up and hearing her already getting ready, thankful that she's twice as responsible as I should be, knowing she'll be wide awake enough to make sure we don't overlook the necessary things for Jake and Natalie.

Part of me wants to tell her about Nicole, but I decide to wait until I'm home. I don't know where to begin, what to tell her and what to leave out. I still remember telling her everything about Nicole during our college dating years. Isabel never held this over me, not once. But she also knew there was something I couldn't give to her if we did marry. All she could accept was my regret.

I hang up the phone and once again feel the seclusion of space, the distance of unfamiliarity. I open my laptop and plug it into a phone jack by the desk, deciding to check e-mails just for something to do. I know myself well enough to know it'd be pointless to try to actually write. Too many thoughts distract me.

The phone by the bed rings only five minutes after I hang up. I assume it's Isabel again, and I pick it up absently.

"Steve?"

a whole world away and the very utterance sounds the same

"Yes" is all I can say.

"It's Nicole."

"I know."

My voice is steady, more assured than I actually feel. So many emotions fill me as I sit on the edge of my bed and look out the window onto the snow-blurred lights of Manhattan.

"I saw you. In the lobby."

"So you were there."

"Yes."

A pause. The receiver feels like a lifeline I'm holding. I grip it harder than I should.

I wait for her to talk. She called. She initiated this. All of this.

"I'm sorry I didn't— There's like a million things I want to say right now. I didn't think I could say anything if I went up to you."

"What are you doing in New York?" I ask her.

"I came to find you. To talk with you."

"How did you know?"

"You said something in your e-mail about the *Today* show thing. And it was on your Web site."

I'd forgotten that somebody put that information on my site. I'd certainly forgotten writing to her about it.

"But why?"

"Why what?" Nicole asks.

"Come all this way. After all this time."

"I wanted to see you. To explain things. Set a few things right."

"It's been a long time," I say.

"I know. I— This is really weird. I feel like a teenager again."

A small wave of irritation passes through me. So many years later, so long after she left, and she's telling me she feels like a teenager.

"I don't—I didn't want to do this on the phone. Or in an e-mail."

"Do what?" I ask.

"Talk to you. I want to see you."

"I don't know."

"I need to make sure you understand."

"Understand what?"

I pull myself off the bed and move toward the window. Flakes flutter around as the wind blows in a hundred different directions.

"Do you believe people can change?"

I think for a minute.

"Of course."

She says nothing. I don't understand her question. Is she saying she's changed? And if so, how?

Both of us have changed, obviously. We were teenagers back then. What did we know about the world and about responsibilities and about love?

"I need to tell you so many things."

"I don't know if that'd be a good thing."

"I'm not asking you to do it now. It's just—when I left—"

"Don't," I say.

"What?"

"Not now. Not after all this time."

"But I need to explain to you, Steve. You deserve to know."

"Our lives are completely different now. I—this conversation prob-ably shouldn't even be happening."

"I promise you, I'm not here to hurt you or your family."

But you don't understand and will never understand how I feel and have always felt about you.

"I should go," I say.

"Can I see you tomorrow morning?"

"I don't think that would be a good idea."

"Steve—just this once. I'm not asking for anything except the chance to explain some things."

"What kind of things?"

"Tomorrow. Please? That's all I ask."

I rub a hand through my hair and close my eyes and still picture her. So many years later. It doesn't feel magical though. It feels strange and confusing. And wrong.

"Nicole—"

"Please, just breakfast. Simple as that."

"Okay," I finally tell her.

She asks me to meet her in the Soriale lobby at eight in the morn-ing, and I say yes. She says good night to me, and when she does, I feel goose bumps cover my body. I don't reply. I don't say anything. I hang up the phone and continue to look outside and wonder why God is allowing this and why in the world she has come back after all these years, after our paths split and headed in different directions.

What do you want with me, Nicole?

The clock reads 9:25. The New York night is still young.

I know I should have never picked up the phone. I should have never gone to the Soriale. I should have never replied to that first e-mail.

Do you believe people can change?

Has Nicole changed? And how so? What has life brought her? If I see her again, will I still feel a longing for her to be in my life? Will I be able to listen to her stories and not feel the urge to rescue her?

I need to do something right now. Watching television doesn't work. Sitting on my bed doesn't work. I don't dare get near a phone. It's as though I don't trust myself anymore.

What's happening to me?

It's as though spirits wage war inside of me. I'm afraid of who will win.

In my bag is a Bible Isabel gave me years ago. A thinline volume of the New Testament, it stays in my travel bag, even though I rarely open it. Now I grab it and flip it open, searching. This moment calls for Scripture, something beyond my power to compete with the thoughts and impulses racing through my mind and my heart.

I read a portion of Romans 6. But this is evidently not one of those divine moments when someone opens a Bible and God speaks then and there through what is written. Romans 6 just doesn't leap off the pages. I read bits of Romans 7 and, not much of it seems to register either. Until I reach the twenty-first verse.

> It seems to be a fact of life that when I want to do what is
> right, I inevitably do what is wrong. I love God's law with
> all my heart. But there is another law at work within me
> that is at war with my mind. This law wins the fight and
> makes me a slave to the sin that is still within me. Oh, what
> a miserable person I am! Who will free me from this life that
> is dominated by sin? Thank God! The answer is in Jesus
> Christ our Lord.

The words sound simple, profound, and right. I do feel miserable, and I know that the war going on inside me is not something I can win on my own. I know I need to rely on Jesus Christ.

I wonder what the beautiful people of New York City, the city dwellers and literary crowd, the publishing masses and artistic packs, would think of such thoughts. How foreign they might sound. Yet I know I've been given a precious gift, and that gift also requires obedience. Something I don't always give.

Lord, help me.

I ask for caution. For wisdom. For victory over temptation.

And for answers on what to say and what to do about Nicole.

I know I still love her. A part of me still wonders why we never married. Even after she left, I held on to a bit of hope, even though I knew it never would have worked out. Her wavering and constantly changing faith, the little faith she claimed to have, contrasted with my own. What would I have been like living with her? Pining away and hoping she would come to understand that Jesus died for her sins. She thought that sort of talk was foolish and childish, and the way I acted didn't help her think any differently. I only managed to prove that I could be no different than the rest of the world.

I tried to be an example to her. Tried to rescue her from a lifetime of men letting her down. Yet ultimately I rose to the top of that hurt list. I was no different from any of the rest.

I want to be different now. I want to be an example, make amends for those mistakes. But I don't want to fool myself.

Lord, help me not to fail.

TWENTY-FIVE

I mean it.

No, you don't. You can't.

I mean it more than I've meant anything else in the world.

We can't, Steve. It wouldn't work.

Yes we can.

We're too young.

It doesn't matter. We can make it work.

Please, Steve.

Listen—

No, you listen. This is a bad idea.

Why are you doing this?

You might understand one day.

Now is that day. Tell me.

Look, I'm leaving. I'll be living across the country. It just won't work.

I want to go with you to California.

Do you understand what you're saying? How ridiculous you sound?

I'm only saying the same things you've said to me.

I'm sorry.

And just like that, she left.

Nicole and her mother headed west again. Away from Knoxville, out of my world, far from my love.

I remember the last-ditch effort, the final chance. I remember thinking it would work, that I would finally manage to get through it all. I honestly thought Nicole would let me, that she would understand.

I think back to that afternoon, to desperate pleadings from a high-school senior who thought he knew what he wanted from life. Yet this younger girl simply walked away without another word. The final ones would come a couple of months later, in a letter from California, placing a simple period at the end of a remarkably short sentence.

Late at night, in the darkness of an unfamiliar room, I wonder what life would have been like if Nicole had agreed to marry me. I know the decision would have been a rash and wrong one, but at the time, I still believed it was the only thing left to do.

Despite her passionate nature, I know Nicole was far more mature than I was.

I wonder if she still is.

I think of calling her. Knowing I wouldn't have an inkling of what to say. Knowing I'd probably wake her up, that a call at 2:34 in the morning would wake up almost anyone. Knowing she'd probably ask me to save my thoughts for later in the morning.

Perhaps.

I am restless. I remember when she told me about her mother's decision. We had already felt the consequences from our night together after my parents grounded me and forbade me to see her. We managed to talk a little at school, but not much. Nicole's mother reacted even more strongly, ultimately deciding to move both of them back to California.

Nicole told me this, and I initially said it didn't matter, that nothing mattered, that our love would last, that nothing could keep us apart. Sophomoric babbling. Childlike declarations that even Nicole couldn't swallow.

Nicole changed after hearing her mother's decision. And when she understood that she and her mom were truly leaving Tennessee, leaving for good, a part of her died as well. I think in a way she already knew we were done. Everything that had happened was simply a prelude for this final act. But her conclusion shattered me. And the epilogue lingered another twenty years.

What if she had said yes?

I remember Nicole telling me that if God allowed things to happen, then this obviously was his judgment on her. I told her no, of course not, don't say that sort of thing, but part of me wondered as well. She blamed God, even said she couldn't help hating him, and I told her to please not say such things. She wondered if there even was a God, if perhaps her guilt was all for nothing.

We are a culmination of our mistakes and fortunes, of the paths we wander down with reckless abandon and the dead ends that block our supposed destinies. I remember holding Nicole in my arms and feeling her weep against my chest and trying to think of something to tell her about her move. I thought about saying something like "Just trust God" or "All we can do is pray," but those phrases seemed trite. I believed them, but they would have sounded ridiculous at that moment.

So I proposed. And she never even said no. She simply ended with an "I'm sorry."

All I could do then was hold her. Twenty-four hours later she was gone.

For the rest of my life. Until now.

TWENTY-SIX

I've decided not to meet Nicole for breakfast this morning. It's past eight o'clock, and I know she is waiting for me in the lobby of her hotel. There will be no greeting, no breakfast, no baring of souls. I know my decision is final. And right.

The news says that today's flights are on schedule. I watch *Today* and find it amazing that I sat in the same studio just twenty-four hours earlier. I wonder what the reaction in Johnson City will be, what my relatives and family will say once I get home. I find myself impatient to get on the midday flight heading south.

After a quick shower, I put on the same pants I wore yesterday and a fresh, ribbed turtleneck sweater and head downstairs. The outside air feels brisk, as if the day is holding its breath and wants me to do the same. I walk and find the empty, freshly shoveled sidewalks refreshing. A few blocks from my hotel, I pass by the window of a French café. La Cencaise, the banner reads. I scan the menu posted outside and figure it sounds good enough. I'm dying for a cup of coffee to warm me up.

I sit at a table not far from the window. Looking out, I can see piles of snow in the gutters and people picking their way around them, probably on their way to work. Inside, out of the frigid Manhattan morning, I sip from an oversize white mug and find the coffee delicious, almost as good as the heavy stuff we brew at home. I order French toast, wanting something different for a change, and enjoy the quiet atmosphere of the elegant café.

Looking back, I realize that the aftermath of the storm, the night I spent with Nicole, seemed anticlimactic yet powerful. Nothing was ever the same between us after that night. My guilt, my fears, my longing to be with her—none of this could compare to the change in her once she realized she was moving. And all the things she told me not to worry about—we were in love, so nothing else mattered—suddenly *did* matter to her. And the faith we had spoken about—my faith in particular, the beliefs I had abandoned for a night—suddenly became real to her when she knew she was going to leave.

Nicole simply walked out of my life as easily as—

she might walk down a New York sidewalk on a weekday morning.

"No," I say out loud, under my breath but still audible to anyone around me.

But yes, there she is, walking directly toward me, toward the restaurant, stepping softly, casually.

It will be a scene that I know immediately will be replayed in my head for however long God grants me to live.

Years from now I know I'll remember the smell of fresh-baked breads and pastries complementing my half-cup of vanilla latte. Taking a sip, then glancing ahead and seeing her.

After all this time, she still carries an ironic air of passion and sadness mixed with unattainable beauty. The years have been kind to her. I can picture her smiling even though she glances straight ahead, her lips tight in the cold.

She looks taller than I remember her, and I assume she is probably wearing heels or boots. Her tan leather coat flaps around her knees. Darker pants and a light cream turtleneck complete the ensemble. Her hair is long, past her shoulders, the color of golden honey. It no longer curls the way it used to; the straight locks sway gently. Her walk is steady, her expression distracted. Perhaps I imagine this.

Beautiful—what a trite nine-letter description. *Rapturous. Divine. Sincere. Finally.* Words that come to my mind when I see her.

I never thought I'd see you again.

Yes, the years have been kind to her. She is still magnificent. Can this really be the woman—and the word *woman* sounds so strange referring to Nicole—who e-mailed me?

She walks and glances into the restaurant, and I believe in my heart that she sees me eyeing her, gawking at her with my emotions fully visible. Much as I must have done years ago when she first walked up to me at school.

Yet she looks away quickly, no change in her expression. The glare on the windows and the reflections apparently block her view. She doesn't see me.

I wonder whether she will come into the café. Wonder what I will say. *Good to see you. I'm sorry I didn't come this morning. You look more breathtaking than I even dared to imagine. What are the chances? What happened to twenty years?*

Yet any remotely decent greeting is overshadowed by her figure walking by in front of the restaurant. I see her plainly as she moves past the large window several tables past me.

no

not again

I lost her once. I let her go without having a final word. Not again.

She's not yours to let go.

I sit still and see the last few seconds of her slide away, a vision of stunning class, a picture of sweetness and strength and a million could-have-beens.

This is our last good-bye.

No, I think. *No.*

Chase after her.

To say what?

To say something. Anything.

Yet I have nothing to say. Not after everything I said years ago. When I bared my soul and almost discarded my future. Despite guilt and despite the acknowledged mistakes.

I believed I'd be with her the rest of my life.

The coffee cup, the hard chair, the small table for two, the vacant sidewalk. They all beckon me to get up. To go find her.

If I'm going to go, I need to do it now.

Now.

Yet it's not the same. Not anymore.

I still owe her thanks. Owe her gratitude. She doesn't understand what she did for me.

Yet my lover, my friend—her name is not Nicole. Her name is Isabel. Despite my past failures, she took me. We made a life together.

And Isabel waits for me now.

Why, I wonder. *Why is it so simple?*

She waits. Go to her.

I'm going. I sip my coffee and wait for the taxi that will take me by the hotel and then back to the airport. Back home. Back to the woman I love.

I imprint the image of Nicole's passing on my mind and my heart, for I know I'll never see her again.

Twenty-Seven

Please stop writing. Stop calling. It's over. I told you once, and I'll tell you again. How could anything work? I've allowed you to fail, telling you it was fine. I think I understand things better now. I know it was not meant to be. Perhaps. But perhaps God allows things to be.

You asked for a word. For something final. Something to leave you with. So I'll give it to you now.

Follow your dreams, Stephen.

Don't follow me.

TWENTY-EIGHT

I took Nicole's advice. Even now, twenty years later, I find myself heeding her written words. But there has always been this tiny tug inside, this whispering voice, that wonders. Were we truly meant to be together? What would life have been like had I not given up on her so easily? Why had she ended things so abruptly?

A couple of months after my New York trip I find the doubts seeping back into my thoughts. Yet something simple, something remarkably simple, finally allows me to open my eyes and see what I've been given.

I drive the SUV. Isabel sits with Jake in the backseat. Natalie sits up front with me, as she often requests. We've just finished dinner at the Applebee's in Johnson City, and as we drive home we're all wound up and feeling good. I slide a disc into the stereo that I know will get everyone singing. Sure enough, Jake is the first to join in with the *Sound of Music* soundtrack. We've watched the movie numerous times as a family, and we all know the songs by heart.

Track seven is the one that gets us all singing. Julie Andrews sings about brown paper packages tied up with string and other favorite things. Jake and Natalie have every word down pat, and they continue to belt them out as we drive home.

"When the dog bites!" we all scream in unison.

As a father, I love moments like this. Moments when our family acts corny, when we laugh at how corny we're being, when we don't care what anyone might think simply because we're enjoying ourselves.

We sing a rendition of "Do-Re-Mi" together, then I skip ahead to two more of the livelier tracks. When our voices and our energies are exhausted, I turn down the stereo as the slower songs play, and we drive in darkness. Jake talks quietly to his mother and asks if we can ever go to Europe. Natalie slips a hand over the seat and grabs my own as naturally as one might take a breath.

The darkness surrounds us, yet I'm suddenly conscious of the bond between us. It's a connection I sometimes neglect to work on. But it's strong. It holds us.

This is my family, our family. Regardless of choices made and past mistakes and all the million could-have-beens in my life, these are the people God has given me. I believe this. And I know there can be nothing greater than what I have here, in the cabin of this vehicle, with these lives that have intersected and been allowed to grow and prosper along with mine.

Natalie holds my hand the rest of the way home. I turn slightly and see Isabel's grin as she listens to Jake tell jokes that don't make sense.

Thank you, Lord, for this. For us.

I know that as long as I live, images of a snow-covered house and a passing beauty will never leave me. And perhaps they shouldn't. Perhaps they remain in my memory like warning signs.

Warnings against losing my way. Reminders that it could happen, that it's not so far out of bounds. One step, one choice, one easy slip, and I could lose these ones I love.

Lord, let that never happen.

Let me be the father, the husband I need to be.

And let the past remain in the past.

TWENTY-NINE

I know the manuscript is too big. Most novels hover around the hundred-thousand-word mark, and most of mine have ended up around that size. Yet, as I stare at the five-hundred-plus manuscript pages stacked on my desk, I already know this one will give my editor a challenge.

One hundred sixty-five thousand words. It's a whopper.

Thank goodness I have a name as an author. I think new novelists shoot themselves in the foot trying to get an eight-hundred-page book published. If no one has heard of you, what makes you think somebody will devote half a summer to *one* book you've written? That's probably why my novels have grown longer and longer. The first one barely made it past seventy-five thousand words.

I pick up the new manuscript, knock it against the desk to square off its pages, and fit it into the mailing box I've been saving. I'll e-mail the electronic manuscript to Alan, but he always likes to read hard copy first. The manuscript fits neatly in the box, the title page on top.

Whiteout.

Already I've gotten some comments from Isabel about my working title. "Isn't that the stuff you use to cover ink?" I've told her yes, but add that it obviously refers to a blizzard or a snowstorm. After the success of *Immersion,* both Alan and I like the idea of a concise one-word title.

The title fits, too. For many reasons I feel good about it. And about the story of a man coming to grips with his past life.

The June sun has already climbed high in the sky. I know this summer day will involve yard work and playing outside with the kids. I love summertime, when the kids have as much time at home as I do—especially when I've finished a project and earned a break. We're planning a trip to Orlando in a few weeks—a celebration of my finishing book number eight.

The stereo pipes in soft music as I look over the cover letter to Alan on my computer screen. As I send it to print, my computer announces that I have a new e-mail. I click the icon on my screen and allow the message to fill the screen.

I immediately recognize the address in the "sender" box.

What now?

The e-mail is long, that I know. I wonder whether I should simply delete it and move on. But instead I read the words from Nicole.

> Dear Steve,
>
> New York's snowstorm seems like a far-off dream. I half believe my trip to Manhattan was simply a mirage, a blinding vision in a blizzard.
>
> I write one last time, asking for no reply. I write to tell you something I wish I'd had the courage to tell you years ago—the same thing I wanted to tell you in person in New York. I've always wanted to explain to you the few weeks after our night together. Why I did what I did and said what I said.
>
> I know now there can be things we do in life that we dearly wish we could change or take back. Things that affect the rest of our lives for good or bad. I wish I could take back those last few days, Steve. Not because of the decision I made, but because of the way I acted and the way I hurt you.
>
> Saying no to your proposal was and will always be the hardest thing I ever had to endure. I loved you. And though I am no longer the girl I was back then, I know that part of me will always love you. Nothing can ever change that.
>
> Remember when we used to talk about God? How you were so strong in your faith and I seemed so ambivalent in my views? I want you to know I did believe in God when we were together—but my feelings about God were all mixed up. I believed the same God who put us together was judging me for my sins that night we were together. I believed his judgment was forcing me to move away from you. And I believed that

if I stayed with you, that judgment would follow us the rest of our life together.

Whether that would have been true, I honestly don't know. I guess I'm still unsure about that. But I do know I handled everything wrong. Instead of explaining, I turned down your love and disappeared. Maybe I couldn't explain it back then. But I could have said *something*.

When you proposed, I knew I could not say yes. I *allowed* you to fail, Steve. After you had been so strong and made it so clear to me that we needed to wait. For that, I've never been able to forgive myself.

When I saw you in New York—in the lobby of the Soriale—I couldn't help thinking back to the night of the storm. Part of me knew, hoped, that you would come to my door. Part of me always realized what was going to happen. And in New York, I realized the path we were walking down, even if those weren't the intentions either of us had.

Mostly what I wanted to do in New York was to say something I've needed to say for many years. So I say it now. Good-bye, Stephen Conroy. And I hope you take it as the good-bye I never offered you years ago. I want you to know that I didn't end everything because I fell out of love. I ended everything because I didn't want you losing what I held most dear about you—your convictions and your faith.

Remember my last letter to you, after you wrote me many letters asking why I was doing this, asking to talk to me, telling me you'd give up everything to be with me? I felt that God didn't want us together, that it wasn't right. So I finally told you to follow your dreams and not me. And so many years later, I see that you did exactly that.

I still search for the faith you hold and for the joy that existed once between the two of us. I ask that you don't e-mail me again, that you simply keep me in your prayers. You found your love and your future in your family. I pray that I might find one of my own as well.

I hope you grow old with your wife, Steve. And that you can let our past—and the memories of us—go. I think that finally, after all this time, I've been allowed to do that.

But always know this. The teenage girl I was—the one who will always live inside me—still loves you, Steve. She always will.

Nicole

I shut off the computer and lean back into the soft leather of my chair. My eyes close, and I can still picture the woman, a vision of rapture and escape, walking toward me. Just as she did years ago when she approached a guy she didn't know and started to talk with him. Speechless, both times, I knew that neither intersection was accidental. And now, with time having passed, I wonder if the first directly affected the second.

Nicole is no longer someone I can save, no longer someone I can embrace. For a brief season the two of us shared something wonderful, something magical. Something I know now, much later, was never given to us. Something that changed both of our lives, our paths in life, and the roads we would inevitably take.

Where are you now?

It is not my place to know.

I once loved you.

And I guess probably always will.

I wonder if, ten years from now, I'll look back on that morning in New York with the same clarity as I look back on it now. If I'll know without a doubt that I made the right decision.

At this moment I believe with all my heart that it was the right one.

Time can be a gift. Sometimes it allows you to look back in the silence of a solitary moment and remember your mistakes. Sometimes you recall brief, passionate, daunting moments. Moments that wash away like chalk on a sidewalk, lovely and innocent and quickly gone.

On the desk in front of me is a photo of the four of us. I'm in the middle with Isabel, Jake, and Natalie grouped around me, leaning in close. There is nothing I can do to deserve my place in that picture and the love I've been given. And despite my loyalty to them and their abiding trust in me, I know that nothing I can do or say will ensure I don't lose them forever.

All I can do is ask the Lord to watch over us.

Protect us.

A simple prayer. And it *is* simple.

I know that I'll never e-mail Nicole again, that the good-bye I always dreamed of hearing has finally been given.

Are we allowed to say good-bye?

Perhaps not always. And sometimes, when the good-bye comes, it's not packaged the way we wanted. How could we possibly say everything?

I know I once loved Nicole. That we once loved each other. Yet another life awaited me. And Nicole somehow knew that. Even in her own disbelief, she knew something else awaited me.

Are we allowed to say good-bye?

This is the moment. In my heart. My eyes closed. Alone. Simple.

good-bye

Still Life at Sunset

GENEVA

She heard the brush of footsteps before she saw him. When she looked up, she noticed the unbuttoned top of a dark blue shirt that had probably hidden behind a coat and tie earlier that day. A full, indulgent smile greeted her.

"Hello."

The lobby was vacant except for an elderly couple sitting in chairs next to an unlit fireplace. Anna sat alone in a corner spot, comfortably reading a novel. The man slid into the seat across from her. She focused back on the hardcover.

"Can I get you a drink?" he asked, ignoring her silence.

Her eyes broke off the page and assessed the man. *Fifties, slim, handsome, business, well off*—the terms rang off in her mind in the second it took her to shake her head.

"Are you here by yourself?"

Anna brushed her dark hair away from her face and refused to let herself smile. Even a polite smile could be misread.

"Look, I'm sorry, but I'm sort of in the middle of something."

The stranger's eyes flickered with energy, like those of a poker player ready to show his cards.

"What are you reading?"

She closed the book and put it facedown on her lap. Normally she would have just said "Jacquelyn Mitchard" and showed the cover and left it at that. Instead, she shook her head and let out a sigh.

"Exactly what part of 'I'm in the middle of something' don't you understand?"

The man, probably a V.P. of something in town for a conference, leaned back and took a sip from his glass—some executive drink like scotch and soda. The effect he was obviously going for was relaxed and suave. The latter term fit this man well, Anna thought. *Suave.* She had always hated the word, as if applying it to someone immediately defined that person in a derogatory way.

"Just trying to be friendly," he said, crossing one leg over the other. "The place is pretty quiet tonight."

Normally Mr. V.P. wouldn't have bothered her. Normally Forbes 500 could've been ignored with a polite smile and a few minutes of well-mannered but pointed chitchat that told him she wasn't interested and never would be and would he please leave as fast as he'd sat down.

It's probably this place, she thought to herself. *Something like this shouldn't happen here. Especially not here.*

"It was a lot quieter a couple of minutes ago," Anna told him, her eyes unblinking.

"Come on. What would be the harm in just letting me—"

"Hey, there you are."

Anna and the businessman both looked up. A man in his late twenties approached them with his hands outstretched toward Anna. He wore jeans and a button-down, short-sleeved shirt.

"I was looking for you," the younger man said to Anna, his face lit up and smiling. He looked at the man sitting across from Anna as if to trying to place him.

"Hey, uh, excuse me. I was supposed to meet her half an hour ago. I was thinking it was going to be outside."

The animated newcomer, stocky but fit, with wavy brown hair, shot a pointed look at the pickup artist, who finished his drink and stood up.

"You two have an enjoyable afternoon."

Anna watched and laughed as the gray-haired man walked away, only to be replaced by another stranger.

"I've seen him annoy women around here for the last few days. Sorry. I hope I didn't interrupt something meaningful."

His boyish grin made her laugh. "No. It was just ending."

"Good." The man clasped his hands and looked around the room. "I'm Derrick. And before you say anything, I want you to know I'm *not* trying to pick you up or buy you a drink or anything like that."

Anna nodded.

"I just—I saw you earlier today when you were checking in. We've had this business-meeting thing going on here for a while now. For about five days. And I've been getting a little tired of this place, even if it is pretty swanky. You ever stayed here before?"

Again, Anna confirmed this without a word.

"Yeah, our company wanted to do something unique. We're from Wisconsin, but the company is located in downtown Chicago. They're having a retreat for the directors, and, well, this place worked out. That guy's been around acting like he's James Bond or something. The women in our group have been creeped out by him. So I saw him over here and thought I might—"

She gave him a small smile. "Thanks." She glanced down toward her book. A hint.

He looked at her and appeared to be thinking for a few seconds. "Can I just say—and this is not a line or anything—but—"

"If you have to say that, then it probably is a line."

He raised his eyebrows as if to say, *good one*. "You're one of the most vibrant women I've ever seen."

"Hmm," Anna replied. "Vibrant? Looked in the thesaurus for that one, did we?"

"No, I'm serious. I'm mean, even when that man was talking with you, the smile—it's hard not to notice even from across the room."

"It just radiates, doesn't it?" she said.

"It does. I'm serious. Don't laugh."

His innocence and honesty could have been appealing any other time. But not today. "You know, Derrick—"

"No, wait." He held up his active hands in a stop mode. "Look, I didn't say that to sound like some cornball, okay?"

"I appreciate the compliment."

"I just—I've probably been in too many meetings. I just told myself that I should say something, you know. It's not every day a stunning woman walks by you."

"Sorry to hear you don't put your wife in that category."

Derrick paused for a second, almost as if he didn't understand what she just said.

"No, I didn't mean, not that—"

Anna stood up, holding her book in both hands and staring down at the flustered man. Of course she felt the attraction—handsome yet endearing, bold yet also self-conscious.

And that was what made his attempts at—at whatever it was he wanted—all the more pathetic.

"You could be the man of my dreams, you know. If it wasn't for that tiny tan line around your finger. Now I could be wrong. You could be a grieving widower who usually wears a ring in memory of his loving wife. Or you wear it as a good luck charm. Or perhaps you're divorced and you just managed to get the tight thing off your finger minutes ago. But I have a feeling it's none of the above, right?"

Derrick rubbed the twitch underneath his eye and chuckled. "Smart lady."

"Hope you make it home safely," she said, wondering what exactly she meant by that last word, knowing that Derrick surely must be wondering the same thing.

As she walked to her room, her conversation with the stranger reverberated in her mind.

Once there, in the muted darkness of one lit lamp, Anna put her book down on her open suitcase. She picked up her purse and looked through it. Inside her wallet, tucked safely inside a pouch, she found the rings. She slipped them on her finger and held it up. Even in the dim light she could see the way the stone sparkled. Perhaps it was a trick of the light. Perhaps the diamond wasn't as big or bright as it seemed. Perhaps it was an ordinary, simple wedding set.

But there was no perhaps about the way she had felt when she wore it.

The only question now was whether she would ever wear one again.

The river glinted with sun-soaked creases, moving steadily this calm morning. From her bed Anna watched through glass-paneled doors that opened up to a small deck edging the water. On the opposite shore, two bikers coasted through a park. A plane droned as it set out on its course, probably after taking off from O'Hare. Anna sipped her coffee and felt dwarfed by the king-size four-poster bed.

Next to her, on a cherry table that held her travel alarm, the five-by-seven package waited, her name scribbled in black ink on the front. It was one of those padded envelopes. Its contents bulged the center.

Anna knew it was early yet. Too early to open the package. But part of her wanted to finally break the seal and get it all over with. She expected anything. Nothing could surprise her now.

She took another sip and knew that she would wait. She had waited this long. Another few days wouldn't be too difficult.

Being in this room at the Herrington Inn brought back memories, of course. Perhaps she was kidding herself that she could stay here without harm. But she was testing herself. If she could bear the hotel, the room, she could probably go through with everything else she had planned for this weekend. She really could let go of the past.

Fifteen years. Could it really have been so long? Fifteen years, with so much in between. Sitting underneath the down comforter, drinking coffee that had arrived at her door half an hour ago with an English muffin and some fruit, Anna still felt like a young woman on the threshold of her life. A new bride, glowing in joy, anticipating a long life ahead.

It had been a good feeling once, thinking of the future. Little had she known their future would be so short. So unbelievably short.

She had requested the room months ago. Room 116. She had spent quite awhile looking up the room number. She remembered that it faced the Fox River on the first floor and that it featured a fireplace with a king-size bed and oversize bathroom. But she didn't remember the bathroom being as opulent as it was now, with its two-person marble Jacuzzi and glass-encased shower. Part of her felt embarrassed for being in such a room. The guy behind the counter must have wondered what she was doing checking into this honeymoon suite by herself.

By herself.

It seemed impossible that she was here at all. She kept questioning her motives behind this trip to Illinois. It had been years since she had been back, and the life she once led here was forever gone. She couldn't even think of this trip as "going home."

Along with the small suitcase, Anna carried enough memories and photographs in her mind to keep her occupied during this trip. Self-doubts were unusual for her. She had spent many years building up her confidence and her barricades in order to block out any reservations that might come her way. But regardless of how secure she felt in her life now, there was one area where she still felt like a small child. This area she was entering now. The one where she had failed so miserably before.

Don't lose your faith, a voice encouraged.

Anna was putting on the last touches of her makeup when she heard the phone ring. She breathed in and hesitated for a moment, letting it jingle a few times. She finally walked into the room and grabbed the receiver.

"Hello."

"Ms. Williams?" A male voice.

"Yes?"

"You have an overnight package waiting at the desk. Would you like someone to bring it to you?"

For a few seconds her mind shuffled through the different files that separated her life. Work. Home. Family. Personal. The first dossier was crammed full, overstuffed. Each subsequent file contained less, with the last one almost empty. She knew that the package probably had to do with work, but she had no idea what it could be.

"Yes," she said, "that would be great."

In a few minutes she answered a knock at her door to find a young man with curly blond hair and a Federal Express overnight envelope. She thanked him and took the slim cardboard package, glancing at the sender's address and seeing it was from her partner.

Well, what do you know?

She ripped open the package and pulled out the stack of papers clipped together. The front page of the contract held a yellow Post-it note from Joel written as eloquently as he usually spoke: "Sign this ASAP."

Anna knew what the contract was for and why it had been overnighted. She had asked Joel, Mr. Kick-Back-and-Take-It-Easy himself, to FedEx it to her if it arrived. But she couldn't believe he had actually followed through with her request. Joel was a likable partner—levelheaded, good-natured, and able to do anything with computers and Web sites—but he tended to leave the detail work to her. Joel had worked with Anna for several years at Events Unlimited, a business she operated out of her home in Asheville, North Carolina. The Web site had been up and running for a couple of years now, and so had the national interest. Business lately had been good enough for her and Joel to hire another full-time person.

She began to leaf through the contract until she caught herself and set it down on a table. *Not now,* Anna told herself. Business could wait, at least for the weekend. She could read the contract on the flight back home. She wanted at least to enjoy this Friday, this weekend, and to try not to think about work.

But Anna doubted if she could let the whole weekend pass without looking through the contract. It was from the Pilano Company, a cosmetics firm in Atlanta, and she knew that it would be a lucrative one. Anna's company would be handling their trade show in Charlotte later this summer. This was Pilano's draft of the contract, the one where they went through and marked out clauses and costs and made their offer. Eventually, Anna hoped, Events Unlimited and Pilano would agree on the terms, and then Anna would send out a fresh contract ready to be signed.

If I sign it.

She picked up the contract and glanced through it. After several pages, she stopped counting the mistakes and the changes that needed to be made.

An urge to call Joel filled her. Another urge to abandon this foolish fantasy and go back home. With so much on her proverbial plate, this trip was downright irresponsible.

The contract felt heavy. Anna set it down again and thought for a moment. Signing it could change everything. Most contracts did. You signed for loans, for mortgages, for licenses, for life-changing deeds. And, as much as she didn't want life to change, Anna faced a decision. Signing this contract meant more busyness, more responsibility.

More work.

And she didn't want to think about work now.

She had been looking forward to this trip, if for no other reason than to spend time on Third Street shopping. Dozens of small craft shops and boutiques lined the street and its surrounding avenues. A day like this—upper seventies, bright and sunny—would be perfect for shopping.

Who are you kidding?

She hadn't come here to shop, any more than she came to read novels. This trip was about the past, about finally dealing with mistakes made and never forgiven.

The picturesque day called to her.

It had been a perfect weekend fifteen years ago too.

Anna sat on the wooden bench outside the Sweet Tooth, a delightful bakery that specialized in chocolate treats. Her lunch consisted of a chocolate-and-nut-covered pretzel log. Salty and sweet, just as she remembered it. She remembered coming here years ago and sampling one of their pretzel logs for the first time. They came in semisweet chocolate, milk chocolate, even white chocolate. She had picked milk chocolate today.

She watched a couple stroll by on the sidewalk in front of the porch where she sat. Probably in their late twenties or early thirties. And hand in hand, of course, as if to flaunt their love. Both looked well dressed, he in khakis and a blue, button-down casual shirt, she in well-fitting khakis and a white shirt tied above the waist.

How cute, Anna smirked to herself. *They even sorta match.*

But a voice inside whispered, *You're just jealous because somebody's not holding your hand.*

There was a time when she'd thought she could have it all. The tailored but casual wardrobe. The hand-in-hand closeness. The house in the suburbs, Geneva being her first choice and St. Charles her second, with all the clichéd amenities—white picket fence, a welcome mat at the door, a flower bed in the back, two-point-five bathrooms. She never moved into that house, though for a while she'd occupied a nice townhouse with one-point-five baths and three bedrooms. For a while, she'd been on her way.

She sighed and wondered if she'd be able achieve that dream now. Not that she could see moving back to Illinois. Too many memories lurked here in the Chicago area, and she was glad to have let them all go. They didn't burn inside her deep at night, keeping her awake, nor did they haunt her in the mornings when she woke up alone.

That wasn't always true, of course. There had been times when the demons and nightmares came and made a mess out of her. First when she found out about the other woman. And then again later, after she'd moved to North Carolina. After the funeral and its aftermath.

But not now. Now, all the nightmares were in the past.

She loved that word. *Past.* Whenever she had cynical or humorous and even sad thoughts about what had happened in her life, she could always tell herself they belonged in the past. Not only was the past a different time, but she had been a different person back then. Now, at thirty-four years old, she still felt as though life had just started, that she was seeing things fresh again.

Even this part of Illinois, with its miserably cold winters and the stifling summers she used to bemoan, a place that was flat and hectic and expensive, could be seen in a different light. Coming back here didn't feel as bad as she had thought it would.

Of course, the weekend had just started.

She began to walk down Third Street, looking for the next cute shop to patronize. She'd been wandering through the historic district for a couple of hours already, but so far she hadn't purchased anything. Many interesting items had caught her eye, but reason always held her back. How many souvenirs could she take with her on the plane, crammed in a suitcase small enough to be stowed in an overhead bin? If she found something small, unique, it would be hers.

Something small and unique—like, let's say, a man?

Her friend's voice spoke up loudly in her mind. Kiersten from back home, always looking for someone new to set her up with. Always looking for Mr. Right, as if someone like that existed. Before Anna left for this trip, Kiersten had told her to bring home a man. Anna had replied that she would bring back two, one for each of them.

Many of the quaint stores on this street occupied former private residences, some with two stories, each room stuffed with thousands of knickknacks. You could walk down a sidewalk and see a garden path heading off toward what looked like someone's home. Instead, you'd see a sign outside beckoning you to come in and shop. Scattered among these homey shops were occasional strip centers, designed to maintain the vintage look, and a few larger buildings that might once have been offices or department stores.

One of these that Anna strolled by held a directory on a wooden board—a kind of minimall. She read the list of stores: The Card Company. Scent of Pine. The Geneva Winery. Corbin Photography.

Her neck suddenly prickled and felt taut. The sensation flowed to her arms and then continued through the rest of her body. She didn't recognize the sensation immediately because her mind was racing.

For several moments she stared at the sign, reading it over again, then decided to follow the walkway toward the building. Her face felt flushed, her entire body warm even though she wore linen slacks and a white halter top. She hesitated, wondering whether she should go into the building, until somebody opened the glass door and held it for her, beckoning her in.

The Winery was located down a set of stairs to her right. She walked past the first store on the left, The Card Company, which appeared to house thousands of one-of-a-kind stationery items. Another worn wooden staircase led her to the second level of the building.

Scent of Pine, the first shop at the top of the stairs, featured Christmas and holiday items. She was tempted to stop, but pressed on to find the last store listed. The wood floor underneath her creaked, and she knew it had to be original to the house.

Corbin Photography stood at the end of the hallway, with a modern-looking sign and a black-and-white photo next to the door. The picture, blown up to poster size, depicted a blond girl six or seven years old. The background faded away, but she was outside somewhere, possibly near a river. The girl looked away from the camera, smiling at someone or something. The shot was classic, something that could have graced the cover of one of those old magazines like *Life* or *Look*. The photographer obviously knew what to do with a camera.

She entered the compact, light-filled room. An array of photographs decorated the walls, most displayed in simple black frames with white mats. Against one wall stood a backdrop for portrait sittings. A desk stood in the corner behind a glass counter that held various photo albums, but no one was at the desk. No one was in the room. Rock music played from a small boom box on the cluttered desk.

Anna swallowed. Everything about this felt strange. Vaguely familiar. Startling, surprising, even overwhelming.

She examined one of the photos on the wall, another black and white. It pictured a train moving late at night. The lighting was deftly handled, and the photo felt more like art than simple photography. A dozen shades of gray played out in the photo, hauntingly suggesting the motion and the romance of the train. Next to it was a more conventional family portrait in color, one that could have been taken in this room in front of a gray background.

A bead of sweat distracted her for a moment. She wiped it off her forehead and caught her breath. She suddenly wondered how she looked as she smoothed out hair that had gone limp in the heat. She knew she couldn't do anything about it now.

Anna walked over to the counter and saw a handwritten sign: "Yell for Service." She almost turned and walked out, but something held her there. It was the last name, of course, but still. It'd been years since she had heard the name *Corbin*.

"Hello?" Her cracking voice barely rose above the sound of the radio station.

She glanced around and waited for a moment. She knew her feeble attempt to call out had gone unheard.

"Hello? Anyone?" she said a little louder.

An open doorway close to the desk led to a hallway or another room. She heard footsteps and fought the urge to run. Then he appeared in the doorway. Cropped and somewhat messy blond hair, blue eyes that seemed more striking against his light tan, an amiable smile that stopped half formed before he could say anything. The look of surprise filled the tall man's glance.

"It *is* you," Anna let out without thought.

He began to speak and then stopped, completely taken aback. Stunned silence filled the room.

"You know, that look would probably scare away most customers," Anna said with a smile, doing her best to keep things light.

He nodded and approached the counter. He wore a collarless long-sleeved shirt and dark jeans. Again he opened his mouth to say something but shut it.

"It's Anna. Anna Williams. You remember me, don't you?"

"Let me think," he finally said, playing along. "That name rings a bell." Hearing his voice relaxed her. She thought of the years that had passed since she saw him last.

She picked up a business card from a holder on the desk. "For appointments, call 645-4234. So this is your shop then?"

Brad nodded and gazed at her with a look of amazement. His face showed a couple of days' worth of beard.

"I didn't realize you…worked around here."

"I moved out here about a year ago," his low but friendly voice said.

"So you're living in Geneva now?"

Again he nodded. "You're the last person I ever expected to see in this studio."

"Why's that?" Anna said. "It's not as if I don't have any connections here."

"So that's what you're doing—visiting family or something?"

She paused and looked down. "Something like that."

Brad rubbed the side of his face. "You, uh, look very nice today."

Anna laughed. "Thanks."

His look probed her, trying to read her thoughts.

"What— Where are you—"

"Spit it out," she said, unable to keep herself from needling him a little.

"I don't know what to say."

"So don't say anything," Anna said.

"No, it's just—first I meet you in Mexico, and then—"

"Mexico was a while ago."

"And that changes things?"

"I didn't say that."

"I know. I just—I never had the chance to say good-bye."

"You can say it now."

"Do you want me to?"

"Not if you don't want to."

Anna could see the torture on the man's face and knew she shouldn't be so nonchalant.

"I didn't know you had a photography business."

"It's relatively new."

"Relative meaning what?"

Brad finally turned down the music. He fumbled with the mess on his desk for a few seconds and then seemed to realize it was futile.

"I've owned it for a couple of years now."

"So how's business?" she asked him.

"Good. I mean, there's the whole photography studio thing where I take shots like the good ol' family shot on the wall over there. I do weddings and events, the sort of thing that pays the bills. I also do a lot of custom photography. I have a Web site and everything that people can log on to and—"

Brad stopped in midsentence.

"What is it?" Anna said.

He appeared dumbfounded.

"Look, I'm sorry if I... It's just, one moment it's like we're... I mean, I gotta back up here."

Anna shifted on her feet, glancing around the shop. Avoiding his eyes.

"What happened in Puerto Vallarta?" he said.

"Don't—," she began.

"Don't what?"

"I didn't come to... I mean, I wasn't even sure it was you. I don't know what to say. I guess I don't have anything to say." He nodded, and suddenly she knew *that* had been the wrong thing to say. "I didn't mean—"

"No, it's okay. You don't have to say anything. It's just—here I am talking to you as though you live right down the street."

"For a day or so, I do."

Brad looked at her to try to see what she meant. An unrecognizable expression registered on his handsome face.

"You know, when I left Mexico, I thought that week had been some sort of a dream, that I'd never see you again. I've wondered whether I should contact you again."

She looked away. She wasn't ready to address Mexico. Not now. But she should have known it would be an impossible issue to avoid if she ever saw Brad again.

You knew that could happen the minute you saw the sign. So why are you here?

"Are you still in North Carolina?" he asked her.

She nodded. "Yes. I live in Asheville."

"A little more hilly down there, isn't it?"

Anna laughed at his comment. "Yes, it is."

He just looked at her and nodded. "Did that sound as stupid as I think it did?"

"Probably not," Anna replied.

" 'A little more hilly down there.' I'm quite observant, aren't I?"

Anna laughed. They both stood, facing each other, and neither said a word for a few seconds. Then they both tried to speak, interrupted one another, stopped again.

"You go," Anna said.

"Are you here for a while? Yeah? Did you come with anyone? Oh. Okay. What are you doing, let's say, at this moment?"

She couldn't help but let go with a giant grin. Seeing this man stumble and stutter around her made him so much more appealing than if he knew exactly the right things to say.

"That smile," he said.

"What?"

"I've thought of that smile for a long time."

She tried to rein it in but didn't do a very good job of hiding it.

"Are you busy now?" he asked.

"I don't want to keep you from anything."

"From sitting in here waiting for maybe three people to wander in all morning? Please, it's no big deal."

"Seriously, I don't want to—"

"What?" Brad asked.

"Be a bother."

"Right. You're a big bother. You want something to eat? Coffee maybe? Chocolate? There's this great place just across the street called the Sweet Tooth."

Anna didn't want to tell him she'd just visited this shop. In fact, there were many things she didn't want to tell him.

At least not yet.

"Is there a Starbucks around here?" she asked, knowing the answer.

There was so much about this man she still didn't know, so much she had only managed to glimpse before. Three years had passed since they'd met in a faraway place, a seemingly faraway time. Now, in the picturesque town of Geneva—not her home, but the home of her childhood—she sat across the table from Brad Corbin talking as though the trip to Mexico had happened days ago.

So much has happened.

They sat at a table nestled in a corner of the Starbucks. Forgettable piped-in pop music created a backdrop of sound for the usual activities—orders placed, espresso brewed, customers sitting quietly by themselves or in the midst of conversation. Brad worked on his iced tea while seeming more his usual laid-back, good-humored self.

"How's that mocha concoction?" he asked her.

"Wonderful. Want a sip?"

He wrinkled his nose. "No thanks."

"Still not big on coffee?"

"Thank goodness, no."

"So do you find time to actually take photos for your own enjoyment?"

"Yeah. Actually, I have more time, now that I have the studio instead of a day job. Of course, now all my work is potentially part of the business, even the stuff I took before I opened. You remember all the photos I used to take? I always thought it was this great little hobby. Then one day I went through all my pictures and was just blown away. I have thousands. Some really aren't bad."

"So now you're selling them? In the shop?"

"Actually, most of them are on my Web site. I license them to be used. You should see it. I have a bunch of photo albums, too. Professional albums, really classy ones. I've got them arranged by year, and also by color and black and white. I've even got a sepia-tone album I'm making."

"I'd love to see them."

"Yeah, I could show you. I live just…well, close by. A little too far to walk."

She noticed him studying her and being bothered by the silence.

"I mean, that's just a suggestion—"

"That's okay. Yeah, maybe sometime."

Anna glanced into his familiar eyes and found herself thinking of North Carolina for some reason. Something about the expression.

"How long are you here for?" Brad asked.

"My flight leaves Sunday afternoon."

Brad nodded and took a sip from his drink.

"Gives me time to go by the church," she added.

"Riverside Church?"

"Of course."

She could see his eyebrows shoot up in surprise. She smiled, knowing much of this was new ground, not sure where to start.

"Have you been there recently?" Anna asked.

"No. Not for a while. Did you hear one of the pastors there, a fairly young guy, walked away from that plane crash that went down in Nebraska?"

"I bet the church was in shock."

"Yeah, I think so. Especially right when it happened. He was in the news for a while. Pastor Williams even gave some good quotes for the papers."

"He's always good for some nice sound bites." She grinned.

"Does he…does anyone else know you're here?"

"Actually, no. This was sort of a spontaneous trip."

She could see the confusion on Brad's face. There was so much she wanted to tell him, but not here, and not like this. She needed to edit certain things, skip some things altogether, and somehow still be completely honest. And honesty hadn't been one of her strongest traits over the years. But ever since Mexico and what happened afterward, she knew that Brad deserved to know.

How do I tell him?

That was still to be determined. So was when and where.

"Brad, I…I'm not ready to talk."

"What do you mean? We're talking now."

"No. I mean, I can't read your mind, but I know you have to be wondering about everything. What I'm doing here and, well, everything."

"Yeah, 'everything' sounds about right."

His grin gave her a little more confidence and relaxed her.

"I just…I didn't think…I didn't expect to run into you and then hang out in Starbucks."

"Weird, isn't it?"

"Very," Anna replied.

"Remember the first night in Puerto Vallarta? The show and then the beach and everything?"

"It's kinda hard to forget."

"You know the best part of that night?" Brad asked.

"There's a lot to choose from."

"For me, it wasn't the show or the beach or the dinner or any of that. It was the first time I saw you that evening, waiting at the table for me."

"What do you mean?"

"That was when I realized you didn't mind me hanging around you. When I had a clue you might be...well...interested."

"Interested?" Anna asked.

"Okay. Bad word choice. It's just—I remember that so clearly. Seeing you smile and not ever wanting that smile to go away."

Anna looked away from him for a moment, her face warm. She knew she was probably blushing.

"I know you don't want to talk about any of that," he said.

"Not right now. Maybe later."

"I understand. I won't bring it up unless you want to."

"That trip changed many things for me, Brad."

He looked as though he was going to ask for more, but then he let it go.

"Me, too," he finally said.

For another hour they spoke about every single safe topic they could find. Photography, movies, music. Anna's business and her home in North Carolina. Brad's former job with the stone company, the Carolinas, and his old home in Elgin, Illinois. And even though she knew both of them felt the unspoken tension, Anna never felt awkward or at a loss for anything to say. Just the opposite. It was as if they had only been there for a few brief moments and there was still so much left to say, even if it was just about the world they lived in and life in general.

As six o'clock neared, Brad confessed that he had to leave.

"That's okay," Anna said, getting up, not asking why.

Halfway through their walk to the Herrington, Brad told her what his plans were.

"I've got a date tonight."

"Oh," she said, giving more away than she should have, knowing he could probably read right through her reaction.

"Look, it's, uh—"

"Brad, please."

"What?"

"I'm not here to invade your life. I didn't come here for that. I didn't even expect to see you."

"I know. It's just, it's really nothing serious."

"It'd be okay if it was."

They arrived at the front of the inn, at the steps that led down to the main entrance at river level. Brad took a look down the steps toward the river, then glanced back at Anna. He looked as though he was about to say something to her, then he stopped himself and looked around again for a moment.

"Can I see you again?" he asked. "Tomorrow sometime?"

She smiled and said yes. To just call her at the inn.

"Just call you at the inn." He smiled.

"I'll be there."

"Look, if I didn't have these plans, we could've gone out tonight—"

"That might not have been the best idea."

"Maybe not." He looked at her, studied her for a moment. "You know? There's something remarkably different about you."

"Think so?" she asked.

"Yeah."

She looked at Brad and remembered her last words to him in Mexico. She knew them by heart. She had often wondered if she should have been so direct and honest. And now, long afterward, she found herself wondering if she might have to say them again.

"Have a good evening," she said.

He stopped her from leaving and took her hands in his. "Anna—"

"No," she said.

She looked up and glanced at lips she once had kissed. She knew she was still not ready for this, that this was exactly what had happened in Mexico.

"I should go," she said, loosening her hands from his grip and walking down the stairs.

She glanced back once before closing the door, and his eyes hadn't moved. The door closed behind her, and she walked into the riverfront inn by herself.

The clear, open canvas of sunlit sky had been replaced with a twilight study in gold and gray. The hum of suburban life harmonized with the sound of gliding water in front of her. Her little deck held only a single chair. All this gave Anna a sense of loneliness, especially in light of the unexpected events of the afternoon. She sat watching the river pass her by, wondering if her life was doing the same. In the soft glow of the room behind her waited her future. She knew it, and she knew what needed to be done.

How could she even begin to tell any of this to Brad?

It had started months ago as she began to make changes in her life, opening boxes that had been ignored for years. Literal boxes, stowed away in an empty bedroom of the house she occupied, untouched and abandoned until she could decide what to do with them.

In those boxes were a hundred thousand memories she had fought for years to stow away and forget. But she was learning that getting on with your life was partly a matter of consolidating your storage space. You couldn't keep your past packed away but easily available. You eventually had to do some housekeeping.

For a week she had worked on the project—sorting through the boxes, throwing a lot away, forcing herself to keep only what was truly essential. And she had found herself remarkably controlled about the whole process until she came upon an average-looking sealed package with her name scrawled in ink across the front.

That package now lay on the nightstand of her hotel room.

She had almost opened it the night she found it but had stopped herself. The real significance hadn't hit her until she began to count the years and suddenly realized how ironic it was that she'd found the package when she did.

That had prompted the trip here, this sentimental journey she had made. But was it sentimental or simply absurd?

I need to let go of the past.

That was her intent, and this trip—everything she planned—was her way of dealing with the past. Was it overly dramatic? Perhaps. But she knew it was something she wanted to do. Needed to do.

So much was unknown. But first, what was in the package itself? What if she opened it up to find something meaningless?

You know that's not going to be true.

What if it ended up breaking her heart?

It already broke years ago. And it's mending. All this package can do is possibly give me some closure.

She absently thought of the old Bee Gees' song, "How Can You Mend a Broken Heart?" Was that even what it was called? She didn't remember.

Who even uses the word mend *anymore? Besides someone being melodramatic?*

The package. The date. The inn. The church. So much to take in. So much to let go.

Brad Corbin didn't fit into that picture, into her plans. He was a surprise. And she wasn't sure she needed a surprise right now.

At thirty-four years old, she needed to start again. She wasn't too young to hope for something else, for something new, for something good to happen to her.

What about someone else?

She had tried going out with men she met. But every single date had ended in disaster. She hated the cliché that all her dating prospects ended with disaster, but they all had. So far, the one and only good experience had been in Mexico with Brad. But even then, there had been too much she couldn't handle, too much of her past she couldn't release.

So instead, she had turned him away.

Can I really, truly start over again?

It was a prayer. She wanted God to answer her right away. She knew that perhaps he had, but she couldn't let herself dwell on that.

You walked into Brad Corbin's life. Again.

But surely that wasn't a sign. That was simply an accident. They had their chance once and let it pass them by. She couldn't begin again with someone she had turned away.

He might turn me away.

But things had changed.

Tell him the truth.

What would he say or do? Things had gone well in Mexico until they had begun to open up to one another. But in the end she'd been unable to be honest, to tell him the things she wanted to say.

I was different then.

Was it true that you became a new person? She didn't know. She wondered about that. Even Brad said she looked different. Remarkably different.

Was it true? Had she really changed?

She walked back into her bedroom. She saw the half-finished bottle of water and bag of chips that had been her dinner. She still wasn't hungry. Thoughts continued to drift to Brad and his date. His "nothing serious" date.

The clock told her it was nine o'clock.

Anna sat on the edge of the bed and read the three-paneled brochure for the Herrington Inn. She learned the site was a popular venue for conferences, banquets, and weddings. And that it had been first settled by a couple named James and Charity Herrington, who traveled west from Chicago in 1835 in search of a new beginning.

Anna put the brochure down and looked toward the still-open door to the deck. Now, so many years later, someone else had ventured out here in the month of April in search of a new beginning.

Can I really call this a new beginning?

She didn't know. Perhaps it was the inevitable conclusion to a long, sad story.

The fireplace...the bed...the river outside flowing at nighttime... promises made. And forgotten.

She glanced at the package on the end table.

I haven't forgotten. Have you?

* * *

"Is it too late?"

"For what?" Anna asked.

"To talk."

"Where?"

"Here. On the phone."

"Oh, okay."

"No, I'm not going to—"

"That's fine."

"Were you sleeping?"

She thought about lying but couldn't. "No."

"You sure?"

"Yes."

She lay on her back and looked up at the ceiling, wondering where Brad was and what he looked like at this very moment.

"How are you?" he asked.

"A lot different from this afternoon," she answered.

"How so?"

"I'm kidding."

"Oh."

"How was your evening?" She tried not to sound too interested, too desperate for details.

"That's what I wanted to call about."

"What?"

"My evening," Brad said.

"What about it?"

"It ended abruptly. I told the woman I was with—"

"The woman you were with?" Anna interrupted, amused by his phrase.

"Sandy. Sandra."

"Okay."

"I told her about you, about seeing you today and how we met and basically everything."

"Had you ever said anything about me before?"

"I told you, we aren't—"

"Serious," they both said in unison over the phone.

"I'm sure she loved hearing about me."

"I was being honest," Brad said.

"Doesn't surprise me." There was a silence. Anna wondered if her comment had hurt him.

"I just—I couldn't help thinking I should've been doing something with you. I mean…"

"You already had plans."

"It was only our second date."

"Is there going to be a third?"

He chuckled. "I'm thinking probably not."

"I never expected to—"

"I know," Brad replied. "I didn't think I'd move back to Geneva either. Things happened. That's what I want you to know."

"What?"

"When I left Puerto Vallarta, after everything that happened with us, you need to know why I didn't…I didn't give up, Anna. I know you might think that—"

"No—"

"But you have to know I didn't. I just… Well, I did feel embarrassed, hurt, however you'd describe it. I didn't know what to say. And then I got the news that my father had had a stroke. He died during my flight home."

She gasped in surprise. "Brad, I'm so sorry."

"Yeah. I just—I didn't know what to say. I didn't want you to think I was asking for your pity—"

"I wouldn't have thought that."

"Probably not. I was confused. I mean, our time down there—it was sort of this magical fairy tale. I just—"

"I know," she said. "I understand."

"I've wanted to contact you. I just— After the things you said, the stuff you wrote—"

"You weren't the only one who was confused. Part of me still is."

"Then why did you come here? I mean, I was thinking about it. I know you said it was to see your family, but I'm not sure that's really why…"

"No, you're right."

"Then why?"

Anna couldn't tell him. Not over the phone.

"I told you I'll tell you. I'm staying till Sunday. There's time."

"For what?" Brad asked.

"For a lot of things. Answers, I guess."

"What about tonight?"

"It's 11:30, and I'm already in bed."

"Put on some jeans, and let's go to Starbucks."

"Right," Anna said. "I'd look pretty funny."

"It's physically impossible for you to look bad."

Anna laughed. "Tomorrow's almost here. Let's make it tomorrow."

"Do you have plans?"

"Nothing official."

"Can I spend some time with you? No pressure? No weirdness?"

"Well, if there's no weirdness, I'll think about it."

"I'm serious," Brad said.

"You act like I'm frightened of you."

"Not of me. Of us."

"A lot has changed since Puerto Vallarta."

"With what?"

"With me. Don't you remember? You said I looked different."

"I did," Brad said. "So how are you different?"

"In time. Okay?" She turned on her side as if leaning toward him.

"Part of me always thought you'd never want to talk to me again. I had to leave just like that. I never said good-bye."

"It was sort of a crazy time."

"It was my fault," Brad said.

"No. It was mine. So many things couldn't be said. Even now, I don't know where to start."

"Nothing has to be said, Anna. We don't have to dwell on things that happened yesterday."

"Sometimes you do have to."

"Why?" His voice sounded sad, confused.

"I had a great time this afternoon," she said to change the subject.

"Me, too. I haven't felt— Ah, there I go again."

"It's okay."

"What?"

"Don't edit yourself," she said.

"What I wanted to say is I haven't felt that good in a long time. It's like today was meant to be. You know? It felt so natural. Going to Starbucks and chatting with you like it was no big deal. Like it wasn't some strange coincidence or fate that brought you here."

"It'd be nice if it was natural or meant to be."

"And it's not?"

"I should probably get going," Anna said.

"Okay."

"Thanks for calling."

"Anna?"

"Yes."

"I've thought about what an amazing person you are ever since I left you. You still are, you know."

"I'll take that sweet compliment to bed with me," Anna said.

"Good night."

She turned on the light. When her eyes adjusted, she checked her travel alarm. The delicate hands pointed to 2:34. Next to the clock on the table, the package with her name on it still waited.

Anna leaned back against the pillows, took a deep breath, let it out, then glanced at the package again. She couldn't sleep, couldn't wait any longer.

There's no magical time. No magical date. No magic whatsoever except in my head.

But she had to admit her head had been a little loopy recently—ever since she'd realized the date that was pending. The same date that had officially arrived two hours and thirty-four minutes ago—make that thirty-five now. This date. This day.

The realization had hit her in a grocery store, when she noticed the expiration date on a package of sliced turkey. Not the sort of romantic notion one sees in the movies. They don't make scenes for movie stars like Julia Roberts where she's standing in the deli aisle and looks down at her bag of freshly sliced ham costing $3.67 and suddenly realizes that in two months a major milestone will arrive.

Now it had arrived, and Anna knew she couldn't wait any longer.

She reached for the package and fumbled to open the seal. The tape that held it together forced her to rip at it and pierce the container's sides, and she broke a nail before she finally got it open.

Inside was something she wasn't expecting, something so normal she wondered if it indeed was a joke.

Her hand grasped the VCR tape and slipped it out. No note nor label explained its contents. It was a plain black videotape. The kind that could be played in any VCR.

She held it and wondered what could be on it. Ideas came to her—a funny gag reel, a series of movie clips, snippets of her from college, a montage of people talking into the camera. It could be anything—or nothing. But she couldn't help feeling slightly disappointed at what the box contained.

She had imagined many possibilities, most purely romantic. A love letter, though she knew that wasn't likely. A collection of photographs with special meaning—that would make more sense. A poignant gift that would make her marvel at its appropriateness. Something more than this, this ordinary tape.

She glanced across the room at the television housed in its elegant armoire. It wasn't a very big television, but then again, most of the people coming here didn't spend the money to lie around watching movies. When people thought of the Herrington, they envisioned long bubble baths and fireplaces glowing late into the night, not movies and popcorn. Nevertheless, the little TV included a built-in video recorder. And a part of Anna wanted nothing more than to slip this tape right in and watch what was on it.

But a part of her feared what she would find. And yet another part of her hated to give up the anticipation that had brought her here. Once she watched the tape, in a sense, it would all be over.

Wait until later today, she told herself.

She had already opened the package. It wouldn't hurt to let her mind keep on wandering for a while, trying to guess its contents.

Why in the world was it ever made?

And why had it taken her so long to finally view it?

* * *

She walked slowly down the sidewalk this Saturday morning, relishing each step. It could be called nondescript, this neighborhood, this street named Maple, this concrete pathway lined with middle-aged trees and middle-income homes. Yards were plots, squares carved out years ago when neighborhoods followed cookie-cutout diagrams. The houses were ranch homes built on slabs, with dreams of basements and play-rooms and extra space relinquished long ago.

The light blue house she stopped in front of had been recently painted, but the paint job looked like a glamour shot done on a seventy-year-old. No matter how much makeup and color were added to this structure, she would still consider it over the hill.

Staring at the structure, Anna vividly remembered standing here a thousand times, just home from school, preparing to lug her backpack inside and get started on her homework. She found herself amazed at the emotions that touched her as she walked. The last thing she expected to feel was joy.

She had deliberately parked down the block, allowing herself a chance to walk past homes she could picture blindfolded. There was something exciting about this walk, this homecoming of sorts. Anna could barely contain the smile on her lips as she walked up to the front door and knocked.

Chances were high she knew who would answer the door.

"Anna." The word had tried to come out as a shriek, a cry of surprise and joy. Yet the voice failed, and her mother simply choked out her name.

"Surprise," Anna said, hugging her mom for the first time in four years.

"What— Dear, are you okay? Where'd you come from?"

"Everything's fine," Anna said, understanding her mother's con-cern. "I parked down the street. I didn't want to alarm you by parking in the driveway."

"Your father is gone."

"I knew he would be."

Patricia Williams looked up at her tall daughter and began to cry. Anna hugged her mother again and whispered in her ear.

"It's okay. I'm not going anywhere."

* * *

Anna had talked with her mother recently. In fact, their last conversation had been four days ago. But they had not actually seen each other since the funeral. Since the bitter argument with her father. Since her world cracked open and swallowed the last meaningful thing in her life into its empty black hole.

Back then, anger wasn't an emotion. It was a defense, a way of life. And her anger had been directed at anything in her path.

Little had she known how many things would have their beginning at the funeral.

So many things.

She sat at the kitchen table telling her mother about the Herrington, about the decision to come to Illinois, about how her business was doing. Her mother moved restlessly, tidying up the counters while they talked. She asked Anna four times if she wanted her to make coffee before Anna finally let her do it.

"How is everything? In North Carolina?"

Anna glanced at her mother. "It's good."

"Are you in trouble?"

"No." Anna laughed.

"Have you seen your father?"

"No."

"You should see him," her mother said.

"I know. I will. It's just that I wanted to see you first, spend a little time together. And I…I thought maybe you could tell him I was here."

Her mother nodded. "I will."

She had cut her hair, Anna noticed. She couldn't remember ever seeing her mother without the long, flowing hair she'd always encouraged Anna to keep.

"Your hair is pretty. Makes you look younger."

"Thank you," her mother said. "It's easier to manage."

"How long have you had it short?"

"A few years."

Anna nodded, looked down at the wood floor, touched a finger to the corner of her eye to catch a tear.

"So what else is new? How's Dad?"

"He's about the same. Things are the same."

Anna looked around the kitchen and remembered the smells. Certain, distinct smells. Toast. Gas from the stove. Pepper. The wallpaper, the wood floor, even the kitchen table where her father had sat across from her countless times. Sitting in the padded chair, Anna could feel his presence, hear his adamant voice and his unwavering emotion as he shared some conviction with the family. Her father was a man of many convictions, all of them passionately defended.

Including the conviction that his only daughter was going to hell.

She shook her head to resist the familiar thought. She was beyond that kind of thinking now. Or at least wanted to be.

"How are things with you?" Anna asked her mother.

"Pretty good. I've joined a book club. We're reading the latest Scott Turow novel. I was going to go buy it this morning, but then you—"

"I was going to tell you I was coming. This sorta came up out of the blue."

"You sure there's nothing wrong?"

"Yes, I'm sure."

"You wouldn't tell us if there was."

Anna laughed. "That's probably true."

Her mother brought a cup to the table and set it in front of Anna. "Pretty day, isn't it?"

Anna nodded, glanced out the window beside the kitchen table. The long yard with the meticulously kept green lawn looked inviting. Well cut, well fertilized, well maintained, just like everything in Henry Williams's life. Everything except his one and only daughter.

For a moment, Anna found herself at a loss for anything to say. There was so much she wanted to tell her mother. Yet the things she needed most to say seemed impossible to utter, while talking about the weather and the lawn felt easy enough. She searched her mind for a way to start.

"It's nice outside. Do you want to go sit on the patio?"

Patricia studied her daughter. "Sure."

"I've got a lot of things to tell you."

"Good things?"

The joyful look Anna gave her mother answered her question.

* * *

It had turned out better than Anna had dared imagine.

A sense of relief filled her now as she walked down the steps toward the front door of the Herrington. More than relief, in fact. With every step came the powerful sense of being loved, the feeling that every minute here was part of an answer to prayer.

She had known there would be tears when she told her mother why she came. She had always cried easily, a trait she got from her mother. Over the past several years, as she struggled to regain control of her life, she had learned to push the tears away, to numb herself to anger and pain. But lately they had been close to the surface again. And just as she suspected, both she and her mother had been sobbing by the end of the conversation.

Anna's steps felt lighter than usual as she walked down the hall to her room. Her eyes were no longer full, but her ears rang with her mother's loving words.

I've never stopped praying for you.

Her mother's words had soothed her guilt, smoothed aloe over the lost years, massaged her stiff soul.

"I know," Anna had replied. And she knew the prayers had worked. Even now, she could feel the tightness in her soul unwinding, though in the back of her mind lurked a small fear, a slight hesitation.

There's still Dad.

He would question her, of course. Press her, with that eternally skeptical attitude of his. For a while, he would be in disbelief. But in the long run he would be left with nothing to say, because he would have to see how much had changed in her.

She hoped that she could still be strong. And that he could, for once, refrain from preaching. That he could simply tell her and show her how much he loved her. For the first time in many years, she thought both might be possible.

As she opened the door to a freshly cleaned room, she noticed the blinking light on the phone. She thought she knew who had called. She reached for the receiver but then hesitated.

This visit was going as planned except for one thing. One complication she had not counted on.

Brad.

She sat down at the edge of the smooth bedspread and thought for a moment. Part of her said not to answer the phone, not to check voice mails, not to let anything bother her this weekend. Not even Brad.

But he's not really bothering me.

And did she really want to tell herself their meeting here was accidental? She knew it wasn't. Not this weekend. She couldn't shake the conviction that somewhere, somehow God was showing his face in what was happening. She wondered if he wore a grin.

"We're heading downtown."

Brad shifted into fifth gear and nodded his head. They had just merged onto the Eisenhower freeway, and the distant skyline of Chicago winked at them straight ahead.

"And you're not going to tell me what we're doing?"

"Nope," Brad said. "There's a thing called patience."

"Ah. Should I be worried?"

"On a day like this? You know they said it might reach eighty-eight degrees?"

"It feels wonderful now."

"That's about twenty-five degrees warmer than usual for this time of year," Brad said.

"It's 'cause of me. I brought the sunshine."

Brad laughed. "Maybe you did."

"How long have you had this nice little toy?"

"Not long. About six months or so. Just came out."

"Tell me what it is again?"

She knew the car was a two-seater, silver, and built by Nissan. The black leather seats, the fancy control panels, the loud stereo—all of it spelled lots of money.

"It's a 350Z. To be honest, I wish I hadn't been able to get it."

"Too many speeding tickets?" Anna asked.

"No. I bought it with some of the money I got after Dad passed away. It was a fair-size estate, especially after the business was sold. I used a lot getting set up with the studio and all. But this car was my little indulgence. Paid cash for it."

"I really am sorry about your dad. It must have been awful."

His smile was sad and philosophical. "He was a great guy and had a good life. And he went the way he always said he wanted to go—quickly. It helps to know that. It helps to know where he is, too."

The 350Z sped down the Eisenhower, unhindered by the minimal traffic. The closer they got to the city, the more Anna wondered what Brad's surprise would be. When they were about five minutes from the Chicago city limits, she guessed it.

"You should've known the moment I picked you up," Brad told her.

"How come?"

"Note the shirt."

"I'm a ditz."

Brad glanced at her, his face reminding her of a teen's youthful grin. The oversize Chicago Cubs T-shirt looked good on him.

"You might be many things, but you're not a ditz."

"So. Do we have good seats?"

"The best."

The best seats ended up being the only kind Brad would ever consider—the bleacher seats at Wrigley Field, where you paid general admission and fended for yourself. The afternoon game was scheduled to begin around four o'clock. They arrived half an hour before that and managed to find decent seats near the top center of the outfield bleachers. Perhaps Sammy Sosa would slug one out their way.

"How long has it been since you've gone to a baseball game?" Brad asked her.

He was smiling, taking in the crowd, watching the picturesque green of the field below them from behind his shades. Anna could sense how much he loved being there.

"Quite awhile," she told him.

"Is this okay?"

"Yes. Unexpected, but yes. Thank you."

Brad took a sip of his Coke as they watched the batting practice.

"I used to think baseball was everything, you know? I mean, when I was a kid, I used to imagine that the one and only thing I could ever see myself doing was playing ball. First base, probably."

"And now you're just a suffering Cubs fan, right?" She laughed.

"Like every other poor soul out here, yeah. Just when you think they might have a chance, they rip your heart out. I don't follow them too seriously anymore. Actually, I haven't been to a game in a while."

"What about playing?"

"No. I mean, there's softball. But, no."

Brad looked away. She wished she knew what he was thinking. What memories were running through his head? Regrets and unfulfilled dreams? A sadness about the long-lost days of playing baseball? Something else, perhaps something deeper?

"So," she said, "the baseball player became a photographer."

"Yeah," he said with a grunt. "After a thrilling stint as a hotshot executive at Corbin Stone. You should hear some of my friends when I tell them what I do now. I don't think they consider it a real job."

"Whatever a real job is."

"I know. I don't think I ever really considered photography growing up. I mean, I always liked fooling around with a camera. But it's really only been in the last few years that I really discovered my love for taking pictures. I have a decent eye for capturing shots."

Anna pointed to the camera bag strapped over his shoulder.

"You going to capture some good shots of me?" she asked.

"You mind?"

"Only if they're bad."

Brad unzipped the bag and pulled out a small, sleek, silver box.

"I thought your camera was one of those big, heavy jobs."

"Yeah, that's my Nikon. I might get it out later. But this little point-and-shoot Olympus makes surprisingly good shots."

He held up the camera and shot a few photos of her in the seats. He even moved down several rows to take one of the pictures. She felt a little embarrassed when Brad asked people to slide over for a few seconds. His charm and eagerness allowed him to get his way. She wasn't surprised.

He sat down again. "Want a hot dog? burger? anything?"

"How about peanuts when they come by? And let me take some pictures of you."

"Oh no. I'm not very photogenic."

She glanced at the handsome man beside her and laughed.

"That's not true."

"It really is," he said. "If there's ever been a person to mess up family pictures, it's me."

"Oh, come on. You know that's ridiculous. I remember some shots of you I took in Mexico."

"You still have them?"

"Well, not with me, but I got them developed."

"Am I squinting in each of them? Or looking off into no-man's land?"

Anna shook her head. "You look very cute."

"Cute?" he exclaimed. "Cute? That's what every man loves to hear."

"You know what I mean."

"That I'm cute?" Brad said, teasing her.

"Okay. Handsome. Good-looking. Every girl's dream. How's that?"

"Yeah, I'll take that."

"Give me that camera."

Anna took several shots of Brad with the little silver camera. She asked him to take off his sunglasses for the last couple. She wanted to see his blue eyes.

I wonder what he's thinking about all of this?

Before the game started, Brad excused himself for a moment, asking her again if she wanted anything. She said no thanks and watched him sidle past the people next to them. She let the sun warm her face and thought back to the last time she had attended a Cubs game.

That was so long ago.

Her life had turned out so different from what she once expected. Like Brad's dream of playing baseball, her dream of getting married and living happily ever after used to be everything to her. She could still remember the moment when she finally knew it was going to happen, when she was finally asked. For her, it had been an answer to a prayer she had never actually prayed. A gift from a heavenly Father she hadn't completely believed in.

We did come close, she mused. *So close to happily ever after.*

Anna had grown accustomed to not thinking much about the past. There were so many things locked away, barricaded off, silenced. So many names and faces and memories.

Isn't that what this trip was all about? Finally saying good-bye to those names and faces and memories by facing them again?

Going to a Cubs game with Brad wasn't really part of the plan though. What was this anyway? A date? A date for what? Where could it possibly go? She would leave tomorrow and tell him good-bye again—and then what?

What am I thinking?

She already knew the answer—that she wasn't thinking at all. That wasn't what this day was about. She hadn't felt anything like this in a while. Certainly not with the men she had dated recently, the losers she seemed to attract.

But Brad's different, she thought, and then she had to laugh at her own ridiculous thought. Of course he was different. And now she was here with him again, sitting at a game talking about hot dogs and Sammy Sosa. And not really wanting to examine the situation too closely.

I've been angry and hurt too long. It's time I begin to live again. Nothing wrong with having a little fun.

She would have plenty of time to crash down to earth again. Later tonight, for instance, when she played the videotape that was in the package. The tape might well be a disappointment—or worse.

I won't let that possibility spoil the afternoon.

Brad came up beside her holding another soft drink and a bag of peanuts big enough to feed four people.

"Think this will be enough?" he asked.

He sat down next to her and began talking about the lines of people in the concession area. Without hesitation, without thinking, Anna took Brad's hand and held it. It just felt right.

Anna sat on a bench gazing out across Lake Michigan. If you didn't know otherwise, you could almost believe this was an ocean. Sailboats and other vessels skimmed over the tranquil waters in front of them, coming into port as daylight slowly evaporated. Brad sat next to her, his sunglasses off, his shaved face red from the sun. She noticed the contentment on his face as he stared at the horizon.

"You're burned," she told him.

"Can't help it. That's what I get for being blond."

She took a bite of her ham-and-cheese sub. They had purchased sandwiches down the street at a small deli after joining the mass exodus from Wrigley Field. Anna had asked if they could eat them by the lake.

"Are you sure this is okay?" Brad asked her.

"Of course it is. It was my idea, wasn't it?"

"A thousand incredible restaurants in Chicago, and you want a ham sandwich to go."

"I ate a lot of peanuts at the ballpark."

"That was the longest two-to-one game I've ever been to," Brad said.

"Sorry about your Cubs."

"Hey, you're a fan too."

"I gave up on them after I left Chicago."

Brad laughed. He had already finished his sandwich.

"Tell me something," he said to her.

"Yes."

"Why'd you come back to the area? I know you said you were going to tell me, and I've waited, and you still haven't said anything."

"I know."

He waited for more of an answer. Anna took a final bite of her sandwich and thought about what she wanted to say.

"Awhile ago—a few months ago—I was going through some old stuff. Stuff that had been put in boxes when I moved. I wasn't sure I'd ever open them again, but for some reason I decided to go through them. I found something that I wanted to open here, in Illinois."

Brad looked at her without blinking.

"What was it?"

Anna took a deep breath, not sure she wanted to tell him, wondering how he would respond.

"It was a package," she said.

He simply nodded, the expression on his face neutral.

"It was given to me on my honeymoon," Anna added. "I never

really paid much attention to it. I mean, I was supposed to open it if…"

She glanced at him, wondering if she could continue. Brad obviously wanted her to, even if she needed to compose herself and strengthen her voice.

"I was supposed to open it if we ever went through tough times. If I ever—we ever—fell out of love. I mean, I thought it was just a symbol or something like that. Then—after the divorce and everything—it was so many years afterward that I simply forgot."

"Did you open it?" Brad asked carefully.

"Yes. It's a videotape." She sniffled and tried to regain her composure. "I was going to watch it tonight."

Brad simply nodded, not saying anything more.

"It's probably stupid. I mean, I know it's stupid. But that's the main reason I came here. To open it."

"Why?"

"Because this is where it was given to me."

"I don't think that's stupid," Brad said.

"It's just something I have to do. On my own."

Brad nodded. "I understand. I think."

"Then tomorrow, I'm going to go to church. Dad's church."

Brad's eyes leveled on her.

"Really?"

"Yeah. It's been a while. I think maybe it's time."

"I thought church was one of those things other people did, not you."

Anna felt a little better, knowing that the discussion had changed a bit and that Brad wasn't pushing her for any more information.

"Do you know that before I left Mexico, I prayed? Prayed for the first time in years?"

"Why?" Brad asked.

"Because of you."

"Because of me?"

"Everything you said back there about…your beliefs and all. You handled it so delicately. That was something new for me. I mean, faith always got jammed down my throat growing up. I wasn't used to someone talking about something other than sin and hell."

"I was just telling you the things I'd been through."

"That's what impressed me so much," Anna said.

"I just finally got to a point where I knew I couldn't do things on my own."

She nodded. "It's taken me awhile to get there. Even after Mexico, it took awhile."

An understanding filled Brad's face. She was grateful that he didn't push for more. Instead, he gave her a small smile. "Your father's church tomorrow. That's a big step for you."

"Is it? I feel like a coward for being away so long."

"You're not." Brad took her hand and held it.

A slight breeze lifted strands of her hair and blew them in front of her face. Brad gently moved them away so he could see her.

In that moment Anna wanted to say so much, to open up and tell him everything and anything, to just forget the past and let the future be what it could be. But she didn't. She couldn't.

"Remember that glorious sunset in Puerto Vallarta?" Brad said, looking out over the lake.

Anna nodded.

"Do you remember what I asked?"

Anna wrinkled her lips. She would carry that memory for the rest of her life.

"Of course I do."

"Should I ask again?"

"No. Not right now."

She moved over and touched his lips with her hand, then kissed them even as she continued to smile. The kiss lasted a long moment, and Anna felt her body shudder as Brad brushed her cheek with his hand. He was the one to finally pull back.

"Anna, I…," he began, stammering for the right words. "I never thought this could happen again."

"Maybe it's not happening. Maybe this is…I don't know—"

"*Something's* happening," he said. "You know it too. Maybe it was meant to."

She pulled back a little and examined his face. "Do you really believe that—that certain things are meant to be?"

"I think so," Brad said.

She studied him for a long minute more. "I used to think that too. But then I woke up one morning, and my life was totally turned around. Everything I thought was meant to be disappeared, just like that. So I get a little nervous when I hear that phrase."

Brad took her hand and looked intensely into her eyes.

"I understand why you might feel that way. I really do. But I've come— I mean I believe that everything does work together somehow. That God has a plan for how things turn out, even if we can't see it at the time. I think your coming here—now— This really could be meant to happen."

"Or not," she said, though she wanted it to be true.

Brad kissed her cheek, his touch gentle. He whispered into her ear.

"Don't you think that sometimes we're given second chances?"

"I thought that in Mexico," Anna began, her words drifting into nothing.

"What?"

"I thought that's what I was being given."

"Then what went wrong?"

"I was afraid."

Brad kissed her again. "Are you afraid now?"

"Very."

The trip back to the suburbs was short and quiet. They spoke in spurts, but both were tired from the earlier conversation. Brad still held her hand, still let her speak about whatever she wanted to. But in no way did he push her. Sometimes he simply fell silent, lost in his own thoughts.

They pulled up to the Herrington Inn around nine o'clock. After everything that had happened between them, the words and emotions expressed, the intimacy of their kisses, Anna didn't know how to end this evening.

"I don't know if I should tell you good night," Anna said.

"I don't want you to. But I probably should anyway."

"I know."

"This day—"

"I know," Anna repeated. She did know how he felt. The words and feelings inside her were too complex for mere words to do them justice.

"Are you going to watch the video tonight?"

"I think so."

"And if you do, tell me this. Will anything change?"

"I don't know."

"So then what is the point?" Brad asked.

She sensed confusion in his voice.

"I don't understand."

"I mean, how will things be different if you watch it?"

Anna thought for a moment. She had never considered *not* watching it.

"I don't know if they will. I just…I just need to see what's on it."

"Do you? I mean, really, do you?"

Anna looked at Brad and didn't understand what he was trying to say.

"I probably should go." She opened the door, and the inside light of the car came on.

"You can't change the past, Anna," Brad said to her.

"I know that."

"Reliving it all, watching this video—"

"Brad, why do you *not* want me to do this?"

Brad swallowed and gripped the steering wheel. He glanced down for a moment.

"'Cause the guy who gave it to you is gone, Anna. He's no longer around. And he's not coming back either. Not tonight, and not tomorrow. I'm sorry to say that, but it's true. You have to move on."

"That's what I'm trying to do. Don't you see?"

"You have your whole future ahead of you, Anna. It doesn't have to start tomorrow, Anna. Why can't it start now? Today? You know how they say this is the first day of the rest of your life? Why can't that be the case for you? For…"

"For what?" Anna asked.

"For us."

Anna looked at him confused, surprised.

"No matter what happens tomorrow, I need to deal with my life up till now. That was my whole point in coming here."

Brad shook his head, his body language calling a truce and giving up.

"If I don't watch the tape," she said, "I'll always wonder what was on it."

"It's all right. I understand."

"I don't want to end an incredible day with you upset at me," Anna said.

"I'm not upset with you," Brad said. "I'm…" He stopped for a moment, then finished by saying "crazy about you."

"Do you want to go to church with me tomorrow?"

He shook his head. "I should probably let you go on your own."

She studied him for a moment and thought about his answer. And realized he was probably right.

"My flight leaves tomorrow afternoon," she said.

"Can I see you before you leave?" he asked.

"I would hope so."

Brad smiled. "This time I'll see you before one of us leaves."

Anna leaned over and kissed him on the cheek.

"You're a surprising man, Brad Corbin."

"I hope…the video and all—"

"It will be fine," Anna said. "Good night."

She walked away from the car and forced herself not to turn around and wave like a teenager might wave to her jock boyfriend dropping her off for the night.

So long ago.

Fifteen years, in fact. Fifteen years to the day.

April 24.

At this hour fifteen years ago, in this very room, she'd been preparing to go to bed a new bride. At nineteen years of age, she had believed that her future would be glorious and happy and that all her dreams could and would come true. As long as they were together, all would be wonderful.

It hadn't happened that way, of course. The dreams that weren't shattered eventually withered away. Happiness had ceased to be an expectation. At one point she'd tried to assign blame, but now she knew that blame was beside the point.

They had tried to do it on their own. They'd tried to build a relationship on their own terms and their own promises, with God as nothing more than a colored backdrop in a photographer's studio. No wonder they had failed. The wonder was that they had held on as long as they did.

But now it was over, and she refused to dwell anymore on what had gone wrong. The whole point of this trip was to take the last step. The last step in coming to terms with those lost, past years.

Anna turned on the TV and slipped the videotape into the recorder. The first few seconds of the video showed an empty bed in what looked to be a hotel room. With a start, she recognized the room. The bedspread was different. But the background, the layout of the room looked the same. It was the same room she was sitting in now, the same bed where she now lay crosswise, chin on her hands, watching.

A man dressed in black tuxedo pants and a white shirt unbuttoned at the top entered the picture. He called her name and looked into the camera and smiled.

Seeing him again caused her to stop breathing.

"You don't know I'm filming this. You're still back at the reception with everyone else. And you might think I'm crazy. When you play this, you probably will. But there are some things you need to know. Some things I need to say right now, this night."

For another ten minutes, the video played. And with each second, the rift in her heart grew deeper. Seeing him like that, hearing his words, knowing he spoke of a love and a marriage that would fail just six short and miserable years later—it was too much for Anna to bear.

Perhaps she shouldn't be watching. She should have heeded Brad's warning that she couldn't change the past, that it was gone, that the young man in the video camera was no more. Yet she sat there mesmerized, in tears, shaking, listening to each word he said.

This is the first day of the rest of your life.

Anna wondered how she could have made such a mess of it up to now but thought she knew part of the answer.

But you're starting over again.

The video message ended, and the screen turned to fuzzy static, then went black. She turned it off and lay there in the darkness of her room. She continued to cry.

Why, God? Why was I allowed to see that so many years later? After everything? Why did I even have to find that video?

Deep down, she already sensed the gleam of an answer. It lay there shining in the depths of her heart, not yet ready to emerge. It had something to do with why, on this of all days, she had been allowed to watch this long-lost message from her long-lost husband.

She lay there alone, begging God to give her peace, hope, love, anything.

Maybe Brad will call.

But he never did. Anna fell asleep still draped sideways over the bed. Letting go. Letting it all go.

Tomorrow will be a new day.

Anna wore a flowing red skirt and a white blouse. She listened to the closing benediction from the tall, tight-lipped pastor with lush gray hair and a thinly cut white beard. She sat in the fifth row from the pulpit, close to the center aisle, and watched him walk down the aisle next to her in order to stand at the back of the church and greet the congregation as they left for Sunday lunch. He didn't acknowledge her. Didn't even look at her.

She stood up and breathed in.

Be strong.

She walked out of the pew and up the same aisle her father had led her down on her wedding day. It was one thing having a father lead you down to the man of your dreams and give you away. It was another to have that same father step onto the platform to perform the wedding ceremony.

Pastor Henry Williams stood near the main entryway talking with some members. Anna knew he had seen her as he preached on a text from Matthew. She knew he was aware of her presence right away. Yet he continued with his duties. As she approached him now, he remained upright and undistracted as he spoke to an elderly couple.

"Dad," she said.

He nodded his head and held out a hand that said *just a minute.* He listened to the couple and let out a laugh, a little more exaggerated than it should have been. Anna stood to the side, waiting for her father to greet her, maybe even to hug her or introduce her to these people he spoke to. She stood, waiting. Waiting.

More than four years since she had last seen her father, Anna stood waiting for him to admit he'd seen her.

The pastor glanced at her briefly and continued talking. Anna felt that enough was enough. She began to walk away, toward the doors of the church and away from this place once and for all.

"Annie. Wait."

She closed her eyes, fighting back tears. She had cried enough of them in the last two days to last her for another year, possibly another decade.

Anna turned back and saw the wounded, hurt face of a father she didn't recognize.

"Please," he was saying, "please don't go."

She didn't know what to say. For a moment she had been sure he wouldn't say a word to her, wouldn't acknowledge her, would turn his back on her just as he had years ago. Now he was walking toward her. Waiting for her to say something. Anything.

And there would be much to say. Much that he would want to hear. Good things, too. Things that any pastor and father would cherish knowing about a wayward daughter who had finally come home.

The first day of the rest of your life.

There would be time for all that. But now she simply threw herself into his outstretched arms.

"Oh, Annie," he said, letting go a long sigh.

It had been years since anybody called her by that name.

"I'm sorry, Dad. I'm so sorry."

He looked at her with broken eyes. "The Lord is gracious. Even when we're not." He gave her a sad smile, and she realized he was talking about himself and not her. Those words and that smile said more than an apology ever could.

They walked out of the church together. For Anna, for now, it was enough. All she had hoped for, all she had wanted, was for him to be at her side.

The rest would come.

* * *

Anna stood in the Herrington's octagon-shaped atrium, which over-looked the Fox River. The water outside flowed gently, the sun brilliant in the clear sky. Anna had been surprised to find the doors open, had walked in to remember the place where her wedding reception had been held.

"Hey," a voice called from behind her, "I've been looking for you."

"I'm here."

"Thought I might find you here."

She turned around to see Brad. He wore a blue suit with a light blue shirt and yellow tie.

"You look nice," she said. She still wore her church outfit. There hadn't been time to change before Brad arrived to take her to the airport.

"How was church and everything?"

"Fine. He actually talked to me."

"That's good. Right?"

She nodded. "We left things on a positive note. He promised they'd come out to visit me. Soon."

"That's great."

"Yeah. Some things. I don't think we'll ever completely get over what happened between us. But at least he's acknowledging that I exist."

Brad nodded and walked up beside her.

"This is quite romantic in here," he said.

She grinned. "I've always thought so."

"So…shall we dance?" he gave a comic sweep of his arm.

She smiled but shook her head. "I have to go soon."

He nodded, suddenly serious, and she felt the melancholy creep over her. How could she say good-bye? Again?

"Tell me," he said, "how was…everything last night? Did you watch the tape?"

"I think you were right," Anna said.

"How so?"

"I hoped that watching that tape would help me let it all go. You know, just put it on a little boat and watch it drift out onto the river and float away. But it didn't work."

"Maybe not. But do you really want it to?"

Anna stood gazing at the river through one of the open patio doors.

"It was so long ago anyway," she said. "People change. The video—
It was probably foolish even to go there."

Brad walked up beside her and put a hand on her shoulder. She
slowly turned around to see him in the process of kneeling on the
wooden floor.

"What—"

"Anna, I want you to know something. Before you leave."

"Brad—"

"I want you to know that…if the stars somehow all fall, and the sun
gets stuck…" He smiled, and something passed between them.

"And if somehow this feeling I have fades, I want you to remind me
of this moment."

"How?" Her voice was shaking.

"I never said good-bye to you in Mexico. I let you go. I don't want
to let you go again."

"Brad—"

"I know you'll never be able to forget about the past. I don't even
want you to. But I also know I want to grow old with you. I want to
never give up on you."

Anna started to say *stop it,* but she couldn't find the strength to do
so. Her hands trembled as he took them into his own, and her mind
raced in a dozen directions.

"Anna Williams, will you marry me?"

how…God, please…what

She shook her head, wiped tears she didn't know were there, and
laughed at the familiar face smiling up at her.

the first day of the rest of your life

How could he—

"Anna?"

She didn't know what to say. She remembered his words—not typical words for a man like him. Carefully thought-out words.

If the stars somehow all fall, and the sun gets stuck…

"Marry me, Anna Williams. Marry me and never leave me."

the first day of the rest of your life

And in the next instant she realized she could do it. She really could see living that life with this man. This kind and gentle man, this careful soul who wanted the best for her. She could see growing older with Brad Corbin. Regardless of what had happened before. She knew he could help her let it go.

Anna inhaled, and her body shook. Then she smiled and nodded and finally knelt to kiss the man she would grow old with.

PUERTO VALLARTA

"I swear, she looked just like Denise."

Brad glanced at his friend and made a moaning sound.

"When was the last time you saw her?" he asked Jay.

The stocky, dark-haired figure next to him shrugged. "I don't know. A few months ago."

"A few months?"

"Yeah. She came by work one day when you were out."

"You serious?" Brad asked.

"Yeah. Looking for your father."

"Oh. He told me about that. Looking for more money."

"And?" Jay asked.

"He gave it to her. You know how he is. He'd give a crack addict money if he thought he was a nice guy."

"You're comparing your ex to a crack addict. Yet another reason I'm never getting married."

Brad shook his head, his eyes examining the pool from behind amber-tinted shades.

"I was making a point about Dad."

"And about Denise."

"Whoever you saw, it wasn't Denise," Brad said. "She has a phobia about going anywhere outside the U.S. That's why we ended up going to Florida for our honeymoon."

"What? She thought you'd get sick or something?"

"Yeah. I told her most of these resorts are safe—the water and everything. But she wouldn't listen to me."

"Fairly typical for you and Denise, right?" Jay asked, sounding serious.

"Shut up."

Jay finished off the beer in his plastic cup. "I'm getting another one. Maybe I'll go find her and see if she really is Denise."

"That wasn't Denise," Brad said.

"It'd sure make for an interesting time, huh?" Jay laughed. "Want anything?"

"I'm fine."

"Remember, you're on vacation. You can loosen up a little, pal."

Jay stood, wearing only red trunks and sandals. His farmer's tan made his arms, neck, and face several shades darker than the rest of him.

"And you can get a little sun. Man, that's embarrassing."

"This is from a little thing you might not know. It's called *work*."

Brad feigned a laugh as his friend sauntered off toward the bar next to the pool. He closed his eyes and turned his face up toward the sun. His forehead and shoulders were already dotted with sweat. Only three hours into his vacation he could feel the strain of the last week, and the last year, slowly evaporate.

He thought of Denise and then reminded himself what he was doing here. Taking a vacation. Getting away. Going on a trip with a friend.

And, oh yeah, contemplating changing my whole life.

Brad took a sip of his soda and chewed on the remaining cube of ice. He noticed Jay walking back, taking his time and eyeing the women around him.

"Here, I brought you one just in case," Jay told him, setting the cup of beer down next to Brad's lawn chair.

"It's just going to get warm."

"C'mon man. One beer isn't going to damage your soul."

"No. But going to Mexico with you might," Brad joked, prompting a hearty laugh from Jay.

"Oh yeah, by the way. I saw the girl again. Not Denise."

"Told you."

"She took off her glasses and looked about forty-five years old. Leathery skin, too."

"Yeah, that sounds just like Denise."

"She had the same hair, though. Dark, sort of a modern cut."

"I'm going to cut you off," Brad joked, glancing at the cup in Jay's hand.

"No way. I'm getting my money's worth. All inclusive, baby."

Brad leaned back in the lawn chair and closed his eyes. For the moment, he didn't think about anything. The exhaustion had caught up with him. With a hundred different thoughts that could have battled against each other, he waved a white flag and now heard nothing but silence.

The lull would be short lived, he knew. Right now he intended to take full advantage of whatever peace he could find.

The clock in the room said it was 6:45 in the evening, but Brad didn't believe it. By now he had usually eaten dinner and settled into his spot on the couch to watch television. It wasn't that he enjoyed TV all that much, but he needed the relaxation it provided. The escape from his worries and regrets.

Now, many miles away from his couch in scenic Puerto Vallarta, the regrets seemed far away. He didn't feel hungry even though he still hadn't eaten dinner. And he didn't feel tired since he'd been lounging around all day. He might as well have gotten rid of the clock. Who needed it?

He opened the bag on his chair and took out the heavy camera. The Nikon F2 felt good in his hands. Substantial. Nowadays everyone had their tiny digital cameras. But Brad had learned photography as a kid from a friend of his father's—learned the art of adjusting shots and composing pictures in the viewfinder. He'd even tried his hand at darkroom work. As far as he was concerned, there was no comparison. He couldn't see ever letting go of the standard way of shooting and processing photos.

One of the things Brad had looked forward to on this vacation was finally having enough time to get in some good shots. Not of the resort necessarily, but of the surrounding countryside and the beach and the sunrises and sunsets. It had been a while since he'd carried the camera with him. Now he felt like a hunter finally reclaiming his long-lost rifle, or a fisherman holding his favorite tackle.

Wasn't that really what this trip was all about—embracing some long-lost dreams? Remembering who he used to be and grabbing hold of the passion he used to feel back when he was in school? Not that he wanted to go back, even if he could. There was so much more he wanted to do in his life. But there were parts of himself he wanted to reclaim. If all went as planned, who knew what could happen?

The door to the room opened, and Jay walked in. He looked darker from the half-day's worth of sun. A tank top covered his hairy chest.

"This place is like a singles' heaven."

"What do you mean?" Brad asked.

"There're lots of women around here on their own. In groups of two or four. Some of these resorts only have married couples and families."

"I told you you'd like it."

"Some of the women could be friendlier though," Jay said, taking a chair near the window.

Brad put the camera back into his suitcase and sat on the edge of the bed. His hair was still damp from the shower. "What'd you do now?"

"I saw a couple of ladies out by the pool lounging, so I went up to them. Both of them very fine. I was thinking, it'd be fun hanging out with girls like that this trip."

"That's *you* thinking, not me."

"Seriously, these girls were hot. I'm tellin' you. Anyway, I went up to them and started talking and got major attitude. Total cold shoulder."

"Maybe they don't want to be picked up on their vacation," Brad said.

"I was just making conversation. I told them about you. I don't know—they really didn't want to talk."

"I can relate," Brad said.

"No, listen. You gotta help me. I told them I'd bring you around. They'll think you're cute. Girls always do. Then I'll have a shot."

"So you want to use me as bait?"

"I'm telling you, you gotta see them. Anna and Kiersten."

"What did you say?"

"Anna and Kiersten. Anna's tall and dark-haired, and Kiersten's a blonde. I forget where they're from. Well, actually, they didn't tell me."

Brad thought about his friend's interaction with Anna and Kiersten and winced. He could picture the women and the glares they'd given Jay. How could he possibly talk to them after Jay had tried to pick them up? "So what'd you say?"

"Nothing. Just small talk. I don't know—they were annoyed. The tall one actually stood up and left."

"And they didn't say anything else?"

Jay thought for a moment and shook his head. "No, not really."

"You need to tone it down a bit."

"I will. I was just being friendly."

"You can come across a bit strong," Brad said.

"But wouldn't it be cool to have some people to hang out with during our vacation? Some girls, I mean?"

"Sure, but don't force the issue."

"I'm not forcing anything," Jay said.

"Well, how about you force a shower right now?"

"You saying I stink?"

"I'm saying there might be certain odor issues. Hey, maybe if you clean yourself up some and shave that chest of yours, the women won't run away in repulsion."

"Hey, you're just jealous of my manly mane," Jay said with a smirk as he grabbed some clothes and headed for the shower.

Brad wondered if they would run into the women Jay had met and surely offended. He mostly hoped they didn't, that the night would pass without seeing Anna and Kiersten. He could envision an awkward, embarrassing meeting if they ran into them.

Then again, another part of him hoped they would. He thought of Jay's comment.

Wouldn't it be cool to have some people to hang out with during our vacation?

Brad wondered if they stood a chance.

The ocean rustled in the background. Brad and Jay walked back from the restaurant talking and laughing about work. Jay had worked with Brad at his father's stone company for the past four years. This was the third vacation the two of them had taken together.

"I'm telling you, that guy was out cold. We walked in, and he was still in the corner from the night before."

Brad laughed. "Dad should fire him."

"At least he's not a driver. Can you imagine?"

"Yeah. I could see him driving into a Dunkin' Donuts shop."

They walked through an open door toward the grand lobby with its high, arched ceilings and plush couches.

"Hey, there they are," Jay said.

"Where?" Brad felt his stomach sink.

"Over there. Playing chess. Hey, they play chess. Maybe they're smart."

"Do you know how to play chess?"

"No."

"Right," Brad said, standing still, close to the corner leading to the elevators.

The tall dark-haired woman sat with her back toward them. Brad looked at the friendly-appearing blonde who talked and giggled with her friend. Looked at the long, slim tan back in its thin-strapped sundress. Looked and just stood there as if paralyzed.

Anna and Kiersten.

"Let's just go over there," Jay urged.

"No, I don't think—"

"Come on," Jay said. "What's the worst that could happen?"

Brad shook his head. He could think of several worst-case scenarios.

"I just don't think so, man."

"We go over there, and if they want us to leave, we'll leave."

"I just...I don't know."

"Come on. You're a single man now, you know. You've gotta get back in circulation. And didn't you tell me when you picked this place that you might be willing to meet someone new?"

might be willing

Brad nodded, remembering his comments to Jay.

someone new

"Yeah, I just—I don't think tonight's the right time."

"Why?"

"I want to figure out what to say," Brad said.

"Say anything. Come on."

"No."

"Aw, come on. Look. They're both hot."

Brad found himself looking away.

What am I doing here?

The same voice answered his own question.

I don't know.

He looked toward Anna and Kiersten and knew he wanted more than anything to simply go up and make casual conversation. He just wondered if it would happen the way he hoped it would. And wondered if he could ever be ready for this.

"Tomorrow, okay?" he told his friend.

"Weak," Jay said.

"Hey, feel free to talk to them on your own."

"I'm telling you, they'll get up and leave again."

"Tomorrow," Brad said to him. "I promise."

"Okay. You don't lie. I know you. I'll hold you to it."

Brad had begun to walk away from the lobby when he heard the laughter from behind him. And froze in place, remembering.

His life had once been filled with laughter like that.

Would he ever have a chance to get it back?

Brad sat in a lounge chair reading the *USA Today* the hotel supplied when she breezed past and settled on a spot facing the center fountain in the pool. The sun hovering overhead, his sunglasses shielding his eyes, Brad stopped watching the people in the pool doing aerobics and let his eyes float onto the dark-haired woman.

Anna, he thought.

He noticed she was alone. And that she looked beautiful. And that she hadn't noticed him.

She stretched out in the chair, long legs crossed in front of her. Elegant fingers with manicured nails held a paperback book. Her dark hair was tucked up under a big straw hat. Her one-piece swimsuit fit well but was obviously not new.

Beyond her, past the palm trees and the kiosks that served food and beverages all day long, past a sandy beach littered with sunbathers and parasailors, the Pacific breathed in and out with vigor. Even twenty-four hours after arriving, Brad couldn't believe he was here.

He could still hear his conversation with his father.

"You're going where?" his father had asked him on the phone.

"Puerto Vallarta."

"Puerto what?"

"Puerto Vallarta, Mexico."

"And what's down there?"

"Resorts. Relaxation. Fun."

"You don't have to go out of the country for that."

"It'll be great."

"What's the place called?" his dad had asked.

"Escape Resorts."

"Well, I just hope it isn't one of those sex-crazed resorts I've heard about. Make sure people wear their bathing suits."

"A very reputable person told me about this place."

"Make sure you get back in time for the Cambridge project," his father had said.

Once Jay heard about the location and the all-inclusive package, he had insisted on accompanying him. Initially Brad had planned on going alone, but having Jay along would be a buffer against boredom. Or against something. He didn't know what to expect from this trip. And it had been years since he had gone anywhere exotic and tropical on vacation.

But is this really a vacation? he asked himself as he peered up into the spotless sky and then over toward the ocean. A dot roamed the horizon, attached by strings to a boat below. He told himself he needed to try parasailing, along with everything else he could sign up for.

How about signing up to change my life?

The dance music blared as the water aerobics gang in the pool continued to bust a move. Perhaps Brad wouldn't volunteer for *everything*. He tried to imagine his father in the water, flailing his arms and jigging his body around as the tanned and attractive woman instructed him in what to do. The image didn't really work.

Brad looked at his watch. 10:37. It was already getting hot, and in his T-shirt and shorts, he felt slightly out of place. He decided to walk around instead of just sitting at the poolside.

He wanted to talk to the woman who had just passed him. But stepping up to a woman in a bathing suit as she lay back with her eyes closed only made him look like a creep. Besides, what would he say? *Hi, there, I'm Brad. I've been admiring you. Care to come back home with me?*

He cringed at the awfulness of the possibilities. His first words—his first sentence—had to be thought through. He didn't want to go up to her and say the first thing that popped into his mind. He'd done that enough in his life, and it had never gotten him anywhere.

Brad stood and began to walk. He glanced in the direction of the lounging woman, but then looked away and headed toward the steps that led up into the open-air dining room.

He could imagine this resort in some commercial for newlyweds. Ah, yes. The long beach. The three-sectioned pool with a fountain bubbling like champagne in its center. The perfectly manicured lawns and the graceful trees and the greenery surrounding the water. An Aztec-style hotel building aligned in a V to allow most of its occupants a luxurious view of the ocean. A courtyard with various games like Ping-Pong and archery and life-size chess to choose from. Tennis courts. "Nonmotorized sports" like volleyball and Frisbee on the beach. Food and drink available at all hours. And everything for a low, low all-inclusive price.

He half expected to hear Enya's angelic voice in the background singing "sail away, sail away, sail away."

Brad thought of his roommate—still sleeping, no doubt. He wondered what Jay would do if he took a pitcher of ice water and poured it over him to wake him up.

That's a great idea, he thought and headed toward a bar to request the pitcher.

At 1:30, with a bottle of water in hand and worn out by the sweltering sun, Brad entered the shade of the roofed dining area and let his eyes adjust to the relative dimness. He wore a bathing suit dried from the sun and a T-shirt oily with suntan lotion, and he kept his sunglasses on as he examined the multilevel area. An amazingly white, European man asked if he wanted to sit for lunch.

"I'll be sitting over there with someone."

"Certainly," the host said, bowing and letting Brad pass.

The flexibility of the staff and the relaxed schedule of meals and activities made this resort a luxury. One moment you could be wading in the pool, then you could dry off and slip on a T-shirt and find a seat in the dining area. You could get a plate full of any of a hundred different things—fruit or pasta or meat or salad or even a turkey sandwich. Someone would ask what you wanted to drink, then you could eat as you looked out on the Pacific.

Breakfast was served like this from 7:00 until 11:00. Lunch from 11:30 to 2:30. And dinner from 5:00 until 8:00. You could eat and then wade in the pool and hope to avoid any nasty charley horses that dared to follow.

Brad took a deep breath and used his fingers as a comb to straighten his thick, messy hair. He approached the table for two that stood next to a plant-covered stone wall that separated the dining area from the pool below. Anna sat with her back to him, facing the ocean and the empty place of her friend, who had left only minutes ago.

He cleared his throat to let her know someone behind her was about to speak. He didn't want this first encounter to start with his sneaking up on her.

"Excuse me."

"I'm fine," she said before she realized he wasn't a waiter.

"I don't work here," he said to the puzzled face that turned to him and stared.

He decided to say something before she did.

"I know this is going to sound odd, but I'm really wondering. Did you have the chicken today? I'm just curious. I'd like to know how it tastes."

She continued to gaze up at Brad with her mouth slightly open. She started to say something, then stopped herself. She looked around the dining area to see if anyone else was near.

"I, uh… Look, I know this is weird and all. But I just happened to be here, and, well, I noticed you sitting alone."

Her expression of surprise quickly turned to…something else. Something unreadable. She carefully laid her napkin on her plate and glanced up again at Brad, her eyes now penetrating and unfazed.

"My friend just left," her voice said.

"Mind some company?" Brad tried, knowing anything he said would sound like a bad line.

"I was actually enjoying the solitude."

"Yeah. I can relate. I'm here with someone. Actually, you met him yesterday. Dark, burly sort of fella. Sorta annoying."

"There are lots of those around here."

"Yeah. Well, we just got here yesterday."

Anna raised her eyebrows and nodded. He couldn't tell if she was about to smile or to tell him to get lost.

"And how'd you find out about this resort?"

He hesitated. "A distant relative told me about it."

"This person—your relative—ever been here before?" Anna asked.

"No, but my relative knows someone who comes here once a year."

"Ah. So, are you enjoying yourself?" she asked.

He studied her. Her voice sounded upbeat and friendly. Confident, sure of itself. But also a bit formal. Noncommittal. "This place is amazing," he said.

"Quite," she replied, a smile on her face.

What's behind that smile? Brad wondered.

He still stood next to her chair.

"Look, I promise I won't bother you."

"Too late for that," she said.

"Okay, I mean I promise I won't offend you. Or I'll try not to. What's wrong with a little conversation between two strangers?"

She looked at him, studied him. He knew that this was a crucial moment, that if he passed this hurdle, the rest would come more easily.

Finally she shrugged. "I guess there's nothing wrong with it."

"So if I sit, will you leave?" Brad asked.

She shook her head and watched him carefully as he sat across from her.

"I'm uh… My name is Brad Corbin."

A half-smile showed off a flash of white teeth. For a moment Brad wondered if she would even answer him.

"Brad Corbin. Interesting last name."

"I think it's Latin."

"Really. Now there's something I didn't know at the beginning of the day."

Brad chuckled.

The woman's eyes dimmed a bit, still studying Brad, carefully weighing each word she said.

"And you're Anna."

"Am I supposed to believe you just guessed that?"

"No, it's Jay—my friend. You'll see him eventually; he's cleaning up our room right now. He's the one I just mentioned. He met you and Kiersten yesterday."

"Ah. Your little spy."

"More like my big spy," Brad said.

"And he's cleaning up the room? Don't they have maids who can do that?"

"I sort of woke him up with a pitcher of ice water this morning."

She tightened her full lips and nodded.

"Mature," she said.

A waiter came by to ask if they needed anything. Another hurdle. She could have exhausted all the light banter she felt comfortable with, and this interruption would give her the opportunity to excuse herself. Instead, she ordered a strawberry daiquiri.

"So, Mr. Brad Corbin." Anna stated the last name authoritatively. "Do you plan on eating any lunch?"

"Probably. Although I have this feeling that if I go to get some, I'll find this table empty when I get back."

"You're a pretty smart man."

"I guess that's better than being a pretty man."

She laughed at the joke. *That's good,* he thought. *Laughter's good. Maybe she's laughing at you.*

That still wouldn't be bad. Amusement, even the kind directed at him, would be better than annoyance or confusion. Better than any feeling that might tell her to get up and get far away from this guy.

He glanced at her and felt overwhelmed at how beautiful she was. Long-lashed dark eyes. Softly curving full lips. For a moment he couldn't say anything.

"Tell me, Anna, what brings you to Puerto Vallarta?" he started, trying for small talk.

"Look," she said, "I think I should tell you something. Be completely honest with you."

He raised his eyebrows, disconcerted by the sudden change of direction.

Anna stood up.

I blew it. I did something wrong. I knew it. There was no way this was going to work.

"The chicken isn't bad," Anna said.

"What?"

"The chicken. You were asking about it. And I can honestly tell you it's pretty good."

He nodded, still uncertain whether she was mocking him or just being playful.

"I'm going to leave now. It was nice meeting you, Brad Corbin."

She emphasized his last name again. This caused him to smile.

"Maybe I'll see you around," he said to her.

"Of course you will." This time she grinned as she walked away.

Ocean waves. Sand between the toes. Shelter from the sun underneath one of the tiki huts. Watching. Reading. Hoping to see her again.

The afternoon blinked by, and Brad felt lightheaded, lighthearted—just generally light. Light as if he could float up high and look down like one of those parasailors drifting high in the breezes of the surf's tide below. He had imagined the earlier conversation going all wrong and felt relieved it had gone as well as it did. So many feelings raced through him. Questions, sure. Doubts, of course. But a glimpse of hope, too. He could tell. Behind her smile, the sarcastic playful responses, something was there. He truly believed it.

And something, even a tiny glimmer of something, meant everything.

While Jay remained by the pool adding another layer of brown to his skin, Brad strolled down to the beach, his shoulders already sunburned. Swimming in the ocean, the waves strong on this June day, then walking back by the swimming pool. Stopping for a lemonade to cool down. Sipping it slowly. Glancing around, feeling like a fool, like a kid again. Then once more past the swimming pool, the sunbathers sizzling like well-done bacon, the resort managers still wandering around trying to get people involved in activities. Nonstop everything.

He walked up to Jay and pretended to pour the half-full lemonade on his head.

"You're already in deep," Jay murmured sleepily. "Don't give me two reasons to whip your hide."

"Not gonna try any of the games?" Brad asked.

"No. This is what I do on vacation."

"You should make an exercise video. People'd gain weight just watching you."

"That's right."

"Hey, you seen the two ladies around here this afternoon?"

"Kiersten and Anna? No. Have you?"

"I actually sat down with Anna during lunch."

Jay sat up in the lounge chair. "Seriously?"

"Yeah. Told you I would."

"And?"

"And I think it went well. She said something like as long as I kept you far away from them, things would be fine."

"You lie like a dog," Jay replied.

"No. It went fine. Kiersten wasn't there."

"Hey, I'm fine going for Kiersten."

"'Going for Kiersten'? You're such a romantic."

"You tell them we'd see them later?"

"Something like that," Brad said.

"My man."

Brad mentioned that he was going back to the room to shower and change. Jay told him he'd come up in a little while.

"Hey, check to see if my bed's still soaked," Jay called after Brad as he headed toward the hotel. "If it is, you're sleeping on it tonight."

The shade of the lobby cooled him. He walked in sandals, a T-shirt, and a sandy swimsuit. He pressed the button for the elevator. Then, down the marbled hallway, he saw her again. Briefly. Walking past, for seconds, then out of view. Wearing a beach shirt over her swimsuit, her long hair pulled back smoothly in a ponytail, her smile evident as she spoke with her friend. Brad stared at Anna, even for the few seconds that he could.

"You going up or what?"

Brad turned to see an older man holding a half-full glass of beer. The man's chest hairs were white under his unbuttoned shirt, and skinny white legs protruded under his shorts. He stared at Brad as if daring him to get on the elevator.

"Yeah, thanks."

Brad glanced to his right again, then got on the elevator.

It could be a long trip if he kept this up.

The same jingle had played on the Escape Resorts television channel at least twenty times that day.

"If I hear that song one more time, I might kill myself," Jay joked.

"Time to celebrate. No time to hesitate. We all have to try to escape." Brad sang in a high-pitched voice with a mock accent.

"Let's all regurgitate," Jay added.

"We'll probably hear it a thousand more times before we leave."

"I'm telling you, just put me out of my misery now."

They were watching to find out the schedule for the evening entertainment. According to the screen, it started at nine—an evening show complete with dancing and singing.

"Where do you want to eat tonight?" Jay asked.

"Let's see. We can do Japanese. We have to reserve seats for the fancy French restaurant. I doubt we'll get in there tonight. There's the place we eat breakfast and lunch. A seafood place—you up for that?"

"Japanese would be better. Maybe I can get some sushi."

"Oech. You really like that stuff?"

"Love it."

"And it doesn't make you sick?"

Jay slapped his stomach. "This machine don't get sick."

"Wonder what Dad would think of this place," Brad said. His father had wondered how the food would be at the resort.

"Still wishing he would've come?"

"Kinda," Brad said. "I mean, he gave me this trip. Or whatever trip

I wanted to take. Said I could go anywhere if I finally finished college. So I did it. Only about a decade after everybody else."

"Was it worth it?"

Brad nodded. "Honestly? Yeah. I think it was."

"Why?"

"I learned a lot. And it was the first thing I'd done for myself in a while. I've worked at Dad's company for how many years now—thirteen or so? I always wanted to go to college, but not for any decent reasons. I only thought it'd be fun. But now, well, it feels good to have that under my belt. Like I have more options."

"You see yourself ever leaving stone?"

Brad glanced over at his friend and nodded.

"Seriously?" Jay asked.

"Yeah. I actually…I'm sorta thinking about doing it pretty soon."

"And doing what?"

Brad picked up the camera next to him and waved it.

"And you expect to make money?"

"Well, that's the problem," Brad said with a smile. "Sort of expensive to get started."

"You know your father—"

"Yeah, I know," Brad said.

He knew what Jay was referring to. Right now, Brad made more than sixty thousand a year in salary, and with the benefits and perks of the job, it was a position he couldn't simply turn his back on. God only knew he had turned his back on so many things in his life. Running from one thing to the next. Failing and then finding something else to try out.

This job had been handed to him by a loving father, and he believed he had done the most he could with it. He was basically second in command, and even though he was only thirty-one years old, the men in the company respected him.

What would he tell his father now? *I'm going to make money taking pictures. Thanks for teaching me everything you know about cutting and laying stone. Thanks for the last thirteen years. I'll see you later.*

Brad knew he could never do it. But something needed to give. He believed that if he stayed much longer, he'd get his fifteen-year pin and his gift and then allow himself to sit on his dreams for the rest of his life. If he didn't act on them soon, he would lose them forever.

Brad and Jay didn't see the women after dinner that night. They ended up eating an enjoyable meal that lasted more than two hours at the Japanese restaurant where chefs cooked in front of them on a grill. Brad figured Anna and Kiersten had probably chosen another restaurant, perhaps one of the more formal restaurants that required long pants and reservations. Perhaps the ladies had gone on one of the advertised nighttime excursions—leaf painting in the jungle or something like that. Or maybe they'd ended up with sun poisoning and needed to stay in for the evening.

Quite possibly they had switched hotels after Brad spoke to Anna at lunch.

But morning brought round two. Brad saw both Anna and Kiersten stroll into the main eating area and start to roam the various food lines picking out their breakfast. Brad had already eaten breakfast, leaving Jay behind in his room just he had yesterday. Now he decided he could stand in line again and fill another plate.

He ended up behind Anna once again without her knowledge. He cleared his throat a couple of times so that she turned around. Gave him a long look before she spoke.

"Coming down with something there?" she asked him.

No *Good morning.* Or *Hello again.* Or *Oh, hi.* No *Brad Corbin* or anything even remotely friendly. Instead, he got a *Coming down with something there?* What did that mean? Of course she was kidding. But why? What was she kidding about anyway?

Before he could think of something clever to say, she was gone.

This wouldn't go down in the history books as a romantic interlude to remember.

A few hours later, on a pool deck blaring American dance music, Brad walked over to Anna and Kiersten. They were back from lunch, still wearing shorts and T-shirts and sandals. He got to them before they reached their beach chairs in the *no comunicado* zone—the area where he'd look like a creep taking a peep if he talked to them while they were in their bathing suits.

"How are you guys?" he asked.

"That's him," Anna said to her friend.

The blonde checked out Brad, shrugged noncommittally, and continued walking.

"What was that?" he asked.

"Oh, I told Kiersten about you."

"What'd you say?"

"That this strange guy keeps bothering me."

"I'm bothering you?"

"I wouldn't exactly say you're charming me," Anna said with a grin.

"Should I try to?"

"No-o-o-o-o," she replied in an exaggerated fashion. "I don't want you hurting yourself."

"That's funny."

"No, the chicken line was funny. Kiersten really liked that one. A lot better than what your friend said to us the other day."

"I don't even want to know," he said.

Anna began to walk past Brad.

"Anna—"

"Yes," she said with the same urgency that filled his voice.

"Look, I'm not trying to be a nuisance here. I'm just...I'm just trying." And then he stopped, not sure *what* he was trying to do.

"Trying for what?"

"I don't know," Brad said. "Just to talk, I guess."

"What would you like to talk about?"

"About everything. Get to know each other."

She tilted her head and gave him a long look over the top of her sunglasses. "The jury's still out on whether that would be a good idea."

Brad wanted to reply, but now he didn't just feel confusion. He felt anger. Not harsh, bitter anger but a frustrated, tired, insecure sort, the kind that demanded self-examination.

He nodded and let her walk away.

Enough with this. I'm acting like an idiot, and that's exactly how she's treating me.

He waited for her to at least turn around. He was almost certain she would. But then he realized she wasn't going to, and by then she was out of view. Eventually he walked away feeling like a moron.

Sunset burned the sky. The restless ocean with the hills on the horizon and the magnificent blazing candle setting them all afire—Brad watched it all from where he sat. In the main dining room again, feeling the damp Pacific's breath on his newly showered skin, he nibbled at his dinner. He found himself even less hungry than he had been at lunch.

How many years had it been? How long since he had tried? Truly tried?

And look what you got.

He studied his hands. They looked worn. Older. He'd just turned thirty-one. But he didn't feel even that old. He could remember being twenty and thinking that thirty felt lifetimes away. In many ways he was still that twenty-year-old with just a little more life experience. And a lot more heartache.

If he could have a conversation now with the guy he was then, what would he say?

If only I could.

In another decade, nine years to be precise, he would reach the big 4-0. What would that forty-year-old Brad have to tell him? What would he say about this little situation right here? Taking this vacation to Puerto Vallarta to what—to find the love of his life? He might as well have gone on television in search of a soul mate. You couldn't orchestrate these things. Especially not after you gave up so easily before.

It's a second chance.

But a second chance for what? he wondered. Probably this was all in his mind. A game. Part of the Escape Resorts fantasy. But no one said that "all-inclusive" included love.

He sat there alone for another few minutes, gazing at the interplay of water and beach and mountain and fire, sitting quietly as the flame-colored sky gradually cooled to a rust-colored smolder. It was almost as if God were speaking, motioning, urging him to see a beauty he had missed for so long. Gently redirecting him to rethink what he was doing and why. A future was staring down at him in the clouds.

I need to get my camera.

He looked over his shoulder and saw Jay piling food onto his plate at one of the buffet lines. He turned back toward the view and didn't want to leave.

Maybe later.

It had been a while since he'd been serious about taking pictures. Sometimes he'd go weeks, even months, without hearing the shutter of a camera. Without framing a vision for the moment. For a time in his life, it had been all he thought about. In addition to baseball, that is. And other things…

Some things are worth trying a second time.

He sipped his water and felt hope gradually rise again. He knew that today could be different. Yesterday was something he couldn't control or change. The days ahead weren't to be expected or promised. All he had was now. This moment. This breathtaking, sunset-hued moment.

"Brad?"

He turned to see the slender blonde approaching. Her red dress accenting her tanned skin. A grin gave her away.

"We wondered if you wanted to join us for dinner?" Kiersten asked him.

He looked in the direction she nodded, at a table up one deck along the railing. It was a table for four. The woman in white smiled his way.

"I'm with—"

"Yeah, your friend," she said. "We asked him, too."

"Oh, okay. Great." He stood up and took his glass of water with him.

Anna sat in front of a plate compartmentalized with small helpings of food. A tropical drink stood next to her dinner. She grinned as Brad said hello and sat in a chair between the two of them. Anna wore a white dress with spaghetti straps that showed off her golden shoulders. Her hair was pulled to the side, accented with some sort of flower. Brad realized now that when he saw her earlier, she'd worn little or no makeup. Now her eyes were more striking, her lips fuller. He wanted to tell her how beautiful she looked.

"Did you already finish dinner?" Anna asked.

"I could get another plate."

"You don't have to do that."

"It wouldn't be the first time."

"This is my friend, Kiersten. You met briefly today."

"Kiersten with an *ie,"* Kiersten said. "Anna's been telling me all about you."

"What did she say?" Brad asked as he glanced at Anna.

"That you gave her some really awful line about chicken or something. But she said you were cute. Hence the poolside examination."

"Kiersten," Anna said, smiling.

"Hey, I agree with you. He's cute. So tell us, Brad. How long are you guys staying?"

"Until Monday," he said.

Jay brought a plate piled with four different desserts. "Evening, ladies," he said to all of them, including Brad.

"We're trying to have a thoughtful conversation," Brad said. "You might want to leave."

"Ha-ha. So, names again. I'm Jay. He's Brad. Kiersten and Anna, right?"

"Yes," Kiersten said.

"So, are we on a last-name basis or not?" Jay asked.

"Probably not," Kiersten said. "But we'll still have dinner with you two."

"Fabulous. Don't mind that I'm already on desserts."

"Leave any for the rest of the resort?" Brad asked. Jay just grinned.

"Brad," Kiersten said, "you know, I was thinking that before you can make any more passes at my friend, I need to get some more information about you."

"Did I make a pass?" Brad asked Anna.

"Look," said Jay, "I don't think he even remembers how to make a pass."

"Where are you guys from?" the freckled-face blonde asked.

"Jail," Jay said.

"He just got out. We live outside of Chicago. Both of us work at the same place."

"Doing what?"

"Corbin Stone. Provides stone for buildings. We cut and deliver it for builders," Brad said.

Anna continued to eat and listen while her friend talked.

"You don't strike me as someone who does hard labor. You, maybe," Kiersten said, pointing at Jay. "But not you."

"He sits in an office and directs others to work. Others like me."

"It's a hard job, but somebody's gotta do it," Brad said.

"I think he's forgotten what real work actually means."

"Note the fine physique of this 'hard laborer,'" Brad said, nodding at Jay in a touché gesture.

"So, Brad," Kiersten continued.

"Hey, what about me?" Jay asked.

"You're next. Now, what's your story?"

Brad laughed at Kiersten's inquisition. She sounded as if she were interviewing him for a job. He kept glancing Anna's way and watching how she reacted to each comment and reply.

"My story?"

"Yeah. Like, have you ever been married?"

Brad raised his eyebrows.

"And what if I had?"

Kiersten's eyes widened, then looked at her friend.

"Are you married right now?"

"Yeah. Actually, my wife's over at the next table. I like to live dangerously."

"All right," she said, making a face. "Have you been married before?"

"Yes."

"Interesting."

Something passed between Kiersten and Anna.

"What's interesting about it?"

"What happened? How long were you married?"

"I could say not long enough and too long," Brad said, looking down at the table. He wasn't sure what Anna was thinking.

"Why'd it end?"

"Kiersten," Anna said.

"She was a monster," Jay said.

"No," Brad said.

"She was. All he ever did was treat Denise right, and she bailed not long after they married."

"Wasn't all her fault," Brad said. "There were issues."

"It's okay," Anna said. "We don't have to talk about this."

"Hey. I'm just trying to get all the cards out on the table," Kiersten said.

"It's okay," Brad said, wanting to talk with Anna and only Anna. "I can see now that I made a lot of mistakes. I was mostly the one to blame."

"No you weren't," Jay said, taking a bite of his chocolate cake.

"How come?" Kiersten said.

"I think in the end it came down to selfishness. My selfishness."

Kiersten took a sip from her glass and raised her eyebrows at Anna. "Hmm. A penitent and wise bachelor. We've got something here."

Brad laughed. "So do I pass?"

"Maybe. But I have high standards for my friend. And by the way," she said, pointing to Brad's glass, "what's up with the water?"

"I have to keep my edge," he said, "especially around ladies like you."

This answer finally seemed to satisfy Kiersten. She stood up and told them she was going to find some dessert. The sun now was already gone, the evening still warm and breezy. For a moment Brad wished that only he and Anna were sitting at the table. But Jay sat across the table from them, watching and smiling.

"I'm sorry about that," Anna said.

"It's fine."

"She's a good friend, but she had no right—"

"It's okay."

"I've known Kiersten for a couple of years. Ever since I moved to North Carolina."

"How'd you guys meet?" Brad asked.

"My... Well, a guy I knew...she knows him. We met through him."

"Your boyfriend?" Brad asked.

"No. Not my boyfriend now. He was. It's a long story."

Brad nodded. "I'm not going anywhere."

"That's quite interesting."

"What?"

"That statement," Anna said.

"I liked yours better. 'Not my boyfriend now.' So what's the long story?"

She glanced up and saw Kiersten coming. "Don't get her started."

"I won't. But I'd really like to hear."

Strands of hair fell across her cheek. Brad fought the urge to brush them away from her face.

"What are you guys talking about?" Kiersten asked as she sat down holding a plate with three different desserts.

"Oh, I was just telling Anna all about myself," Brad said, joking. "She's really quite interested, you know."

Anna laughed, and that laugh was one of the most glorious things Brad could remember hearing.

There was more of it too. Natural, infectious, and constant, their laughter filled the night. After dinner, Brad and Jay walked with Anna and Kiersten toward the platform overlooking the ocean, then through the courtyard and down onto the beach. Brad told stories, joked with Jay about things they'd seen the last couple of days, and teased the women. All the while, he kept thinking the evening was some exotic dream he didn't want to wake from.

As they walked in couples down a hallway leading to the lobby, Anna suggested they all stay together for the night's entertainment, which would start at eight and last a couple of hours. Each night held its unique theme—the seventies, Hollywood, Caribbean Festival. Tonight's theme was Broadway.

"I haven't bothered you enough?" Brad asked her.

"I wouldn't say that," Anna said.

"What would you say?"

"Stay."

Brad froze, stopping to look into Anna's dark eyes. She stopped too, while Jay and Kiersten walked on ahead. Strands of her hair, lifted by the breeze, played around her face.

"Don't say anything," Anna told him.

"But—"

"Shh. It's worked so far."

"What has?"

"Come on, you guys," Kiersten called back from fifty yards ahead.

"This. Everything."

Anna walked toward the gathering crowd of men in dress pants and button-down short-sleeved shirts and women in skirts or dress slacks.

Stay.

Brad followed her and Kiersten and Jay into the crowd.

"Go up there."

Brad snorted loudly to the pounding bass of the dance music. He leaned over to talk in Anna's ear.

"No way."

"Come on. Where's your sense of adventure?"

"You're crazy."

"No one knows you around here anyway."

"I'm not volunteering."

Anna laughed. "They'll come get you."

"My hotel room is sounding mighty nice right now."

"Oh, but it'll be fun."

Members of the entertainment staff, recognizable from being out by the pool all day exhorting people to participate in various games, approached their row in the outdoor amphitheater. The four of them sat in the middle section on one of the aisles. Overhead stretched a canopy. One of the women, dark-skinned with a radiant face you couldn't say no to, told Anna to go up on the stage.

"He wants to do it," she said, pointing to Brad.

"No, that's okay," he said. "But Jay is just dying to go."

Jay, who was sipping on a frozen drink, merely shook his head and grinned.

"You come," the Mexican woman said, tugging on Brad's arm until he finally gave in.

She led him down to the stage, where Brad walked up steps and looked out over bright lights as he was pulled into a rousing chorus of "There's No Business Like Show Business."

He squinted into the audience and found Anna's smiling face.

Back in his seat during the show, Brad could only think of one thing. One person, rather. A million thoughts of Anna juggled in his mind.

Her perfume. Sweet, of course, but tropical, a touch fruity. Her slim brown shoulders, dotted in two or three spots with tiny moles. Elegant cheekbones balancing over an ample smile. Long legs. A beauty mark—and it was just that—on one cheek. A distinct chin and those wonderful full lips.

Yet as cute or beautiful or adorable—and all those words worked with Anna—as she might be, it was more than her looks that mesmerized Brad. He was captivated by her light whispers in his ears. Her spirited applause and expressive eyes during the performance. The playful touches she gave him. Her easy amusement and seeming love of life. The fire that seemed to smolder deep in her dark eyes.

God, could something truly work out between us here? Is this a ridiculous fantasy I'm living?

As the performance concluded and the staff of the resort came on stage to take their bows, Brad wondered about the rest of the night… and the next day…and the rest of this week.

I came here to start again. And this…this is definitely a start.

Anna grinned and applauded next to him. She glanced over and raised her eyebrows. And Brad felt something, an emotion deep inside, that he thought had been forever lost.

Please, God, let there be an encore.

The music softer now, the wind and the waves providing a hypnotic, soothing rhythm section, Brad watched Anna laugh with the bartender. They waited as the man blended icy, tropical concoctions to be served in plastic cups.

"Not much of a drinker?" Kiersten asked.

Brad shook his head as he sat in a plastic chair in the sand next to Kiersten and Anna's empty seat. Jay sat across from them.

"I do the drinking for him," Jay said.

"No," Brad told Kiersten. "I've reformed."

"How so?"

Brad laughed. "A lot of ways."

Kiersten looked at him with curiosity. "Interesting."

She looked back at Anna, then continued talking.

"Tell me, honestly. Any skeletons in the closet?"

Before Brad could answer, Jay chimed in.

"His ex-wife is the only evidence I've seen of something not working out for Brad."

"That's not true," Brad said. "Don't believe him."

"It's true. This guy here—he's a saint. I'm telling you. The best guy you could find."

"And this guy here works for my father. He's got a bad case of brown-nose."

They laughed, and Brad asked Kiersten why she wanted to know.

"It's just—there were several reasons for this getaway. I mean, it's a vacation, but it's more than that. Poor Anna. She's had a rough go of things the last few years. Ever since her grandmother died and she moved to North Carolina. And even before that—"

"What happened?" Jay asked as Kiersten hesitated.

"She'd tell you this. Anna's pretty up-front about things. She was married when she was younger."

"Wow, that's perfect," Jay said, looking at Brad. "Both of you guys are in the same boat."

"So has she vowed never to marry again?" Brad asked.

"It depends on her mood. Sometimes she wishes she had a family, all of that. And sometimes she's glad she's on her own."

"And she *is* on her own? Now, I mean?"

She nodded at Brad. "I guess you could say that. That's why I have to look out for her."

"I understand," Brad said.

"Her track record with relationships hasn't been the greatest."

"I guess we've got something in common then."

Kiersten's smile disappeared into a cold, serious look.

"Don't you dare hurt her."

Brad wanted to say something, but Anna swept up to the chairs and handed her friend a cup.

"What's this?"

"I think he called it a Bahama Mama."

Kiersten sipped it. "Coconut. Mmm."

"Good?" Brad asked.

"Better than Diet Coke." Anna glanced at the cup in his hand. "By the way, what'd you think of the show?"

"I wished you guys hadn't volunteered me to go up on stage."

"Come on," Kiersten said. "That older lady sorta liked you."

"Especially when she sat on your lap," Anna said.

"Brad's had a crush on her ever since he arrived," Jay said.

They all laughed.

"I have to tell you," Brad said, "playing musical chairs with total strangers—and inebriated ones at that—is a little weird for my taste."

"Oh, quit complaining," Anna told him. "You looked cute."

They walked past couples who mirrored them, strolling side by side. Brad and Anna walked alone, Kiersten and Jay having left minutes earlier.

One day they had spent together. One simple day, no longer than any other. Yet a whole lifetime seemed to have passed in those hours. And now that the day was closing its curtains, a million words offered themselves up to be chosen as a farewell.

He started by saying, "This has really—," then was interrupted.

"Brad?"

"Yeah?"

Anna looked at him under the wooden roof that connected the hotel to the dining room. Warm light lit up her face.

"Don't say too much."

Brad considered her words for a moment. "I'm not likely to," he finally said.

"In a place like this, anything is likely to happen."

"Including a girl like you talking to a guy like me."

Anna grinned. "Exactly."

"I hope you know that this day— It's been great being—"

"I know," Anna said.

"Yeah."

She looked up into his eyes, and he almost kissed her, leaning down and then stopping himself, telling himself, *No, not now. Get hold of yourself.*

He heard Kiersten's warning in his head: *Don't you dare hurt her.* And with everything he said and did, he wanted not to hurt her as she had been hurt in the past.

"We're leaving at 7:30 tomorrow morning if you want to come," Anna said. She turned and walked toward the elevator as he stood on the walkway.

Don't hurt her.

The guy sitting next to Brad looked unconscious and smelled like a tequila factory. The bus rolled steadily through the winding streets of Puerto Vallarta and back into the country as they headed toward one of the resort excursions you paid for. All-inclusive *didn't* include outings like horseback riding. So Brad had actually shelled out his hard-earned cash for the opportunity to share a bus ride with a snoring drunk from Texas.

Just my luck, he thought. *I can't get a hung-over Jay out of bed, so I wind up next to this clown.*

Brad looked several seats behind him to where Kiersten and Anna sat. Both seemed highly amused that he'd managed to share a seat with the inebriated kid from Texas who was finally getting some sleep after a night of hard partying. The guy's friends sat in surrounding seats. As the bus rattled through the countryside, they hollered and laughed and told of their exploits the night before. Apparently they had gone into town and spent the evening at local clubs.

Eventually the guy next to him woke. He was just a kid, really— twenty-one at the most, with peach fuzz on his lip and baby-soft skin burned bright red from the day before.

"Who are you?" he asked Brad in a rowdy, ragged Texan accent.

"They're paying me to baby-sit you," Brad told the syrupy-eyed stranger.

"Heh-heh." The Texan let loose with a devilish laugh.

Thus began a twenty-minute dialogue between Brad's loud, obnoxious, and still-drunk seatmate and his loud, obnoxious, and partially drunk friends. They razzed him about the night before, calling him Señor Loco and asking if he remembered anything. He bantered with them loudly, making little sense, sometimes causing Brad to laugh in spite of himself.

Every so often Brad would turn and grin at Anna. He thought, *You're the only reason I'm here.* Seeing her laughing face though was almost enough to make the ride enjoyable.

"I gotta get me one of them big horses, you know," Señor Loco spat out next to him to anybody who'd listen. "Just call me Clint. Get it?"

Brad didn't answer. Talking to the guy was pointless, and you had to be deaf not to hear him. He wondered if there was some policy about drunks riding horses. Could this kid even get up on one?

"Where are you from?" the haggard voice next to him asked.

"Texas," Brad said in a mock accent.

"Really? Whereabouts?"

"Austin," he said. The same place the group of four was from.

Señor Loco squinted at Brad.

"You don't sound like you're from Austin."

"I am. Right?"

One of Señor Loco's friends agreed, seeing the confusion on the kid's face. Everyone laughed.

"My head hurts. Señor Loco done DOA'd on José Cuervo."

He said it in a ridiculous Speedy Gonzales accent. Ahead one seat, the Mexican driver ignored the kid.

The guy then turned around and began a drunken flirtation with a darkly tanned woman holding hands with the man next to her. Possibly on their honeymoon.

"Mucho buenos, pretty señorita."

"Shut up, Stan," his friends said.

After the bus finally stopped, Anna came up behind him, still laughing over Brad's newfound friend.

"You guys make quite a pair," she said.

Brad groaned. "I just hope I don't have to share a horse with him."

"Actually," she said, "I'm a little surprised you came."

"Are you?"

"A lot has surprised me in the last couple of days."

Brad nodded. "Is that good?"

"So far, yes."

The ball of fire shone in the distance, beyond the whitecaps and the curving stretch of land. Sand cooled his bare feet as Brad sat on a lounge chair next to Anna. She held his hand as they watched the sunset.

"It's glorious," she said. He nodded. They sat there in the stillness, watching, until twilight fell.

"Can it already be Thursday?" Brad finally asked.

"I've forgotten," she said jokingly.

"You ever have moments you wish you could freeze in time and go back to?"

"I've had a few."

"This will be one of those for me," Brad said.

"Really?"

"Yeah."

"I think I'd go back to Jamaica. It was so…perfect."

"What part did you like best?"

"Moments like this. Not worrying about a thing, being far away from the rest of the world—I don't know. But that was a long time ago. I was a different person."

They let the silence soothe them. All that day they had spent together, from horseback riding along the beach to lounging at the pool to dinner earlier in the Mexican restaurant with Kiersten and Jay, who was feeling better after a day of napping and drinking water. After dinner, Kiersten had announced that she was going to their room for a while so that Brad and Anna would have some time alone. Jay got the point and said he'd be hanging out by the poolside bar.

Anna had taken his hand, her long, cool fingers gentle in his grasp. The touch moved him more powerfully than he would have expected. It was like being dropped into the belly of the ocean and feeling the rush of water cover him, being whipped toward the shore then tugged back in the warm waves around him. He said nothing, but his body and his hand shook, and all he thought was, *It's been such a long time.* Anna noticed this and simply squeezed his hand, not saying anything, not even looking at him.

"Sometimes I think my father has to be right," Anna said. "At least about a few things."

"How so?"

She had already talked some about her father, the pastor who had distanced himself from his prodigal daughter. Brad had a few private opinions about that situation, but he didn't want to push them on her. He just let her talk.

"About God, I mean. I just—I see something this beautiful, and I know without a doubt that there is a God above. I mean, someone had to have created this. It's just—I get a little more confused when I see the world out there, all the misery and evil. It's like God created this incredibly beautiful world, then turned his back on it. Except, as my father seems to think, he's just waiting for us to screw up so he can zap us with eternal damnation."

Brad nodded. She sighed.

"I didn't mean to bring up that subject. I don't want to ruin this moment."

"You're not ruining it," Brad said. "I want to hear what you're thinking. It matters a lot to me."

"Can I ask you something personal?"

"Only if you don't tell our buddy, Señor Loco."

Anna laughed. "What do you really believe about God?"

He hesitated, knowing her background, not wanting to push. Finally he said, "I believe God is real. And I believe that he grieves just like the rest of the world for all the evil going on."

"How did you...how did you start to believe this?" Anna asked.

"Well, like I told you, I started going to church with a buddy of mine. One morning, I just went up and prayed with the pastor. You know, all my life I thought that people who did that sort of thing were fools. They were just needy people, people who needed some attention or something. Like people who go to those tent revivals to be healed—just get slapped on the forehead, and suddenly everything's fine. But it wasn't like that for me. It was sort of quiet. We prayed, and I went home, and gradually I started noticing that I was different."

"But what got you to that point?"

"Of what?" Brad asked.

"Praying the prayer? I mean, I know what it is. I heard my father tell people about it my entire life. Asking forgiveness for sins, knowing that Jesus died for you. I know all of that. I just—in my heart, I never actually believed it meant anything."

Brad still held Anna's hand, and now it was his turn to give a gentle squeeze.

"I guess I finally realized that my way—Brad Corbin's way—wasn't getting me anywhere. And I've always tried to do things my way. It's not like I've been a bad person. I never tried drugs, never did anything illegal. You know what I mean. But I looked at my life and realized it needed changing."

"Changing how?"

"I was twenty-seven and looked back and saw a life of failures. Mainly with, well, the whole area of relationships, the way I just let them go. You know, I always believed for some stupid reason that there was something and someone that would make me happier. So I just kept looking, and I kept hurting people. Because I didn't realize that it wasn't a person I was looking for."

"I know what you're going to say," Anna said.

"I wasn't going to say it. Honest. Look, I know it sounds kind of trite. But I do believe in Jesus. In a place like this, it's easy to forget about all that. But my life started turning around when I admitted Jesus was the only person who could change me."

Anna didn't answer him. She just looked out into the ocean.

"I'm sorry if I sound like I'm preaching again," he said.

"Preaching was about all I ever heard growing up. But at least you're not telling me I'm going to hell."

Brad looked at Anna. The glowing red embers of sunset burned against her face.

"Anna. I don't know how many men in your life have told you this. Maybe a lot. But probably not enough. But I want you to know something. I want you to know you're an incredibly special woman. Any guy would be incredibly lucky to be with you. And this moment with you…well, it's just one of those I wish I could capture and replay for the rest of my life."

Anna's eyes filled with tears. She dabbed at them with her free hand. "I don't feel so special most of the time."

"That's probably because those guys you've been with just haven't appreciated you."

Anna smiled and sniffed back the tears away.

"Can I ask you something?"

She looked at him, eyes glassy and sad, and nodded.

"Would you mind if I kissed you?"

Again, the smile came. A different smile. Not the passionate, exciting, zest-for-life sort of smile he'd grown accustomed to in the past few days. This was a bittersweet smile, the sort that came after tears, after a life full of hurt and rejection. A smile that called for a kiss of loving grace, not one of passionate fire.

Brad moved toward her and touched her cheek. And then he closed his eyes and brought his lips to hers.

A soft, gentle kiss. Sincere. Delicate. The kiss lasted a few moments. "Anna?"

She opened her eyes, and a new look, one he'd never seen before, floated on her face. Surprise, joy, sadness—so much combined in one expression.

"Yes?"

"I've dreamed for years of something like this happening," he said.

"So when are we going to wake up and go back to reality?"

"Nothing says we have to," Brad said.

Anna met his eyes, and he kissed her again. When they finally moved away from each other, Brad asked her to stand.

"What?"

"Let me take a picture of you."

Anna shook her head. "You've already shot about a hundred of me today. No more."

"I might not ever see another sunset like this in my life."

"You don't think so?" Anna asked, her lips rounding into a tender smile.

"No, I mean with you."

She looked at him and then looked to her left, the magnificent outline of her face gleaming against the smoldering horizon. Brad didn't
hesitate as he picked up his camera and took another shot of her. He
wished he knew what she was thinking as he pressed the shutter release.

"Hey, man."

"And you are?" Jay asked, pretending not to recognize him.

"Very funny. Now shut up."

"You know, I came here with my friend. And all of a sudden, he's
on another vacation. Going out horseback riding and deep-sea fishing
and scuba diving—"

"I only went horseback riding," Brad said, sliding onto a seat next
to Jay at the bar.

"You know, you see a tall brunette and go running after her and forget all about your friends."

"I thought you'd be proud. How often has that happened?"

"I know. I know. I'm just kidding. Where is she?"

"She went looking for Kiersten. She felt a little guilty about ditch-
ing her friend."

"But you didn't, did you?"

"No way," Brad said with a smile. "I'd still be with her if it was up
to me."

"Glad to see that I rate."

They remained under the tiki hut as the piped-in music grew
louder and the crowd swelled. It took Jay the better part of an hour to
ask Brad what he was really thinking.

"I'm sitting here talking and you're just zoning out. What is up with
you? "

"Actually," Brad said, "I'm still thinking about quitting."

Jay looked at him with a blank, confused face. Brad realized the idea
was so far removed from his friend's thinking that he couldn't understand the obvious.

"The business."

Jay shook his head. "I can't believe you're still on that kick."

"It's not just a kick. I'm pretty serious about it."

"Well, your dad's going to flip. He pays for a vacation so you can decide to flake out on him?"

"I'm not flaking out on anybody."

"Then what's all this really about?"

Brad inhaled and looked around him at the people smiling and talking and drinking and applying themselves to forgetting about life's problems.

"It's just—I've never really felt any sort of satisfaction in the job. Except in my paycheck."

"Yeah," Jay said. "I could find a great deal of satisfaction in your paycheck."

Brad ignored him. "It was almost as if I gave up on all the dreams I once had and opted for the safe route. Work for Dad and make money and live out the rest of my days cutting rock. But now I'm thinking that if I don't give the dreams one last chance, I'll always regret it."

"This is a pretty bad time to be leavin' though."

"I know. But there's never going to be a good time. What—Christmas, fall? When? We're always busy."

Jay gave him a long look, then tilted back his cup of beer and finished it with a final gulp. "Well, it's up to you, man. But your dad's going to be disappointed."

"I want to try at least. I've been telling myself that about several things in my life. At least give it one last shot, you know. And if it doesn't work out… Well, that's the way it goes."

Jay nodded and ordered another beer. "Just don't move to Alaska or anything, all right? It's kinda nice having you around."

Friday morning, a little after ten, as the heat began to simmer and the poolside activities began to heat up, Brad lay back on the lounge chair. Sunglasses shielded his eyes as he flipped through a novel.

"Hey, there. What're you reading?" Kiersten asked, sitting up in a lounge chair next to the empty one that separated them.

"Book called *Turnabout.* By Stephen Conroy. Ever heard of him?"

"Didn't he write something like *The Winding Road*?

"*The Long and Winding Road.* Yeah. I read that one and then got this one. I actually like it better."

"Where'd Anna go?"

"I don't know."

Kiersten lay in a revealing two-piece that Brad tried to keep his eyes off. She had to be aware of the glances she received from men in the pool, but she acted oblivious to them.

"Can I ask you something?" Brad said.

"About Anna?"

"Uh-huh."

"You can *ask*. I'm not promising I'll answer."

"Does she ever talk about her ex-husband?"

Kiersten shook her head. "Not really. I mean, he's come up in conversations, but no. Especially not since she's been dating Jon. Or *was* dating Jon, I should say."

"What about Jon?"

"That you can ask her. I'll just say that he was a little whacked. Possessive, you know."

"Were they serious?" Brad asked.

"In Jon's mind, yes. But not Anna's. I don't think she's been serious with any of the guys she's dated since I've known her."

"Really?"

"Yeah. I don't think she's really looking for someone to get serious with. You know."

Brad nodded and made a *hmm* sound.

"Not to discourage you," Kiersten added. "Even if she's not looking, it doesn't mean she can't find the love of her life somewhere like here."

"What if she found him a long time ago?"

"No, I don't think so," she said, facing him as she leaned against a towel on her chair. "My impression is that he never loved her to begin with."

He watched her glide up into the air, her long legs dangling as her hands gripped the nylon cords. The wind carried her up slowly over the capping waves and the ocean swimmers until she floated delicately in the sky, her Corona Extra parachute a bright butterfly against the blue backdrop of the sky.

Lord, don't let her fall, Brad prayed silently as he watched Anna climb higher.

He had already flown up over the Pacific and felt the rush of soaring behind the tow of a motorboat. The fee was only twenty dollars to go up for twenty minutes. Even though he didn't mind heights, parasailing had made his heart race. Every jolt and bump that made the parachute behind him flutter caused a bit of panic inside.

The landing was the most fun, as he maneuvered the chute to glide down over the pool and back onto the beach.

Now he had to endure watching Anna do the same thing. With her shape a mere speck on the horizon, something he could put his thumb over and block out, he continued to watch and pray she'd be okay. And then also to think about this evening, when dinner would arrive and the sun would fall away in splendor and night would be upon them again. He pictured their kiss again, the sweet and delicate kiss that had caused him a night of unrest afterward. He hadn't wanted to tell her good night, to see her get off the elevator onto another floor and tell him she'd see him tomorrow. There were so many things he wanted to say to her.

Can I say them tonight?

Another nagging thought—or more like a voice—haunted him. One that asked him in a murmur what would happen once tomorrow came. Tomorrow Anna was scheduled to leave Mexico for North Carolina. Would they both go back to the lives they once had and remember Mexico with fondness as a vacation interlude? Would they make promises to keep in touch or even to get together? Did any of this make sense?

This makes all the sense in the world, Brad told himself, his sunglasses blocking the piercing rays above him as he stared out toward the ocean.

The only thing he could be, he decided, was honest. True to his heart. He wanted to be as up-front with Anna as he could. He had certainly made plenty of mistakes in the past by not saying enough or doing enough. He had let chances slip through his fingers. This time he vowed not to make that mistake.

As the boat pulling Anna began to head back to shore, Brad chuckled at the fact that he was here in Mexico falling in love. But was it love? Could he really define it as love?

He knew the answer even as he asked the question. But he also knew that telling her might be a huge mistake.

Anna appeared above him on the beach. That wonderful glow filled her face. She waved at him with one hand, then quickly grabbed on to the straps again. She drifted gently toward the sands like an angel with massive wings prepared to deliver joyful news.

Brad wore a black sports coat and khaki slacks with white polo shirt underneath. He paced the tiled floor of the hotel lobby, waiting for Anna. It was already ten minutes past six o'clock, and their reservations at Le Méridien were at six.

Each room was allowed one evening at Le Méridien as part of the vacation package. Anna and Kiersten had planned to go there together on their last night, but Brad asked Anna if she wanted to join him there instead.

Kiersten had insisted she didn't mind, saying she would grab a quick bite and bring it to the room or dine with somebody else. Maybe even Jay, she had joked. Jay had made a face but then hinted that he had no other plans. Brad suspected they'd end up sharing a table with a variety of people Kiersten had befriended at the resort.

Brad heard the elevator ding and looked up to see Anna step out, dazzling in a knee-length red dress with high-heeled sandals. The tiny shoulder straps showed off her tan, and her upswept hair emphasized an elegant neck. Her full lips curved sweetly, their color the same as her dress.

"Wow," Brad said to her as she approached with a smile.

"Sorry I'm late."

"It's definitely worth it," he said.

"Ready?"

"Yeah. I feel I should go change again."

"No, you look great," Anna said.

"Thank you. You look beyond great."

"Stop it," she said, though she looked pleased.

They walked toward the restaurant, and Brad wondered whether he should take her hand. He decided not to, but remained close at her side.

"Table for two for Corbin?"

Brad glanced at Anna and grinned, nodding at the maître d'.

The restaurant held only ten tables, which basically meant ten couples. White linens, flowers, and candles adorned each table. Menus were heavy and brief, with a few select entrées that offered little description—mostly pasta and steak and seafood. A waitress came and asked if they would like anything to drink. Anna ordered wine, and Brad said water was fine for now.

"Thanks for asking me out to dinner," Anna said.

"This could be our first official date, you know."

Anna grinned. "Last night—what was that? Kissing before a first date?"

"True. Not very good relationship etiquette."

"So what do you have planned for the rest of the evening, Mr. Corbin?"

"*That* remains to be seen."

"Uh-oh," Anna replied.

They took ten minutes to decide what they were going to have for dinner. Anna finally chose a chicken dish, while Brad ordered shrimp and pasta.

"I'm going to need to take next week off just to diet," Brad said.

"Kiersten and I were talking about that. All this rich food. After a while you just want to crawl up on a couch one night and have some Cheerios or something."

"Well, tonight at least, you have full permission to eat whatever you want."

"I might have to try one of those banana flambé things," Anna said, her eyes pointing to the waiter who was igniting a banana dessert.

Their conversation drifted from one topic to another. Other places they had vacationed in recent years. Home life. Favorite movies and books. Even music. When Anna told Brad that she recently found herself getting into some of the classic rock music, he laughed.

"I didn't expect that," he said.

"What do you mean?"

"You liking the Beatles. Or early Elton John."

"They've grown on me."

"So you're saying you're changing as you get older?"

"Maybe. Learning to appreciate things I didn't used to."

"Like what?" Brad asked with a grin.

"Let me think," Anna said, acting as though she was trying to solve some impossible math equation. "Well, here's something. These days, I absolutely adore children."

Brad raised his eyebrows. "Hmm."

"What's that *hmm* about?"

"It's just a *hmm*."

"A good *hmm?*"

"Liking children is a good thing."

"Yes, but you see, I never was that interested in children before."

"You said it," Brad offered with a laugh.

"It's just that I've got an aunt who recently became a grandmother. I'm not sure what that makes me—except maybe old. Anyway, it's my cousin's little boy. His name is Benjamin, and he's adorable. I can't get enough of him. His skin is so incredibly soft. And his hair... He's absolutely precious."

Brad loved watching Anna describe Benjamin. Her eyes lit up, and she demonstrated with her expressive hands the feel of the baby's skin and hair.

"With this newfound appreciation of children, can you see yourself being a mother one day?"

Anna nodded. "People used to ask me that years ago. And I'd always say nothing, because I didn't really want to have children, but I was sort of afraid to admit it. But the idea of being a mom has grown on me. Not that it's going to happen anytime soon, of course."

"I hear you on that," Brad replied.

They continued to tell each other things about themselves that they didn't know. How Anna actually loved living in North Carolina and couldn't see herself ever moving. How Brad still dreamed of having his own studio where he could devote his full time to photography. How Anna had met Kiersten more than three years ago, and how close they had grown since then. How Brad hadn't gone on a date since his divorce from Denise. How awful Anna's dating life had been.

After watching the presentation of the dessert and sharing the bananas flambé, Brad asked Anna if he could take her hand. Her eyes squinted in mingled confusion and amusement.

"How come? Going to tell my fortune?"

"No. Just…I'd like to hold it for a moment."

Brad sat next to her at the square table. Anna offered a hand, and he took it gently. She looked in curiosity as Brad held her hand and studied it for a moment. Then he looked up at her, capturing her eyes with his unblinking gaze.

"Do you want to know something else about me?" Brad asked. "Something you don't know?"

"Uh-oh."

"What?"

"This is going to be your deep, dark secret. That's what Kiersten said—that you're probably carrying around some big, awful secret."

"It's pretty big, but it's not awful."

The smile diminished on Anna's face.

"What is it?" she asked.

"Please promise me you won't overreact."

"I won't."

"I just… There's something I need you to know. Something that might, well, surprise you."

"Brad?"

"Just hear me out, okay?"

"What's wrong?"

The look on her face was now full-blown concern.

"It's nothing wrong. It's just—something that can't wait until tomorrow morning or after you guys leave."

"Brad—"

"Anna, I—"

"Please don't—"

"love you."

"What?"

"Anna, I love you."

The concern on her face grew into something else. Something Brad had not seen yet in Mexico. A look of…a look of what?

"Anna?"

She shook her head, tears inching their way out even though she seemed to be fighting them. "No—"

"Anna, what is it?"

"No. This…this isn't right."

"Please, don't—"

She quickly wiped her eyes and then let them penetrate his heart. There was no love in those eyes, no longing or affection, no friendship or thanks. Only distance and hurt.

Hurt?

"Don't what?" Anna asked him, her voice strange.

"Don't— I just, I told you, I needed to tell you that."

"How can you say, how could you think to say something like that?"

"Like what?"

She shook her head, more tears coming. "I don't want to do this anymore. Not here. Not now."

"Anna, what is it? What's wrong?"

She gave him a bittersweet smile, one that seemed to wish he already understood, one that told him he should have known better.

"You just…you just can't say that—not *now.* Not here."

She pulled her hand away from him and looked around the quiet restaurant. They spoke softly, in voices just above a whisper.

"I wanted you to know how I felt," Brad said.

"Really? That's very convenient for you, isn't it?"

"Anna, please. Don't get up."

"I need some air."

"Anna?"

"Please, just…don't… I need to be alone."

"I'm sorry. I shouldn't have—"

But Anna had already risen to go. In the dim light of the restaurant, the meal already finished, empty plates and glasses in front of them, couples surrounding him, Brad was aware he had made a critical mistake. He just wasn't sure what it was.

I needed to tell her.

He heard her words and thought about them as he let her go, let her walk out into the night air and try to regain her composure.

That's very convenient for you, isn't it?

Her words humbled him.

Was he wrong to tell her?

I told myself she needed to know. She couldn't leave without knowing.

He finally stood up and headed out of the restaurant to find Anna. To offer an apology. To explain.

And perhaps to discuss exactly what was going on between the two of them.

That night he didn't see Anna again. He roamed the resort looking, desperate to talk with her. He knew he had rushed things, that he should have waited. What exactly did he know about love anyway? What had he ever known about love? He wanted to explain to her, to apologize. Maybe to blame it on Rio, as the old movie title went.

Instead, he didn't see Anna. But he did run into Kiersten. Or rather, she came looking for him.

"What'd you say to her?" Anna's friend demanded when she spotted him by the pool.

"Where is she?"

"She's in her room. Pretty upset. Did you— What'd you do?"

"Look, I can't explain."

"Did you insult her or tell her you didn't want to be with her?"

"No. I want to talk with her. Could you go get her?"

Kiersten shook her head. "I'm going back up there. I was just letting her have some time alone."

"What'd she say?"

"Nothing. She just said that she can't see you again."

"What?" Brad asked.

"What'd you do?"

"Look, I just—"

"What?"

He didn't want to explain this to Kiersten. He himself didn't understand completely. And he wasn't sure how to correct his mistake.

Was it really a mistake?

He wished he could take back his words, but he had no idea how. How could you erase the phrase *I love you* from a woman's memory?

"Kiersten, please tell Anna I need to talk to her. Tell her I'm sorry for anything I said."

"You *should* be," Kiersten told him.

"Please, Kiersten. I...I don't want to hurt Anna. I'm crazy about her."

I love her, in fact. But I can't say that, can I?

"Please tell her to come down," Brad continued. "I'll be by the pool. Waiting. Just tell her to come down."

Kiersten looked hard at him and then nodded, striding quickly toward the elevators.

Brad walked out and sat on one of the lounge chairs. He leaned back and looked up at the heavens. Patches of clouds allowed him to peer through to an infinite ceiling of stars.

What have I done?

He waited alone through the nightly entertainment and even after it was finished. He knew Jay was somewhere around the resort, but he didn't want to talk to Jay. He'd have to tell him everything, and he didn't want to.

He tried calling Anna's room a few times, but no one answered. So he lingered around the pool just in case.

Past ten. Toward eleven.

Anna never came.

Brad opened the envelope he'd been given at the front desk. It was ten o'clock on Saturday morning, and he still hadn't been able to get through to Anna's room. He had looked around the dining room but didn't see either Anna or Kiersten. Ten minutes ago, when he went to his room, he'd been notified that something was waiting for him at the front desk.

It was a letter. From Anna. Written on Escape Resorts stationery. He'd returned to his room and locked the door before breaking the seal. Even though daylight from the open windows lit up the room, Jay still lay in his bed, slowly breathing in and out.

The letter was short, with Anna's name written at the bottom in short, concise handwriting.

Brad,

I'm sorry to have left you like that, but everything seemed to come to a head last night when you said what you said. Even now, I can't write out those words. You might not understand this, but those words mean too much to me to be tossed around flippantly. I know you didn't mean harm by them, but they were harmful nevertheless. The past is not something I've fully dealt with. In a place like this it's almost easy to forget. Almost. But hearing that word, that phrase—it was too much.

I need some distance, Brad. To think. To know what I'm thinking. The last few days have been wonderful. And I care about you. I've come to realize that. You are—well, there are many things I can say. It's just, now in my life— I don't know what can come out of this. I would like to offer you some encouragement, but I'm not sure I have any to offer.

As much as I'd like to hope that something can come out of what happened here, I don't think anything can.
Anna

Brad held the letter in his hands and looked up from his bed, past the windows and outside where, only a day earlier, the two of them had floated high and life had seemed almost perfect.

His hand tightened and the letter crinkled. He thought of ripping it apart, but instead he flattened it back out and folded it up.

He sat on his bed for several moments, thinking. What to do. What not to do.

How could one word, one phrase, ruin it all?

His jaw clenched, and he was angry with himself. He should've known better. He should've kept his mouth shut. What was he thinking?

Don't regret what you said.

He held many regrets. Far too many. But would this be one of them?

Would she talk to him again?

He reread the last line of her letter. It offered him nothing. No hope.

But perhaps he had time. He could at least talk with her again. Hear how she felt and apologize to her. Find her before they both left the resort and went back to their separate lives.

God, so close. So close. Heavenly Father, how can this be?

He picked up his key card and beach towel and was almost out of the hotel room when the phone rang.

It's her. She's going to talk to me after all.

Brad walked to the stand between Jay's bed and his and found the phone. He picked it up and said hello, hoping, expecting to hear the familiar voice on the other end.

Instead, it was another familiar voice. An alarmingly familiar voice.

"Oh, thank God, it's you. Brad, this is Becky."

His aunt calling him in Mexico wasn't a good sign.

"What's going on?"

"It's your father. He had a stroke."

Silence. Brad didn't know what to say.

"He's in intensive care. Brad, you have to come home."

He didn't need to hear any more.

HARTSIDE

It was far too beautiful a day to spend in a church viewing the dead. Still, dressed in all black, Anna finally opened the door of her rental car and climbed out.

The late September sun forced sunglasses. She walked across the tiny gravel parking lot toward the building from yesteryear. She could remember the church well, with its peeling white exterior and the steeple jutting toward the sky. She glanced upward and felt anger and dread. Nothing about this would be easy. But she knew that coming was not debatable.

Did angels watch her? Did spirits mourn today? Were the heavens crying in sadness or celebrating in glory?

She could hear her father's voice in memory, spouting the phrases he always used on such occasions. Trite phrases like "going home to be with the Lord" and "being at rest now" that did nothing to stop the tears of loved ones. How could anybody offer hope to the hurting when he didn't know with one hundred percent certainty that that hope was there to be given?

Of course, her father would say he did know with certainty and without a doubt. The doubts and uncertainties, she knew, were hers.

She climbed the steps gingerly in high-heeled shoes she was unaccustomed to wearing. The door was open. She walked into the church foyer and was greeted right away.

"Anna, darlin'. I'm so glad you made it."

If only the words could have come from the pastor who would surely be conducting the service tomorrow. But she knew better. She knew they might never come again from him.

Her Uncle Ted was the one giving her a big hug. "How was the trip?"

"Fine. I hope I'm not late."

"No. Family's been here for just under an hour. The public's coming at six."

Anna nodded. Ted Hutchence was her mother's brother, a kind-hearted man with the accent and attitude of a Southerner. He had grown up in Marietta, Georgia, though he and Anna's Aunt Joan had lived for years in Asheville, an hour away.

The entrance hall to the church was filled with people she vaguely knew. She couldn't see her parents yet.

"Are you still living in Seattle?" Ted asked her, making conversation.

"Yes."

"Enjoying it out there?"

"Very much," Anna said.

"And what do you do again?"

"I work at a publicity firm in the city."

Ted raised his dark eyebrows and looked impressed. "A business-woman, huh?"

She forced a grin. "That's me."

"I always wondered what it'd be like if Joan worked, you know. But with the kids and everything, it's just never been possible."

Anna quickly changed the subject. "Have you seen my mother?"

Ted glanced around, looking uncomfortable in a red-and-blue tie that ended inches above his belt. "Uh, I think I saw your father in the, uh, viewing room over there. This isn't exactly a funeral parlor or any-thing, but Emma's request was to have everything in the church. Including the visitation."

Anna nodded. She looked toward the open doorway that led to a room full of hurt and death. She excused herself from Ted and walked a few steps down into a large open area that usually served for after-church socializing.

Even though it had been years since she set foot in a church, Anna felt strangely at home here. Why shouldn't she? She couldn't even count the hours she'd spent at churches like this one, always coming early for Sunday school and hearing her father preach and then usually staying for lunch afterward. And then, of course, coming back for evening serv-ices and midweek prayer meetings. As a child, she had practically lived at the church. Or at one of the churches. Her father had gone through four, staying until some big controversy boiled over and they were forced to leave.

It was always in the name of doctrine. In the name of right belief and purity of thought. In the name of doing God's will. Her father, Pastor Henry Williams, had a tendency to confuse his stubbornness with God's will. He mistook his anger for righteous indignation. And when he offended enough church members, causing them to rise up and demand change, he had only platitudes to offer his uprooted family.

God's will. This was at the top of his excuses list, his cheat sheet. Whenever a problem with a congregation came to a head, whenever the church elders demanded his resignation, Henry Williams would just purse his lips and claim his leaving was God's will.

It's God's will to drive people away by being belligerent over little issues that nobody knows the answer to anyway?

Anna couldn't believe how raw her memories felt. Twenty-nine years old, months away from turning thirty, she still found herself obsessed with childhood resentments. Leaving churches, friends, family. Changing schools again and again. Finally moving out of state, heading up to Illinois. As if driving miles and hopping states could change a life and family. Anna knew better now. She knew much better.

I guess I'm more like my father than I'd ever admit.

She greeted family members she had not seen in years. Her father stood in one corner, talking seriously with another man. Henry Williams looked older, with more wrinkles on his face and more gray in his hair. His eyes found her, their dark brown irises unwavering, piercing. She glanced away before he did.

Anna approached the open casket and embraced this moment with her deceased grandmother. Grandma Em, her mother's mother. Her last grandparent to pass away.

Anna had visited Grandma Em only months ago, and now she was grateful she had taken the time to fly out and spend time with her. She had not seen her parents for several years—three and a half, to be exact—just talked with her mother occasionally by phone. But she'd always stayed in touch with Grandma Em, who never judged Anna for her failures, just loved her.

Anna composed herself as she stared at the lifeless body. A plastic half-smile, sleeping eyes, a pretty blue suit. This was not Grandma Em, who liked to make jokes and laugh. She was full of life, full of vigor and spunk—all those things people liked to say about older people to compliment them. But with Grandma Em, those things were true. Or they had been true.

Tears stung her eyes at the thought, but Anna willed herself not to cry. Over and over, she said one thing to herself. *I will not cry in front of him. I will not give him the satisfaction.*

She knew Henry Williams was watching her.

Anna gazed at her grandmother's body and then at the large photo resting on display next to the casket. It had been taken with the family years ago. When Anna was still part of that family.

What am I going to do without you, Em? What are we going to do without you?

The question scraped her soul. Did her grandma hear her? Was her grandma truly still living? Grandma Em had been one of the most spirited and passionate Christian women Anna had ever known, and one of the most loving. That love, which some people called Christlike, made her faith seem real. Real if it ever was real.

Can you hear me, Grandma?

She finally stepped away from the casket. Her father still watched her as she approached him.

"Hello, Dad."

He stood alone, still taller than she was, still looking down at her. He stared at her for a moment, saying nothing, then finally uttered her name. Not a *Hello*, not a *How are you?*—just her name. The name he had given her.

"Is Mom around?"

He nodded, his eyes unblinking, his face tight and humorless. "In the kitchen. Over to the left."

She stood, waiting for something more, hoping for something. But nothing came.

After all this time, he still wouldn't talk to her. Really talk to her.

She sighed and turned around to head toward the kitchen to find her mother.

* * *

What am I doing with my life?

Anna looked down at her hands open and stretched wide. She wanted to claw at her face, her heart, her soul, her entire life.

Alone in the cozily furnished room, after the visitation and an evening of meeting and getting reacquainted with a family she'd left behind, Anna felt imprisoned by silence. Her mother had told her she could stay with relatives, and many of them had gladly offered rooms to her. But Anna had decided to stay at a nearby bed-and-breakfast. She was counting on the solitude to give her peace of mind.

Instead, she was wallowing in misery.

Don't do this to yourself, she thought over and over again. It didn't do any good.

The day had been exhausting, yet she couldn't sleep. She wished she had someone to talk to. Her mother, as usual, had been gracious and loving, but there had still been a distance between them. After so many years apart, that was probably normal. Besides, she couldn't go see her mother without seeing her father, too. And she couldn't bear another encounter with those stern eyes.

I'll never earn his forgiveness, Anna thought with anger, knowing she shouldn't have to.

One thing about the day she was proud of, however. She had never broken down in front of anyone, not even once. Her eyes had never wavered, her disposition never appeared defeated. She had managed to perform and perform well. But now, at the end of the day, she could feel herself on the verge of breaking down.

I will not cry, she told herself. Not today. And not tomorrow. Not with her father so close. She couldn't afford to be so vulnerable. And she suspected that once she gave in to tears, they might never stop.

She distracted herself by remembering that her grandmother had lived a good life. She loved and was loved. She left the world with a rich treasure of memories. A life well lived.

What will they say about me?

But this day wasn't about Anna. She had to keep reminding herself that. Nor was it about anyone's soul. Or about eternal life. If there really was such a thing, that was simply a bonus. Maybe Grandma Em was up there, preparing for whatever everlasting life meant. This day wasn't about that, however. It was about saying good-bye. About celebrating her grandmother's life—and facing the reality that it was over.

A life well lived. But what about yours?

Ghosts. Demons of doubt. They haunted her now, as she had known they would.

Her father had not said a word to her all day, or at least a meaningful word. She could still see the disdain in his eyes.

What about love, Dad? What about gentleness and kindness? I might have failed. But so did you.

It was so easy to preach to others, so very difficult to live what you so often preached.

You're judging. Just like he does.

She opened up her laptop to do some work. To read e-mails and answer them. To open spreadsheets and continue to add to them. To write plans and create ideas. To do something, anything, to help her leave behind the thoughts that haunted her.

It didn't work.

Grandma Em—my life could have been like hers. I was on the way to something full, something meaningful, something lasting.

Why did it all simply go away?

Because he did.

She wished, after all this time, there was something big and awful she could blame for their breakup. Something scandalous, evil, wicked. But in the end, she knew, it came down to simply giving up. Falling out of and failing to give love. Selfishness. Pride. Stubbornness.

Such ordinary failures to complicate and alter her life so. To leave her so alone.

What I would give to have it all back. To be able to start over and make amends.

Or simply, finally, joyfully to move on.

This wasn't a prayer, she told herself. It was simply thinking, wishing. And wondering what moving on would mean. How would it ever happen? Who could it be with?

But I have moved on, she protested. *I no longer think of him, of us. What we had is simply a part of my distant past.*

Anna found it amazing that here, in the small town of Hartside, North Carolina, her walls of determination were breaking. They had held strong for so long. They would have to hold a little longer.

Maybe I can start over again. Maybe I can start another life.

She felt the jab of a painful reminder.

He certainly did.

Anna had to admit that her father was good. His funeral message, based on Romans 6, managed to praise Grandma Em and make it clear that she was on the way to eternal life while insinuating that everyone else in the room was in danger of eternal damnation. And he did it all while stressing the eternal love of God.

Anna wondered how so many pastors could go on and on about God's tender love and yet be so callous and unsympathetic when it came to their personal lives? But even as she thought it, she had to admit she didn't know that many pastors. All she knew was one, and he always claimed to be practicing tough love. *Tough love?* As if that meant turning your back on your own flesh and blood.

Well, your tough love accomplished one thing, Dad. It created a tough daughter. A daughter who said she was leaving years ago and who said it was up to you to find her. A daughter who has never waved a flag of defeat. A daughter who has never come home.

The funeral service ended with a prayer. Then they moved out of the pews to go bury Grandma Em. It was already close to noon. Anna had tickets for a flight out of Charlotte late this afternoon. And she already had plans for tomorrow and the next day and the rest of her life.

She had wondered if anything said during this service might change her mind. She knew the stories. God chiseling through a hard heart. Someone who's known the gospel message through and through and yet never truly heard it, someone who finally, at the end of her life, is touched by something or someone. Anna had even seen it happen in church growing up. And a small voice had murmured that this could happen to her, too.

Yet her case, her life, was different. She had walked down the aisle at a young age, afraid of spending an eternity in hell. Afraid of all the things her father preached about, plus all the many things a normal third grader would fear. So she'd walked down the aisle after one of her father's sermons, during the altar call, as the congregation sang "Amazing Grace." She hadn't felt amazing though. She hadn't even understood the word *grace*. She hadn't felt her spirit moving or her soul opening up. She'd felt afraid, the way she might in a scary movie, hoping it would end.

That Sunday had ended with her at the front of the church praying a prayer—the Sinner's Prayer, they called it. Had she become a Christian then? Born again, as her father put it?

So many years later, she didn't know for sure, but she didn't think so—mainly because she didn't think anybody was listening. She believed there probably was a God in the heavens. She even believed his son, Jesus, had probably come down to save the world. But that had been a different world, a world worth saving, with good people still around. The world she lived in today—it just seemed logical that God must have turned his back on them.

Or maybe, just maybe, God had turned his back on her. On Anna Williams. Her life already had managed to have its share of train wrecks. Maybe she didn't have to wait until an afterlife to experience eternal damnation.

Stop this, Anna. You're being foolish.

She walked out through the front foyer of the church and into the outside air. She followed her weeping mother closely, not looking at any of the others in the church, not noticing the strangers and the faces that passed her by.

She simply wanted to get this finished and move on with her life.

Uncle Ted was asked to give the closing prayer. In the warm midday, the blue sky above them granting a welcome sense of peace, Ted's voice was deep and pronounced. Anna stood next to her mother, close to the hole that would swallow her grandmother's coffin within minutes. Her father stood on her mother's other side. He never looked at Anna.

"Dearest heavenly Father, we thank you for the life of this woman,

Emma Hutchence, for the family you gave her, for her friends and loved ones, for a life rich in Christ. Thank you for her testimony, for what her love meant to all of those who had the chance to experience it. We thank you for giving Emma to us, Lord, and now we give her back to you. We pray that she may find rest in you and that her life goes on through all of us. Help us to keep in mind her spirit of love, of faith, and most of all, of grace.

"We thank you for this glorious day and for this glorious life. And we ask that we continue to honor you in our lives, in whatever we do. Help us have the impact that Grandma Em had for you, Lord. In your Son's name we pray. Amen."

Anna opened her eyes and watched as the coffin began to descend into the hole. Her mother began to weep, and for the first time in many years, Anna held her mother in her arms, trying hard once more to keep her own tears at bay. She thought of Uncle Ted's prayer and replayed some of the words.

Her life goes on through all of us....

Her spirit of love, of faith, and most of all, of grace...

Help us have the impact that Grandma Em had for you....

Anna knew this prayer was not for her. The "we" of her uncle's words didn't apply to her. She could never be like Grandma Em. She would never have the same kind of life, could never have the faith and love and *grace*, would never even be associated with the word *impact*.

She was almost thirty. She'd lived perhaps a third of her life, perhaps more. And as far as she could see now, things weren't likely to change much. She'd just have to live with her reality—being a middle-aged woman with a pretty good career and a failed relationship and serious estrangement with her family.

And why is that?

The doubts in her head were only foolish afterthoughts. People didn't change course in the middle of their lives. Perhaps when they were young, but not in their late twenties, when they were finally realizing the truth about life and about being a grownup.

My mother and my father are the same as they were when I left them. So am I. People don't change.

* * *

Anna assumed she would leave without any fanfare. She would eat lunch at one of the round tables set up in a meeting room, and then she would politely and graciously say good-bye to those who knew her. She would hug her mother and tell her she loved her. She wouldn't even bother with her father. He had made his choice, his move, and his actions spoke for themselves. So did his words from the pulpit this morning and his lack of them elsewhere.

When it came time to leave, Anna hugged relatives and walked toward the front foyer with her mother. She had almost reached the front doors when a loud voice startled her and caused her to stop.

"Anna!"

She turned around to see her red-faced father approaching them.

"Henry, please," her mother said.

"Stay out of this, Patricia."

"Henry, please don't," she said again. But he was talking to Anna.

"Were you just going to walk out of here, just like that?"

Anna faced her father without fear. She used to cower and avert her eyes when he grew angry like this. Not anymore.

"Yes," she said. "I'm leaving."

"Just as you did three and a half years ago."

"I'm surprised you even noticed," Anna said.

"Please, not here, not today," Patricia said, standing between them.

"You can't escape your mistakes by running away," the pastor told his daughter.

Anna let out a harsh laugh. "Really? Is that true? Then tell me, *Father*, how many churches did it take for you to finally find a congregation that would put up with you? How many times did you run away? Oh wait, that's right. That was *God's will.*"

"Anna—"

"You will never understand the choices I had to make," her father said, his face hard.

"Maybe not. But you didn't have anybody standing over you, telling you what a *failure* you were, did you?"

"You can't compare the two things. Everything I did, everything I've ever done, was out of love for this family. All I've ever wanted was to keep this family together."

Anna laughed again. She felt tears coming and summoned the will to hold them back. She would not break down and weep as she had done years ago.

"Telling me what a disappointment I was—what was that? Tell me, Dad. Was that your way of keeping your precious family together? Oh, you couldn't have a daughter who got divorced. The ugly little D-word. Isn't that right? You weren't acting out of *love* for our wonderful, godly family. You did it because of the way it made you look. You raised a daughter who didn't believe all the things you preached. And who—oh dear heavens help us all—got *divorced*. You could never even say it out loud, could you?"

"Anna, stop."

"I was hurt, Dad. The only man in my life I *ever* loved, the only man I ever trusted, the one I thought I'd love the rest of my life—he left me. He fell out of love. Did you hear that? *He* was the one who left. And when I told you guys, when I needed someone else's love, another *man's* love, what did I get?"

"Sweetie—"

"No," Henry said to his wife to stop her from hugging Anna.

"I got denial. I got anger. I got the same thing I've *always* gotten from you, Dad. Preaching. Well, you know what? God didn't work this one out for his glory. We got divorced. We moved on with our lives. Your one and only daughter is alone. And you know what? She'll probably be alone for the rest of her life."

She waited to hear what her father would say. Maybe, just maybe…

"There are consequences for sins," the pastor told her.

Anna let out another exasperated chuckle and nodded. "Yeah, I guess there are. And we'll have to live with them the rest of our lives."

"Anna, come back here," her mother said.

Anna didn't even look back. She stepped out of the doorway, breathed in, and continued walking, heading to the back of the church where they had just buried Grandma Em. She heard her mother's voice calling her name several times and her father's domineering voice quieting her.

I'm going to forget all about this and move on. Just as I always do.

She would be leaving soon. She would just cool down and see the grave one more time, say a last good-bye to Grandma Em, and then leave. Nothing could stop her now.

As she walked once more down a hill decorated by gravestones, finally arriving at the fresh dirt and the machine that had lowered the coffin into the ground, Anna stared toward the horizon and tried to compose herself.

Tears finally flowed. She wept into her hands and let it all come out. She knew she was alone, and she knelt on the ground.

And then she heard the voice.

"Anna."

From behind. From above. She looked behind her, up, hearing the steady deep voice, thinking it could be her father's but knowing it wasn't, recognizing it instantly.

How—

Blue eyes looked down at her, familiar and sympathetic.

"I'm so sorry," he said.

This was unexpected and momentous. She wiped her eyes and looked around to see if anyone else was nearby. No one. She sniffled and breathed in deeply and stood to her feet again. Her head spun, and she felt the desire to suck in as much air as possible and yet she couldn't manage the breath to say even a word.

"Are you okay?" the tall man in front of her asked.

She nodded, wiping her eyes again and trying to get rid of the tears. "How long have you been here?"

"Long enough."

She felt embarrassed, humiliated, and angry. The argument with her father suddenly seemed minor. For a moment she forgot where she was.

"I saw you leave the church. I heard you talking with your father."

"Pretty hard not to hear that."

"I'm sorry, Anna."

She nodded.

"I'm sorry about Grandma Em, too."

She looked into his eyes and finally realized she had regained her composure. She studied him carefully, deliberately. He looked different.

"What are you doing here?"

"I…I know how much your grandmother meant to you. I just—I felt like I ought to be here."

"Well, you're here. You made it."

She began to walk away, past him up the hill.

"Anna, please."

"What?"

"Can we please talk? Maybe not here. Maybe somewhere else. Please."

"I have a plane to catch."

He ran a hand through his blond hair and looked at her with surprisingly desperate eyes.

"Please."

She finally nodded, glancing back up at the church where she could see several people coming out the front doors.

"Just not here," she said.

"Anywhere. I don't care."

"We can talk at the bed-and-breakfast where I'm staying." She saw relief in familiar eyes. "And, Brad, I mean it. I can't talk long."

Brad Corbin nodded and followed her up the hill to the parking lot in silence.

They sat in a lobby that felt more like a family room with its soft couch and armchairs. Anna's suitcase and carry-on bag stood waiting next to her chair. To her right, Brad sat on the edge of the sofa rubbing his hands.

Things don't change, do they?

"I'm sorry about that scene at the church," Anna said.

"Your father deserved it. Probably even more."

"I shouldn't have said those things."

"He was wrong."

"I wish you hadn't seen it."

Brad looked at her, his eyes unmoving. He looked good. The years had treated him well. But there was something different about him too. Something she couldn't quite categorize.

"I didn't know exactly how to approach you. I tried at the church this morning after the funeral service. And then outside. At lunch I stayed in my car mostly. I didn't know what to say."

"You could have tried 'hello.'"

He smiled. "Would that have worked?"

"Probably not. But compared to my father's greeting, it would have been remarkably successful."

"Hello then."

This time Anna smiled. "Hello."

"I know it's been…well, too long."

"Almost four years."

"Yeah," Brad said. "How have you been?"

"Fine."

"Really?"

"Yes." Anna looked around to see if anyone was listening. The rustic, dark-wooded room was empty except for the two of them.

"I wish I could say the same."

This surprised Anna. The statement, the way it sounded, the way he looked when he said it. She squinted her eyes.

"Was that true what you said back there? About your parents, your father?"

Anna nodded.

"Man. I…I would've never… I can't believe that."

"Yeah, me neither."

He gave her an odd look. Sad. She couldn't remember ever seeing a look like that on Brad's face.

"The few years… Anna, things have really changed. I mean, in ways I never knew possible."

"What do you mean?"

"I don't—in light of everything… I'm not sure where to begin. You probably don't want—"

"Just tell me," she said.

Brad nodded and looked down at the floor, his hands still writhing with nervousness.

"You heard about Denise? I still don't know… I can't take that back. All I can say is that was a mistake."

"I'm sure you feel the same about me."

Brad shook his head, looking at the ground for a minute.

"No. No, I made some mistakes with you. But I... Everything about Denise was wrong. Everything about you and me, all the choices I made—"

"It's over between us," Anna said. "I've moved on."

"Yeah, I know. But you need to know something. A year and a half ago, I went into a church and came out a new man."

"What?" Anna said.

"I've changed my life, Anna."

She shook her head and stared at him. Too much was happening today. Too much.

"I can't believe that."

"I don't blame you. And...well, now might not be the time. It's just—for a year and a half I've wrestled with what to say to you—"

"What to say to me?"

"Yes. I know—"

"What to say to me?" Anna repeated.

"I know that sounds crazy."

"Brad, there is nothing to say. Nothing. You said it all when you said good-bye to me. You made it very clear how you felt. About the things you didn't feel."

"I know."

"Have you forgotten?"

"No," Brad said. "I couldn't—"

"Then what is this? Some kind of sick joke?"

"No. Anna, please—"

He reached for her hand, but she moved back.

"I knew you'd be here, and I thought this place might be different. That here perhaps I wouldn't be invading your life."

"What do you call this?"

"I..." Brad let out a sigh. "I don't know. Maybe this is a mistake."

"I think the mistake happened years ago."

"Anna, I know it did. And I know it was me. Almost all me. I just—there were things we never had in our relationship. Things that you said yourself you doubted we'd ever have."

"I didn't tell you to just give up and leave."

"I know."

"So, telling me this now. What's this all about? What's the point?"

"Did you really think you'd love me the rest of your life?" Brad asked.

He had heard her talking to her father. She swallowed and knew it'd be stupid to lie. It had almost been four years since Brad left her and their marriage. Four years since she had seen him face to face like this.

"Yes," Anna said, "I did."

"Did…these past few years… Have you—?"

"What?" Anna asked.

He rubbed his forehead, then looked up, and she suddenly realized what was different about him. The empty look that had filled his eyes years ago was gone. The silence when looking at her was no longer there. He was opening up, talking to her, speaking his heart and mind.

Is this the same Brad Corbin who fell out of love with me?

"Have your feelings changed? About us, I mean?"

She couldn't believe the question. She couldn't believe this whole conversation.

"Brad, how can you even ask that? You left without much of a reason. I guessed and assumed. You said you felt there was something else out there, something you were missing."

"I just didn't know what it was," Brad said.

"Obviously you thought you could find it in somebody else."

"I know. I was wrong."

"So what—you go to church and find religion, and now you want to make amends?"

"No. It's not like that."

"Then what is it like?" Anna asked.

"I just want to know. I… Do you… Could you ever be able to forgive me?"

Anna looked at him, the man she had married a decade ago, the man who never offered apologies and never expected them either.

Can people change?

"I don't know," she told him.

"That's okay. That's better than I thought I'd get."

"What do you mean?" Anna asked.

"I thought you'd say no and leave."

"I probably should."

"I know you probably should," Brad said. "But you're still here."

"Actually, I have to go. It's a pretty long drive to the airport."

Brad reached over and took her hand. She was struck by how normal it felt for him to touch her. This was a man she'd once given her body and soul to, a man she was once comfortable in touching and embracing. They had shared a future once, shared a life, shared a love.

"Anna, I can't begin to tell you how sorry I am for everything that happened. For leaving you. For falling out of love with you. What you said to your father—it's true. I let you down. I told you over and over that I wasn't going to be like my parents. I'd never get divorced, never give up on us. But what did I do? The exact same things I said I wouldn't."

He paused and looked at Anna, pleading with her to hear him out. She knew him so well, his mannerisms and body language. He was different. She knew that. He looked the same, but in so many ways, he was different.

"What I didn't realize was that there was no way I could do it alone. No way we could have done it alone. You know, you see these glamorous Hollywood couples who have everything—everything—and they almost always end up divorced. And people shake their heads and wonder why. It's the same reason why people who have money or success or anything fail."

"Is Brad Corbin actually preaching to me?"

"I'm just telling you what I believe," he said. "What I know."

"Which is?"

"Which is that people can't do it on their own. The only way anybody can make it—the only way a marriage and a love can survive—is through the help of God."

"You sound like my father," Anna said.

"I hope I don't. I just—I'm just telling you the truth."

"The truth is that I have to leave."

"Wait. Please wait. Just a few more minutes."

"What for?" Anna asked.

"It's just—there are a lot of things I want to say to you. I've thought about writing, but you know I really can't do that. I even thought of sending you a videotape, but then I thought you wouldn't understand. I mean, how could you—"

"Brad, you've already apologized. And I appreciate it. But now—"

"Anna—"

"What?"

"Anna, I want to start over again. I want us to start over."

She shook her head hard. "No—"

"I mean it."

"You can't, not now. Not after… Brad, this is too much."

She fought the tears again, but her eyes filled.

"I don't mean to hurt you. I just—maybe this is my only opportunity that I'll have with you, Anna. And I don't want to blow it."

"You already blew it. Years ago."

"Maybe so. I just—I needed you to know this."

Anna waited.

"Is there any way—"

"Brad, please."

"I'm just asking. I don't know how to even begin."

"Would you be asking this if I had remarried?"

"But you didn't," Brad said.

"And you did."

"Denise left me after I became a Christian and started going to church. I woke up one day and realized my life was in the sewer. That life changed. And she didn't want anything to do with it."

"That's not my fault."

"I know it's not. And I know I don't have a right to even ask you this. I know I don't. You have every right to get up and walk out and never speak to me again."

"I do," Anna said. "And I'm about to."

"I just—I'm asking for another chance."

Anna looked around again and still found nobody in the room. "A second chance at what?"

"At us."

Anna shook her head. She couldn't take this in. She didn't know what she would say if she had clarity of mind. But clarity escaped her.

"Brad. This—now—I just need to go back home. Think about things. I can't have this conversation right now."

"But what if you met me in another place? In another time?"

"What do you mean?" Anna asked him.

"I mean, what if you and I just forgot about the past? What if we started over from scratch, as if we didn't even know each other?"

"That'd be impossible."

Brad slipped off the chair and knelt down beside her. "You're talking to me now. Again. I once thought that would be impossible too."

"You don't just start over. That's a fantasy."

"Yes, but what if we did? What if I earned the right for you to fall for me again?"

"Brad, this is ridiculous. You don't just start over again in life."

"But that's just it," Brad said, kneeling before her as if he wanted to propose to her. "I did start over again. I was given a second chance. And then I thought, if the Creator of the universe could give me another chance, then maybe, just maybe, the wife I left four years ago might give me another chance too."

Anna wiped her eyes and shook her head and stood to gather her bags.

"Please, Anna," Brad said. He followed her out to her car, carrying a suitcase. "It's worth a try."

They didn't say anything until she had opened the door of her rental car and stowed her bags in the backseat.

She glanced at Brad and didn't know whether to slam the door in his face or embrace him. Yet when he looked her way, she did what felt right. She opened up her arms and pulled him close.

"Anna, I'm so, so sorry," he whispered in her ear. "I will do whatever it takes, go wherever I have to, to win back your love."

I have to be dreaming.

The embrace opened up something inside of her. Perhaps it was a combination of everything that had brought her to this embrace. Perhaps this was her reconciliation with him. This would be it, and nothing more would happen.

Tell him how you really feel.

Yet she couldn't say anything else. No words felt right. No *I know* or *I love you* or even *Good-bye.* She held on to her husband, her ex-husband, the only man she would ever consider to be her one true love, the only man she could ever see marrying, and she realized that people could change. That people could start over. That maybe, just maybe, God was in control of things.

Grandma Em, did you have anything to do with this?

They let go of each other and simply looked into each other's eyes.

"Don't say good-bye, okay?" Brad said to her. "Don't say anything. Just know that I'm trying Anna. I want to start over again. As crazy as it sounds, think about it."

She nodded and thought for a moment.

"It is a nice thought."

"What?" Brad asked.

"Having you earn the right to be with me again."

She actually grinned. She couldn't help herself. The hug—the embrace. It meant everything. And it changed everything. She had never thought they would ever speak again, much less hold each other.

"I'm serious, Anna," Brad said.

"I am too. I just don't know what that means."

She climbed in her car and looked at Brad.

Don't say good-bye. This isn't a good-bye.

"I'll be here—out there, that is—if you need anything," Brad said.

"I have a lot to think about."

"I know you do. But just remember. Someday you might have a guy named Brad Corbin walk up and introduce himself to you and try to get to know you."

"Should I let him?"

He shut her car door but looked at her through the window.

"That is entirely up to you," Brad said. "But I'm going to pray every single day that you will."

"And the past? I should just act like it never happened?"

"No. There's a lot of our past that I would never want to change. Memories I never want to forget. And I can't change the person I once was. Can't go back and slap some sense into that guy, even though I wish I could. Yet I think I'm different now, and you might like getting to know who I am now."

A wave of both regret and delight flowed through her as she looked at her ex-husband and searched for an appropriate response. Finally she just said the first thing that came to her mind.

"Maybe I will."

Anna smiled and turned the key in the ignition and shifted gears to pull out of the parking lot. In the rearview mirror she saw him watching her go.

She believed she would see him again.

GENEVA

He slipped out of the crowded room and walked down the hallway with a small video camera in one hand. He felt elated, higher than he'd ever felt before, moved by the entire day that was coming to a close. He knew that he never wanted to forget these feelings he carried inside. The passion. The love. The belief that they would live happily ever after.

This would be where they would spend half their honeymoon, courtesy of the Herrington Inn. Part of the wedding reception package was a luxurious room looking out on the river. Brad had the key to the room, and they both had already stowed clothes and personal items there. But Anna was still at the reception, still talking and laughing and drinking punch, her dark hair and bright eyes beautiful against the white cloud of her dress. Brad entered the room again, closing the door behind him and bolting it shut to make sure he remained alone.

This was crazy, sure enough. Maybe it was the champagne filling his head with bubbly thoughts. More than that, he knew it was everything that had happened that day. It was watching the woman, the woman he'd dreamed of marrying since the moment he met her, appear at the back of the church. It was seeing her walk down the aisle with her father, place her hand into his, look into his eyes, and say, "I do."

Anything is possible, he believed. *Anything.*

He spent some time fiddling with the video camera, which he'd borrowed from a friend. He'd gotten pretty adept with a regular camera, but he'd never done much with video. He checked the controls, made sure the tape was in there, then tried putting it in several different spots—on a table first, then on the television, and finally facing the bed on the shelf that held the television. He checked to make sure he could get all of himself in the viewfinder, then he sat on the edge of the bed facing the running camera.

"Hi, Anna," he started out. "You don't know I'm filming this. You're still back at the reception with everyone else. And you might think I'm crazy. When you play this, you probably will. But there are some things you need to know. Some things I need to say right now, this night."

He breathed in, smiling at the camera. They would be here later tonight. They would be together for the rest of their lives. *Till death do us part.* Seemed like a simple proposition. Like a wonderful idea.

"I just want to tell you just how lucky I am to have met you back in high school. Meeting you and falling in love—I will never know why I was so fortunate to end up with a girl—a woman—like you, Anna. How you stuck by me as you went off to college and I managed to do nothing with my life. How your love for me has grown over the years.

"Today, we spoke our vows and exchanged rings and kissed. I said words I meant, but not ones I came up with. They were the right things to say—all those traditional promises. But now, I want to say things that you know I'm not very good at saying. I've never been good at expressing my feelings. Heaven knows I couldn't ever *write* them down, so that's why I'm sitting in front of a video camera, talking, telling you.

"I don't know exactly how I will ever feel like I truly deserve you, Anna. This feeling inside—it burns. I still smell your perfume from dancing, and I can envision kissing you a hundred times today. I'd replay this day over and over if I could. Seeing you never look happier. What I ever did to deserve you, I will never know. Never.

"I'm saying all of this… Well, I think I'm saying it more for me than for you. But I want you to keep this tape on hand for the both of us. I want you to keep it safe so it will be a reminder, just like our rings and our photos and the video of this day. I want this to remind us both how much I love you.

"I know it sounds like such a trite and insufficient phrase. But it's true. So that phrase—I love you—will have to do."

Brad paused for a second, thinking, trying to make sense of the thousand thoughts that galloped around in his head.

"I want you to know that I promise never to give up on you. Or us. This is my pledge. My vow—my complete promise to you. I promise I will always love you.

"I will fight for us and do whatever it takes to keep you. I'm absolutely sure of that. Yet if five, or ten, or twenty years pass, and those feelings change—everybody *says* they will, and I assume that perhaps they won't be as intense as they are now—I want something to remind me. To jump-start me. To recap this incredible day. To remind us.

"Keep this video and these words and hold them close to your heart. And if things ever get rough—truly rough—watch this again. Make me watch it.

"I want to grow old with you, Anna. Life—whatever it's going to be—with the two of us side by side—it's just—I can't wait to live it. I wouldn't be anything without you."

He laughed, thinking how unusual this was. Just sitting there, spewing forth all these sentiments of love and hope and the future and the two of them. But they were true. And he wanted to make sure he remembered how he felt today. What he'd promised.

"Oh, Anna," he said. "I love you. Thank you for loving me back. I just—I know I've said probably too much, rambled all over the place, but I don't care. We have our whole lives ahead of us. It's pretty unbelievable. A few days from now, we'll be in Jamaica on our honeymoon—our second honeymoon, because our first one will be right here in this room. But after Jamaica, then we'll start our life. Together. And that's what I'm *really* looking forward to."

He sat there for a long moment, long enough to wonder if he should turn the camera off so he could collect his thoughts. He even half-stood, but then he sat down again, because he knew exactly what he wanted to say.

"I want you to know something, Anna. I want you to know that if the stars somehow all fall, and the sun gets stuck..."

He smiled. "And if somehow this feeling I have fades, I want you to remind me of this moment and of these words. They're all down here, every one of them, captured for eternity.

"Never let them go."

ABOUT THE AUTHOR

Travis Thrasher is the author of *The Promise Remains, The Watermark,* and *The Second Thief.* He and his wife, Sharon, live in suburban Chicago. He welcomes e-mails sent to him at TT@Tyndale.com. For more information, visit TravisThrasher.com.